COME HERE OFTEN?

COME HERE OFTEN?

Ellie Center

bookouture

Published by Bookouture in 2022

An imprint of Storyfire Ltd.
Carmelite House
50 Victoria Embankment
London EC4Y oDZ

www.bookouture.com

ISBN: 978-1-80314-420-7
eBook ISBN: 978-1-80314-419-1

To my mother and father.

CHAPTER 1

MONDAY

"Break my bed, not my heart."

To sweat or not to sweat. That is the question.

I'm standing in front of Great Fitness, one of Nashville's most upscale health clubs. It's a two-story building with a brown brick façade, massive Greek-style columns adorning the entrance, and big reflective windows. 1609 Greenview Drive. I'm at the right address for sure, but it feels like I'm in the wrong place. Story of my life.

I've never been one to exercise, God knows. Lifting glasses filled with vodka and ginger beer is about as aerobic as I get, and with this hangover crushing the space between my temples, I'm not certain I can muster the energy to even tie my running shoes. But here I am. Ready. Set. Go... home?

Just do it. See what happens. Get this over with.

I take a deep breath and summon the courage to walk through Great Fitness's daunting front door. My heart pounds with anticipation as my hands slicken with sweat. I find it humiliating, being unfit and entering a health club. It's actually downright scary. Thankfully, the air-conditioned reception area brings some relief on this humid Monday morning, typical of Nashville's sultry, summertime heat.

Approaching the front desk, I whip out my brand-new membership card, paid for by Sam. "For the improvement of our overall health," he had said, grinning at me. "We can work out together. It'll be fun." *Fun?* Not so sure about that. Still, I have to face it: I am a thirty-two-year-old dental hygienist who's about thirty-two pounds overweight. But at least there's a certain symmetry to those numbers.

"Hi!"

I blink when I see who takes the card from me—a Jake Gyllenhaal lookalike, for sure. Wearing AirPods in both ears, the guy's the spitting image: tall as an oak, ocean-blue eyes. He rubs his scruffy beard as he shoots me a welcoming smile.

"And how are we today?" Fake Jake Gyllenhaal's loud greeting rings in my ears, making my poor head thud even harder. He swipes my card through a digital verifier. It clicks green. "Ready for a grrrrreat workout?"

Actually, no, Tony the Tiger, I'm not even ready for a mediocre workout.

"Well, this is my first time here." I swallow as my stomach tightens, my mouth turning beach-sand dry.

"That's great! Just great! My name's Lee!" Lee speaks as if there's an exclamation mark after everything he says, making him sound oddly invigorated. He reads the name on my black-and-gold membership card, squinting at it, then eyeballs me as he hands it back. "And you are Katherine, uh... *No-Add?*"

I sigh. I always have to explain how to pronounce my name. "It's Noad. As in 'toad.'"

"Oh, sorry. Noad."

"And it's Katherine on the card, but"—I blow a stray blonde hair from my messy bun out of my face—"I go by Kat."

"That's just great! Great! Welcome to Great Fitness, Kat! So glad you came!"

I wince. Lee's exhibiting way too much enthusiasm for 9:42 a.m. as far as I'm concerned. I can't believe I'm even up this early on my day off. And what's this "great" business about? It all seems so fake, like the slogan on the wall behind him, a light-blue sign that commands me to *Be Your Best!* in big, black lettering. The same message is imprinted on the front of Lee's tight blue shirt.

In my Whack-A-Mole of a life, I'm not even *close* to being my best. In fact, I may be hovering around the dark nether regions of my very worst, physically, emotionally, and every other kind of "-ally" you can name.

The next thing I know, Lee's exuberantly extending his huge mitt of a hand, which I stare at before shaking with far less enthusiasm. I bite the inside of my lower lip, a sign that my anxiety is watching all this with significant interest. Anxiety follows me almost everywhere I go. Excessive worry and fear triggered by a negative event, then, God only knows how, it turns into a kind of general nervousness. I call it my Big A. It's practically my other shadow.

I start blinking rapidly, as my chest gets tight. I feel like bolting.

"You're going to love it here!" Lee exclaims. The guy's so keyed up, he reminds me of a dog who's treed a squirrel.

"Thought I'd give it a try." I shrug, trying to exude a defiant nonchalance. "Today's supposed to be my Day of Change, you know? Kind of like the first day of my new life. I've been planning this for weeks, actually, getting up the nerve."

I don't know why I'm even telling him this. I'm babbling. This entire exercise thing, it seems so unnatural. I'm normally working on my second breakfast croissant about now.

"Good for you!" he says. "That sounds gre—"

"Oh, yeah." I interrupt him before he can say that word again. "Put it on my iCalendar and everything. Been counting down the days."

"That's just—"

"I know. Great, right? Hey. So I made an appointment for someone to show me around. Do you have me down? It's for nine-thirty. I'm a little late. Sorry."

Lee checks his computer monitor. "No prob. Be right back! Wait here!" He literally jogs down a hallway, disappearing into the front office with the spirit of a young stallion. The guy's a human can of Red Bull. *Oh, God. My head.*

A tall, twentyish blonde woman comes up to the desk and scans her card. It clicks green and she's on her way, her body as tight as a gold-medal gymnast's. I can't help but compare myself to her and then move down another notch or two in my overall self-confidence. I bet she's never had a second croissant in her entire life.

Oh, well. Some people have it and some people don't give a shit. I stand a little taller as I readjust the gym bag that's slung across my shoulder, mentally cataloging the bag's contents. Brand-new workout outfit. Check. Towel. Check... God, I'd so rather be home right now, burrowed on the couch and doing something seriously important like finishing *The Crown* on Netflix. I mean, Queen Elizabeth is nearly one hundred. *She* doesn't work out... Can you imagine the Queen in Lululemon? I smile to myself and continue my checklist. Let's see, pink one-piece bathing suit, which still just about fits. Clean underwear. Deodorant. I'm about as ready as I'll ever be—I guess.

But how are you supposed to exercise when it feels like a slab of concrete has filled your skull? I stare at the sign again. No, I'm definitely *not* being my best right now. Especially not after what happened last night with Sam.

Though we *do* have a meaningful and caring relationship, last night we had one of our big disagreements, which seem to be getting bigger and more frequent by the week. After berating me in his condescending way for going out "practically every night" with my girlfriends, Sam actually had the audacity to call me a "lazy narcissist" for not cleaning up around the apartment. I called him an "obsessive clean freak," which obviously didn't help, but it's true, and he proved me right by marching into our bathroom and pointing at all the makeup jars and tubes that were on the counter. It wasn't that bad—at least I didn't think so —but he got all up in my face about it.

"Can't you clean this crap up?" he asked, wrinkling his nose as if he'd just inspected my laundry basket, which could, I admit, contain something archaeologically interesting deep down in its primordial strata.

"I will in a bit," I said, rolling my eyes.

And then—because he was being all huffy with me—I went clubbing with friends, got into a Bacardi party, and wound up drinking with some bachelorettes from San Antonio until I threw up in the bathroom at Billy Ray's Ale House. I got in at 2 a.m. So really, it's his fault I'm so hungover.

I love him to death, I swear. But there are times when I just want to wring his—

"I'm back!" Lee announces. He's with another employee, who's clearly the Hemsworth brothers' closest cousin.

Hemsworth takes Lee's place behind the desk and greets another member. Tall and gorgeous, she laser-beams a smile at him. Come to think of it, there's quite a bit of Margot Robbie in her. What is it with this place? I wonder if I'll find a Brad Pitt clone in the weights area.

"Okay, then! Let's do this!" Lee rubs his hands together, excitement flame-broiling in his eyes. "You're going to love it here! No doubt about it!"

As my Big A simmers on the back burner, Lee walks me through the facility, talking non-stop about how *great* it is here. With an array of members and other staff circulating around us, he leads me past a bubbling fountain that's been erected in the very center of the huge, blue-and-green-carpeted lobby with its off-white walls and high ceilings. A sense of exclusivity abounds. Membership must cost a fortune, so I vow to try at least a little bit. Sam can afford it, though. He really brings in the bucks as part-owner and head chef at Prime House, one of Nashville's most popular—and expensive—restaurants.

Sam hasn't been to Great Fitness yet, but will surely love it when he does. Everything's immaculate, orderly, sparkling, and there's a refreshing lavender scent in the air, which is slightly calming my Big A. The fountain rises at least twenty feet into the air, spilling over at the top to create a vertical river, like something you'd see in a five-star hotel. Great Fitness is a workout cathedral.

Mirrors line every wall; they're all over the place, reflecting images of me from more angles than I would ever want to have access to. It's almost psychedelic, extra-dimensional. I feel like Alice in Blunderland, walking around hungover, still wondering if I've made a mistake in coming here.

After Lee leads me past two swimming pools and the Pro Shop, which carries women's apparel and a variety of sundries, we stand outside a yoga studio where about a dozen women are lying on mats, their hands on their abdomens as they deep breathe. Through it all, I can hardly catch what Lee's saying because he speaks in machine-gun fire and my brain's in a fog. I rub my temples, trying to reduce the size of the watermelon in my head.

"Sure is a big place," I interject just as Lee takes a breath. "You could get lost in here."

"So true! So true!" Lee laughs as if I just told the funniest joke he's ever heard. "Biggest in the city, probably in the southeast! We've got everything and then some. Besides the latest equipment, we've got saunas, massage rooms, and, if you need nutrition along the way, there's an excellent restaurant and juice bar. They make killer smoothies! Seriously! We've got it all!" He waves an arm in the air. "You could practically live here!"

Sure. I bet. Who would ever be stupid enough to do something like that?

Lee walks me past another of the club's many weightlifting rooms in which three versions of The Rock are lifting hefty pounds of iron. He turns toward a buff guy strutting in our direction. I can't help but notice his dark, wavy hair, killer blue eyes, and muscles in *all* the right places.

"Marcus!" Lee says. "My man."

"Hey, Lee." According to the logo on his shirt, Marcus is a personal trainer. He gives us a friendly nod. "How's it going?" Marcus's smooth voice and casual style strike a startling contrast with Lee's hypermania.

"Marcus, meet Kat Noad, brand-new member," Lee says. "She's all excited about her first day here!"

I am?

"Hi." I force my lips into a token of a smile.

"Nice to meet you, Kat," Marcus says. I can't stop my eyes from taking a visitor's tour around Marcus's handsome face—his straight nose, his full lips, his bold chin. He extends his hand and we shake. His hand is so soft yet very strong; I don't want to let go.

"Welcome to the land of being the best you can be," he says in a voice as mellow as a Caribbean breeze.

"Thank you. It's quite a place. If you're into this sort of thing, I guess. You know, getting healthy and all."

"Of course. And who isn't? Great Fitness is the best. I've worked all over town and trust me, nothing comes close." Marcus flashes me a smile that makes my stomach flip-flop. His white-as-snow teeth are impressive, causing my dental hygienist brain to kick in. Yes, that's me, the eradicator of tartar and plaque and periodontal disease. I wonder which whitening method he uses. Crest at-home, or the quicker Zoom in-office variety? In-office is so much better.

Marcus's laidback approach is putting me a bit more at ease.

"Have you shown Kat the calorie monitor?"

"No," Lee says.

"What's that?" I ask.

"Oh, it's great!" Lee says. "We have a computer system that keeps track of your calories burned and posts them on a big screen. We call it the TWR: Total Workout Rating. It's kind of a healthy competition; members see who's burned the most calories for the week, exercised the most. It's for those who want to participate, of course. You can tap your card to use machines or go into classes if you want to in order to log your calories."

Me? Logging calories? That's a joke. I'm way more focused on *consuming* them; the more the merrier, I say.

Lee and Marcus lead me to another workout room to show me the huge TWR monitor. I notice this one person named Lura tops most of the lists. She must be a fanatic.

"Have you considered registering for some personal training sessions?" Marcus asks. "I'd highly recommend them as a way to get started, and the initial consultation is complimentary."

As his eyes roam down to my midsection, then back to my face, at first I think he's checking me out. But then his eyes descend to my midsection again—quickly, but not quickly enough—and I get the message.

"Maybe later," I say through clenched teeth as I tilt my head downward. "I want to get my bearings first."

"Well, you can sign up any time. I'd be happy to work with you." He gives me a wink. "See you around, Kat. Later, Lee."

I frown as Marcus walks away from us. I feel my face burn, and then a flash of gratitude for Sam: He doesn't judge me based on external factors, even if he does judge me pretty harshly on other things. We connect on far more important levels than mere appearances—we love to discuss food and art, travel, and wines—and although we do fight from time to time (e.g. last night), our relationship has still held together for five years, braved the storms.

I scratch my wrist and feel a sharpness in the center of my chest. I should have just cleaned up my side of the bathroom counter and been done with it. And I shouldn't have stayed out so late, come home so drunk. I must have been a mess.

As Lee and I walk past the juice bar and restaurant, I come to find that there's actually a real bar here! This is no mirage. I stand there, dazzled, hardly able to believe my own eyes. Maybe this is my kind of establishment after all. A broad smile breaches my lips. An adult beverage is the perfect reward after a strenuous workout. Genius, really, whoever thought of this.

It's located in an alcove with wood walls and gray carpeting, set back and isolated on its own. They even have Picker's Vodka on the shelf and seeing that makes me grow a little warm and fuzzy inside. Picker's and I go way back; we're practically high-school sweethearts. I picture myself exercising on a stationary bike while sipping a Picker's and tonic. That's my kind of multi-tasking, for sure.

"Kat?"

"Huh?" I say, turning to Lee. I have no idea what he's been saying. I was too busy considering how Picker's goes so well with a splash of cranberry juice over ice.

"I asked what kind of workout you're interested in."

"Oh. Oh, yes. Hmm... I'm... Let me see now." I clear my throat. "Actually, I'm not really sure what kind of workout I'm interested in." I tug on my gym bag nervously. "Any suggestions?"

Lee starts bouncing on his toes as if he's jumping rope. "Sure. We have Barre, yoga, aqua aerobics, kickboxing, spinning, aerobic dance, Zumba. You name it. And you can schedule them all on our app. It's great! Me, I'm a treadmill freak. Oh, and we also have Pilates, if that's your thing."

"Did you say pie and lattes?" I joke.

"Huh?" Lee stops bouncing and stares at me with a deer-in-the-headlights look.

"Never mind."

We come to the entrance of a large room housing countless spinning bikes and wall-to-wall mirrors. I guess the mirrors are there in case anyone forgets how stupid you look on a bicycle that stays in one spot no matter how hard you pedal. I point toward a bike. "I think I'll start with the... uh, bikes. They look simple enough."

"Sure! And there's plenty of time to try everything else too. Anything your heart desires. We're open from 4:30 a.m. till midnight, seven days a week, so..."

God, these exercise fanatics, this entire workout business is like a cult.

"So, no room for excuses then, right?" I raise an eyebrow and try to contain my sarcasm.

"Nope." He shakes his head. "None at all."

Well, I'll find one. Don't you worry about that. When it comes to finding excuses, where there's a will there's a way.

When Lee smiles, his white teeth glisten. He has a bit of gum recession. Not uncommon. He's probably a nighttime grinder. Most people are and don't even know it.

"Thanks for the tour," I say when Lee and I have returned to the fountain.

"Sure thing. And remember"—he gives me a wink —"be your best."

I wink right back at him. "Of course." Easy as pie and lattes.

I change into my workout clothes in one of the massive locker rooms. I still cannot believe I'm doing this. Humans weren't meant to exercise like gerbils on running wheels, pay for expensive gym memberships, and lift weird-looking artificial weights.

I quickly realize that the women in the locker room are all part of the cult. Tight bodies, lean, physically fit. There doesn't seem to be anyone else here like me. Anyone normal. I'm surrounded by goddesses like the one blow-drying her hair with a white towel wrapped around her. And that one, putting on her leggings: Salma Hayek incarnate. I feel so out of place, so out of my league that I change awkwardly under my towel. Maybe Sam should have set us up at a less posh club—something next door to a Dunkin' Donuts, for example, and suited to more average people.

My stomach turns over as I leave the locker room. My Big A keeps tapping me on my shoulder, demanding attention. As a weight claps down on the floor nearby, making a huge clanking noise, I gasp. For a moment, I lose my balance and nearly trip over myself. My heart patters in my chest. I have to stand still and take a breath.

Shake it off, Kat. You can do this.

Another breath, and then I enter one of the gigantic rooms where about thirty bicycles are lined up with eight TVs hanging on the walls in front of them. I grab a bottled water—evidently, they give them out free here—and stand next to one of the bikes, studying its buttons on the panel: Calories. Time. Speed. Distance. Resistance. Watts... Wait. What are Watts?

Staring at myself in one of the many mirrors, I start making little warm-up moves, stretching, tilting my head right and left, pretending I know what I'm doing. My bones pop and creak in protest, as if they're saying, *"No, Kat. You do not know what you're doing!"*

Still, I take another long breath and exhale slowly. The sounds of the bikes whir around me. I calm down as my Big A begins to go into mute mode. It does that occasionally, which is fine with me. As crazy as it seems, perhaps I could get into this. I even start to feel pumped. Maybe it's the environment itself, the fountain, the cathedral-like setting dedicated to Narcissus and the goddess Aphrodite, or maybe it's being around all these devotees of the body and the good-looking staff. Or the fact that I'm in a health club with a bar. Whatever the case, it's all somehow rubbing off on me. Maybe it's the endorphins. I can practically inhale them. It's like one hundred percent pure optimism is blowing through the air vents.

I check myself out in the mirrors—Kat Noad, multi-dimensionally, side, front, rear. My dimpled chin, my broad forehead. My round face. I don't look too bad, pale as I am, but those circles under my eyes... and my gut. It really has to go. Somehow. My nose is too big for my face too. That's always been a problem. Oh, well. At least I'm dressed the part: black leggings with cutouts at the knees and a gray, wick-away tech T-shirt. I turn from side to side, studying my reflection.

If only Sam could see me now—he'd be proud. And maybe, just maybe it will bring us closer. After all, he is the one, my "it" man, the man I intend to marry someday, the man I am *determined* to marry. We've already "married" our bank accounts—isn't that a start?

Still, I wish we didn't fight so much. And yet there are other times when we're in perfect sync. Like just a month ago—or was it two months ago? Hmm—Sam made me this fabulous chicken soup with these crazy-good spices and brought it to bed for me when I had a cold. He fed the soup to me, and we kissed when I was done. He said he didn't even mind if he caught my cold. How sweet is that?

Just as I'm about to hop on a bike, my phone buzzes. The caller ID says it's my boss, Dr. Jane Pierce, DDS, Doctor of Dental Surgery, a dark-haired petite workaholic whose personality straddles the line between science nerd and robot. The thing is, she *never* calls. I may get a text from her once in a while, but that's about it. A flurry of panic strikes me and I blink rapidly.

"Kat? Hello? Kat?" Dr. Pierce's voice is strident and deep. She could probably moonlight doing evil cartoon character voiceovers. "Kat?"

I blink. "Yes. I'm here."

"Oh, hi, okay. Getting right to the point." Her voice turns root-canal serious. "I'm afraid we have a problem."

My stomach roils. I speak slowly. "What kind of a problem?"

"I just got off the phone with Mr. Goldbaum. He was *very* unhappy with you, Kat. In fact, he's filing a complaint against you with the board."

Mr. Goldbaum—what a patient! There *was* a bit of an episode with him last week, but I thought I had smoothed it over. Besides wanting to babble about how global warming's nothing but a conspiracy created by the air-conditioning industry, he kept getting up to go to the bathroom every five minutes, and I couldn't finish the cleaning. His teeth were a mess too, total bruxism. Plus, I had two patients waiting for me and I was running behind. It was making me so anxious, I snapped. My Big A was in control and I was its puppet. All I said was, "Please, Mr. Goldbaum, can you keep your butt in the chair for one more minute so I can get to your goddamn molars?" And I may have called him a pain in the ass. As soon as I said it, I regretted it. It slipped out.

"God, no!" I say now. "I immediately apologized. A complaint with the board? Really?"

"Kat, it's not just Mr. Goldbaum, either. There've been other complaints. Mrs. Roth said you were rude to her daughter when all she wanted to do was take a photo of her mouth while you were working on her and you said you didn't have time."

"Well, I didn't! I mean, she wanted me to pose with her and everything, right while I was suctioning. And I had two patients waiting. It was too much."

"A simple photo? How could you not have time for that? We have to coddle our patients, Kat. Indulge them. I've also heard you make jokes with the male patients about trying on latex gloves together after work and how you look good in latex."

"I'm just kidding! They know that."

"Still. It's not appropriate. And when a female patient with an eight-millimeter gap between her two front teeth says she wants to keep it that way because it's great for sucking her thumb and quote, 'other things,' unquote, you don't say, 'Wow! Sounds good to me!' You encourage her to get it fixed! But seriously, Kat," she takes a breath, "Mr. Goldbaum was the last straw."

I bite my lower lip. What does she mean by the last straw?

"The truth is, it doesn't seem like you care about your job anymore."

"That's not fair! I do care about my job!"

"You don't seem as interested as you used to be, and the patients are starting to feel it. *I'm* starting to feel it. And this is after your vacation too. I was hoping you'd return in much better spirits. More relaxed."

"Well, I was helping my Aunt Gladys move into assisted living. It wasn't exactly a vacation."

My Big A is back with a vengeance. My hands start shaking uncontrollably. Blood rushes through my ears and when I stare at myself in one of the mirrors, I see that my neck has turned a flushed red. I can't catch my breath. I so wish I had Lilly with me right now. Poor Lilly. My emotional support dog, a sparkly-eyed, golden Labrador. She helped me face the world until she got cancer and died six months ago. It ripped me apart.

"Nevertheless, at this point," Dr. Pierce goes on, "I'm calling to tell you that I'm going to have to let you go, as of today."

"Are you serious?" I shriek the words. Heads turn my way. The red blotches spread from my chest to my cheeks, my entire face is on fire.

"You're calling to say that you're firing me?" My head pounds and throbs. My lower lip trembles. It's as if my mind goes numb.

"Yes. I have no choice."

"But... but... I *need* this job." Thank God my student loans are paid off, but I do have a fairly sizeable car payment, plus my share of the rent, plus food, plus a variety of important and necessary entertainment expenses, plus everything else that's attached to my life, like my precious T-Mobile account, which is basically the very heart and soul of my existence.

"But I have a loyal following," I say in my defense. Just last week, I went out of my way to squeeze in a patient and stay past my shift. Miss Zimmerman. A crotchety old woman with perio out the wazoo. And this is what I get? I've been working for this dentist for almost, what... five-and-a half years?

"Honestly, I don't have a problem with the way you perform your work. It's not that at all. You utilize the Cavitron and the laser as well as anyone," she states in that mechanical voice of hers. "But it's your *attitude*. It's far too..."

"What?"

"Surly, I'm afraid. You've changed in the last six months, Kat. Mr. Goldbaum, he's been with me such a long time. And now he says he's going to find another dentist!" Her voice stretches up a notch. "At any rate, I've come to the conclusion that you're not the right fit for our office. I'll have Sara call you about your final paycheck. I'm giving you the next two weeks' salary as part of your notice. It's the best I can do. There's no need for you to come in again."

My nostrils flare as I grab the phone so tight it nearly slips out of my hand. My eyes moisten with tears, my teeth clench together, and my jaw aches. I wouldn't be surprised if I'm giving myself TMJ, something else to add to the growing list of shit in my life.

"I'll start smiling more. I promise. I-I'll do whatever you want. I'll give Mr. Goldbaum a free cleaning next time, I'll—"

"Kat. I'm sorry. I've made my decision. Best of luck."

And before I can say anything else, she hangs up on me, the sound of the phone clicking off in my ear at the same moment a heavy weight crashes to the floor. It leaves me feeling like I'm falling down an elevator shaft. Just. Like. That.

I stand here next to the bike, shaking and blinking rapidly, trying to process what happened. My head is a cannon, ready to explode. This is insane. It's totally and completely insane. I've *never* been fired before—not in my entire life. Not even when I worked as an ice-cream scooper in my teens and accidentally locked a customer inside the building when I closed up for the night. Finally, a security guard let him out. But not before he'd eaten almost all our pistachio ice cream.

I've got palpitations and I'm hyperventilating, waves of adrenaline rushing through my body. My lungs hurt as I gasp for air. It feels like I'm breathing through a straw, barely able to inhale enough oxygen. And, what's worse, I don't have a single Xanax with me. I grab onto the handlebar of the stationary bike like a lifeline. This is so cruel. Life is so cruel. Screw dental hygiene! I should have gone into teaching kindergarten like I'd originally planned. Taking care of children who don't have an attitude like Mr. Pain-in-the-ass Goldbaum.

Gaining control of my breathing at last, I hop on the bike, as if to seek revenge. I go at it furiously, legs pumping faster and faster. Pedaling as if this bike's somehow attached to the electric grid and *I'm* the one who's got to generate electricity for the entire building.

I'd hate to ask my parents to support me until I find another job. No way is that happening. I've already been enough of a burden to them. My reflection in one of the mirrors shows sweat beading my wrinkled brow, my eyes still glistening. I'm a five-foot-six-inch whirling blur. Damn that Dr. Pierce. I hope the crown she did for Mrs. Puglisi on Friday blows up in her face.

Exactly four minutes, sixty watts, and a gallon of sweat later, I'm totally exhausted. I stop and get off. I can barely catch my breath and my heart beats as fast as a rabbit's that's being chased by a hunter. But at the same time, I now actually somehow feel... I don't know... better? Yes, I do, crazily enough. I swipe the sweat off my brow with a towel and as I stand there, blinking, staring at myself, a newborn confidence takes root inside me.

So what if she fired me? I don't need nerdy Dr. Pierce. I never really liked the woman to begin with. There are a ton of dentists who'd be thrilled to hire me. New dental practices are springing up all over the place, and I have connections all over town. Besides, I may not be Miss Congeniality, but Dr. Pierce has the personality of a rock. She's as dull as a wet weekend. *She's* the reason her practice isn't taking off like she wants—not me. I'm good to her patients. I do a great job. And she knows it.

I'll start sending out resumes this afternoon. Two weeks' pay coming? "Great!" as my new friend Lee would say. I'll be fine.

Head held high, trying my best to ignore the wounded feeling in my heart, I march over to the weightlifting area and spy a gray-haired woman doing basic curls. I pick up my own ten-pounders to imitate her. Maybe exercising isn't as bad as I thought. Maybe I *could* start to like it around here. Maybe I could even turn Sam's head again. I'm going to focus on that, not my job, or lack thereof.

Finishing my set of ten curls and feeling a nice tension in my arms, I walk into a smaller weight room and phone Sam. I want to tell him how cool this Great Fitness place is and how I think I might like this working out business after all. But even more, I suddenly feel this huge need to apologize to him for last night. I'm a brat. What can I say? I don't think I'll give him the news about my job, though; I'll lay that on him tonight—in person. He'll be pissed, for sure, disappointed. But still... I'll convince him things will turn out for the better, that maybe losing my job was even meant to be. After all, when one door closes, another one—

"Sam!" I say when he answers on the third ring.

"Kat. Hey." He sounds tired, strangely depressed, not Sam-like at all. I'm taken aback.

I get right to it. "Look, Sam. I really want to apologize for last night. I was being an asshole. I know. I need to clean up more. You're one hundred percent right. How do you even put up with me?" Before he has time to answer, I go on. "Hey, I'm over here at Great Fitness. Do you want to meet for lunch later? I'm buying. How about sushi at Ichiban? You know you like the—"

"Kat, look," Sam says, interrupting me before I can finish.

"What?" The sad tone of his voice makes my heart pound in my ears again and my hands re-slicken with sweat.

"I'm tired, okay? I hate to say this, but, well, I'm exhausted. And no, I don't want to meet you for sushi."

I look around the club at all the gorgeous people working out, then run a hand through my hair. Behind me, I hear sudden laughter. *He's* exhausted? Thinking about getting fired, my anxiety starts building like crazy again, going from embers to flames in seconds. I can't stop it. It's like standing on the edge of this high cliff and looking down, afraid that you're going to fall, that you're even *going to make yourself fall* and you don't have the power to stop yourself. Or afraid that you won't be able to take another breath, that you've run all out of breaths.

"Exhausted? Why?" I ask, lowering my voice as a sense of dread overtakes me. "Sam, I'm sorry I woke you up when I got in, but—"

He sighs gravely. "It's not that. Well, it is that. But there's so much more. The thing is, it's getting hard living with you. I'm sorry to say, but it is. Very hard."

"What do you mean?" I can picture him sitting on our couch the way he does, his legs crossed in a yogi position, ear pressed to the phone.

"You know. The way we argue all the time, and it's not getting any better. It's made me all discomposed."

Discomposed. That's Sam. When he gets nervous he starts using these weird, stilted words. He has, like, three degrees, and can't help himself. He can discuss the poetry of Auden in one breath and in the next, talk Einsteinian physics and space and time.

"What are you talking about?" I ask cautiously.

"I really don't think I can take it anymore." Again, he sighs through the phone, one long, painful, unmistakable exhalation that seems to reach into me and dig down deep. "You know? The way you sleep whole days away when you're not at work. Hardly caring about anything. The drinking. It's simply too much. And ever since Lilly died, you've only gotten worse. I know it's hard without Lilly. But come on, Kat. You've got to get over it and move on. You've got to let Lilly go. Honestly, some-times I don't think you even care about yourself anymore. But on the other hand, you can be so self-involved too. It's like *you* are *all* you care about. Whatever the case, it's all falling apart for me." He pauses and for a moment I hear nothing but static between us. "Look," he says, his voice growing more distant. "Let's wait until you come home, and we can talk about it then."

"No, Sam. I'm not waiting until I come home. If there's something you need to say, then say it. I'm a big girl."

"Okay, then." Another long breath. "So, I've decided, see?"

My heart kettledrums. I wipe a tear away. I have no idea what he's talking about. I'm so confused right now. But my Big A isn't. My other shadow is right by my side, its vicious teeth ready to bite.

"Decided what?" I demand, angrily spitting out the final "t" like a tack.

"I've decided that I can't be around someone who's so completely and irrevocably given up on everything."

"What the hell? I haven't given up." The words come fast and in a deep whisper. My eyes begin to burn with fresh tears.

"But you have, Kat. You have and you don't even realize it."

Hearing these words, my heart starts to squeeze shut. "I'm tired of being desultory about this."

"Desul-what?"

"What I'm saying is, I need to take action. I can't do this anymore. I'm sorry, I really am, but I just can't do it. Things have changed between you and me, so... I'm moving out."

"You mean you're... *you're leaving me?*" I put a hand to my chest, then wipe my cheek as another tear sputters down my face. My breaths come in quick succession. "And you're breaking up with me over the goddamn phone? What the hell is wrong with you?" I cannot believe this is happening. I uttered the words so loud that a wrinkle-faced woman wearing pink Lululemon—headband and all—raises an eyebrow at me.

I look away, hardly able to catch my breath, and go to an out-of-the-way corner. My latest reflection is not a pretty one: Kat Noad. Hair frizzy. Face red. Eyes red. Angry as spit.

"You're leaving me?" I ask again, my voice lower, quavering. I feel like one of those people stranded on a rooftop during a flood, waiting for a helicopter to save them—except there is no helicopter in sight. None. Nada. Nowhere.

"Look, Kat. I know this might be kind of unanticipated."

Kind of?

"I'm sorry. I really am. But I'm pissed at you right now. Mad and exhausted and well... fraught."

"Fraught, huh?"

Stab me with a butter knife, why don't you? Get it over with. He's making me so angry I could scream at the universe right now. Just because I didn't clean up my side of the sink? It's not me, it's him—*he's* making himself fraught. Besides, what kind of a word is "fraught"? My muscles quiver and my body tenses up as my throat closes down and goes dry.

He sounds sad, tired. "I'll be back to collect my things. You can have the food processor, by the way, but I'm taking the Nespresso."

"I don't care. Whatever."

"Then..." He sighs. "I'll take that too." Another pause. "Also."

"Yes?" I shut my eyes and rub my temple with one hand, waiting for the other shoe to drop.

He sounds brisk. "I'm taking my name off our bank account. I'll leave you with half the balance—you'll have a bit over eight thousand dollars, and that's being generous, as you well know."

I stand here, not knowing what to say, as my marriage plans sink like a blown-up battleship.

"But—"

"Anyway," he falters, his voice getting quivery and edged with hurt, "I'll move in with my brother until I get my own... place."

"Sam." I don't know how to respond. My mouth gapes open. It feels as if termites have started renting tiny apartments in the inner lining of my stomach and are already gnawing on the drywall. "You can't... can't we talk about this? I just got—"

"I'm leaving you a crab cake eggs Benedict in the fridge," he continues. "I've been working on the recipe for weeks. I hope you enjoy it. I mean, I don't want to be an asshole about this."

"I don't care about that! I want you, Sam. *You!*"

"There's key lime juice in the hollandaise. Goodbye, Kat."

"No, don't say—"

"And I cleaned up your side of the bathroom sink." His voice sounds hollow. Resigned.

"Oh, God! This is crazy. Sam! Listen! Please! I'll come home right now and we'll talk. You can't mean this. What you're saying... We have fun together. We click. I know I drink a bit too much, but I'll slow down. I promise! Do you realize I've just been on a stationary bike? This is my Day of Change, remember? I'm going to—"

"But that's the thing, Kat. You always *say* you'll change, but you never do. And last night was it for me. You went partying with those crazy girlfriends of yours, you came home drunk at two in the morning, you threw up—per usual. You were a mess. And you didn't clean up your side of the bathroom like I asked. It's chaos living with you. I can't take it anymore. I'm sorry, but I've made up my mind."

"Sam! Please—"

"Goodbye, Kat."

"No, don't—"

He ends the call and I drop my jaw. I cannot believe this is happening; it's a nightmare. Here I am at this stupid health club while the man I love is parachuting out of my life like it's a burning plane, right after I got fired in the cruelest way possible. Another tear leaks down my cheek. My chest feels both hollow and tight, if such a thing is possible. My breaths are still coming short and quick.

I look around at all the people working out, movie-star lookalikes, Adonis types, people with bodies to die for, the kind who seem to have it all. Lifting, pulling, bending. And then there's me. I feel like I don't have any of it. Not a soul notices me—they're all too locked up in their own calorie-burning soap operas. Their attractive faces contort as they pump weights, and run on treadmills, sweating, fat-burning—moving their bodies with grit and determination, while I am suddenly and horribly lacking even a minute piece of grit. I feel like a plain old square surrounded by a variety of fascinating and gorgeous hepta-grams. The truth is obvious; I don't belong here. Besides, I couldn't exercise now if you paid me. Everything's blowing up in my face. Some day of change, huh?

I stomp back into the locker room, thrust open my locker in a fit of hurt and anger, and put on my street clothes, wiping away hot tears. Talk about discomposed! I need to get out of here and find Sam. He's either off to the restaurant or headed to his brother's. I *have* to talk to him face-to-face and put a finger in the dike of our demise—even if it kills me. I can't lose him.

CHAPTER 2

I make a beeline for the front door. But as I pass the indoor fountain and a pack of gray-haired seniors all outfitted in some sort of Team Great Fitness uniform, my heart starts pounding so hard I have to stop dead in my tracks. Suddenly, it's here—panic. My Big A's bigger, more ominous brother. There's no avoiding it. I have to grip the edge of the fountain. Heart knocking in my chest, lungs seizing up, sweat dribbling down my sides. I've hit a wall.

This attack is major—almost as bad as the one I had in Walmart ten years ago when I got so panicked that I wound up sitting on the floor in the drug aisle right next to bottles of pink Pepto Bismol and... *Christ. Don't even think about it.*

Never have I longed for a Xanax so much. One five-milligram pill. But I ran out five days ago, and since it's a controlled drug, I can't refill it for at least two weeks. Should I call Dr. Baldwin and beg? He'd refuse me in a New York minute. I'd have to go in and see him. I guess this is what I get for not taking my therapy sessions seriously and for missing so many of them. My expensive therapist, Dr. Rhonda Sharp, warned me in her British accent, "Be careful, Kat. You're still healing."

Healing is right.

Breathe... That's right... Breathe. I take a second and sit down in a chair near the fountain. My hands are shaking. My brain: muddled.

Breathe. Slowly. Breathe...

Okay, one step at a time.

An older lady walks up to me and says, "Dear, are you okay?"

I snap at her. "I'm fine!"

She scurries off, looking offended, and I feel guilty for being so rude. I'm always snapping at people. I don't even know why.

I manage to stand, but as soon as I do, the panic hits again, this time even harder, slamming into me like an emotional car wreck. The next thing I know, my body starts trembling and my knees wobble as if I'm shivering from the cold. And yet, I'm sweating all over. All I can do is sit back down before I collapse in front of all of Great Fitness. All hell is breaking loose inside me.

My breath—too quick, too fast. I'm inhaling from my shoulders—shallow breaths that are thin and painful. My pulse races, NASCAR-style. My chest aches. My panicked mind unfolds everything and nothing simultaneously, an unstoppable merry-go-round: Sam, Dr. Pierce, Dr. Pierce, Sam. Fired. Dumped. Fired. Dumped. How will I get health insurance? All the emotional landmines out there awaiting me: eight thousand in savings—how long will that last?

My car payment, my phone bill. I'm going to have to cut back on everything. I'll have to keep the essentials, of course: food, rent, cellphone, internet... what about manicures? They'll have to go. And drinking... that's one thing that should be cut back on but I'm going to need plenty of it at a time like this. Clothes? I just bought this stupidly expensive dress at Anthropologie—it cost over two hundred bucks. It looks fabulous on me. I think I've taken the tags off anyway.

Sam is *definitely* going to pay his share of the rent this month. But what about next month? My hands go slick thinking about it. Even *with* a job I can't afford the apartment on my own. How long will it take to get a roommate? Could I convince Sam to pay his share of the rent until I find someone? I rub my face and blink as all these thoughts build into one giant mountain of trepidation.

I'm going to be alone, without Sam, for the first time in five years. No one to share my life with, my dreams of having children one day—vanished. The thought of this makes my heart go Novocain-numb. I've always wanted children—two. Hopefully, a boy and a girl. I close my eyes and rub my temples.

Marriage, children, a home, the proverbial picket fence. I was sure we would go through life together, me reveling in his rising chef career, Sam, reveling in, well, the beauty of "us." We'd talked about Bali, renting an Airbnb right on a white sandy beach. I had a real *life* with him. A man to love and be with.

I was a much more confident woman once upon a time. Good-looking and sassy enough to attract a man like Sam. There was a kind of vibrant, positive energy about me. There still is, somewhere underneath. But it's been clouded over by so much else. Sam said that after he met me, for the first time in his life, I inspired him to see his dreams through—to *make* things happen, not to sit on his hind legs anymore and watch the world go by, to sharpen his skills and become the successful professional chef that he is today. He said our love changed his life and he came to see a future with us, together. He'd never felt that way before with anyone else—ever. I can't believe how much has changed.

I know my positive energy has diminished for the past six months ever since Lilly died. My true companion. My golden

Lab. Poor Lilly. It hurts so much every time I think about her. Sam kept on at me to get a new dog, but I couldn't. Lily was irreplaceable. She was my anchor and my sail. Sometimes I think she knew me better than I knew myself.

Now that Sam and Lilly are gone, I'll probably shrivel up like a prune. When I'm old, I'll live in assisted living, alone, getting smaller and smaller apartments, from a two-bedroom to a one-bedroom, then a cramped efficiency, then finally the smallest of all: a twenty-four inch by seventy-four inch coffin— not even enough room to turn around in.

Or maybe I'll wind up moving in with my mother, a resident of the Villages. My mother, a consummate boozer in her own right, about as stable as the wind and as hard to pin down. She's so busy with her clubs and being in second-time-around heaven since she found her new man, Sidney Ensworth. When they aren't golfing or playing bridge, the two of them are always off traveling the world.

I've never been close to my mother. I frighten her, have done so ever since I was a teenager due to my anxiety and all I've been through with therapists, counseling, medicines. Out of sight, out of mind: I think that's how she deals with me now. In a way, I can't blame her. If I could go hang Kat Noad in some closet, I'd forget about her too.

Breathing deeply, I slowly become a little more aware of my surroundings again, the gush of the fountain, the ping of the elevator. I eye the front door of the gym as it swings open, members going in and out. My one way out of here. But the problem is that outside, out there in the warm bright sunlight, under the big blue sky— *out there* seems like about the scariest, most frightening, most devilishly unfriendly place, where any misfortune can happen at any time. As a matter of fact, while I was driving over here, I nearly hit a phone-mesmerized carrot-topped teen who appeared out of nowhere on the crosswalk, just as the light turned green. What if I'd hit him? I'd probably already be in jail now. Disasters can happen in the blink of an eye. You wake up thinking it's going to be a normal day and the next thing you know, you're being handcuffed for involuntary manslaughter.

I squeeze my eyes shut and then slowly open them. I swallow and wring my hands together. That door is *still* daring me. *"Come on, just try to cross my threshold, baby! Let's see you try!"*

This is ridiculous. *Grow up, will you? Have some balls!* I stand, clutching my gym bag, grip it hard, determined to get the hell out of here. Surely, I can do this. Step by step, I move closer. Breathe. Step. Breathe. Step. But a second later, I stop.

It's crazy and bizarre and everything else. Cause and effect. The closer I get to the door, the more panicky I become. I can't even take a single step without my body going into full-fledged revolt.

I grow nauseous and my head spins... My head! My aching head! It's my hangover combined with the panic attack. Instead of exiting the building, the only thing I can do at this point is to make a break for the nearest women's locker room. I barely arrive in time to find a toilet in one of Great Fitness's clean-smelling, white-tiled bathroom stalls. I throw up. My heart is careering like a thoroughbred racehorse galloping away at Churchill Downs—hands cold and clammy—hot and cold sweats. Throwing up brings relief in a way, but it doesn't diminish the hammer of fear that keeps pounding inside me.

"Are you all right?" I hear someone asking me through the door of the stall as I flush. Lord, I made a racket.

"Fine, sure. Ate something bad, I think. I'll... live," I manage to say. My voice echoes against the tiles as if I were calling from down in a well. It's like a bad dream, I swear.

I exit the stall and find two women staring at me, eyebrows raised. They watch me as I go to the sink and throw cold water on my face.

"Got hold of some bad *tom yum* at this Thai place." I make it up as I go and feel even more uncomfortable as they continue staring at me.

"Hmm... Happens more than you'd think," one of the women answers. She gives me a sympathetic look, and there's real care in her eyes—even if her botoxed forehead is as smooth as a placid lake. I don't perceive any snootiness at all, for which I'm grateful and a little surprised.

The two are perfect gym specimens, dressed in brightly colored workout clothing, lithe and lean, two versions of the anti-me, yet both around my age. The other one says, "My husband got food poisoning at a restaurant once. He was miserable for two days."

Oh. Your husband? Right, okay.

"I'm better now, I think. Just needed to get it out of my system."

I give them a good-old American can-do smile, then turn and stare at my face in the mirror as the two women, seemingly satisfied by my answer, exit the bathroom. God. I look awful. Pale and puffy cheeks. My eyes seem unfocused and fogged over by a hazy curtain. My Big A is still hovering.

If I try another exit, will it end in another panic attack? I don't think I'd be able to handle that at this point. I grow dizzy again just thinking about it. I need fresh air. Surely, that's the ticket. And so, I slink out of the bathroom, look right and left, and spot a sign that says: POOL AREA AHEAD. Sounds good to me. Instead of facing that dreaded door, I follow the directions and plop down on a lounger beside the outdoor swimming pool. The door to the pool? I walked through *that* with ease. Not even an issue. Go figure.

Outside beneath the electric-blue sky, relief rushes through me. I take a deep breath of fresh air, put my gym bag on the ground next to me, and then lie back in the increasingly stultifying Nashville heat. God, yes! Out here, I feel *much* better. My body seems to uncoil. My breathing returns to normal. But still, it's as if that big blueness up above is laughing at me. A bird skitters around me on the concrete, chirping and pecking, and then flies off like it's the easiest thing in the world. Now, that's what I call freedom.

It's 10:30 a.m. Sam's no doubt long gone from the apartment. I call him, hoping I can say the exact right thing to win him back and change his mind, while also hoping that the sound of his voice will ease my frazzled nerves. But my call goes straight to his voicemail. How could he do this to me? I don't leave a message. I don't text.

Oh, Kat. What have you gotten yourself into? Dumped and fired within the span of an hour? How could that happen?

All I can do is lie back in the chair and listen to the sound of splish-splashing water. Letting it curl around my ears, I take long, deep breaths and count backward from one hundred. There. Better.

Slowly, my composure returns. I sit up. Finally, my heart rate returns to normal. My breathing is steady. After a panic attack, it's always the same thing. A kind of inner calm settles into me, embracing me.

In front of me, a cute little girl in a red bathing suit plays happily in the water. I smile at her and she smiles at me. Once upon a time, I was that innocent. I remember how my father, a successful real estate developer, used to play with me in the pool we had in our backyard. Now he lives in Marietta, Georgia, and I hardly get to see him. He's always doing a deal somewhere.

"Mommy," she says. "Watch me! Mommy!"

She's so cute! I'd love to take that little girl in my arms and cuddle her. There are times when children awaken my maternal instincts so strongly it hurts. And yet, how can I take care of a child when I can barely take care of myself?

Lying here a while longer, I'm so exhausted and confused that all I can do is fall asleep.

According to my phone, it's nearly noon when I wake up. Seriously? Okay, okay. This is insane. I stare up at the now cloudy sky and look around the pool. God, it's so mother f'in hot. Humid. Sticky. I'm sweating like the outside of a cold can of Mountain Dew. I feel sunburned.

Pool-people are all around me, a variety of age groups, lying about, swimming, staring at magazines or books or their phones. I've been at this place since around nine-thirty. Is this incredible or what? Here I am, a non-celebrity lookalike, well maybe a bit like Amy Schumer, stuck inside Great Fitness, afraid to leave the building. I sit here shaking my head.

I still can't believe Sam. The words he said to me over the phone come rolling through my mind: *"I can't do this anymore. I'm so sorry, I really am... Things have changed."*

We've been together five years now, long enough to know each other's habits, wants and needs inside and out. Like the way Sam loves it when I rub the back of his head while he's driving. He has a knot from childhood on his occipital bone. It soothes him, he says. He knows exactly where to rub me too. And trust me—it's *not* on my occipital bone.

Is this how Sam and I end? A distinct heaviness fills my body as I rub the back of my neck and sigh. I guess our relationship dwindled as time passed and before we knew it, it changed. Like the way enough raindrops on the ground finally make a big fat mess of a puddle. There was no inciting incident; I haven't cheated on him, he hasn't cheated on me—as far as I know anyway. Nothing like that. It was simply time doing its day-to-day thing the way it always seems to do, making two people in a relationship care less and be careless with each other as the months drag on, emotional drip by emotional drip.

Of course, my behavior hasn't always been that great along the way. I mean, I'm definitely not the easiest person to live with. I'm peculiar. I know that. I have my issues. But isn't love the one thing that's supposed to help you climb those mountains and get you over to the other side? Has Sam's love for me died? My heart skips a beat at the thought.

Before it turned sour between us, before our arguments began, Sam and I were running on all cylinders, holding hands and kissing, making early-morning love, treating each other with tenderness, eating his famous and fabulous chocolate cheese-cake in bed, and making plans. Big Plans. We had a great thing going.

And now... it's like being in this fantastic dream and you're eating the best hot-fudge sundae of your life and then waking up to find that you're doing nothing but chewing on a frickin' pillow.

I stand and shake myself off. Ready? Not really. I'm *still* afraid to face that damn door again. But wait a minute. I glance around.

"No, Mommy," a little boy with blonde hair is telling his mom. "Don't wanna get out of the water! Wanna stay!"

I wanna stay too. What's the big rush? Where do I have to be? My stomach grumbles. I'm hungry, which is a good sign. I've found that when I'm hungry, I'm not anxious, and when I'm anxious, I'm not hungry. I need to eat and since I'm here and all... I gather my things. Why not grab a bite?

"Yummy's" is conveniently located on the first floor to the right of the fountain, past the workout areas and the juice bar. There are all kinds of close-up photos of fruits and veggies on the walls. Apples, asparagus, bananas, all photoshopped and looking luscious. In big letters above the fruit hangs that same slogan: *"Be Your Best!"*

I emit a hollow chuckle. Maybe one day.

After ordering and sitting alone at a table, I feel like a lonely tourist on some island. I find myself staring at a grilled chicken salad—organic chicken, of course—accompanied by an organic Fiji apple. I take a bite and chew. Mmmm... The salad *is* quite yummy, although Sam, I'm sure, would have all kinds of critical things to say. When it comes to food, he's a fanatic. French, Italian... He knows it all. It's kind of like living with a gustatory Michelangelo—to watch him make Red Snapper Livornese is a thing of sheer beauty.

Dr. Pierce's voice starts reverberating inside my head: *"Nevertheless, at this point, I'm calling to tell you that I'm going to have to let you go..."*

I rub my temples and stare into space for a moment, then take another bite. This could easily be the worst day of my life.

As I sit here, I can't help but listen in on the conversation of three well-groomed women at the table next to me, all decked out in colorful workout finery.

"And we snorkeled with the sharks in Belize!" one of them is saying. I fiddle with the bracelet on my right hand. Wearing a pink outfit with a cut-out cross in the back, she's sporting a perfect tan. "The water was simply amazing!" She has gorgeous red hair flowing down to her shoulders and a ring on her finger that looks as though it's worth a small country's GDP.

I stare at the ring on my right hand; it suddenly looks smaller than ever. Sterling silver, sapphire and topaz. Hers is probably worth a fortune; I bought mine for fifty bucks over the internet from Jewelry by Delores.

"Ed and I are heading to Majorca for a month. We have a villa there," the dark-haired woman says. *Oh, really?* Puffed-up lips, definitely a boob job, not too over-the-top, though. "It overlooks the Mediterranean. I can't wait. Anything brewing in your world, Sue?"

Sue is a sleek, auburn-haired beauty with a swan neck.

When she smiles, I see that her teeth are white as could possibly be. "Bob and I are planning a trip to Hawaii. His company pays for it. One of his ophthalmologist conventions, you know? He'll probably be playing golf most of the time."

Bob, huh? He sounds like a real dick.

The women laugh as I sit here, unable to close my mouth for a second. My stomach hardens. Here's a lifestyle that I'll probably never come to know. It's like we live in different dimensions. I'm in the world of barely making ends meet, haunted by anxiety to boot, while these women are apparently dancing in the lap of luxury without an anxious bone in their bodies. I take another bite of my organic chicken salad and feel even more isolated.

As the women continue gabbing away, Marcus strides by. I can't believe it was earlier this morning that I met him. It feels like a lifetime ago. He gives me a hello and a friendly smile.

"Well, well. Nearly one in the afternoon and you're *still* here," he says, glancing at his fitness watch. He raises an eyebrow at me as if I'm a curious member-specimen that needs exploring. The comment annoys me no end.

Yep, still here.

"Just getting my money's worth," I say with a forced smile, trying to impart a sense of grand, health-club contentment, which is the absolute opposite of how I feel. "Really went at it hard."

I feel myself blushing.

"Remember, you don't want to overdo it on your first day." He looks me over, scrutinizing me—God only knows what he's thinking. "But anyway, I'm glad you're enjoying it. Keep it up. By the way, Yummy's has the best kale and mushroom dish ever —it'll knock you on your taste buds." He laughs, gives me a wink, and then a white-tooth grin, as cute and handsome as they come.

"I most certainly will," I say, trying to keep up the banter and lifting my cup of filtered water at him as if to say, "Cheers."

He walks away and I catch myself watching that well-built body of his. He seems nice too. Maybe he's not as judgmental as I thought. I hope I bump into him again...

After eating, I decide to keep moving, putting off everything that I know needs to be done. Procrastinating. Yes. That's the spirit. It's one of my God-given talents. I should write a book about procrastination one day. I'll call it *Wait! Wait! Don't do it! The Very Fine and Exquisite Art of Procrastination* by Katherine Jane Noad. I smile. It would probably sell millions—if I could ever get around to starting it.

With my panic attack still a fresh memory, I don't go anywhere near the exit. Instead, I start walking up and down between floors, checking things out all over again, keeping a tight smile plastered on my face. I pretend I'm a reviewer of upper-end fitness centers, flying around the country quality-testing sun loungers. Do a YouTube documentary about it.

I come across a daycare facility that's large and roomy, enclosed with glass windows so that nothing's hidden. It's filled with children of all ages. I smile at the thought. Cute kids running around and annoying daycare workers as their parents exercise and have time to themselves.

One girl, hardly more than a year old, with big blue eyes, a dimpled chin, and a round angelic face smiles at me, and then stands up and walks toward me carrying a doll in one hand. Oops. She falls, but gets right back up, her flushed face flickering between smiling and crying.

I watch as parents pick up their little ones, their eyes lighting up when they reunite. One mother with long red fingernails hugs her energetic four-ish-year-old daughter who starts chattering about a new toy she's been playing with as she comes out into the corridor.

"And he jumps when you push the button, Mommy! He jumps! Like this." The girl jumps herself to show the mother what she's trying to describe.

"That sounds so cool!" the mom replies.

"He's called 'Jumper.' Can we get one?"

"We'll see, we'll see."

The mother catches me looking at them and gives me a knowing smile, as if I too am in the motherhood club.

But I'm not. Nope. Not me. I smile back, but it hurts. I've had this knee-jerk reaction before: watching mothers stroll with their children, gazing their way as they play with them in parks, their proud looks, that motherly nurture written on their faces. But now, without Sam, my chances of becoming a mom, of taking part in that wondrous part of newborn life myself, look slim to none. A new relationship? Maybe years from now, when I'm, like, forty. Artificial insemination? Not likely. I cannot see myself going through it alone. I rub the heel of my palm against my chest. My heart feels squeezed. My eyes moisten again.

I wander on. I check out the massage rooms, then the pools. I also explore the Pro Shop. Lee is right—this place *does* have everything. There's a hair and nail salon that's extremely busy, and what's called a float room. Evidently, you lie naked in a tank filled with water and Epsom salt and relax for an hour. The tank is covered by a dome-shaped top that looks like a turtle shell. It sounds awesome. Yes, sir, children are dying around the world due to malnutrition, poverty, wars coming and going all over the globe, but the lucky few are luxuriously floating in Epsom salts.

Still wanting to avoid the front door, I head back to the locker room and put my workout attire back on. My goal is to blend in with everyone else. I feel like I've somehow put on a new face as well, replaced my old personality with this new one:

Workout Kat. The new me. Quite a change from Couch Kat, or Afternoon Snooze Kat, or... Boozed-up Kat. Maybe I could spend the rest of my life here. Would it be so bad? Isn't this place about as close to utopia as you can find? Minus the exercising, of course.

It's 5:15 p.m. now—my, how time treadmills along. I pass a spin class on the second floor, men and women biking and sweating to "Little Lion Man." Suddenly an idea pops into my head.

Yes! I know *exactly* what I'm doing next. And nothing's going to stop me either. I quickly take the elevator down to the first level, make a right, march past a weight room, where the clank-clinking of weights resounds, past a locker room and Yummy's and then... After all, I *do* tend to gravitate in the direction of the nearest watering—

"So, what can I get you, ma'am?" the bartender asks as I pull up a barstool and sit down. He's fortyish and has a blonde beard, piercing blue, deep-set eyes, and an angular face. Handsome in a rugged way—his buff chest indicates that he's definitely someone who works out.

The fact that there's a bar inside this health club still blows my mind. I shake my head in wonder as I look around. I feel a little giddy. It's discreetly yet conveniently located not far from Yummy's, guarded by a row of glossy green potted palms. Even the plants look healthy here! The bar, with its wood-paneled walls, and hidden-away-feel, gives the club an extra upscale sense of coolness.

I try but fail to close out thoughts of Sam and his goodbye words. One pea in the pod instead of two now—that hurts. I rub my hands together, feeling the pain of what he said all over again. But I also feel resentful and irritated. Breaking up with me while I'm here at this health club engaging in my Day of Change? Telling me over the phone? That's almost as bad as a text break-up, which, of course, is the absolute worst. (*Hi. I'm breaking up. Thanks.*) How dare he! Screw his fancy education and his big words like "fraught" and "discomposed" and his... his... better than thou attitude and that miserable Dust Buster of his. Screw him!

A new, heady sense of anticipation courses through me. Since I'm trapped here and all—at least for a while—why not have a little fun? It's not like I've got anything to do tomorrow anymore. Why not get Sam off my mind with a bit of a buzz? And then, once I'm feeling nice and high, I'll try the door again. It's like being stuck in an airport when your flight's delayed.

The nametag on the bartender's white shirt reads, "Jack Hammer." I have to smile. *He's kidding, right?*

"Ma'am?" he asks.

"Oh, yes. Hi. Hmm... Let's see now, Jack Hammer." I shoot him a playful smile as I twirl a strand of my hair. He puts out some raw cashews in a bowl for me. I take a few in hand. "I'm in the mood for... Make me a..." I think for a second, looking at all the bottles lined up on the wall behind the bar. What's the appropriate drink for a health club? This is indeed quite the issue—an interesting "philosophical conundrum" as Sam would say.

Finally, after running about half a dozen different cocktails through my computer-brain, comparing flavors, I decide that I need something with a few healthy ingredients in it. And then it hits me. "Okay, then, Jack. Set me up with a Moscow mule." Lime juice, ginger beer. What's not to like? "And use the Picker's, if you don't mind." God, I'm good. Problem solved. Still, there goes my Day of Change. But isn't having a major panic attack workout enough? I've burned God knows how many calories.

"You got it. Comin' right up," Jack says in a yeehaw, down-home drawl. His eyes stare into mine and for a second, it's as if he's peering into the very heart of my soul. It's like Jack *knows* I'm one of those types: the heavy drinker species, *genus*

Drinker-Under-The-Table-Asaurus. Something like that. The kind to watch out for. I don't know how he knows, but he does, and I know he knows I know. We connect, communicate instinctively, wirelessly. The guy's reading my mind, I swear. At least I think he is. Sometimes, when I meet certain people, I get the feeling that they have this mind-reading power. That I'm nothing but an open book. Jack Hammer is one of those people. Our eyes meet and hold each other's for an intimate stretch.

As I suck down the mule, which tastes perfect and tangy and immediately helps to soothe my frazzled nerves, a short, fat man with wispy light-brown hair and a walrus mustache sidles up to the bar and sits down two stools away from me. He grunts, gives me a nod, and orders an IPA.

We don't say a word to each other. I'm praying he doesn't try to strike up some sort of a conversation, or, God forbid, try to flirt. As a sign, I turn on my phone and flick around on it. I land on the Facebook page of The Dental Clinic, "home of Nashville's friendliest dentist." Dr. Pierce's cold eyes glare out at me. The bitch! There I am, one of the team members. *"Katherine Noad, dental hygienist with six years of experience."* My smile is bright, eager, teeth milk-white. I had only recently joined "the team" when they'd taken that photo. I looked so much better then. My shoulders sag as I realize that Dr. Pierce was at least partly right. I *was* much happier on the job at one time.

I can't help it. I swipe over to the photos of Lilly and immediately my eyes tear up. Why do I go there? She's gone.

Lilly was a tail-wagging, wet-nose, busybody, loveable mess of a pet. When the cancer came, Val, my absolute best friend and a super veterinarian in her own right, couldn't save her. Val said she never got emotionally involved with her patients, but with Lilly, it was a completely different ballgame.

When my Big A was really bothering me, it was Lilly who healed me, soothed me, served as my best therapist of all. People with anxiety are sensitive types; we resonate and empathize with the pain of others. We're simply built that way. I started feeling Lilly's cancer-pain all over my body; whenever she winced, I winced right along with her—just like I'm sure Lilly felt my anxieties. She knew I was an anxious human; I'm sure of it.

I got Lilly as a pup, the runt of the litter, on a farm in Fairview, about ten years ago. I had no idea she'd become my emotional support dog, but she did. As she grew, we bonded, cuddled, and played, went through life together, and when she looked into my eyes, I not only saw a true companion staring back at me, I felt real, honest to goodness security. A kind of home base for me. Sam loved her too. Who wouldn't love a dog like Lilly?

When I grew anxious because of something that happened during the day, when my Big A was really hammering me, Lilly was there to snuggle up with me and to calm me; she eased me. She was even better than a Xanax. When she looked up at me with those big doggie eyes of hers, it was as if she was speaking to me: "Come on, Kat," she was saying. "You can handle this. Find your calm place. Take it easy on yourself. Relax." She was another reason why I thought I didn't need therapy. I had Lilly as my therapist, I told Dr. Sharp, who adamantly disagreed.

"You need real counseling, Kat," she would say in her calm, objective manner—too calm for me. "A dog simply isn't good enough."

I had to disagree.

Oh, dear Lilly... About a year ago, she started getting sores that wouldn't heal, unusual swellings, and she lost her appetite. That sparkly look in her eye faded away and she simply moped around her bed all day. Val gave me her diagnosis: cancer. Hemangiosarcoma, a fast-spreading form. She developed tumors all over her heart, lungs, and spleen. She lived in such pain and her last days were awful.

She was so loyal. Completely there for me in every way. She

would have sacrificed her life for me—I'm sure of it. Watching Lilly die was like watching the sun fade away and never return. Val did everything in her power to save her and to help me through my loss.

Everyone, my parents included, told me to get another dog, like the answer was that simple. But I couldn't do that; I wanted Lilly. How do you replace a companion that seems to see into your heart, a trusted friend? How do you replace the dog that turns your sad day around and comforts you inside? How do you find a new safe place to run to? I *couldn't* get another dog—it would be a recognition that Lilly was gone, the Final Recognition, and that I could not handle. Watching Val's somber face when she took me into her office to tell me Lilly had passed was a pain that shattered my soul. I wept for days.

I think of losing my job and of losing Sam, his quick and wise mind, his gentle touch, his body next to mine at night, all in addition to losing Lilly. Sadness, like a rushing river, streams through me and I stare down at my hands, sniffing back tears. I hunch over on my stool, leaning against the bar, and stir my drink as a new tightness forms in my chest and limbs. Life's a bitch. No doubt about it. I raise my glass and finish my drink as I let out a long, troubled sigh.

There's only one thing to do at a time like this, of course—order one more.

As I sit at the bar, my sadness turns into a bad mood that descends over me like a thunder cloud, gray and dark. I run a hand through my straggly hair. I feel heavy. My thoughts are weighty.

"Thanks, Jack," I say when he sets another Moscow mule down in front of me. "You've made my day."

I wish. I put my phone away, look around the club, stare at those healthy potted plants, and feel lonelier than I've ever felt in my life. It's the kind of loneliness that stretches for miles. I start to feel the buzz of alcohol in my blood, but it doesn't begin to numb the pain.

Even walrus-mustache guy ignores me, as does Jack Hammer, who is serving a tall woman in a blue dress who has just sat down. They're laughing about something, like they have no worries at all. I take another sip and shake the ice in the glass around. How am I ever going to find the courage to walk through that front door and face the outside world?

CHAPTER 3

Three's the limit. It's my rule. Any more and I start tapping into my Obnoxious Self. After thanking Jack for the drinks, I make my way to the nearest bathroom, feeling a little floaty, and check my face in a mirror. It's not good. Not. At. All. I'm definitely *not* being my best, as the signs instruct. I am still candle-wax pale. The whites of my eyes are lined with red and there's a sadness deep down in them that I can't deny. Sadness and fear and a certain ghostly ghastliness that really sinks its teeth into me. In fact, I look like an extra in some *Night of the Living Dead* movie. My hands won't stop shaking and my stomach feels like a plane crash.

I wish I could do something with my hair too. It's always so straggly and oily. I run a hand through it. When did I last wash it? I shouldn't be wearing it down to my shoulders because of its unruliness, but I don't have the courage to cut it short. I've tried every shampoo and conditioner on the market but nothing will make me look like Blake Lively.

I exit the bathroom and find a chair near the fountain. Here, it's better... Yes. The gurgle of the fountain is soothing, as is the lavender scent that permeates the air. Minutes later, I start walking around again, and before I know it, it's close to seven-thirty in the evening. Members are still arriving in droves, going and coming. It's busy. The health cultists all have that serious workout look on their faces. They're not kidding around.

I still have my buzz going, which is not un-nice. The air is so clean and pure here. I take in a deep breath. I'm sure they have expensive air filters working overtime. It's so tranquil. In a way, it's like a fancy hotel—the Ritz Carlton of health clubs. Most of the members walking past me are stunning and... it's so serene...

So when are you going to get the hell out of here, Kat?

I stand. *Now. Do it.*

But as soon as I move toward the door...

I sit back down in a chair near the fountain and take deep breaths. The need to throw up dissipates, but I'm left with a sick feeling and a disturbing lightheadedness that makes my ears ring. I need to face it. Once again, I am unable to walk through that door.

I need to phone a friend. It's like what they do on that show where you can win a million dollars—Phone-A-Friend. Yeah. My life is one frickin' game show, all right. Too bad there's no *Wheel of Fortune*.

But it's true: I'm not going to be able to do this on my own. My Big A has me by the throat. Dread takes over. Am I actually *stuck* inside this health club? Am I seriously trapped? The high of the Moscow mules has drained out of me and I feel a new headache coming on. I continue sitting here, taking deep breaths.

Val Ambrose comes to mind as my first friend to get me out of this mess. I call her "Val Pal." We went through so much together with Lilly and now, when I'm with her, I spread my wings and get loose. I party with Bacardi, I dance with Jose Cuervo, in hopes that all the pain that I've felt in my life will disappear for at least a few hours. Of course, Sam the Asshole, as I shall now refer to him, disapproves of her. He doesn't seem to take to Val. And Val doesn't seem to take to Sam. Maybe they knew each other in past lives and Sam was Val's drunken dad. Who knows?

Unfortunately, at the moment, Val Pal's in San Diego on vacation, something she's been planning for a year. We were college roommates at Lehigh and met at a party, during which she tried to talk me down from jumping naked into a pool one boozy Sunday morning around 3 a.m. But irrationality won and in a fit of "screw the world!" we both stripped and did it. Ever since then, we kind of stuck together. She went on to become a fantastic veterinarian, and if I don't go out with her at least twice a week for drinks, I feel like something's not right with my life.

But since she's out of town, I try Gloria, my next-door neighbor. Gloria doesn't answer. Does anyone answer their phone anymore? I honestly don't think so. Actually answering your phone is as primitive as snail mail these days. I decide not to leave a message. How am I going to begin to explain my situation to her? She doesn't even know I have anxiety. It would be so embarrassing telling her I'm stuck inside a health club because I ran out of Xanax. I can hear it now, "You did what? Where?" She's probably out of town anyway. She's some sort of sales rep and is always on the road.

Next, I text Carla.

Hey! Give me a call when you can. I need you to help me with something. ASAP.

I don't want to alarm her, but I do want to make her realize that I'm in a bit of a pickle. We've been friends for quite a while now. We met through Sam, actually. She's a high school English teacher who also works at Loser's—one of my favorite bar/restaurants—as a server on weekends. She knows I have an issue with panic attacks, but she doesn't know how bad it is. Probably because I tidied up my story for her, shrugged it off like a cold when I explained it to her one night over vodkas and tonics. I do that every time I get close to talking about my Big A. It's my little secret. I have my psychiatrist, Dr. Baldwin, and Dr. Sharp, my too-calm therapist, who know all. I have no desire to tell the world. I do not want to wear my mental illness on my sleeve.

Typically, when I wind up in a predicament, Sam comes and helps me out. But not now. Definitely not now.

Man, what I wouldn't give for one five-milligram Xanax.

CHAPTER 4

Okay, then. I can't believe this is happening, but the true-blue fact of the matter is that it's now *11:43 p.m. And I'm still here!* I've made multiple attempts at leaving this place, but every time I try, I'm unable to do it. The same things happen each time I approach the door: nervousness, anxiety, panic, then fear and dread. It's like there's a force field that doesn't allow me to take another step further. DANGER! My mind screams when I approach the door. I succumb to a kind of full-body paralysis. I cannot move forward.

As I stand next to a yoga room, not knowing what to do, I start to hear this voice, lulling me like a hypnotherapist: *"It's so comfy here... so healthy... so heavenly... with all the movie-star lookalikes... and the gurgling fountain... and the cleanliness and the orderliness, the tranquility... Why even leave?"* the voice says. *"Stay. Make yourself at home right here at Great Fitness."*

So there. It's called "stuck." I find a comfy leather chair near a weight room and sit down.

Lee said the club closes at midnight, then opens back up again at 4:30 a.m. So... now what?

Yes. Now what?

If I'm unable to leave the building, my only other choice is obvious: I must stay for the night.

Are you serious?

What if I'm caught? Would they call the police? Or would they bounce me out of the club on my ass? I can always say I accidentally fell asleep, worn out from too much exercise on my first day—as well as maybe one too many Moscow mules? Something like that. Play innocent.

In my mind, I run through the scenario, something like: "Sorry, let me grab my things and just..." What, leave?

Right!

But what other choice do I have?

Couldn't I hide away somewhere inside this humongous facility? Find total seclusion and sleep on a yoga mat? Stay for the night and, in the morning, after a good night's sleep—*a good night's sleep? Really?*—just grab my things and go? I mean, how hard could it be?

Obviously, the idea is crazy, sordid, and desperate. And yet, there's a certain ring to it as well. Maybe it's possible after all. I smile to myself as I shift in my seat. I pretend to stare at my phone, while two members, young guys talking about sports—"That's how the Bruins *are* these days!"—walk past me, not even noticing me. In my mind, I run through the different rooms I've peered into today and my heart gives a leap as I remember the massage rooms. Yes. What about the massage rooms? Is it possible? Or do they keep that section locked?

Maybe I *can* do this, maybe I *could* spend the night on one of the massage tables, and then in the morning simply vamoose as soon as the doors open. Surely, I'll be over this in the morning. Surely, by tomorrow, I'll have gained the courage to leave.

A massage table isn't that comfortable but, hey, it's as close to a bed as I'm going to find in *this* joint. With no other plan that comes to mind, and the anxiety building inside me once

again, I head up to the massage area on the second floor and
tiptoe around—just to see what's what.

I discover that it's actually not locked at all. The massage
section is simply an open area that winds down several halls in
its own maze. As I wander around, attractive members pass me
by. Some staff too: a youngish male trainer who uncannily
resembles the actor Rufus Sewell, wearing a tight-fitting shirt
that says, *"Be Your Best, Get Trained at Great Fitness."*

"Closing soon," he says. "Great workout?"

"Uh... Uh..." I can barely mumble a word.

He gives me an odd stare as I quickly walk past him, feeling
so bad about myself, so frickin' inept.

It's quiet up here in the massage zone. Not a soul around.
So safe. Comfy. Calming. Why can't life be one big massage
zone? I take a deep breath as I find myself passing through an
entire hallway of small, dark rooms with massage tables in them,
one right after the other, all blessedly empty and dimly lit. The
massage personnel must have gone home long ago. Once again,
I get jittery as hell thinking about trying to leave the building.

There are ten rooms in total, each with all kinds of lotions
on the tables. A mix of pleasurable aromas wafts through the air,
vanilla, peppermint, lavender. Clean, white, fluffy towels are
neatly folded on the tables. In one room, music still flows from
speakers set against a wall: soft sounds, harps and strings,
abstract melodies designed to put you in a blissful state of mind,
the harmonious music of the spheres. Someone must have
forgotten to switch it off.

I yawn just being in here. Surely, I could lie down on one of
these tables and stay the night without being discovered,
couldn't I? I mean, Great Fitness is so huge—no one would
notice one lone sleeper in this giant building.

*And then you're leaving in the morning—ASAP. No fooling
around. 4:30 a.m. sharp. Right on the nose, as soon as the doors
swing open. You're outta here. Right?*

But what if there's a night watchman? I swallow. Or a midnight cleaning crew? Or security cameras!? On top of everything, I'm breaking all the cardinal sins: I have no toothpaste, electric toothbrush, or dental floss. This is a dental travesty.

11:50 p.m.

Oh, God! What should I do? An announcement comes over the intercom, making my heart thrum and my mouth fall open: *"Ladies and gentlemen, we will be closing in ten minutes. We hope you've enjoyed your workout today and thank you for choosing Great Fitness."*

Are there cameras all over the place?

This is ridiculous.

You CAN'T spend the night here. Be reasonable, Kat.

And so, with nine quickly dissolving minutes to go, I traipse down to the front again, march toward the reception area, carrying my cellphone and gym bag, then linger by the fountain as I enviously watch everyone else in the building walk out the front door and depart. To them, it's a cinch. I fidget with my hands and blink rapidly as I stand here. There's an empty feeling in the pit of my stomach and my nerves are zinging all over my body. I'm a tragedy waiting to happen, that's what I am. I sniffle and wipe my eyes. *Oh, Kat. What is wrong with you?*

It's now or never.

11:55 p.m.

The tall male with an earring in one ear at the front desk stares at a computer screen while he's on the phone. He doesn't even see me. I feel invisible. It's so dark outside too. What kind of fool would exercise at this time of night?

Maybe I could ask the guy at the desk to help me leave. Tell him I'm anxious and... I stare at him. He looks pissed about something. His face is flushed and there's a sneer on his lips. No. I don't think he'd be helpful.

There are only three members left in the building now and they walk around me as I stand here, frozen in space and time.

These bulky macho guys—would one of them be willing to lend a hand? I'd be so embarrassed asking them. They'd think I was out of my mind. At this point, I'm not sure I could even muster a coherent string of words.

No. I need to do this myself.

Go! Go! Go!

A few more tentative steps toward the door. And then... One more... One more...

That's it. I can't. It's like trying to break through a wall.

I can't do it.

The Big A is inside me now—one more step toward that door, and I'll be done for. I'll collapse right here and now and they'll have to call an ambulance. There's a giant nervous energy that has grabbed me by the shoulders and is holding me back—immobilizing me.

I can't do it. No. No. No.

I wipe away a tear, and my stomach tightens with dread as I give the door one final glare. I stand on the spot, thinking maybe I *should* ask someone for help. But I have to pay the price for my hesitation; by the time I get up the courage to approach the last two members, they're all out the door and then I turn around and I don't even see the front desk guy anymore. I'm alone in the entire building. Shit! In the end, all I can do is head back toward the massage rooms—it's like a walk of shame after sleeping with some bad-news guy—and take the elevator. Alone. All by myself—like that song by whoever.

I find the most out-of-the way massage room possible and close the door behind me. There. It's done. My whole world comes crashing down right in front of my eyes. All I can do is hunker down, sit on the floor in a corner, and cover my face with my hands, knees up to my chest. Tears are rolling down my cheeks, thick globs of tears. I feel so lost, so isolated, so different from every other human being on the planet. Whatever malevolent force has arisen in my mind, it owns me; I can only obey it.

Oh, Kat, look what you've done now.

Midnight. 12:00. That's what my cell says.

A minute later, the doors to the facility slam shut. BAM! BAM! BAM! The lights in the entire place go out. Darkness. Complete and total. It's a nightmare. I'm stuck here. I want to scream.

But I don't scream. I can't scream. I'm afraid to even whisper. All I do is listen intensely as I shift around on the floor. But it's hard to hear anything when your heart is booming in your ears, as if it were in a symphony performing Beethoven's Ninth. I manage to make out faint voices rising from the parking lot outside. And there's some sort of electric humming noise inside the building now; maybe it's the security system turning on? And then I hear three loud, quick beeps like the buzzer at the end of a basketball game. BZZZZZ... BZZZZ... BZZZZ... Oh, God! I startle, then clench my teeth and freeze.

Now silence. I look around. There's nothing but darkness, thick and dense, a "fog of darkness" as Sam once said while reciting one of his high-brow poems. I can't even see my hand in front of me. But a red light has somehow turned on, arising out of the darkness like an eye staring straight at me, blinking from the other corner of the room. Blinking... blinking... I have no idea what it is. Some sort of sensor? A motion detector? If it is, I'm screwed.

I don't dare break the silence. I rest my head against my knees.

What would Sam think of you now? Huh? Wouldn't he be thrilled?

This is wonderful, isn't it? Isn't this, as Lee would say... *great?*

Minutes pass. More minutes. Handfuls of minutes. Pitchers, gallons of miserable, unforgiving time. And still, nothing happens. Not a sound. Not a blip. I hear no signs of anyone walking around, humans or aliens, no security guard. Nobody. I'm on Planet Screwed, its only occupant.

Finally, I find myself yawning in the continuing galactic silence. After all, it's past midnight and I have worn myself out today, physically and emotionally. No doubt about it. I am beat.

Thank God I had the common sense to keep my cellphone with me. When I press the activation button, the warm glow of the pixilated screen lights up my face. Digital fire. I feel like a cavewoman hovering around my only source of light. Is this how humanity ends, the few remaining souls gathered around the dying embers of a digital glow two hundred years from now?

I check my messages. Ah! Val's texted me and I read it like a prisoner starved of news from the outside:

You should see it here. It's gorgeous! Went sailing today! So beautiful! Luvvv San Diego!

Dear Val. But there's no way I'm going to tell her about the predicament I'm in when she can do nothing to help. No reason to alarm her. Besides, how would I put it? *Glad you're enjoying yourself. Just got anxiety-locked inside a health club. No biggie. Have fun. Let's talk soon.*

And then a text from Carla pings in at last:

Hey, got your message. Lost my phone today. Just found it. What's up?

Not a whole heckuvalot.

I turn to my emails. There's one from my ex-employer's accountant asking me a question about my W-2. I don't even understand what he's talking about. An email from Angela Ackerman, another dental hygienist I know, asking me if I happen to know of any job openings. Yeah. Actually, I do, come to think of it.

There are about ten spams... new ways to make money instantly, new ways to lose weight instantly, even one about new ways to make money instantly *as* you lose weight instantly, a home security systems offer, Travelzoo's latest bonanzas—man, that trip to Aruba looks amazing!—all of which I delete. And an email from my mother telling me she's in Hawaii for a week. She still doesn't feel comfortable texting, God bless her. She says she can't get the hang of it.

It's marvelous here. Tomorrow we're going horseback riding! How are you doing? How's Sam?

The thought of how much my mother adores Sam makes me hurt even more. I swear, my mother likes Sam so much it's like *she* wants to marry him. All those embarrassing too-long hugs she always gives him whenever she visits, ruffling his hair, staring into his eyes... not to mention her absolute adoration of his cooking, Sam always plying her with mini beef Wellington bits, scrumptious Brie, and these amazing Belgian waffles that he makes to perfection. And oh, that raspberry en croûte. Like heaven on the tongue. She still can't believe I landed him. Honestly, *I* can't believe I landed him, either. She's going to be heartbroken when she learns we split up... or that he split up with me—whatever.

12:35 a.m.

Phone's down to its last bar. I have no charger. *I'm* down to my last bar.

I use the flashlight mode and shine it all around, aiming the light at the bottles of oils and lotions, which now cast monster shadows on the walls. Scents of vanilla and peppermint waft in the air. I focus the light on the strange red blinker, which is emanating from a small black box in the corner. Is it somehow watching me? What the hell is it? Is it some kind of charger?

Searching for a security camera, I shine the light at the walls and the ceiling, but find nothing. Not a thing. This is good. And then, with the flashlight's glow all around me, I slowly and carefully find the courage to stand. I take off my shoes, grab a few towels, and creep toward the massage bed, inch by inch, fully expecting a motion detector to go off at any moment, or an alarm, or something. My body tenses. Wait. Motion detectors?

Are you serious? This isn't an art museum. Where do you think you are, the MOMA?

I carefully crawl up on the massage table—which is hard and narrow and not very welcoming at all. Since I'm low on juice, I switch off my cell. I merge back with the darkness, then, after one long and tremulous sigh, as if life has hurled its final arrow at me, I curl into a fetal position on my side. I ball up one towel and place it under my head and put the other one over me. But without a real blanket, it's agonizing. I am so scared. I wipe away another tear. I've done some crazy stupid ass things in my life, but this? This takes the...

As soon as this place opens up, I'm outta here.

I can't sleep. I lie here, listening to my heart pound away.

Slowly, like the carefully guarded memory that it is, my Infamous Walmart Incident surfaces, rising out of the darkness like a scary blue whale until there it sits in my inner vision, filling up my entire consciousness. It always seems to come to me when I'm in trouble; I hate to think about it, and try not to. But it's like saying, "Don't think about elephants." And then elephants are all you think about.

Ten years ago, I was standing in line at the super Walmart on Nolensville Road, waiting to pay, minding my own business, when before I knew what had hit, a full-blown panic attack seized me. It was as if the right hand of fear and the left hand of dread, fear's more evil sister, literally grabbed me by the throat, kicked me in the butt, and stomped all over my entire nervous system. I could not catch my breath. I started hyperventilating. Totally from out of nowhere. Maybe it was the crowds packing in tight, or the noisy atmosphere. And then there was the Big Emotional Fact that my parents were getting divorced. Earlier that day, I'd driven by and stopped in front of my childhood home, sat in my car, and cried as I stared at that stinking "For Sale" sign. What made it even worse was the red PENDING sign on top. I couldn't help it. I felt demoralized. I could hardly breathe. That house represented "us," our family, my mother, father, my brother, and me. And though there had been times when it was difficult for my mother and father to be together— days of slamming doors and angry outbursts, followed by periods when they hardly spoke to each other, nights of dreaded silence between them—still, I had hopes that their love for each other would carry them, and "us" through. The sale of our home banished that hope completely.

And so, in that frustrating, slow-moving line, this bearded man in dungarees breathing down my neck with the odor of a sweaty horse, and all the problems of my life surfacing before my eyes. Bryce, this marriage counselor guy I was dating, had just broken up with me—there's something about breaking up with a *marriage counselor*; it's depressing and I don't even know why. My heart started palpitating so hard I thought that was it. Death by anxiety. I found myself literally *unable* to make my way out of the store. Instead of paying for my items, I backed out of the line and started wandering around for a while, checking out this and that. I finally wound up plopping down on the floor, right next to the drug aisle that sold Pepto Bismol, Imodium and other anti-diarrheals. I had to ask someone if they could please call 911 for me—my hands were shaking too much to even use my own phone. It was your basic variety nervous breakdown—nothing fancy about it at all. What made things worse was that I uttered to the wrinkle-browed pharmacist who'd suddenly turned pale, "Oh, God. I just want to kill myself." That kind of talk really gets someone's attention. I drew a crowd of onlookers.

I wound up being escorted by ambulance straight to a psychiatric hospital, St. Regis, where a well-built, hunky doctor stung my butt with Ativan, a major tranquilizer. "Are you sure you're not an actor? Haven't I seen you on a soap opera?" I jokingly asked him before I finally fell into a deep, untroubled sleep.

I was court-mandated to stay the night and throughout the next two days for observation. It's the law, I later discovered, once you say you're going to kill yourself. Trust me, yes, they *can* take your freedom away if they think you might be a threat to yourself or to others, and a person who has a breakdown inside a Walmart is a complete unknown variable—they don't know what you might do.

It was horrible. For starters, there was this short, bald psychiatrist who had a superiority complex going on, as if I was some sort of semi-human, and he was a giant among men and women.

"I am the medical doctor in charge of this ward," he'd said. "And you are a sick young woman. Do not question me and we'll get along fine."

When I said that I wanted to go home, that I didn't need to be there, that I was totally fine, he talked to me like I was a child or some sort of complete idiot. Or a childish idiot. He said, "If I decide to, I can keep you here for at least a week. So do not argue with me, Ms. No-Add."

"It's Noad, please," I'd said staunchly. "As in toad."

If I wasn't panicky before, I sure was then.

Good old American healthcare. Best in the world, right?

Being among the patients and all those sad and confused people—the suicidals, the drug-addicted, the schizophrenics—only sent me into a further tailspin. Was I going to wind up like them? That's the kind of fear that roots around inside you and doesn't let go. I felt so sorry for them. I did, however, manage to find a bit of a humorous angle: some of them were walking around in creepy-looking pajamas, talking to themselves as if they were preparing for their own stand-up comedy routines. As if Jimmy Fallon was calling their agents and this was going to be their big break.

A red-haired, gaunt woman, smelling of a mixture of Chanel No. 5 and sweat, came over to me while I was sitting in the TV room. She whispered in my ear, her voice so grainy it sandpapered my eardrum, "There's no trusting the FBI. Beware. It's every woman for herself."

"Okay," I'd replied in a whisper, turning back to my *People* magazine. "If you say so."

But then, even worse, she added, with a bright, effervescent smile, "By the way, I absolutely *love* your hair. How'd it get so thin and straggly?"

I felt like weeping...

Finally, after sifting through this memory and letting it fall through the hourglass of my mind, I descend into a dreamless, pitiful sleep...

I awaken in a state of unbridled agitation, eyes blinking rapidly, heart pumping. An electrified adrenaline rush sizzles through my body. For the longest, most terrifying moment, I don't even know where I am. Sam? Is he here? Then it all comes back to me in one fat wad of memory regurgitation. Great Fitness. *Be Your Best!* Exclamatory Lee! Treadmills... Rufus Sewell. Yummy's. Moscow mules.

I turn on my cell. It's 1:47 a.m. Christ! Barely an hour has passed. I have a long, long way to go until 4:30 a.m., when the club reopens. Time is creeping by. Time is my enemy. Time is a traitor. I listen for anything outside my room, listen with all my might, ears straining, but all I hear is the sound of my own breathing and the bass drum of my heart in my ears. A few creaks here and there—pops and grinds, as if the facility itself is shifting around, trying to get comfortable. I take a long, slow breath. Eyes wide open in the deep dark and suddenly, I recall that movie, *The Shining*. Could a health club be supernaturally evil as well? It was only a movie, of course, but still... what about: *Attack of the Evil Treadmill?* Stephen King's probably working on it this very minute. *Once you get on, you never ever get off!*

About ten minutes pass and now, a new problem arises: I have to go to the bathroom. Maybe if I hum or something, the urge will pass. I start humming a Backstreet Boys song—"I Want It That Way," catchy as hell—sitting up on the table and moving around, squiggling, trying to get my mind off my bladder... A few minutes later... Nope. Still gotta go.

I'd noticed a bathroom near the entrance of the massage area. Dare I head out into the hallway? What if I run into a security guard? Or a cleaning person? What if there's someone else staying here overnight like me? That would be a trip, both of us backing into each other in some dark hallway and scaring ourselves to death. Like something you'd see in a movie with, who knows? Ben Stiller? I am so obsessed with celebrities. I really need to stop it. I started reading the magazines at the dental office and couldn't get enough. Before I knew it, I was an authority on things like Camila Mendes's latest boyfriend. It's like I get lost in their lives so I don't have to think about my own —another form of me not facing reality and...

Either use the bathroom, Kat, or pee in your frickin' pants.

I have to go, goddammit! My bladder's about to burst! I tiptoe out of the room in my bare feet, ears perked, nerves set on maximum alert. Silence is a cacophony. It crawls into my ears like a bug and rattles the pots and pans. But you know? In a way, this is kind of—I don't know—almost fun. I try to think of it as an adventure and a smile appears on my lips. Dungeons & Dragons in a health club? Yeah. Let's make a game of it.

Step by step, letting my cell's high-beam flashlight lead the way, I inch down the hallway and find the bathroom. I open the door, which creaks enough to wake the dead, then step inside, slowly shutting the door behind me. My footsteps echo on the tile floor, no matter how lightly I tread.

I shine the light around and see that this is more than a mere bathroom. This is another huge locker room with at least ten shower stalls and a sauna, lockers, a long line of sinks and mirrors. It's so quiet, and yet it's exploding with the silent sound of dread. My hands tremble and there's an ache in the back of my throat. For a few seconds, my teeth chatter and the tips of my fingers feel cold.

I pass five urinals—wait, urinals?—then enter the nearest bathroom stall. After I do my business, I stand and the toilet flushes automatically. It's so surprisingly loud, I nearly jump out of my skin. No. This toilet is *not* a whisperer. It's one of those perfectionistic models designed to remove every single speck of effluence there could ever possibly be in the entire known universe, the noise resounding all over the bathroom, if not over the entire health club and beyond. Would you shut the F up? Well, if anyone else is here, they'll certainly know about me now.

I hold the light in front of me and swallow. My heart is pattering like a drummer practicing paradiddles in the ribcage of my chest. I catch a look at myself in the mirror as I pass by— face all flushed and big-eyed.

You really know how to do it, don't you, girl?

And then just as I'm about to exit, I freeze. I hear a tap-tap noise coming closer, echoing, closer still. Footsteps! It has to be!

A security guard. No doubt about it. What should I do? For a second, I don't have any answers. I look right and left, heart booming. I'm trapped. This is it. I'm going to jail!

I snap out of my indecision at last and rush into the very back stall. I sit on the toilet, drawing my legs up against my chest. Sweat is streaming down my sides. This is it. I'm going to be caught. Sayonara, freedom.

A few minutes later, the door creaks open and a light shines inside. Shadows spread out, large and ghostly. Now footsteps resound, slow-moving, careful footsteps, a flashlight beam leading the way. I hold as still as I can. *Don't breathe. Don't breathe. Don't breathe.*

Surely, it's a security guard, but whoever it is walks around the bathroom, footsteps tapping on the tile floor, echoing. Then no more footsteps. Everything is totally still. I grow dizzy with fear. When the footsteps begin again, the path of the light beam moves closer to where I am. It traces arcs around my stall. The steps come closer, closer still...

The footsteps stop right in front of my door. The light shines bright around me. I hear breathing, kind of wheezy-sounding. Not very healthy. My heart is pounding so loud I'm afraid he can hear it. Blood rushes through my ears. Finally, after what seems like an eon, the footsteps head off in the direction of the urinals.

"Another damn ghost flush," he mutters in a strangely high-pitched voice with a thick Southern accent. "Need to call the plumber again."

Next thing I know, he turns on the light to the bathroom, blinding me momentarily. I hear him unzipping his pants, and then he takes a long piss—don't mind me, fella!—the strong force of his urine streaming against hard porcelain. It's the longest pee ever, as if the guy drank about five gallons of water or a six-pack of beer. Suddenly I have the need to cough. *Don't you dare!* I manage to cough just as he flushes.

Finally, I can hear him zipping back up, and then he starts humming a song. Then he sings, "Man, she's one pretty momma... Sure would love to be with her tonight... she's got what I liiiike... Oh, yeah... that's riiiiight... one pretty momma..." It's some country tune I vaguely recognize. Oh, God. He's still standing there, probably staring at himself in the mirror, singing away, his voice echoing all over the room. He's actually a pretty good singer, kind of reminds me of Garth Brooks. "Gonna treat her riiiight..."

Would you please leave?

Finally, he turns off the light and shuts the door behind him. I hear his footsteps down the hall, fading away.

Jesus!

Hardly able to breathe, my limbs shaking, I tiptoe into a shower stall and curl up on the floor. The showerhead drips water on me as if to accentuate the ridiculousness and the absurdity of my plight. The entire thing would be funny if it wasn't so damn sad.

I barely sleep at all. Time isn't time. It seems stuck, frozen, glacier-like, refusing to move forward, refusing to do what it's supposed to do. I feel so ashamed, so dumb, so wrong. As I remain sitting in this tiled shower, all balled up and afraid, feeling the plunk of cold water on my head, tears come slowly at first, dripping from my eyes like drips from the shower head above me, then harder, until finally, I'm sobbing because of everything, the entire whacked-out entity I call my life, sobbing so hard that I can't stop.

CHAPTER 5
TUESDAY

When I wake up, I've been dreaming of Sam... Sam... We were buying a red Audi together... Standing in the lot of some huge car dealership. The Audi was brand-new and beautiful and Sandra Bullock was the salesperson. All smiles, with gorgeous teeth, teeth like no other teeth in the entire universe—but then she turned into an old woman with no teeth, just a pair of sore gums... and the Audi crumbled into dust right before our eyes...

What the hell does it mean?

I check the time: 5:35 a.m. WHAT? The club opened at four-thirty and I was still snoozing away? I can't believe this! I've overslept, just like I did with my ex-friend Janice Hudson and her airport ride. I promised her I'd take her to the airport for this important job interview in Chicago one early Monday morning. I overslept, she missed her plane, and lost the job. She still sends me nasty texts about it. What is wrong with me? I am always oversleeping!

Heart fluttering, I scramble out of the bathroom, then look around as I stand in the hallway, all disheveled and confused. I'm in my bare feet, still wearing my workout attire, my street clothes stashed in locker 806-A.

I'm groggy, hazy, frightened as shit. My mouth is cotton-dry and I need to brush my teeth real bad. I know I must look like a zombie. I feel totally displaced. What the hell am I doing waking up in a health club?

The next thing I know, I do a double take as someone I recognize walks past me. It's that same guy who was at the bar last night drinking IPAs. He nods stiffly as a trail-scent of cheap cologne follows him. It almost makes me sneeze. I nod back, pretending all's right with the world. Our eyes meet for a second. I don't even think he recognizes me. He's dressed in crisply pressed slacks and a blue golf shirt, holding a communicator-thingy in one hand, the kind with the rubber antenna. So, he works here? Is he in maintenance? Security? Is this the guy who was in the bathroom last night? Other than him, however, the hallway is mercifully empty. I turn to my right and nearly bang into a filtered water machine.

Rubbing my eyes, I jam my hands underneath my armpits, then jump up and down a bit, trying to get going. I remember that I left my phone in the shower stall and dash back to get it. I come out again just as a big man with long black hair and a bulbous nose enters, giving me an odd look. His gnarled up face makes me think he could pass as a professional boxer.

"Ooops," I say with a laugh. "Wrong door."

He breaks into a gracious grin. I walk away from the locker room and shiver, then return to the massage room and quickly tidy up. Not knowing what else to do, I head toward a yoga room on the same floor. It's empty and I look around as if I'm waiting for a class to start. Two women pass by and I smile and nod at them. They smile back.

I yawn and slowly, amazingly enough, I start to relax. I made it through the night without being caught! I feel safe and actually quite confident now. I did it, pulled one over on Mr. Great Fitness himself. No one can accuse me of anything. I'm a paid-in-full member and it's after 4:30 a.m. I'm firmly within my legal rights. I square my shoulders and hold my head high.

Already the workout machines are clank-clunking, treadmills whirring.

"I need coffee!" a woman shouts from somewhere and others laugh.

Just do it.

I'm going to grab my gym bag, take a shower in the women's locker room, change into my streetwear—the same jeans and blouse I came in with yesterday—then eat breakfast at Yummy's. I'd like to try their oatmeal with blueberries. Rinse my mouth with water because of Dental Hygiene 101: When you don't have access to a toothpaste and a toothbrush, rinse with water. It's the next best thing. I'm *not* going to panic.

And then, yes!

I'll just get the hell out of here. Make like a tree and leave. Exit Hotel Great Fitness, and head home to my empty, Sam-less apartment to begin the rest of my miserable life. Turn the page. Get outta this cage. Begin a new chapter. All that stuff.

It's nearly 7 a.m. now, my stomach's full, and I am so determined, so full of resolve, I think I could march across the entire state of Tennessee once I get out of here. Nothing's gonna stop me now! (Is that a song?) I'm showered, using their wonderful peach-scented shower gel—I so love the water pressure here, way better than my apartment—and, after changing into clean underwear, which I brought with me, I'm ready to go.

Lee's at the front desk wearing his AirPods and he waves to me as soon as he spots me. He's as exuberant as ever, Mr. Red Bull himself, all fired up. I'm definitely on his radar now.

"Hey, Kat! How are you? You got here early. That's great! Dedication, huh? Didn't even see you come in." He furrows his brow. "And I got here as soon as we opened."

How about that?

"Guess we missed each other." I shrug, giving him a smile as I shift my gym bag to my other shoulder. "How's it going?"

His voice booms. "It's going *great!* How are you?"

"I'm burning it," I say, feeling myself flush. "Trying to, anyway."

"Well, keep it up!" His eyes go wide. "I'm already impressed!" He laughs ridiculously loudly, evidently forgetting the fact that I "somehow" slipped in without him noticing.

"Thanks!" I flash him my best Life-Is-Great smile.

But when I turn away from him and move toward the front door—drawing to within three feet of it—it's as if all hell breaks loose inside me once again. I freak. My mind starts scrambling and basically, like a replay of an old song by Metallica I know too well, I go haywire. Emotional fireworks light up my dark mental sky. Sparks, flames. Lights flashing. Panic strikes again, hitting me so hard that I nearly fall back and collapse on the spot.

My mind whirs. I grow dizzy. What the hell is wrong with me? I break out in a cold sweat as I blink rapidly. If someone were to try to talk to me right now, I'm not sure I'd be able to respond. A dull pain followed by a sharp needle-like sting penetrates my chest as if someone were driving it through with a hammer. I immediately go sit down near the fountain. Breathe... breathe... Lee's voice rattles on by the front desk.

It takes about fifteen minutes, but finally, after walking out into the pool deck and doing enough deep breathing, I settle down and my heart rate steadies. I go back inside and sit down near the fountain. Lee is nowhere to be seen. Another person is at the front desk. Club members of all shapes and sizes enter and exit the building. Coffee-cup carriers, bottled-water carriers, athletic-looking teens bursting through with their lithe, invincible bodies, seniors trundling past, business executive types marching toward exercise glory, no doubt recalling their nimble college days, all of them, each and every one, with determined expressions scrawled all over their faces.

It's getting busy now. The world has woken up.

I see through the windows that an orange sun has risen in the distance. And there's my car still sitting in the parking lot. I wonder if it was noticed? Did someone write down the license number? My poor red Camry, ready and willing to whisk me away. It's the one with the dented rear bumper, on which a decal reads: *"Clean ' em before you lose ' em."* Windows all fogged up from spending the night ungaraged. *I'm* all fogged up. My car looks as lonely as I feel. If it had a mind, it would likely be wondering, "What is wrong with you? Let's go! I'm bored!" It would be honking its horn!

This is awful. I blink back tears and for a moment close my eyes. I suck in a breath. I wish I was Dorothy in *The Wizard of Oz* and I could just click my heels and...

I can't even leave the building, I can't even...

Suddenly, a new thought washes over me: Wait a minute. What's the rush? Seriously. *What is the rush?*

The idea hits me, staggers me, the possibility so raw and interesting and powerful that it makes me quiver inside. Why do I even *want* to get out of this place so fast? Maybe it's better if I stick around for a while. Hang out. Relax. Work out. After all, I *am* a paid-in-full member. I can stay here as long as I want —up until midnight, of course.

Besides, what's so great about returning to an apartment without Sam and without a job, where Hugh's Muffin and Pastry Shop is so close by, a fine place, indeed, but it's also my favorite entry point into the wilds of overeating. Not to mention the couch on which I perpetually laze. It would be calling my name too. I'd surely fall back into my old ways of binging on food and Netflix. Not to mention, boozing it up and throwing a pity party, inviting me, myself, and I as the only guests. Fact:

There's not a single barbell at my apartment, while in here at Great Fitness... I'm a step away from any kind of exercise machine I could ever dream of.

I remain seated as more members stream past and every few minutes the guy at the desk is shouting, "Great! That's great!" Oddly, I find a kind of satisfying comfort in his exuberant "greatness." A few minutes later, I'm *much* better. The sound of the fountain's calming, bubbling water is tranquilizing. The lavender scent is comforting. All the good-looking members, men and women... Who knows? Maybe there *is* a movie star hanging around here somewhere.

Lee returns to the desk and chatters away. "Hey! Mr. Quentin! So good to see you!" "Hey there, Brandy! Working those abs today? Great! Great! Yeah! I saw that about quinoa too. I guess it *does* have more protein than soymilk! That's amazing!"

And on and on.

Of course, I *could* call Dr. Sharp, my thin, willowy therapist, and explain to her that I'm panic-locked inside a health club. But I'm sure she'd only tell me to call 911. And if I phoned Dr. Baldwin, my portly mustached psychiatrist, that's what he'd say too. Call 911. 911. 911. That's all doctors say these days. They don't want to get involved with anyone who doesn't come into their office—too many potential lawsuits out there. Let the emergency rooms handle it. That's what they're for.

No! I'm *not* calling 911. I'm *not* winding up in a psychiatric hospital again—not yet anyway. I have to figure this out on my own. Should I call Carla? Not now. It would be way too embarrassing.

There's got to be a way to leave this building on my own without going into panic mode.

Should I try the door again?

I stare at that ominous front door and instantly feel that quaking in my stomach, the edges of panic. Considering the possibility makes me uneasy. No. Not now. I don't think I could take it. I have no desire to wind up in the woman's bathroom puking out my breakfast.

I simply do what comes naturally: I head back to the locker room, cram my stuff into a locker, change into my workout clothing, and start walking around again. I badly need to brush my teeth, though, and fortunately, I find a solution. Amazingly enough, I am able to purchase both toothpaste and toothbrush at the Pro Shop. Besides women's apparel, they conveniently sell a variety of deodorants, lotions, razors, and other sundries. I'm in luck.

After brushing my teeth and as I'm standing near a weight room a few minutes later, I hear someone singing in the background. I tune in and I realize who it is: *"Hey, pretty momma..."* I turn and stare. It's Mr. Footsteps from last night, no doubt about it. He's tall, wiry, wearing a white golf shirt and brown slacks, with a bunch of keys hanging from his belt and a Great Fitness logo on his shirt. So he worked the night shift as a security guard and he's here during the day? I wonder if he sleeps here in some out-of-the-way room. I can't catch a glimpse of his face, only a spot of brown spiky hair, as he moves away from me, but just the sound of that song sends chills down my spine. Is he the only one? Is there an entire staff of security personnel?

He turns around, and starts heading my way. He keeps singing. I freeze, then take a step, but the next thing I know, I'm right in his path and damn if we don't start dancing with each other, both trying to move right. Then both of us stepping left.

"Excuse me," he says in that Southern drawl of his, looking straight at me, scrutinizing me.

"Excuse me," I say, looking down, blushing. "Sorry."

He shoves his hands in his pockets, and then moves on as he starts singing again in his super-fine voice.

He only has one good eye. The bad one is all clouded over; a gray mess. I wonder if he forgot his eye patch. And there's a scar down his cheek. Imagine that—a security guard with only one good eye. I hope he has two good ears.

I stand there, frozen as ice, as my heart flutters and my hands go slick with sweat. Finally, I go drink some water from one of the fountains and try to relax. Heart still pattering, I sit back down in a chair and get my bearings, take deep breaths. Wow.

Okay. What should I do now?

There's only one thing *to* do: exercise—again. After all, I'm definitely in the right place.

The morning progresses and time comes unfrozen and liquefies. I lighten up as what I went through the night before seems to vanish in the haze (is that a song?). Eight, then 9 a.m., and I settle in. I spy on a Barre class through a glass window and marvel at how well the instructor moves her fluid body as she leads the fifteen or so women. A real pro. I might like to try that class. Note to self: Read up on Barre.

Instead of exercising though, I take the easier way out. I head outside into the increasingly warm, clear-sky day and plop down in a comfy lounge chair near the outdoor swimming pool. Hey, I'm on vacation. Look at it like that. What's not to like? I'm in between jobs. No big deal at all. Relax. That's the ticket. Take a load off and enjoy. A smile blossoms on my face. Poolside, it's easy not to have a care in the world.

Out here, I don't feel trapped at all. The swimming pool water is clear and blue and sparkling and clean. The sky is infinite and vast. An airplane flies by, cutting across the sky. Too bad I'm not on it.

Summer has brought the kids out to the pool, along with mothers, teens, a few fathers and singles, and a group of four women about my age, sun worshipers with lotion, and white buds in their ears. It's definitely going to be another hot day. That's what Nashville is: humid summers, sweet iced tea, lots of bars and churches—I once went to a church that had a bar in it! —and country music downtown. Tourists galore. I guess you learn to get used to it.

Staring at a wild herd of kids playing in the pool, I lie on a lounger and recall my father teaching me how to swim. I was probably five or six. He was so patient with me, showing me the proper form, the right ways to move my arms.

"Kick your feet too," he'd said, his eyes shining. "It makes you go faster. And cup your hands."

I smile at the memory. When I was a child, my father was always there for me. And even as an adult, he's always been a safe place for me to run to. After Lilly died, my dad was right there with me. I'd feel so ashamed bothering him about my situation now though. He'd come running down to rescue me in a heartbeat. I really don't want to worry him; I've worried him enough over the years. If I have to call him, maybe I will, but only as my last resort. I still believe I can solve this, ahem, problem, on my own. I'm good for now. After all—come on. How hard can walking through a frickin' door be?

Once, my father saved me from nearly drowning when I was almost seven. I had snuck into our pool's deep end along with Sara Jane, my friend, talking her into it, when my parents were having a few neighbors over for a summer cookout, thinking we were strong enough swimmers to handle it. We had both taken lessons, after all. But I found myself struggling to stay afloat, kicking my arms and legs and feeling overwhelmed. Panic set in—yes, dear panic— and I was choking on water when he found me, rescuing me.

"It's okay," he'd said as he pulled me to the side of the pool. I remember his face had gone pale. I was gasping for air. That fear in his eyes—it was something I'll never forget. And the panic I experienced throughout my body? I'll never forget that either.

Finally, he handed me off to my mother who bundled me up in a towel. I was shivering.

"Oh, Kat, darling," she'd said, putting things bluntly in her way. "You're not ready for the deep end yet."

That sense of struggling out of the water, of fighting for my life, that ultimate desperation, has stuck with me all these years. Panic. Blind, heart-racing panic. It's probably written itself into my bones. That's how I felt when I tried to walk through that Great Fitness door too—fighting for oxygen, my very breath, for my survival, for my life. Panic.

Not ready for the deep end yet.

Ten minutes later, a water aerobics class begins in the shallow end. Eight or nine gray-haired women, all wearing flowery bathing caps, start swaying to the music of Michael Jackson's "Beat It." I smile and feel sad at the same time as their bodies move to the rhythm. I guess this is what your life boils down to in the end—trying to fight the inevitable time-eroding process of aging and ultimately losing that fight year by year no matter how hard you try. Is that something to look forward to or what? In the end, maybe *this* is our real purpose in life: water aerobics.

"Okay, ladies," the instructor calls, a tall, twentyish female in a one-piece bathing suit. She has a whistle around her neck and walks on the side of the pool. "Stretch those arms. Move it! Let's get down!"

The precious ladies stretch and bounce, propelled by the rhythm of the song. They seem to be enjoying themselves. They look to be in their seventies and eighties, though one could easily be in her nineties... Oh, my God. No! Don't do that! Please! Miss Ninety-Year Old suddenly starts to shake her butt and sway back and forth while the other girls break out in hysterics. "You go, Gloria! That's right, girl! Shake it!" So, this is what I have to look forward to. Not a bad life.

Suddenly, an image comes to mind: I'm seventy-five years old or thereabouts, still wandering around Great Fitness. Doing water aerobics. Still sleeping on massage tables at night. Still eating at Yummy's. Still ordering Moscow mules and telling myself, hey, at least they have lime juice in them.

CHAPTER 6

Back inside the building, good-looking, fit members circulate around me. A few glance my way, and one well-built sixtyish man with gray hair raises an eyebrow at me, studying my face. I probably look distressed. But I raise my own eyebrow right back at him. *Mind your own business, pal.* Overall, I go unnoticed. Nothing special about me. The other members are all too wrapped up in the revolving kaleidoscope of their own lives. These "chosen ones." The Special People. They remind me of a herd of a certain exotic species—with their backpacks slung over their strong shoulders, their Under Armour fitting their tight, sleek bodies, their Nikes or New Balance footwear and their graceful movements.

I place my dead phone in one of the charging stations, which I've only just realized they have—how convenient!—located around the building, and ten minutes later, I'm at it: walking on a treadmill having slightly upped the incline, studying myself in the mirror. The New Kat Noad.

I intensify my movements, upping the incline even more, going faster, faster. After a while, I actually begin feeling, well, not great, but at least... better. Surely, better is on the way to great, isn't it?

One thing's for sure: Whenever I do get home, I'm flushing Sam's crab cake Benedict (key lime juice or no key lime juice) down the drain—pronto. It's Sam's creation, and I don't want any part of it.

Work it out, Kat! That's right! Take all that negative energy and... go!

Next thing I know, I'm really getting into it, really stepping it up. Is this the same Kat Noad who wakes up at noon on Saturdays and, instead of walking, drives the two blocks to the Starbucks for a Venti Frappuccino? Maybe it is! Of course it is! But now, here I am, running on a treadmill, well, jogging anyway, feeling the blood rush to my face and a sense of newborn determination in my heart. Yes! Exercise! It *is* great! Is that an endorphin I feel? Maybe getting anxiety-locked in this club is the best thing that could have happened to me.

I take all my deep-down anger at Sam out on Mr. Treadmill, who doesn't seem to mind. Maybe he's the best therapist of all. I glance around to make sure no one's laughing at me: the straggly-haired blonde chick on the Nordic Track X22i, huffing and puffing away, all red-faced and sweaty. But they're not. Once again I feel extremely *un*noticed here, almost invisible. No one can even begin to guess my secret. It's freeing in a cloak-and-dagger way. Exciting.

Suddenly, I take off. I pound it. I move faster and faster, upping the incline and the speed. I'm exercising Sam out of my mind. Why not? I guess it's better than *exorcising* him out of my mind with Father Jack Daniels presiding over the ceremony, accompanied by Brother Jose Cuervo.

As I keep moving, I feel like I'm back in high school, running track. I was actually pretty fast at the 800-meter relay and the individual 800-meter race. I even won races. Coach Mills said I had potential. He was so wrong about that. Last I heard, Coach Mills went to prison for embezzling school funds. I guess he thought he wouldn't get caught. He was wrong about that too.

Look at me now, coach. Remember Kat Noad? Here I am haulin' ass.

The TV in front of me draws my attention. I have my earphones in and I laugh at something on *The View*. Lord. Whoopi is such a wit. As I continue burning rubber, the well-coiffed women talk about how we still haven't found equality with men—even now, in this post-feminist world, this #MeToo generation. Hear, hear, I say. Shouldn't the hand that rocks the cradle rule the world?

Twenty minutes later, breathing hard and sweating, I hop off. I realize that, miraculously, my overall nervousness seems significantly reduced, the blood is circulating head to toe, and my head even feels clearer. Fogginess—gone, evaporated like mental dew. Wow. This exercise business really has something going for it. I feel so much better! It's kind of crazy, really. I actually feel on top of the—

"Hey. How's it going?"

A gorgeous woman is speaking to me as she gets off her treadmill. I am shocked, not only by her good looks, but by the fact that she noticed me at all, and then by the fact that she seems a bit familiar.

How's it going? Ha! *You really don't want to know.*

"It's going great!" I say with a buoyant smile. Even my bones seem awake, snapped to attention. More pep in my step.

"Great!" She hands it right back. She gives me a dazzling smile. Whoever did her whitening surely knew what they were doing. Perfect gums, too. All pink and moist. Healthy gums, healthy life—that's what I say, anyway. "You were really rocking that treadmill over there."

"I was?" I ask, surprise ringing through my voice.

"And I love your outfit! Where'd you get it?"

"Uh..." I blink. "Oh. The W-workout Store in Green Hills."

I look straight at her... Wait a minute. It *is* her. *All the news that's fit for the news.* I can't believe it, but I'm talking to none other than Veronica Ray, Channel Five news anchor herself. She comes on locally right before Nora O'Donnell on CBS. My hands suddenly turn into brand-new appendages that I have no idea what to do with.

"Oh yeah, I know that place. It's cute!" When she smiles, her entire face lights up.

"Thanks!" I say, feeling myself blush. I'm at a loss for words. I curl some straggly hair around my ears, and then wipe my forehead with a towel. I take a sip of bottled water.

"Come here often?" she asks.

I take another sip. "It's just my second day."

"Cool. You'll love it here. I sure do." She touches my shoulder. "Best juice bar in town. Anyway, have a great day."

She leaves me with another camera-ready smile and I am floored. Me, talking to Veronica Ray. Who would have thought?

Anyway, I need to keep up my momentum—there's no stopping me now (is *that* a song?)—and so I head on over to an elliptical machine and start it up, hopping on. Slow at first, though. Don't overdo it. A few minutes later, I'm going at it and that same euphoric feeling flows through me again. What anxiety? Right? Ha! I feel so much better! My thoughts don't seem so strong and overpowering either. I feel like I'm in control.

Dr. Sharp has always tried to urge me to exercise to allay my Big A, but I never listened. She also told me that thoughts are nothing but mental bubbles—pay attention to those bubbles and they grow stronger, don't pay attention to them, and they pop and disappear; they're actually weightless. I never believed her until now, but it might be true. I can either pay attention to the mournful bubble or the euphoric bubble.

Sam tells me the same thing, that I always focus on the negative. I sigh and slow down a bit, checking out my calorie expenditure. Sam. My heart plops into my stomach and feels like it fizzes. Will we ever get back together? Is it really over between us?

Sam was a patient at Dr. Pierce's when we first met five years ago. I was cleaning his teeth—he's going to need his lower wisdoms extracted (and there's a crack on number twelve that will one day need a crown—though he refuses to believe me). A week after his cleaning, we ran into each other at a Starbucks on West End near Centennial Park, started talking, and right there, as we were holding our tall Peppermint Mochas—mine had whip, his didn't—he asked me out. It was one of those life events that falls into your lap. When everything works out easily, for some strange reason. As if it was meant to be. I don't know, maybe it *was* meant to be.

One week later, we were going out, having drinks almost every night at a variety of downtown bars. We threw back Moscow mules, lemon drops, Long Island iced teas, whiskey sours, sidecars, daiquiris, martinis, cosmopolitans, mojitos, spritz venezianos, gimlets, margaritas, even a few Tom Collins for the history of it. Sam educated me on how certain drinks originated. He told me that the black Russian—part Kahlua, part vodka— actually began in the Soviet Union during the Cold War and was the preferred drink of CIA agents living in Moscow. The guy knows everything, I swear. Besides a degree in physics from Stanford, he's got degrees in philosophy and art history from Oxford University in England, before he spent time in Paris studying to be a chef.

We had dinners at a smorgasbord of restaurants, and engaged in long, starry-eyed conversations about how he was dreaming of becoming a master chef, and I started dreaming along with him... We spent hours talking about food and wine and traveling and what we wanted out of life. He liked me because he said I gave him a sense of groundedness, a home for his heart. I was *his* safe place. He said he felt totally comfortable with me and I was comfortable with him. We simply came together that way; we fit. When we held hands, we didn't need to say anything. The touch of our hands, fingers exploring, said all that was needed. There was a transmission between us, I swear. It was uncanny.

We moved in together not long after we met and soon he was bringing home lobster bisque—his own secret recipe—from the restaurant, along with an array of dishes. Moroccan quail with rose-petal sauce and cucumber relish, celeriac velouté with chive cream and crispy pancetta (you haven't lived until you've eaten crispy pancetta). Our sex was incredible. He was kind, happy, and in love with me, and I felt the same.

Such is life. Such is love. All I know is that it hurts like hell. Losing love feels as if I've lost my home, my direction. Sam was my emotional GPS. And now I feel directionless. Unanchored. What if this feeling lasts forever? It feels like the loss of a limb, the loss of a part of me that was as close to me as my own heart.

I retrieve my phone from the charging station—it's all juiced up—and stare at it, hoping Sam has called. No such luck.

An hour passes and now—speaking of juiced up—I'm sitting at a table in Great Fitness's juice bar, green juice in hand, feeling relaxed. Hurt. Regretful over Sam. But relaxed. One out of three ain't bad. My Big A seems to have practically disappeared, though I know he won't be gone long.

I've never had a fresh juice before. My choice of refreshment is typically Diet Coke or Mountain Dew. But this turns out to be delicious. Better than expected, as the stock analysts say. Mine's called the Super Buff and has kale, spinach, apple, pear, and lemon. I should start making these at home. I *need* to start making these at home. I feel my face turn red and my hands grow wet.

If I ever get home again.

Where are *my* ruby slippers?

Looking around, I sense a new vibe to the club, which seems to be hitting a mid-morning high. Lots of activity. It's 10:30 a.m. and a kind of exercise-excitement is in the air. Most of the people who come here don't seem to be saddled with a little thing called "work." Yes, it's ten-thirty in the morning, and while the average person is at a workaday job, these people are all parading around this club, pulling in with Jags and Ferraris. My phone beeps.

Breaking news:

1) Text from Sam.

2) Heart leaps into throat.

CHAPTER 7

Are you all right?

I wait before I answer, a long, pissed-off eternity while I sip at the dregs of my green juice. Then:

At Great Fitness.

Great!!

I roll my eyes. There's that word again. It's following me everywhere. Maybe he's changed his mind. Maybe he's going to say he's totally come around.

I put it bluntly:

What do you want?

Can you understand where I'm coming from?

No!

I'm sorry, Kat.☹

Ok.

I feel bad. Didn't want it to end this way. Let's talk soon. I'll be over to get the rest of my stuff. Please don't be mad.

I'm not mad. I'm just hurt.

I'm sorry. I know. This isn't easy for me either.

So, he hasn't come around. I don't respond to the rest of his texts, his insistence that he's doing the right thing, that in time this will all heal over, and on and on. I will not beg.

This is it, then. This is the truth and the light. Sitting here at the juice bar, I can't believe it, but it actually *is* over. Happily ever after? Not for me in this life! His mind's made up and whatever we had has come undone. Maybe I could live with Aunt Gladys and all her cats and forget men entirely. After all, cats are such low-maintenance animals.

Another hot tear wanders down my cheek, one lonely liquid representative of my one lonely life. One: the loneliest number of all. (Is that a song?) All I can do is start screaming at the universe again.

After getting another sauna and a shower, wondering if I can maybe somehow slip out a back door, I receive a text from Val. It's 2:10 p.m. I'm sitting outside of a weight room, staring into space. I can't believe I've hung out here this long. Val Pal. Someone to talk to.

Drinks on Friday when I get back?

I reply:

Absolutely. How's it going?

It's amazing out here!

I believe it.

What's up with you?

Not much. Mellowing out at this huge health club. Exercising for once in my life.

I've been telling you to exercise! That's great

I know. Sam's an asshole though.

Why?

He moved out.

WHAT???

She calls. I go grab a bottled water, return to my seat, and fill her in on the whole absurdly ridiculous debacle. My hands get sweaty as I recite the events of our break-up. My Big A seems to be dwelling at around a six or a seven now, creeping in the back of my mind like the horrid monster that it is.

"Are you serious?" she asks. Val has this high feminine voice that can sometimes sound hysterical.

Another swig. "Dead serious."

"He actually moved out?"

My throat gets tight and for a minute I squeeze my eyes shut. "Moved in with his brother. But as far as I know, he may have moved into Prime House and now he eats and sleeps there." Now that would be a laugh; he's sleeping at Prime House and I'm sleeping here. "He works so much, and he's so into his food creations, he'd probably like it. Anyway, it looks like he's gone for good. Unless I can somehow convince him to come back, which doesn't seem likely at this point." I sigh. "I'm so mad and hurt. It's so unfair, you know? Life is so spectacularly unfair!"

"Wow! I'm so sorry, Kat." Val's sympathetic voice makes me want to cry right here and now. Just. Plain. Sob. I choke up.

I drink more water, gulp it down, hoping to liquify my problems away and then turn them into condensation. "He thinks I party too much. That I haven't grown up. He thinks I've given up on life. And that I'm a narcissist. And... he says I drink too much too. Other than that, we're cool."

"I say you don't drink enough." Val giggles.

"I know. Seriously." Another swig.

"Are you depressed?"

I wait a minute before answering, checking my mental outlook. "Kinda."

"Hey. Listen. I'll be home Friday and we'll go out and party Friday night. I'll get Sam off your mind. Don't you worry about that. If he doesn't see what a good thing he had, screw him. There are tons of guys who'd love to meet you. Trust me. We'll go to Jake's Animal House and flirt like crazy."

I wish that were true—about the tons of guys wanting to meet me. Oh, yes, they're all lined up, ready and waiting.

I don't want tons of guys. I just want Sam.

Should I tell Val about my little health club problem? I want to in a way, but since there's nothing she can do... why get started? Besides, I'm too embarrassed and even ashamed to bring it up.

"But do you think he's right, just a little?" I ask, the possibility creaking open the lid of my mind.

"What do you mean?"

"About what he said and all. That I haven't grown up."

"Of course he's right," Val says all too quickly. "But that's what I like about you. You've got this Peter Pan side."

"My what?" I frown.

"You know, Peter Pan." Val laughs.

"What do you mean?"

"Oh, don't worry about it. It's nothing."

"Come on, Val. It's not nothing. Tell me. Spit it out."

Val sighs. "Oh, Kat. You know. Don't you think you're maybe a wee bit immature? And that there are times when you're seriously... I don't know... pretty darn *capable* when it comes to the avoidance of responsibilities?"

"You think? Me?"

"Kinda."

This hurts. We grow silent and I ponder what she said.

"Sam says I'm narcissistic."

Another sigh from Val. "Kat, dear. I love you to death. You know I do. But don't you think he's right? At least a little?"

"No. I don't think I'm narcissistic. No way," I say as I stare at myself in a mirror and smooth an eyebrow.

"Whatever you say. But one thing's for sure; I hate to say it, but you could practically give seminars on How To Avoid Responsibility. Travel the country and everything."

I am taken aback by her upfront honesty. But is this her opinion, or are these facts? Instead of arguing with Val, for some reason, I take it in and listen. There's a small whisper inside of me that says: *Maybe she has a point.*

"I have a job," I counter. Did have a job. There's no way I'm telling her I just got fired.

"I know and you do it well, I'm sure. But there are times, I don't know, I don't mean to be harsh, but see, sometimes..."

"Yes?"

"It's just that sometimes, it's like you only think of yourself and you don't see things from someone else's point of view."

"Well, I mean... I may do that occasionally..."

"What about when you say you'll call but you never do?"

"Well, sure, I do that. I know. I don't follow through. I admit it... But..."

"And there are times when you don't even apologize when you do something wrong, Kat. Admit it. You know you don't."

"I'm sorry, okay? Does that make you feel better?"

"And when we go out," Val continues, "you're always late and you never apologize for being late, either."

"Go on," I say. I narrow my eyes. I didn't realize I was that bad.

"And you never compromise, either. It's always your way or the highway. You cancel plans at the last minute and think nothing of it. Sometimes when I talk, you don't even listen."

"What'd you say?"

"See? There you go! And you always talk about yourself too. Hello...! Other people's feelings? Sometimes you don't consider them. I mean, I'm sorry Kat, but I could go on. Trust me."

"So why do you put up with me?" I ask after a long pause, all confused and downhearted; what she's saying unfortunately hits home. Am I really that bad?

"Because you're a hoot, that's why. You're entertaining as hell!" Val laughs.

"Well..." I have nothing to say, an unusual event in itself.

All right, so I'm emotionally blind—but how could I be a Peter Pan? Surely I've grown up. I have—had—a job. I'm living on my own. I pay taxes. Sam and I were planning on marriage and kids... That doesn't sound like someone who avoids responsibility, does it? Why does she say I haven't grown up? Because I go a little over the top on the drinking side of life and every now and then forget to apologize? So sue me.

"Hey, look. I've gotta run," Val says before I can say anything in my defense. "We're heading out to Flat Rock Beach. God, it's so beautiful here! The water, the weather's fantastic... I'm seriously looking into moving here. Would you ever consider it?"

Moving to San Diego? Maybe that's exactly what I need—an entirely new change of scenery. Sure. My anxiety wouldn't dare follow me to San Diego, would it? I give her the kind of answer that deep down, I don't really mean. Saying it practically breaks my heart all over again. "Now that Sam's history, I've got nothing to keep me in Nashville."

"Right! There are billions of teeth to clean in San Diego, you know? Think positive. If you can't move on, at least move forward. Screw Sam." Val speaks louder. "I'm glad he's out of your hair. He was holding you back, in my opinion."

"Holding me back?" I blink.

"He was limiting you. You were always down when you talked about him. I could sense it. You two were drifting apart. You said he hardly paid any attention to you anymore. Besides, you're a party animal by nature. You work hard and you party hard. He doesn't understand you."

Party animal by nature?

"But—"

"Hang in there, sweetie. Talk to you soon, okay?"

"Okay."

Ending the call, I do nothing but sit here for the longest while and stare into space. Val's right. Just like the millions of mirrors inside this club, she's showing me the reality of who and what I've become. I *see* what she's saying, which makes it hurt like hell. I *am* emotionally blind. I don't take other people's feelings into consideration. Selfish? Yes. Shortsighted? That too.

Peter Pan in action: I recall the rainy night I got pulled over for a DUI, about a month after Lilly died. Two o'clock in the morning. I was coming back from a party at a friend's. This short, dark-haired policeman pulled me over, examining my license under his bright flashlight.

"You know it's the little men who need to puff themselves up by being cops," I said, slurring my words.

"Ma'am, out of the car, please."

"But I only had a few cocktails, officer," I said.

"Stand your ground, ma'am."

Wobbling on my feet, I pointed at his belt. "Is that a night-stick you're carrying, or are you just happy to see me?"

"Stand your ground."

My cellmate for the evening was a thin woman with raven hair and raccoon eyes. She didn't say a word. Sam had to come bail me out. Boy, was he pissed. I spent the next day in hangover hell. Yeah, that's a Peter Pan lifestyle for you.

But there's more to me than that. I want to settle down. I want to get married and be a wife and... I want that maternal feeling, those innocent baby eyes staring up at me. But let's face it. The evidence says that Val's right. I *am* a DUI-enhanced Peter Pan of sorts, and Sam was a saint for staying with me as long as he did. If I wasn't complaining about something, I was making a mess or eating or snoozing on the couch or talking about moving to Wyoming and living in one of those Tiny Houses... or... coming home at two in the morning all zoned out and drunk. I guess I'd balanced that Peter Pan part of me by also working hard, being a bit of a grown-up at least—but after Lilly passed, I couldn't keep it up. Things definitely went downhill. I swallow against a dry throat as I clench my hands into fists.

"Having a problem?" I hear a male voice behind me. It's a half hour after my phone call with Val, and I've moved away from the juice bar to the weights area. I'm still whirling with all the new insights that she threw my way. The truth hurts. Love hurts too. (Now that's *definitely* a song.)

I turn around and blink. It's Marcus, the personal trainer I met yesterday, gorgeous as ever, and for a long, interminable second, I absolutely do not know what to say. I am trying to adjust the weights on one of the Nautilus machines when I jam my finger in the mechanism that holds the weight-separating pin. Ouch!

"Uh, yes." I finally find my voice as I shake my hand in the air. "How do you lower the weight? It doesn't seem to want to budge—can't get this pin-thingy to work."

I feel myself blushing and then, knowing I'm blushing, I blush even more.

In one quick move, he pulls the pin in and out with ease, and takes the weight down to a manageable fifteen pounds, the lowest weight possible.

"That ought to do it." He gives me a cute, boyish grin that lights up the area. A flashlight of a grin.

I clear my throat. "Thanks," I say, staring at the adjusted weight and feeling like a fool.

"Like I said before, you might want to sign up for an introductory personal training session. It helps people orient themselves to the equipment. It's totally free too."

"So, when can I get one?" I ask, sitting on the machine, blinking up at him.

He's carrying an iPad and he opens up a screen and swipes down. "Let's see." He knits his brow the same intense way Sam does, all furrowed and deep. So manly. Marcus reminds me of a living and breathing statue, sculpted by Michelangelo or someone all Italian who likes bruschetta. "How about tomorrow at one-thirty? Does that work for you?"

"Actually," I say without hesitation, "it does. I'm totally free this week, if you want to know the truth."

. . .

Later, sitting at the juice bar, I'm sipping my second green smoothie of the day. Paying for everything on a credit card, I know I should be careful with my money since I'm jobless, but being here around all these rich and famous-looking people has put me in splurge mode—I can't help it. I'm contemplating staying another night at Hotel Great Fitness—it's either that or face the Horrible Door again—when I hear: "Uh, Ms. Noad? I believe you dropped this?" A rich, baritone voice rings out behind me. I'm amazed. Whoever it is pronounced my name correctly; they must be some kind of genius.

I turn around in my seat and find a smooth-faced man with short black hair standing not more than two feet away. His dark eyes are scrutinizing me. Tall and handsome, early fifties, broad shoulders with one heck of a statuesque physique. He's wearing a Great Fitness uniform like the other employees, but his seems to be somehow specially made. If *"Be Your Best!"* is the slogan here, this guy embodies it. Then I notice gold bars above the pockets.

With a gracious smile, the man hands me my Great Fitness membership card. "Here," he says. "This is yours, I believe."

I'd put my card on the table and must have knocked it off accidentally.

"Oh, thank you so much." I smile, running a hand through my hair.

"I'm Jim Flanigan, President and CEO of Great Fitness."

What?

I'm so shocked that I drop my phone, pick it up, then drop it again. I stand and he extends a hand and I shake it, my hands suddenly slicking up. I gulp. "Uh, hi," I say, my voice squeaky.

"Are you enjoying yourself here?" he asks. His broad smile reveals great teeth. A crown on number nineteen. Very nicely done. Pink, healthy gums—no recession anywhere.

"Oh, yes! It's great!" I say. "I love it here! Maybe too much!" I laugh too hard, emitting an ugly sounding snort.

"Well, if you ever want to give us any customer feedback, please remember that we do have a suggestion box near the front office, plus there's a place on our website. Don't hesitate at all."

How about more comfortable massage tables to sleep on, pal?

He turns serious. "If you don't mind me asking, Ms. Noad, what do you like most about Great Fitness?"

I answer without hesitation. "I like *everything,* really." And I realize that I honestly do. I wave a hand in the air. "I like the saunas and the steam rooms and the hot tubs, of course. And all the great equipment, especially the treadmills and the bikes. The food's fantastic too, and the pools, just love the pools, all of them, and of course the b-bar."

He laughs heartily. "Well, that's wonderful. I'm so glad. If you need anything, don't hesitate to ask one of our staff."

"The staff's amazing too," I say, thinking of Marcus and that well-built body of his, those finely toned arms. The guy's got guns for biceps, truly—what more can I say?

"That's great, really great."

I sit back down in a cloud of trepidation as he strides away in all his presidential glory. *Now you've done it.* I've been able to remain pretty much under the radar so far—except for the fact that now the *President himself* knows who I am.

Great!

I did some leg lifts, tried this ridiculously hard climbing machine called Jacob's Ladder for about two minutes, then took a swim, a sauna, a steam, a delightful shower, and now before I know it, it's six o'clock and time for dinner.

Thoughts of leaving have crossed my mind, of course, but I'm having such a good time that I find myself procrastinating once again and when it comes to procrastination, I am, ahem, one of the best. Just ask Val.

But as I make my way toward Yummy's, passing the clinking sounds of a weight room, I feel so up in the air. I want— no, need—to get out of here, for sure. I really do. I don't even have a change of clothes. I've got the rest of my Sam-less life to live. My car's still sitting in the parking lot. I have an apartment to maintain. And besides, it's ridiculous hiding out at a health club, as posh as this one is.

And yet... the other side of the equation seems to somehow make sense as well: Why *not* take a vacay for a few days? Why *not* spend another night on one of the massage tables, wake up at 4:30 a.m., and basically hang out and work out, swim, sauna, steam, get in better shape, flirt with Marcus? Wouldn't that be fun? Here, I can work on my bod' and my mind. Out there in the real world, there's the House of Cookies no less than a mile from here. Plus, I have time to think about my next stage of life —without Sam—as I reinvigorate my career.

Should I look into doing something other than dental hygiene? Maybe I could start a website on say... Hell, I don't know. Health clubs? Or maybe go back to school and get a master's or even a Ph.D. in biology or biochemistry. Or become a massage therapist. I think I'd be damn good at that. I know a dental hygienist who quit the profession because she got burned out and now raises goats on a farm in Fairview. Maybe I could raise, I don't know, free-range chickens.

Besides, I have no desire to go through another panic attack when I try to make my exit. As long as I stay away from that door, I'm actually okay.

But when will I leave? I *can* buy a change of clothes at the Pro Shop, so that shouldn't be a problem. I noticed they sold underwear there too.

Okay, then. Let's see now... My father's coming to town on Friday to work on a real estate investment and I'm supposed to pick him up at the airport around two o'clock. Other than that, I have no pending appointments, no commitments. So, basically,

I'm free to stay until Friday. My father and I are going to have dinner Friday evening—which reminds me, I'd told Val we could get together Friday; I'll have to scratch that. Anyway, this Friday, it'll be my father, me, and Wanda, his young—for him—fortyish red-haired girlfriend. I like Wanda as a person, but I don't like her scooping up my dad.

Thursday afternoon. Definitely. That's when I'll check out of this place for sure. Yes, 3 p.m. I'm going to make that my deadline. It's Tuesday now. Surely, by Thursday, I will have summoned the nerve to leave.

Two more days of staying here incognito? Sleeping on massage tables at night? Are you serious? You could get caught. Don't you see that?

Well, maybe. But maybe not. I grin to myself. If I stay low-key and mind my business, I think I'll be okay, that nosey security guard notwithstanding. This place is so huge, and there are so many people tramping around day and night, I'm sure I can lose myself in the sheer volume of members and just be part of the crowd. The more I think about it, the more I like the excuse: "Oh, sorry, I fell asleep on the massage table." What's so bad about that? What's the worse they could do to me? Surely, they'd understand. That Mr. Flanigan seems like a nice enough chap, I think.

Okay, then. It's settled. I have the next two days to take it easy and relax. I won't even go near the Horrid Door.

As I go through the line at Yummy's, I hum a tune I can't get out of my head. It's one of the songs they keep on rotation here: "High Hopes" by Panic! At The Disco. I order eggplant parmesan, which looks delectable. I dig in. It's really very good. Cheesy and moist, and the marinara sauce is really tangy. Living with a professional chef has honed my taste buds. Note to self: look into doing food blog.

After I've eaten, a strange magnetism pulls me toward the bar. I am completely under this invisible force's power. Still, one or two drinks. What's the harm?

Bartender Jack gives me a hello and makes my drink. He hands a Moscow mule to me and places a bowl of mixed nuts in front of me without saying much at all. I get a kind of suspicious look from him, though. My stomach turns over. I wonder if he's on to me. He couldn't be, could he? Or maybe he thinks I drink too much, which, obviously, I do. Whatever the case, I need to draw him out and find out what's going on in that yeehaw brain of his.

"What's the latest, Jack?" I say after a while. The mule is already doing wonders for my mood. Sweet temporary sanity, here I come.

"Not much." He shrugs. "Got my kid coming in from San Francisco next week. He's going to be living with me for a while. He's got a job here in Nashville."

"What does he do?" I take a long, sweet sip.

"He's a server." Jack wipes his hands on a white towel.

"Cool. Maybe I can hook him up with Prime House. My boyfriend, well, my, uh, ex-boyfriend is head chef there."

I hate speaking of Sam as my ex. Just saying it makes the truth hit home.

"Really?" He cocks his head at me with interest.

"Yes, sir." I finish my drink faster than I realize. "Hit me up with one more, Jack Hammer. I'm on a two-drink minimum, doctor's orders."

He laughs. "You got it." Jack expertly fixes me another mule, places it before me on top of a white napkin, and I take another sip. Ginger beer—what a great invention of modern-day life! I'd put it up there with the internet and solar power any day. "How come he's your ex, if you don't mind me asking? Pretty girl like you?"

I smile and blush, flashing him a good look at my dazzling

white teeth. I run a hand through my hair and then lean closer
to the bar. "Well, it's a long story." I munch on some cashews.
"But basically"—another sip —"we kept getting into these arguments. You know, he was blaming me for all kinds of things, and
I was blaming him for all kinds of things. Anyway, he had
enough. Restless type, I guess. You can't cage the wind, you
know." I take another long pull of my drink.

"Sounds like me and my ex," Jack says. "How do you pin
down a cloud?"

"Well, anyway, I'm still hoping it's not *totally* over," I say,
swishing my glass around and listening to the tinkling of the ice.
"Maybe there's still a chance for us. But he just moved out, so
it's not a good sign."

Jack waves a hand in the air. "If he moved out, it's over.
Trust me."

"You think?" I raise an eyebrow at him.

"Yep." Jack moves away from me and pours someone else a
drink. Hearing his opinion, my mood, buoyed by the booze,
sinks like an anchor. He probably *is* right. Once they move out,
they're gone. Doesn't that make the most sense?

A group of three older women is sitting at the bar and Jack
starts to chat them up. As I drink, I watch him in action. The
women look to be in their fifties or even early sixties, a pack of
cougars all beautifully dressed in casual attire. They are all over
Jack, flirting, laughing with him, soaking in his every word. Jack
is now holding the redhead's hand as he gives her ring the once-
over. They laugh about something again. Jack leans closer to
her. She leans closer to him.

The cocktails are really soaking into my brain now, just how
I like it.

"How's the mule?" Jack asks when he returns to stand in
front of me.

"It's perfect."

"Great." He sighs. "Too bad I can only make the basics here. Ever been to Bourbon Street Blue?"

"No." I thought I'd been to every bar in town, but I haven't heard of that one.

"It's new. They have this piano player hanging from the ceiling and he sounds just like Billy Joel. And the cocktails are cool—all kinds of amazing flavors. They're really impressive. I saw Jake Gyllenhaal there last week."

I perk up. "Oh, yeah? Really?"

"Sure did. He was with some actress. I think they're making a movie in Nashville. Some kind of country music theme, you know? Girl wants to be country music singer—guy is some big producer who discovers girl. They fall in love. They fall out of love. One dies, or nearly dies. The usual story."

"Jake Gyllenhaal, huh?" I think about Lee. "Are you sure it was him? Maybe he was a lookalike."

"No. It was him all right."

I take another sip of my drink. "Do you know Lee at the front desk?"

"Sure. We call him Red Bull."

I laugh. I'd called him the same thing. "Don't you think he looks like Jake Gyllenhaal?"

Jack doesn't even hesitate. "Of course. Everybody says that. People stare at him all the time. A few have even asked for his autograph. It's a hoot. So how do you like Great Fitness?"

Another mule later—God, I'm describing the passage of time by how much alcohol I'm consuming—we're really hitting it off and we're in each other's contacts.

I say, "Well, that's it for me. Got to get home and feed my, uh, dog."

I wish.

Jack gives me a long look. Something about that look isn't quite right. *Is* he on to me? Does he really believe I'm going home? Suddenly, I'm not so sure about him again. Or am I being paranoid?

"What kind of dog?" he asks. "I love dogs. I have two myself."

"He's a Chihuahua. His name's Moses."

How on earth do I come up with this?

"Moses, huh? Yippy little things, aren't they?"

"You bet. Talk to you later, okay?" My stomach twists inside as I hop off the stool.

"See ya round," he says with another strange wink—as if we are co-conspirators—his voice lilting as he speaks.

Still, I don't think I gave anything away. I'm probably being overly anxious—per usual. Jack is completely unaware of my situation. How could he draw any conclusion from our interaction?

I leave the bar and head in the direction of the door, turning right past the healthy potted palms. But after I'm out of Jack's view, I turn back around and traipse toward the locker room.

I finally hole up in the massage room once again at around ten minutes to midnight, eschewing all eyes that might notice what I'm doing, and close the door behind me. I'm beat. It's been a tough day. I'm still wearing my workout attire. But I don't feel that bad about staying overnight again. I view it as a necessity—just for the next two days. I should probably call Aunt Gladys and see how she's doing. I haven't heard from her since I helped her move in and usually she calls me and complains about something. I wonder how she likes her new place. She's such a fusspot. Loves her sherry, though. For her, Sandeman Don Fino is the third food group after fruits and vegetables.

Earlier today, I did my due diligence. I made a rigorous, but casual-appearing search for any and all security cameras. I found that they are all over the place, fifteen in total. Not good. I did some snooping around and discovered a security guard office not far from reception. It was locked, but I looked through the window and saw that there is, indeed, what appears to be a living quarters within the security area. "Larry Johnson, Security," is inscribed on the door. A picture of him as well. Hmm... So I guess the one-eyed guard and I are spending the night together, so to speak. Lovely. Still, if I stay quiet and out of the way in the massage area, and don't go to the bathroom in the middle of the night, I see no reason why we'd come face-to-face.

Once the doors bang shut at midnight and the buzzer goes off again, I lie on the massage table, merging with the surrounding darkness that covers me like a blanket of its own. Time to recharge my batteries. There's that red blinker light again. And the creaking and groaning of the facility as it settles in for the night.

What a life you have, Kat Noad.

My mind turns to Sam, what we had, what we lost. The next thing I know, I'm crying again. So, this is what the downside of love feels like, the opposite of the high of those early days when you're seeing the world through rose-colored glasses. This isn't fun at all. And to think, he once wrote me a poem about how much he loved me. It was funny and terrible and touching all at once:

"I'm so fondue of you... My heart's been broken into... by you... All my defenses, all my false pretenses, you found the key to me and walked right in."

Wordsworth, he's not, but it was sweet all the same.

I checked out his Instagram today and there was a picture of him working in the kitchen at Prime House, standing there among all those stainless-steel pots and pans. He was wearing his white chef's hat and looked adorable. A gorgeous woman with red hair and a creamy complexion stood behind him, her

hand on his shoulder, smiling into the camera almost victo-
riously.

Surely, he couldn't have found someone else already?

The photo brings me back to earth. I should be out in the
real world trying to get Sam back, not hiding in a health club.
Tomorrow, I need to leave. This is nuts.

Suddenly, I hear some sort of clanking going on. It's right
here on my floor. Footsteps? Yes! They come softly and then
they go. It must be a security guard—or could it be someone
else?

As I lie here, unable to sleep, listening out for the tapping of
footsteps again, my mind continues tripping and spinning.
Before I know it, I'm recalling my younger days and my first
memories of anxiety.

I guess it all started with my pet rabbit, Oreo. I named him that
because he was black and white and Oreos were my favorite
cookie. I loved that little creature. I had him for almost six
months. He was so silly and playful and, believe it or not, he
was as loyal as any dog. I'd begged my parents for a pet for at
least a year until I was finally and reluctantly granted one.

I had no idea that on a warm summer's day in June, things
would go awry: I was probably seven, maybe eight, when I was
playing with Oreo in the front yard—something I knew I
shouldn't be doing—showing him off to a younger neighbor and
feeling good that school was out, when suddenly, Oreo escaped
from my arms. Before I could stop him, he went running into
the street.

"Oreo!" I yelled.

But it was too late. As I stood at the curb, the worst thing
possible happened and there was nothing I could do about it: A
red car came barreling down the street and hit Oreo full on. I
witnessed every second of it and froze in terror. The car didn't

stop and I wailed as Grace, the neighbor child who I had shown the rabbit to, ran and told my mother.

My mom came rushing out of the house, looked at Oreo's lifeless body, and then pulled me into her arms, shielding me from the vision as I shook, trembled uncontrollably. Unfortunately, I had seen what I had seen and that memory has stayed with me the rest of my life, reappearing in dreams, in my thoughts, or whenever I get stressed. If I'm thinking about Oreo, I know something's bothering me big time. As far as Grace's concerned, well, I have no idea whether it troubled her or not.

All I knew was that I was so devastated and awash in guilt, I could barely make it through the day. Joey, my brother who was twelve at the time, came out and picked up the rabbit and laid him in a shoebox. That night, when my father came home, he dug a hole in the backyard and we buried Oreo in it without fanfare.

"And that's that," my mother said when my father was finished, wiping his hands from the dirt. "We're going to wait a while before we have any more pets in this house." She spoke sternly, annoyed by the whole situation. "You're obviously not old enough to take responsibility for a pet."

"But Mom!" I cried.

"Forget it," my father said.

For the next few days, I could hardly eat anything. My family, however, didn't, or couldn't grasp how much pain I was in, which made it even worse.

"Oh, it was just a silly old rabbit anyway," Joey said over dinner a few days later.

When he said that, I went straight to my room in tears. Oreo was definitely not a silly old rabbit. He was my pet, my friend. My companion. I had nightmares about it for years. And then when I lost Lilly, it was as if it all connected together, the two losses of the animals in my life merging into a perfect storm of pain.

Honestly, it's not really that hard to draw a line, to connect the dots, from seeing Oreo hit by a car to...

"We've got to get there on time, Daddy!" I yelled. "We can't be late. Hurry!" I was around nine or ten, dressed in my pink leotard, sitting in the passenger seat buckled in, and all I knew was that I *had* to get there on time; *I just had to*. I don't have a great memory about my past—who does, really?—but I'll never forget that singular day. It was raining hard and the traffic was terrible and I was wriggling around in my seat—my father was driving his famous blue Benz, which he kept for years and which he used to call "Saint B" for some strange reason. I was tying my hands in knots. That burning need was bearing down on me: *"DO NOT BE LATE!"* I can't even begin to explain why it attacked me then.

I was having a major case of butterflies, biting my nails until they bled, and I kept nagging my dad. "Faster, Dad, faster!"

We were heading to an important dance rehearsal for our show, which was going to be in two days. I was part of Miss Johnson's Dance Factory. ("We Make the Moves" was her slogan.) We weren't that good—I kind of even sensed it as a child—but we sure had the energy to make up for our lack of talent.

"Don't worry, Kat," he said as he drove slowly through the congestion of traffic, which frustrated me no end. He gave me a kindly smile, trying to reassure me. "And don't bite your nails like that. Why are you so nervous?" he asked.

With the pounding rain and the bad traffic, the windshield wipers clapping, he wasn't going to rush, no matter how hard I tried to convince him. "We'll get there. We might be a few minutes late, but it's no big deal."

When we stopped at a long red light, I began to cry. "No! I *can't* be late! It *is* a very big deal! It *is* a big deal. I have to get there on time! Go! Go!"

His muscles tightened along his jawline. "Kat. Please. I'm not getting a ticket over this."

I knew my behavior was irritating. I was sure he was wondering what kind of child he had. A child who made getting to a dance class on time such a major problem.

We arrived maybe ten minutes late in the end—a horror to my eyes—and for the rest of that day, I was completely out of sorts.

Then, in my high school years, I started getting even more panicky. Not during a test or anything like that. No, my panic feelings basically arose for no reason at all. Appearing from nothing. I'd be sitting, reading a book, or watching TV—anything, really—and suddenly my breathing would get shallow, and I'd feel my heart palpitate, booming hard against my chest. I'd put a hand over my chest and close my eyes and all I could do was ride the horrible wave until it subsided. It could last at least ten or fifteen minutes. And then I'd get panicky about when my next panic attack would come. I hid my problem as best as I could, but I couldn't hide it forever.

At fourteen, one day, I was unable to leave my bedroom. I felt snug and safe in my room, with the curtains drawn, my comfy bed, and posters on the wall of my favorite boy bands, while out there... outside my room, life was far too unpredictable. Too many variations coming at you all at once: what people might say or do to you, traffic—I always had and still have a fear of traffic and cars and pedestrians—the sudden emergence of bad weather—you never know!—and unruly crowds.

Inside my room, I kept thinking to myself: *What if I have a panic attack OUT THERE?* I needed an ordered universe in which to survive, and the safety of my room offered me the best possible solution. The only thing I could do was grab my blanket and pillow off my bed, lie down on the floor, and pull the blanket over me. I felt afraid and sorry for myself.

My mother knocked on my door while I was hunkering down. "Kat, what's wrong? We're ready to go. Are you all right? Kat?"

We were all going out to eat at a place called the Italian Pasta Palace; me, my older brother, my father and mother. It was a restaurant where the waiters and waitresses actually sang opera to you at your table. Some were really good. Crayons were provided so that you could draw or write whatever you wanted on the disposable paper tablecloths.

"Do you mind if I stay here instead?" I asked as I stared at the one goldfish in my fishbowl. I named him Earl. The fishbowl was sitting on top of my chest of drawers, next to a window. Swimming around in the clear water, Earl, a comet goldfish with bright orange stripes, looked about as lonely as I felt, and yet, there was a kind of predictable satisfaction knowing that he was safe in his bowl, that there was no need for him to get out, and that basically, all was well. Earl was imprisoned, but it really wasn't a bad place to be as far as I was concerned. Yes, he was safe and I wanted to be just like Earl. I wanted a safe place just like that.

My breathing grew quick and shallow, my palms wet. "I'm not feeling good," I said.

"But we're ready to go!" my mother said, frustration lining her voice.

"Don't want to," I cried.

When my mother opened the door and came into the room, she saw me lying on the floor, a blanket pulled over me. I stared up at her and my mom's eyes went wide.

"What is wrong with you?"

"I don't want to go," I said, blinking up at her. "Can't I stay here?"

My mother had to drag me from my room as I cried and put

up a fuss. By the time I got to the restaurant with my family, however, I was a different person. I was glad I came and ate a large order of spaghetti and meatballs, drank two Cokes, and had a slice of apple pie for dessert.

My parents sat there, watching me with new eyes, not quite knowing what to say. What kind of daughter were they raising? I'm sure that was what they were wondering. What kind of person would she turn out to be?

A few weeks later, I began my introduction into the world of therapy.

I finally fall asleep and dream of a treadmill. As I walk on it, the incline takes me up and up into an orange sky. Then I'm in this long hallway, at the end of which stands Jim Flanigan with anger burning in his eyes. He keeps saying, "Miss No-Add? Miss No-Add? Aren't you here a heck of a lot?"

CHAPTER 8

WEDNESDAY

My cell softly beeps the alarm, which I immediately click off. I awaken at exactly 4:25 a.m. If nothing else, this little adventure of mine is kicking my lazy bone right in the butt; a good thing, no doubt. The old Kat Noad normally slept until noon when she didn't have to go to work.

I yawn and stretch, then climb off the table and peek out the door of the massage room, making sure the coast is clear. Lights click on all over the building and the AC rumbles. I look right and left; all is good. I head out to join the early birds, quickly deciding that I could use some aqua therapy. Downstairs, I hear doors open, and already the staff is entering along with members. I wait a few minutes in a secluded hall, then shuffle over to the hot tubs on this same floor. I go into a locker room and change into my bathing suit and then come back and slowly melt into the water. My body moans with delight. I become one with the bubbles.

Mission accomplished. I feel tired though. Didn't sleep that well. But on the bright side, I didn't hear a thing from a security guard. And all that exercise I'm doing—my body is not used to it. But still, I'm hanging in and staying under the radar. I'm getting good at this. You know what? This is fun! Is this first-class well-being or what?

At nine o'clock, after doing some early morning light exercises, taking a swim, and eating breakfast, I go to the Pro Shop and buy myself two new sets of workout clothing and some underwear, putting it on my credit card. I'm still okay money-wise—at least for now. If I need to do laundry in the near future, I'll have to figure something out. Maybe wash my things in a shower and hang them in a locker to dry.

Here's the plan for today. I'll work up a good sweat and then hang out, maybe check out one of the Pilates or Barre classes. Grab another healthy lunch at Yummy's. Let my food digest. Exercise full on, take another hot tub soak-session, shower, and then wait around until my appointment with Marcus at one-thirty. Now that, I'm looking forward to.

Around 10 a.m., as I'm heading back to the locker room, I pass by the daycare center on the first floor. Through a glass window, I watch the children inside again. I am mesmerized. The kids are playing with all kinds of toys and games, scampering around as only children know how to do with that intense here-and-now look on their faces. They strike a chord inside me.

My eyes well up at the thought of all those talks with Sam about a wedding, children, a home in maybe Crieve Hall or Green Hills, the entire marital enchilada with chips and salsa to boot.

One little boy, probably about four and with the chubbiest cheeks ever, is building a blockhouse on his own with serious determination, perhaps an architect in the making? A darling blue-eyed girl is playing with dolls and a tea set. She seems to have a pretend friend she's talking to.

But it's the small child sitting alone who really catches my eye, the one looking at a book, turning pages slowly, thoughtfully. She must be about three or four years old and has long black hair and a dark, Mediterranean complexion. She's wearing a blue dress and white socks. She seems sad. My heart goes out to her. I'd love to scoop her up in my arms and comfort her. She suddenly looks up and our eyes meet. She doesn't smile at me, but she stares at me, a puzzled look in her eyes. Finally, she turns away.

There are three daycare workers tending to the children. One's texting on her cell, one's helping a child with her coloring book, and one's sitting there at a table, staring into space and drinking a Starbucks. She looks frazzled. When she catches my eye, she stands and gets busy, helping a little boy with his ABCs.

As I continue watching, the worker who was texting, a short, pudgy woman with thin lips and a deep cleft in her square chin, turns to another of the workers and talks to her, then stomps outside into the hallway. There are tears in her eyes and before I know it, she starts sobbing right in front of me, not even noticing I'm there. She reads her text and then her fingers fly over the keys as she taps out a response.

"Are you okay?" I ask softly. I'm rooted to the spot.

"I have to go," she says. Her eyes are red. "They're taking my husband to the hospital. I need to be with him." And then she runs off down the hall.

Maybe *I* could help out at the daycare. What else do I have to do? I need money coming in and suddenly the idea of being around kids seems pretty fantastic, if not therapeutic. I don't even give it a second thought.

I walk in and blurt out to the worker who was staring into space, "Are there any job openings here?"

The woman looks at me, surprised at first, but then the surprise turns to an increasing expression of relief. She studies me before answering. I feel myself blush. "Plenty. Lately, our staff's been dropping like flies. We're always looking for some-one. Any experience?"

"Yes. I used to work in a daycare when I was going to college."

That's a laugh. I was there two days, part of a class project in child psychology. I had to do it to pass the course. I remember being hungover both days and watching the little tykes wander around with their toys in hand, looking at me like I was an extra-terrestrial creature. The kids were cute, though, runny noses and all.

"Perfect. You can fill out an application online on our website. We're really short on staff right now. They'll give you an interview and if everything checks out, you'll be in business."

At that moment, a little boy begins tugging on the woman's dress.

"I'd better take care of this one. But hopefully I'll see you soon!"

"Thanks!"

I step outside and stare through the window again. My eyes go back to that dark-haired little girl. There's something about her, something that I can't quite pinpoint. She's still reading her book all by herself when suddenly, she looks up at me and our eyes meet again. I smile at her, and again, she doesn't smile back. She has such big, beautiful, coal-dark eyes. There's a sadness in her demeanor that saddens me as well. Somehow I get the feeling that she's trapped in her own way—just like I am.

It's probably my imagination. Who knows? I sigh as I walk down the hall toward the elevator. What is wrong with me? Why can't I shake my anxiety? Why can't I face my fears and get on with my life? I decide that I need to call Dr. Sharp. I need to talk to her. When she's unable to come to the phone, I leave a message with her assistant to call me back. Then ten minutes later, I send in my application for the childcare position using a computer station that's available for members. I want to get it in ASAP.

At eleven, I summon my courage and do a Barre class. The sign on the door says, "Lift. Tone. Burn." I'm not sure about the "burn" part.

The instructor is a fiftyish woman with short black hair who possesses a ridiculously fit body, the Mercedes Benz of bodies, if such a thing is possible. She's wearing an outfit that shows off her tan, flat-as-a-pancake stomach. Her belly button sparkles with a diamond stud as do her eyes.

"First time?" she says when I walk in. It's as if she can read my mind or my body, or both.

"Thought I'd give it a try." I shrug shyly. "I'm trying to open up to new experiences."

"Good for you!" she says. "That's the spirit!"

It starts out easy enough and, at first, I like it. There are eight of us, all lined up facing the teacher. We start deep breathing while lying on the floor and then we do some light stretches. Not too bad. This, I can do. Then we use colorful bands to stretch our muscles. We are pulling our legs so far apart, it's as though some of the stretching would get you ready for the most intense sex of your life. The only problem is, now that I'm single, I don't see the most intense sex of my life happening anytime soon. Depressing thought, no doubt. Next lifetime, perhaps?

Ten minutes into the class, however, and things go downhill fast, or uphill—however you look at it. I'm lying panting on the floor. I'm so exhausted, I'm questioning my entire life cycle from kindergarten on. There's a tall blonde woman next to me who is gliding through the exercises with ease, while I'm dying right next to her.

My body is burning, my muscles are aching. By the end, I am shaking.

"Did you have a good class?" the instructor asks me when it's finally, mercifully over.

"I think I died for a minute or two, but other than that... I guess I made it," I say, sweat streaming all over me, barely able to stand. I hobble toward the door.

She gives me a warm smile. "Oh, good, that's good. Just keep coming back. You'll get stronger before you know it."

No pain, no gain—got it.

The other women leave the class all cheery and chatting to each other, while I have to go sit down, stare into space, drink water, and recoup. I feel like I've been beaten to death.

Twenty minutes later, finally restored to semi-consciousness, I head on over to Yummy's. I feel like an old woman, bones creaking.

A pair of teens sitting at a table next to me are laughing about something on TikTok. At another table, an old man and woman who look like they've been together at least fifty years, quietly chew on their sandwiches. They even chew in sync. They both wear hearing aids and don't say a word. But I don't think they even *need* to speak to each other. They probably read each other's minds at this point in their relationship. It's touching. Will *I* be sitting at a table like that, fifty years from now, *not* talking to the man I love? God, I hope so. I wonder what Sam will look like when he's eighty.

My phone rings. It's Dr. Sharp.

"Kat? How are you?" Her smooth, steady voice is reassuring. She's an expert at showing empathy without getting too close to someone. How she does that, I still don't know. It's a talent, I guess. Some people can curl their tongues; some can't.

"Hi, Dr. Sharp. I don't want to come in just now, but you said if I ever needed to call, I could, so I thought I'd give you a shout."

"What's wrong, Kat? You sound sad."

"I am, Dr. Sharp."

"What's going on? Are you sure you don't want to come in for a session? You missed your last two, no, uh, three appointments, you know. I had to bill you for them because you didn't call to cancel either."

"I know." For a long emotional moment, I don't say a thing. Three seventy-five dollar sessions—down the drain. My insurance policy didn't cover mental health counseling.

She doesn't say a thing. But she's good at that. Not saying a thing is her style. Waiting out the silence. Silence is a kind of therapy in itself, a time to look within and... What's that saying about the unexamined life? Hell, I don't know.

Oh, yeah—the unexamined life is not worth living.

Well, when it comes to anxiety, you can examine your life all you frickin' want, but it doesn't seem to do a bit of good.

I had a male therapist before Dr. Sharp, but that was a total bomb. Dr. Ronald J. Bleekerman, mustache, black curly hair, these big round eyes that kept looking at me, studying me as if I were a research project from a nuclear waste site. He seemed to have the empathy of a wart. But Dr. Sharp... there's something about her as well, her too-calm manner and her businesslike, fifty-minute, time's-up mentality. Maybe all therapists are like that. I can't relax with her. When I see her, it's like she has one eye on the clock. Maybe it's me. Maybe I just try to avoid the whole thing.

"I wanted to say..."

"Yes?"

Should I tell her what's going on? Should I open up?

"I'm going through a rough patch, Dr. Sharp." I whimper, unable to hide the sadness in my voice.

"Is it about Lilly still?" she asks in her calm manner. I always wonder what it would take to make this woman get mad.

I sniffle. "Yes." Then... "No." I squeeze out the words.

Then, "Sam and I broke up, I'm afraid." I barely more than whisper the words.

"Oh. I see. I'm sure that's been rough on you. I'm so sorry."

My heart starts racing and I feel the blood flush my face. "He... he told me we were through. That he couldn't live with me any longer. And now he's moved out."

"I'm sorry, Kat. I really am." She is sincere as she consoles me.

"And since then, well, since then, I've been, see, I've been working out a lot."

"Well, that's good, isn't it? That sounds like a breakthrough! You always said working out was for people who had nothing better to do. I've always encouraged exercise as a—"

"I lost my job, too, Dr. Sharp."

"Oh, Kat. No." She takes a breath. "Listen, Kat. I have an opening tomorrow at five-thirty. Can you come in then? I really think you need to come in."

"Yes," I say quickly. "I will."

"Great. That's the spirit. Let's talk then, okay? Are you going to be okay?"

I know what she's hinting at.

"Yes. I'll be okay. I plan on taking some personal training today. I'm at this health club called Great Fitness and... and..."

"Marvelous! That's great. Listen, we'll have a lot to discuss. Have you talked to Dr. Baldwin about your medication? Aren't you on Lexapro?"

"No." I sigh and I decide right there and then: There's no way I'm going to reveal the truth of my situation. I have to figure this out on my own, number one, and number two, if I told her the truth, there'd be an ambulance heading to Great Fitness in about five minutes, ready to whisk me away to a psychiatric hospital. No, if I'm going to confide in someone, it can't be a professional. I need a friend to help me with this, someone I can trust. But who? "He switched me to Zoloft about a month ago.

And of course Xanax as needed. And I'm out of Xanax." I lick my lips and then suck in a breath.

"Okay, then. Well, look. Let's talk tomorrow, okay? I'll see you at five-thirty. And please, try to make it this time. I can't help you if you don't come in, Kat. I want to help you find a breakthrough."

"Five-thirty it is," I say, my voice cracking, and I hang up before I say anything else. I put my hands to my face as sadness pours through me, over me. My chin trembles. I don't need a breakthrough. I need a breakout.

I hit the showers and take a long hot one, needing it badly.

An hour later, just as I'm finishing a splendiferous veggie sandwich with this amazing creamy sauce, Val texts me:

Got blitzed last night.

Why am I not surprised?

We wound up at a bar with male dancers and I ended up making out with one of them.

Seriously?

☺

You're a trip, you know that?

I try. Whatyaupto?

Not much.

Working?

Yeah.

Are you getting down in the mouth? ☺

Something like that.

She always says that to me, about getting down in the mouth. Her one and only dental hygienist joke was funny —once.

So how are you, really? Okay?

Haven't talked to Sam.

You're going to have to move on, Kat. You're going to have to find someone on your own wavelength.

I guess you're right.

But Sam's my man! My love for him is still alive and breathing, as real as could be. It's not something I can simply put into some sort of box and store in my attic. I need time to sort through this before I can file him away under "One More Relationship Gone Wrong." (OMRGW).

Forget Sam. There is an abundance of men out there.

You're right. I need to move on. It's done.

And there's no undoing it. Listen. You hang in there, okay? See you Friday night?

Oh. Can't. My dad's coming into town. I have to be with him. Maybe Saturday?

Okay, sure. I understand.

I end my conversation with Val, then just as I head toward the juice bar to grab a smoothie, I spy someone who looks like Sam parading into Great Fitness. It couldn't be, could it? I blink, moving closer to the entrance as my hands go slick. No? Yes? He moves like Sam does, but I'm still not sure. A shadow crosses his face. I blink again and strain to see. Same height. And yet, there's something different. Or is there? My pulse races when I realize there's only one possible conclusion. It's Sam.

CHAPTER 9

My heart starts jamming like the drummer for a punk rock band. Nerves zinging all over. I don't want him to see me. Or do I? I feel like a schoolgirl with a crush on a guy and at the same time like a jilted lover on the verge of throwing a green smoothie in his face. I should have expected I'd see him here sooner or later.

I hide behind a row of potted plants. I peek out and watch Sam check in at the front desk. Tall and lean—he eats anything he wants and never gains a pound—wavy, chestnut hair, hazel eyes, and kissable lips. He hasn't shaved in two or three days and I love that rugged look on him. He's looking around now and I think he almost spots me but, thank God, Lee intercepts him and starts giving him the super-duper welcome routine. Quickly, I take my chance and, with my head down, make a beeline for the women's locker room.

I retrieve my gym bag and comb my hair, put on some makeup, and try smiling at myself in the mirror. My mouth turns dry and I gulp down half a water bottle and then I start slow breathing. Relax. Calm down. Just Be Yourself. That's what my mother always told me when I was little.

"But Mom, how can you be anything else?"

She didn't have an answer to that. I don't think anyone does.

I finally step out of the locker room and feel more... composed? No! I'm never composed. I'm discomposed—always and forever. Even now, I can feel my anxiety rattling around inside me like dice.

Get with the program, Kat. It's only Sam, the guy you've slept with for the past five years, the guy you've been in love with. Should I go talk to him? Should I have a face-to-face pow-wow right here and now?

Yes? No?

I *need* to talk to him. As bad as our relationship was, there's a part of me that's now crying: "Give it another chance."

He's wearing simple workout pants and a white T that says, "PRIME HOUSE," in big blue lettering. Standing next to an elliptical machine now, checking it out, he's talking to a short fireplug of a guy who, I believe, works as a chef at another restaurant called Thrills, Chills, and Grills. I'm frozen, staring at him. I'm like a rodent who knows she's about to be eaten by a bat in the next ten seconds.

Before I can move, his head revolves my way and then, as he sees me, he freezes too. We lock eyes. We are both rodents. I don't know what to do. My stomach feels like it's about to split in half. Maybe this health club isn't big enough for the two of us.

Okay, Kat. Get your bearings. You need to talk to him in a calm and adult manner.

Me? Calm and adult?

I look right and left as if I'm about to cross a busy street, then hesitantly make my legs and feet move toward him as he cautiously moves my way. As I walk, I nearly bump into a Leonardo DiCaprio lookalike walking beside a woman who could be easily mistaken for Kiernan Shipka, both in blue Great Fitness uniforms.

Sam and I meet in the middle, next to a rope-pulling machine.

With a nod of his head, Sam leads me over to an isolated corner next to a water fountain. Mirrors. They're everywhere. You can't even begin to avoid them. I want to shut my eyes because I do not want to see the stressed expression that I'm sure is written all over my face.

"Glad to see you're working out, Kat," he says, right off.

Asshole. So, he's taking the superficial approach. Okay, then.

This is the guy my mother adores—the guy my father not only approves of, but gets along with. He strokes his chin and rubs the side of his angular face. His eyes burn into me.

"You were here on Monday, yesterday, and again today? That's dedication, I must say. What's gotten into you, Kat? Quite a change for someone who always said exercise was not for you. What was that you said? Oh, yes. '*My* form of exercise is very brisk sitting'." He laughs awkwardly, then glances at his watch, a rose-gold Vincero that we bought together two years ago. Sam had to have it. "But aren't you supposed to be at work?"

"Just taking a day off." I speak casually. I even surprise myself, making up the lie on the spot with amazing surefooted-ness, then immediately feeling bad about it. Still, the air between us seems saturated with all kinds of heaviness, storm clouds of confusion.

"Are you unwell?" he asks with concern on his face. My heart pounds. I feel so stranded right now. So alone. I've always felt close to Sam, but now, there's a wall between us and it's more solid than I ever dreamed it could be. This painful realiza-tion digs into me, burns with a new sense of loss. "Have you spoken to Dr. Sharp?"

"No. I am not unwell." I take a breath. I draw myself up and try to exude self-confidence. "I have found that exercise is good for me. It helps my anxiety." I speak stiffly. Inside, I feel disjointed, as if my bones want to go in one direction but my muscles want to go in another.

"That's great, Kat. Seriously. I'm impressed." He smiles and runs a hand through his hair. "Good for you!"

He does seem impressed. He doesn't have a clue as to why I'm really here. He's staring at me with eyes that seem to say that he's kind of amazed—dumbfounded, actually. That I'm really here, working out, trying to improve myself.

"Yes, well..."

A kind of thick silence ensues. We both grow uncomfortable. I have to pee all of a sudden.

I see it all so clearly now. He doesn't have to spell it out for me. He may be impressed by my willingness to work out, but he's not going to be my boyfriend any longer. The end is here.

Stuffing down the pain, I hold my head high and stick out my chin even further. "And now, if you'll excuse me," I say, "I have a class to get to."

"A day off, huh?" Oh, God. He's back to that. "But you were off yesterday, too."

Determined to get to the bottom of this, are you?

"Yes. I'm having a second day off. It's PTO that I'm owed. Now if you'll excuse me—"

"So where were you last night?" he asks, looking me up and down.

"Huh? What do you mean?" I swallow. I'm a terrible liar. Already, I can feel my ears getting hot. My ears always get hot when I lie. Sam knows that too. How can I hide anything from him?

He steps closer to me and looks right and left. "I came by around nine-ish to get more of my stuff and you weren't there. Your car was gone too."

I swallow again. He's a cop, I've committed murder, and he's about to put the handcuffs on me. I don't say anything for a long moment. This is chess. I need to make the right moves. I clear my throat. "Obviously, I was out. It doesn't take a detective to figure that out. By the way, I'd like your key, please. Since you're no longer a tenant." I hold out my hand.

"I need more time." His voice suddenly turns stern and a coldness creeps into his tone. "I've got two more loads to haul out. I'm paid up until the end of the month. And listen, Kat..." Abruptly, as if his mind has changed channels, he goes soft and there's a sadness in his eyes, the kind of sadness that grabs my heart and shakes it. He speaks gently, commiserating over the loss of us. Our life. Together. Sam and me. Me and Sam. "Don't worry. I'll pay my share of the rent for the next four months too, because I know this was sudden, and I don't want to leave you high and—"

"Fine," I say curtly, unable to bear listening to another word. I curl some hair behind my ears and feel myself blush. My two weeks' notice pay from Dr. Pierce. Four months of rent from Sam. That's a lot of cash. Getting dumped and fired kinda sorta pays off—I guess.

"Simply slide the key under the door when you're finished. We are done, Sam. Just like you said. You want it to be over, so it's over." I stand there. Cold. Aloof. Ice Woman.

"Where were you?" he calls as I finally walk away. His voice needles through my heart.

"Would you please stay the hell out of my life? I was out, like I said. It's none of your business."

I refuse to give him the satisfaction of any further clarification. I hope he gets a good look at my rear end—since this *is* the end.

But as I pass the weight room, a great big sense of regret hits me in my heart. If I hadn't been such an ass toward him, if I'd cleaned up more and if I hadn't been a depressed complainer all the time... *Oh, Kat. You screwed up big time, you know that?*

I sure did.

CHAPTER 10

After saying goodbye to Sam, I rush headlong toward the treadmills in a different area of the club. I don't even want to be in the same room as him. If he's out of my sight, maybe I can get him out of my mind. But suddenly, I stop in my tracks. I suddenly realize that Sam was wearing black weight gloves, which can only mean one thing: He's turned serious about exercising too and will probably be coming here quite a bit. Exactly what I don't need. One more reason why I need to get out of here.

"My, my, I think I see some dedication, girl. I sure do."

The familiar voice startles me. As I hop on a treadmill, I realize who it is: Veronica Ray—once again.

There's not a single hair out of place: perfect makeup, eyes, lips, red nails that look like they've been worked on by a *team* of super-talented manicurists. I swear, it's as if TV anchor people aren't really people—they're *too* coiffed—or something. They're like human dolls who've somehow been birthed into this world, or living manikins.

Seeing how perfect she looks, how self-assured, I make a vow to myself. I'm not going to wallow around in some desperate pool of pain. I'm *not* going to wait for Sam, hoping he'll have a change of heart. No. This girl's gonna burn it up and tear it down. I'm on fire. I'm setting my emotional GPS on a different course altogether: I'm heading straight for the land of health, and then on to the wondrous and sunny state of finding someone new. Isn't that what they say? The best way to get over someone is to get under someone else? Of course it is. And as far as my career's concerned: I'll open up my own dental hygiene company and start franchising throughout North America if I have to. I'll call it CLEAN USA. I'll show that not-so-friendly Dr. Pierce a thing or three. Ladies and gentlemen: Meet the brand-new Katherine Noad.

Next thing I know, Veronica's getting on the treadmill next to mine, and a thrill shoots through me. She flashes her radiant smile at me, the same one I've seen on TV countless times.

"We'll be right back after a word from our sponsors..." The way she says it, so coolly and confidently as she smiles into the camera.

"Keep it up, you're doing great!" she says.

"Well." I shrug, giving her a shy grin. "I'm trying, I guess."

"I'm impressed!"

She's wearing a Dynamite Brazilian workout jumpsuit with open-air netting that looks fantastic on her. How do some people turn out like this? So perfect and well-adjusted and successful, as if the road of life for them isn't bumpy and full of potholes at all—it's actually nothing but one long smooth interstate highway.

"Love your outfit," I say as we both walk on our treadmills.

"Thanks!" Veronica gives me another camera-ready smile and the next thing I know, we are two women gabbing as we exercise. It's as if it all falls into place.

We start talking about the best place to get your nails done, she tells me about a sale at Nordstrom's—"Got these Vince Camuto block-heel booties for a steal!"—she says she's going to see her mother who lives on Long Island in a week... We talk about how good Yummy's is, and the bar, and even Lee at the front desk who looks just like Jake Gyllenhaal. I tell her I've lived in Nashville all my life, and on and on.

"Sure are some cute guys around here," she winks at me right before we're done. "By the way, we're doing a health segment tonight featuring women who've turned their lives around through exercise and diet. You might want to catch it."

I get the hint.

Then she hits me with a question that bowls me over. "Hey, you want to meet here again and work out together? Weekdays at eleven? It'll keep us both motivated."

"Sure," I say quickly without even thinking about it. I blink, caught off guard, but a second later, I'm doing inner somersaults. "Of course!"

"Okay, cool."

After we say goodbye, I use a towel to wipe my face and drink some bottled water. I can't believe it. Veronica Ray and I... workout buds! How cool is that? I should be excited, and I am, until Sam-thoughts break through my good mood.

I find a chair near Yummy's and sit down for a moment, looking around and getting my bearings. A group of teen girls pass me, yakking about how their math teacher gave them a test that was so hard and no one passed it and it's so unfair! They continue on, lost in their own world. I rub my head, ruminating over Sam. Is it possible that a person's life can turn into an emotional Tilt-A-Whirl ride? I can't handle it. I walk back over to the room where Sam is still working out. He's huffing and puffing as he takes long strides on a treadmill. I drink some water as I watch him staring at a TV screen hung on a wall, watching the Food Network, frowning, his earphones plugged into his ears, sweat beading his brow. He's always losing those earphones and I'm always finding them. Sam is a neat-freak kind of guy, but he's also a major space cadet. He would lose his mind if it wasn't bolted into his head.

On the TV, two bearded overweight men, wearing long white aprons and oversized chef's hats, are making Cajun seafood pasta and telling their audience how it's done. I can't stop myself. I walk over toward him, arms folded across my chest. As he continues on the treadmill, he slowly takes his eyes off the TV, pulls off his earphones, and turns to me.

"Thinking about stealing that recipe?" I ask with a raised eyebrow.

"God, they're doing it all wrong. All wrong." He laughs. "They're not even adding white pepper along with the cayenne. And where's the basil? Don't they get it? This charade should not even be allowed on television." He chuckles again, joking with me, then looks me up and down.

"By the way, guess who I'm working out with now?" I say.

"Who?"

"Veronica Ray. The TV anchor news lady."

"Seriously?"

"Weekdays at eleven." I can't stop myself from boasting about my newfound relationship.

"Weekdays at eleven, huh? Are you serious?" Sam slows down the speed on his treadmill and wipes the sweat from his forehead as he glares at me. *Ooops.* "So, you're *not* working, are you? I knew it! You're *not* on some kind of vacay. Did you get fired? Tell me the truth, Kat." His voice rises. "Is that why you're here in the middle of the day?" His eyes turn sad, sympathetic, as he slows to a walk and then steps off the machine. He lowers his voice and looks directly at me. "Did you lose your job?"

I look down, then away. I say nothing.

"Come on, Kat. Give it up."

Truth always tracks you down, I guess. It's the best private investigator of all. My neck feels stiff all of a sudden. "Well, kinda... sorta," I say. I swallow as my chest tightens. My ears get hot again.

"Oh, man." Sam looks up at the ceiling, then back at me. "What is going on with you? What are you going to do now? This is serious."

I study my nails. I know *exactly* what I'll be doing—this afternoon anyway. It's perfect: After my session with Marcus, I'm going to have my nails done, my hair styled, and a relaxing facial—can't wait to exfoliate right here at Great Fitness. Who needs a job when you're in hiding?

"Look. It's not that big of a deal. I didn't like working there anyway," I say. "She had me on a quota and, I swear, it was clean, clean, clean. Non-stop. That dentist, all she cares about is money. She wants her chair filled every minute of the day. And she only gave me twenty minutes for lunch. I was always rushing. Nashville's friendliest dentist? That's a joke. Do you realize she only chipped in one percent to my 401(k)?"

I don't even know why I'm telling him all this. We broke up. Why do I even care what he thinks?

"It was a job, Kat. A good job. She was paying you well. Now what are you doing to do?"

He sounds like my father.

"It's none of your business what I'm going to do. But if you must know... For starters." I sigh luxuriously, as if I've become another health-club princess like that rich woman who just got back from snorkeling with the sharks. "I'm getting a facial this afternoon." Pissing Sam off is a blast. I love getting a rise out of him. "And I'm having my nails done too." I show him my nails. "I'm tired of this pink. See? I need a new color. Maybe I'll just get a mani pedi while I'm at it."

"A facial? Your nails? *Those* are your choices? Are you serious?"

I walk away without answering. The less he knows, the better.

CHAPTER 11

I've been looking forward to my meeting with Marcus. There's something about him that I can't quite put my finger on, but I feel like, somehow, I can relate to him, even though he gave me that rude up-and-down look when we first met. Now Marcus gives me a Life-Is-Great smile and all my hesitancies about him fade away. It's right at one-thirty as I follow him into his small office, which consists of a neat desk with a Mac computer on it, a chair for him, and a couple of guest chairs. We both sit down. A framed *Be Your Best!* sign hangs on one wall, and on another is a picture of Marcus himself on a water-ski parachute: a close-up of him from a GoPro, grinning big time, his dark hair tousled in the wind. There's also a picture of him standing next to... wait a minute. Is that Liam Hemsworth? It is! Damn! It's a signed photo.

"Were you Liam Hemsworth's trainer?" I ask, aghast at the thought.

Marcus nods, puts his hands behind his head, and leans back in his chair. He speaks as if it's the most casual thing in the world. "I was."

"The *real* Liam Hemsworth?"

"Yep. I was living in LA, working there, and had some celebrity clients. Liam was one of them. Nice guy."

"You mean he wasn't a lookalike?"

He laughs. "Nope. He was the real thing."

"Wow, it's just that... some of the staff here seem to resemble actors and actresses. Don't you think? It's kind of strange."

"Of course."

"What do you mean of course?"

"There's a group of people on staff here who work part-time as actor lookalikes. Have you met Fred Mastruzzo yet? He's a dead ringer for Sylvester Stallone."

"No, I haven't met Fred, but... wow!"

"Yeah. They go to parties and bars, all kinds of events."

Interesting. Once, I went to a party thrown by this dental crown manufacturer at this fancy hotel in Charlotte where a man and woman were dressed as the author F. Scott Fitzgerald and Zelda. They really had their act together, too. Totally convincing and fun. They kept saying things like, "swell," and "toodaloo." It was a hoot. I wound up getting smashed with F. Scott and he kept asking me to come back to his apartment so that he could show me his latest full-length manuscript. It certainly was full-length!

Marcus turns on his computer. He stares at the monitor, the light reflecting onto his blue eyes, and taps the keys.

"So what did you think about living in LA?" I ask.

"Too fast-paced for me, so I moved back here. I'm a Southern guy at heart. I'll take barbeque over sushi any day of the week and to me, country beats pop and rap by far, whatever it is they play out there."

"I agree." I smile and lean forward. "Although I do like the weather."

"I like the change of seasons. In LA, there are no seasons. It gets old. Trust me. Perfect weather's kind of boring, if you ask me. No, I was born in Baptist Hospital, raised up near Nolensville Road, and spent time hunting and fishing in Fairview. That's just who I am, Tennessee through and through. Used to catch fireflies in bottles on my grandfather's farm when I was a kid."

"Where'd you go to high school?" I ask.

"Hillsboro High," he says. "You?"

"Brentwood Academy."

"Oh! Ritzy." He laughs.

"Oh, yeah. Our diplomas were gold-engraved."

"Really?" Marcus raises an eyebrow.

"Just kidding."

We lock eyes and an intriguing pause fills the room. I run a hand through my hair, hoping it doesn't look too straggly.

"Okay, then. Let's see now." He comes around his desk and sits next to me. "So, I've created a schedule for you. It's right here." He opens up his iPad to a screen with my name on it, and then expands it. It's a spreadsheet with different tasks in various colors.

"That looks detailed."

He turns serious, knotting his forehead again. "It's a pretty basic workout schedule. Nothing special." He shrugs. "It's designed to get increasingly more difficult, but it's also designed to be safe. Safety's the key, see? Most people don't even understand that." We stare into each other's eyes. I can't believe how handsome he is. Those ocean-blue eyes are killers. "Actually, around forty percent of people who work out hurt themselves at some point. Did you know that?"

"No. I didn't." I lean closer to the iPad, scooching next to Marcus, so close I can smell his cologne, wafting through the air with a woody cedar undertone and a hint of vanilla. I am a willing student.

"Well, it's true. So, you have to be careful, especially right at the beginning when you're the most gung-ho. That's the most important thing of all."

"I see. Take it easy. Right?"

"Exactly. Yes. We don't want any injuries. Anyway, let's head onto the floor. We'll start with some simple stretches."

"Sounds good to me, coach."

Marcus takes me through an entire one-hour routine: stretches, mild weightlifting—no more than fifteen pounds—jump rope, and push-ups. Something to get me started, but I am huffing at the end. He guides me patiently, which I totally appreciate. When I accidentally bang my head on one of the Nautilus machines, he's sincerely sympathetic.

"You all right?" he asks, putting a hand on my shoulder, a hand that I don't want him to remove. His touch sends a shiver through me that starts at my spine and works its way up and down.

I rub the spot. "Yeah. Sure. It only hurt a little." Dumb me.

"Remember"—he finally takes his hand off my shoulder, but leans in close to me—"you gotta be careful around here." He gives me a wink.

"I'm always careful," I say, with a flirtatious grin. "Until I'm not."

For the last ten minutes of our session, he talks to me as I walk on a treadmill.

"So, what kind of work do you do, Kat?" he asks as he slightly ups my incline and speed.

"Dental hygiene." I beam. I'm liking Marcus more and more.

"You like it?" he asks, interested.

"I do. But it does get overwhelming. And sometimes, I swear, I see teeth in my dreams. Molars, premolars, incisors, cuspids, bicuspids... When you clean teeth long enough, they have a way of taking on their own personalities. In my dreams, sometimes they sing and dance."

He laughs. "My own teeth could use some attention. Where do you work?"

I take a breath and inside my anxiety builds again. "Well, I'm, uh, in between jobs right now."

Marcus doesn't say anything to this, and I have no idea how he's taking it. People who are in between jobs are people who are, well, either hugely successful and don't need to work, or people like me. I guess he's wondering which one I am. He rubs his chin and doesn't say a thing.

Then I go with it and babble on. "Yeah, I'm taking some time off to, you know, mellow out. Explore. Relax." Before I can stop myself, I'm saying, "I'm thinking about changing careers."

As soon as the words are out of me, I realize how right it sounds. But what would I do besides dental hygiene?

Marcus takes me up on the same question. "Really? Like what?"

"I don't know yet. But I'm working on it. All I know is that life's not all about doing one thing. Spending the rest of your career cleaning teeth? That's so limited, you know? There's got to be more to life than that."

"Sure. I know what you mean. Sometimes I want to do personal training the rest of my life. I enjoy it that much. Then there are days when I'm ready to do something else. I have an A Plus certificate, but I haven't used it. You know, computer repair? But it's too sedentary for me. I like to be moving. Next month, I'm heading to the Amazon rainforest for a two-week trip. Me and some friends'll be living in tents, hiking, and exploring."

"The Amazon! How cool is that? Can I come with?" I ask jokingly.

He chortles. "Sure. Why not?"

A little thrill ripples through me. We are definitely hitting it off. He touches my arm and smiles wider. "You can share my tent if you want."

"I won't take up too much space. I promise." But I try and bring myself back down to earth. This guy wouldn't be interested in me. He's a stud. He'd be with a stud-ette, someone with one of those ultra-perfect bodies. (And a job.) Oh, well, it's a nice fantasy anyway.

"Anyway, that should do it for today." He hits "stop" on my treadmill and I stumble off, nearly colliding into him.

"Are you okay?" he asks, grabbing me by the waist, and for a moment, I feel his breath on my neck. A shiver runs through me.

"I'm *great!*" I say. And suddenly, I really am.

I give him an energetic smile and my heart flutters—not from anxiety now, but from a rippling sense of pleasure. He smiles back, great teeth and all.

Most people at this point would invite me back to their office and try to upsell me on a year's worth of personal training. But he isn't doing that. I'm impressed.

Once Marcus is gone, I get a drink of water and the next thing I know, I'm bumping into Lee. Before I can stop it, I splash his shirt with water. I get a peek at amazing abs.

"Ooops. Sorry," I say. I grab a nearby towel and wipe it off.

He looks at me like I'm an alien.

"How's it going?"

He doesn't reply.

"By the way, I was trying to sign up for a yoga class and my app kept kicking me out. Can you please check on that for me?"

Lee still stares at me with a confused look on his face. In fact, he's acting like he doesn't even know me. Does the guy have dementia?

I realize that Lee is decked out in extremely fashionable workout attire and is *very* well groomed. There's a gold watch on his wrist that looks like it cost thousands. He's like an upgraded version of Lee, if such a thing is possible.

"Lee?" I say, peering at him.

"Jake," he finally says in the richest voice I've ever heard. His blue-green eyes light up.

"Oh..." I am totally tongue-tied. "You're... J-Jake?"

He nods.

"Oh, my God."

It's him! I spilled water on none other than Jake Gyllenhaal himself. I can't believe it! I see it now as I stare at him, practically blinded by his star quality. The man is beautiful. I put a hand to my mouth.

He walks on in all his celebrity glory and I quiver inside, jaw dropping to the floor.

It's 2:45 p.m. and I'm still abuzz about meeting the real Jake Gyllenhaal. He's the first celebrity I've ever met, bumped into, whatever. Although I did meet Mr. Rogers once when I was a child and he came to this bookstore in Nashville. Spilled my ice cream cone on him and everything. He really looked annoyed and muttered a few curse words under his breath. I always thought Mr. Rogers never got annoyed about anything—guess he hadn't met Kat Noad yet. It's kind of funny though. First I spill ice cream on Mr. Rogers, then I spill water on Jake Gyllenhaal. Maybe I'll get to be known as the woman who, like, spills things on celebrities. Maybe I'll spill a vodka and tonic on Brad Pitt or Cole Sprouse one day—you never know, right?

I feel embarrassed about calling Jake Gyllenhaal, "Lee." I had no idea he came here when he was in town, or that he was good friends with Mr. Flanigan. But that's what Marcus said when I traipsed back into his office and told him what had happened, hardly able to catch my breath. Marcus laughed at me. Maybe it wasn't a big deal to him, but to me, it was. Starstruck? Of course.

Still, now that I've been razzled and dazzled, it's time to get down to serious business. I'm talking major, heavy duty, primal and important stuff. Earth-shattering action. There will be no stopping me now. I am determined. After a quick shower and a change in clothing, I take a left down a narrow hallway on the second floor—passing by a *Be Your Best!* sign, and a right past a spinning class, then head straight to the most important place of all in this club: the hair and nail salon.

It's an entire suite, with pictures depicting sand, water, sunshine, and blue sky on the walls. A small fountain gurgles against one wall. Scents of vanilla, lavender, and mint hit me as soon as I enter; the atmosphere is calm, very laidback. Wonderful.

I have arrived.

I'd pre-scheduled my appointments on the app and I'm quickly received by a willowy blonde with the smoothest complexion I've ever seen. She leads me to my chair, one of ten all filled with other women getting their nails done as well. She offers me a glass of white wine, which I heartily accept. A short lady, fiftyish, soon approaches me. She gives me a quick hello, and then sets to work. She trims, moistens, and polishes my fingernails in a deep rich red—just like my new hero, Veronica. I try to strike up a conversation with her, but she hardly replies, merely bends down to her task with a studied seriousness as if she were performing a work of art. Maybe she is. I love the new color.

A facial and massage are next. With a twinge of guilt, I remember Val calling me a Peter Pan, and it erases some of the pleasure I'm feeling. But I won't let that ruin this moment. It helps that the massage therapist has hands to die for, and when she finishes, I feel my tension melt away.

Then, the most important moment of all—the hair salon. Let the drum rolls begin. This is what I've been waiting for most of all. Could this be the place that finally makes something of my thin, straggly hair? I float in. Why can't I feel like this all the time? I've had massages before, but the feel-good sensation always wears off. Maybe this time, it'll be different. Maybe I'll be able to keep it going, though I know it's not likely.

I meet my stylist, an Asian woman who wears dark-red lipstick. She has seriously beautiful eyebrows and dark, shimmering eyes. She's petite and slim, reed-like, and has slender hands with fingers that flutter like butterflies as she speaks. I sit down in her chair and she runs her fingers through my hair.

"What are you going for today?" she asks, staring at me through the mirror facing us.

"If you can make it less straggly, I'll give you the biggest tip of your life," I say. "It's so thin. It's oily too." I crinkle my nose. "I've tried every conditioner I can find, different shampoos. Nothing works. It stays this way. Limp and stringy."

"You need to change the part in your hair. Then use my secret sauce. Thin hair's actually not a problem."

"It's not?"

"No."

"I still want it long to my shoulders. Is that possible?" I say.

"Not a problem."

She runs her fingers through my hair again, and then holds up a strand or two so that we can both look at it in the mirror.

I feel relaxed in her hands. After she wets my hair, and begins to shampoo, I breathe in the essence, citrusy and fresh. Her expert fingers lather my scalp. I focus on the sensations. Any remaining tension in my body quickly disappears. She rinses and then re-shampoos and rinses again.

She parts my hair in a way I've never thought of doing before, then cuts and clips as she works with ease and artfully styles me.

When she's finished cutting and clipping, she picks up a silver bottle and uses it to spray my hair. The product has the aroma of freshly cut grass.

"What's that?" I ask. The bottle appears to have Chinese writing on it.

"Oh, this? This is my magic for hair like yours." She gives me a secretive smile. "I'm able to order it from Changzhou, my city in China, as Chinese women often have thin hair too."

When she's done, she turns me around to look at myself in the mirror. I stare at the results and I'm stunned. I break out in a huge smile. I feel like giggling. It's incredible. I run my fingers through my hair – the straggles, the thinness, the stringiness, and that oily, sticky look is totally and completely gone. For the first time since I was thirteen, I have straight, silky hair that's full and rich with bounce. The way I've always wanted it to look.

"I love it! You're a genius! Thank you so much! The way you parted it really makes a difference!"

"You go out tonight," she says, smiling. "You have a good time."

If only I could. The fact that I can't hits me like a brick. "Well, maybe not tonight," I say, feeling a sudden sadness as I think of my predicament. But even so, I know there's a new me rising inside, a new Kat Noad, someone with self-confidence. Someone who will not fall apart simply because her boyfriend has broken up with her. "But hopefully, soon." When I get out of the chair, I give her a hug. "Thank you so much. What's your name?" I ask. "I didn't even get it."

"Cho," she says. "It means butterfly."

"Okay, Cho. You are the best!" She bows to me and I bow to her. "You get five stars from me. No doubt about it."

It costs me a hundred and twenty-five dollars, but it's totally worth it. I put it on my credit card and leave her with a huge tip. I also buy the formula she used and put the precious bottle in my purse.

"Come back soon, okay?" she says, touching my hair.

In the end, I dropped nearly three hundred dollars for the spa treatments. It was worth every Sam-canceling dime. I washed my ex right out of my hair.

. . .

I am a new and improved person. I'm exercising, I'm eating better and, Moscow mules notwithstanding, I am beginning to cut back on the alcohol. Well, maybe not. But still, at least I have the *thought* of cutting back—and that's something. Plus, there's my realizations about me being a Peter Pan and that I'm basically emotionally blind. Now I see, and that's the first step toward healing yourself. Self-reflection. Never did too much of it until now. I must say, staying inside this health club is definitely doing me some good.

I sit down in a chair near the fountain and bring up my resume on my phone, luckily stored in my Word app. I alter it slightly, Google local dentists and fire off resumes in rapid succession. When it comes to references, if I get asked, I'll tell my prospective employer that Dr. Pierce and I came to a mutual understanding. It's her word against mine, plus I do have very good references from other jobs.

I find the dentist I was looking for, someone I worked for before Dr. Pierce employed me. We got along well together: Dr. Maurice Fields. Nice guy. Late fifties. He had to close up shop because he developed thyroid cancer. But he's cured, I heard, and back in business again. I need to give him a try.

I also get an email regarding my application for childcare worker at Great Fitness telling me that everything's in order and it's processing. Wow. That was fast. Who knows? Maybe I'll go back to school and get a degree in education and teach kindergarten or something. What's wrong with keeping a few balls juggling in the air?

I feel so pulled together, so non-befuddled, if there even is such a word, I could even try to make a run for it through the door, now that I'm in such a calm state. No. This mellow mood cost me over three hundred dollars. I'm *not* going to upset myself by facing that horrid door. Besides, I like it here. This place is growing on me. I'm glowing. Why leave now? I'm a new person when I'm in here. A different Kat altogether. Why spoil a good thing?

As I send out my resume, the idea of telling my father I'm unemployed flows through my mind and this, unfortunately, brings me down. I picture the scene. We'll be eating at a restaurant somewhere and I'll say: "Besides losing Sam, Dad, I, uh, well..."

"Yes?" He'll put his fork down and wait, knowing full well that I'm going to hit him with more bad news.

"I got fired too," I'll say, then add quickly, "but don't worry. Dr. Pierce gave me two weeks' salary so I'm good for a while. I'll find a new job. Promise."

This news will kick him in his fatherly heart. My dad is such a successful businessman. He's not familiar with failure the way I am. Whenever he faces a problem, all he does is rear back and knock it in its teeth. But with me—his biggest problem of all—I'm sure there'll be this fleeting disappointed look on his face that he won't be able to hide, and it'll crush me to see it. I'll probably cry right there in front of him, or order another drink and then cry.

"I'm not the kind of daughter you wanted. Sorry, Dad..."

He wanted a daughter who marries the "successful and easygoing nice guy," has cute kids, and lives happily ever after in a safe neighborhood—as does every father. But isn't that what I want too at this stage in my life? So how do I get it? So far, happily ever after doesn't seem to be in my deck of cards. But there's always hope—I guess.

"It'll work out. I'm sure it will," he'll say, trying to reassure me, the same way he's always tried to reassure me. When I was a kid, he used to say the word "pickle" to get me out of a bad mood and I'd laugh uncontrollably. That one word could break me up and make me giggle. If only "pickle" could still do the trick.

I can picture that Big Doubt in his eyes: the hurt I've caused him all these years, me, the daughter who can't seem to get it together—so unlike my older brother, Joey, a successful lawyer in LA, happily married with two young children, his wife a successful lawyer too. Joey and I hardly ever communicate. We live in different worlds. He's always extremely busy. We never were that close. Sometimes I think it's as if we come from two different sets of parents.

My father and I will simply sit there in silence and the mood will descend into a deep, dark pit. Story of my life. My anxiety, the elephant in the room.

My father was the one who suggested I attend Lehigh University, a party school par excellence. Go Mountain Hawks! His brother, Uncle Marvin, a successful radiologist, went there and thought it would be a good place for me.

I majored in chemistry and, during my extracurricular time, found the cure to my anxiety, or at least I thought I had—alcohol. I specialized in the particular mind-numbing effects of Bacardi. But really, I was not limited to any one type at all. I didn't discriminate. Jack Daniels, Jim Beam, Johnnie Walker, Jose Cuervo... (not to mention Ben and Jerry) were all intimate pals of mine and they never let me down. Unlike Sam and the other walking, talking, breathing men in my life.

When I felt anxious, I simply drank. And for a while, I got myself under control. But drinking occasionally in the evenings grew into drinking more than occasionally in the afternoons. In college, I wound up day drinking, missing classes and sleeping more. As anxious as I was, and as much as I imbibed, I still had the mental wherewithal to maintain a solid B average. I even made a B in organic chemistry, which half the class failed. The academic work wasn't that hard for me. How many stereoisomers of phenylpropylene oxide are there? Believe it or not, I know the answer. How to not be so anxious in class and not have to fall back on a few drinks to get me through the day? I didn't have a clue.

I graduated, warts and all, and the next thing I knew, I was back home, worn out, not knowing what I would do with the rest of my life, and for that matter, not really caring.

My parents were patient, and then confused. After a few months they got pissed off and finally, disappointed. I was so unlike my aggressive, determined, goal-oriented brother. I'd graduated with good grades in difficult subjects and now all I wanted to do was to hang around the house and mope. They had no idea how anxiety can overwhelm a person every single day of their life, how it comes to control you and limits you and makes you feel so deeply uncertain about, well, everything. Life becomes a series of going from one thin-ice pond to the next. Walls go up all around you. The certainty is that you're uncertain—constantly.

"What are you going to do with your life?" my parents would ask time and time again. "Do you have any ideas?"

I had no idea what I would do. Twenty-two, twenty-three years old, and there I was, moving in with a friend who happened to be studying dental hygiene. I did some substitute teaching at the high-school level and, for a time, worked in a library, which I liked because it was quiet and no one bothered me.

But to my parents it was infuriating. I had grades that were good enough to get me into medical school, but my anxiety held me back. My Big A.

Medications yielded a variety of results, none satisfactory: Zoloft, Paxil, I even tried Propranolol, which is the stage-fright med that entertainers use. Some of these helped for a while, but either the effects wore off, or the side effects were too strong. Several had weight gain as a serious side effect as well, not to mention dizziness and hair loss. And then, I discovered Xanax, which helped. And yet, it's addictive, so I have to be careful. Too much reliance on Xanax can yield some major problems.

Finally, as time passed, I learned to simply cope—if coping is the right word—by taking deep breaths and lying down until the worst of the anxiety storm passed. With grit, persistence, and determination, I was able to make my way through dental hygiene school and—at last—I made my parents proud—sorta, I guess.

But now, I'm on the verge of letting them down again.

CHAPTER 12

It's nearly five-thirty when I head over to the Pro Shop, which isn't far from the nail salon. I run into Lee and I stop him in his tracks. He's buzzing, as electrified as a Christmas tree—per usual.

"Saw your lookalike here today," I say.

"Who? You mean Jake?"

Lee starts bouncing up and down on his toes, like he's getting ready for a boxing match. The guy cannot stand still.

"Do you know him?"

"Sure do. He uses our facility whenever he's in town. He's doing this movie in Nashville or something. Look." Lee whips out his phone and shows me a pic of him and Jake together, smiling into the camera in front of the *Be Your Best!* sign in the front. They're holding up bottled waters, clinking them together. I swear, the resemblance is uncanny.

"So, I hear people pay you to show up as Jake?" I ask.

"Indeed. Parties, events, you know? Hey. Glad to see you keeping at it, Kat. You're doing great!"

His compliment causes me to flash my own Life-Is-Great smile, something I'm trying to master. "Doing my best."

He turns serious for a moment and points a finger at me. *"Be* your best," he says. "That's the key, Kat. *Be* your best."

Then off he goes like a rocket, practically jogging as he heads toward the front desk. He calls out to a skinny teen. "Hey, Rand! Saw you swimming laps yesterday. Your times are really improving! Good for you!" Then: "Mr. Martin! Wow! You were really getting down on that ab work. That's great!"

Hmm... will have to think about that: *Be* your best? Sounds Zen-like. A philosophical conundrum, as Sam would say. *How does that work?*

The Pro Shop is small, but well-stocked, featuring a variety of high-quality dresses, jewelry, coats, sweaters, and shoes. Three other women are in the store, looking around. Pop music is playing over the speakers. Katy Perry is singing out that she isn't afraid anymore—she's about to roar. Maybe I am too, in my own small way. I scan the selections. A long purple dress? A white dress with sleeves? No. I finally decide to try on a black bandage fringe dress. Standing in front of a mirror, I conclude: This is me. Yes.

The black contrasts nicely with my blonde hair, now shiny and straight. The dress has a slimming look too, with a V-neck. It's sleeveless, cut at a midi length. I like it. I accent it with long silver earrings and a necklace. I buy some black heels with gold patterns—not too spiky, but still showy just the same.

There. The entire ensemble. Staring at myself in the mirror, assessing the situation, I twirl around and smile. I look good, if I do say so myself. Sam doesn't know what he's missing.

"I'll take it," I say to the saleswoman. Thin, with frizzy hair and a pointed nose, if she's in the movie star lookalike club, I can't recognize a resemblance. I love her earrings, though, gold hearts in various sizes dangling from small hoops.

"Would you like me to wrap it up for you?" she asks.

"Oh, no. I'm going to wear it now."

"Really?"

I give her an icy stare. "Sure. Why not?"

I need something dressy if I'm going to hang out here. She gives me an odd look, but so what? I don't care what she thinks.

But then I feel bad. Why am I always so curt with people?

Just because you suffer from anxiety doesn't mean you have to be so hard on the outside, does it?

I give her a smile and say, as politely as I can, "Thank you. Have a great day."

I'm so glad to see her smile back. "Sure. Thanks!"

There. I feel better already.

Leaving the shop, I realize that I'm hard on the outside because inside, I am filled with nothing but fear and anxiety. I vow to be a little nicer to people from now on. Why not? Grumpy gets you nowhere when you think about. Whereas being nice...

My mind turns to Marcus and I break into a grin. Talk about nice! I remember how he joked about us sharing a tent in the Amazon. I imagine *being* there with him, fantasizing the whole thing: It starts raining really, really hard, tons of rain, buckets, and we get caught out in it... hand in hand, we dash to our tent and dive in, laughing and hugging each other, the sound of rain pattering around us, maybe a few baboons hooting in the distance just for ambience... He takes me in his arms and... oh... hell...

Would you cut that out?

I go into one of the locker rooms, put all my belongings in two lockers, and then apply a touch of makeup. I think of Sam, Marcus, Lee... Jack Hammer...

Men.

I really don't get them. In one way, they are so easy to read, they're like dogs with their tongues hanging out who only care about food and sex. But in another way, they're entirely impossible to figure out—as complicated as the Theory of Relativity.

If only I could be a man for one day, just to see what it's like; balls and—

"Love your outfit," a woman says to me, turning my way and interrupting my thoughts.

"Oh, thank you. Just bought it," I say, smiling at her.

"Nordstrom's?" she asks. She's putting lotion on her hands, tall, fit, one of those gym-perfect bodies so prevalent around here while the real world—out there, yes, there is a real world, isn't there?—is so vastly different. Bodies of every size and shape imaginable. Her sea-green eyes sparkle with a kind of strange intensity.

"Actually, I bought it right here."

"It's nice. I'm Lura." She checks herself out in the mirror, fusses with her hair, and then turns my way again.

"Kat," I say.

"Nice to meet you. How long've you been coming here?"

"It's only my third day."

"Oh. A newbie! Well. That's great! Welcome aboard, Kat! I'm kind of the club's unofficial social butterfly. Everybody knows me and I know everybody." She giggles. "The thing is"— she looks right and left and whispers as if she's telling me a secret—"I practically live here."

"Really." I suppress a smile and finger my hair.

"Oh, yes. If this place had a bed, I'd probably be camping out in it."

"Sure, why not?" We both laugh. "Maybe you could even sleep on a yoga mat."

"I've slept on worse things," she says. "Trust me."

Again, we chuckle. She takes out her lip gloss and carefully applies it. "It's just me and me these days. Newly divorced. Kids long gone." She sighs and stares at herself in the mirror again. "I work out a lot, you know? It keeps my mind off everything else. So how do you like it here?"

"I love it," I say and once again, realize how much I do.

"Have you eaten at Yummy's yet?" she asks.

"Actually, I have. A few times." I take out my own lip gloss and slick it over my lips. "I love their food. Their veggie sandwiches are amazing!"

"Well, on Fridays, they have their famous Belgian waffles made out of organic groats—they're so delicious!—and the organic coffee's discounted from 5 a.m until 8 a.m. Don't forget."

"I'll keep that in mind."

Suddenly, she gives me an odd, angular smile, which seems to wobble on her lips. Her eyes darken with a kind of muddled sadness. It looks as if she's about to crack. For a second, the smile reverts to a frown—as if she's in some kind of inner pain—then thankfully returns. She pats my shoulder, and I feel her eyes flick briefly up and down my body.

"Okay, then. Nice meeting you, Kat." She sighs. "You should really try one of the trainers. You won't be sorry. See you around."

Seriously?

Must she jab me like that?

After she leaves, I think about what she says though. Maybe she *has* got the right idea about what fitness can do. It keeps my mind off everything else. To be honest, I hate to admit it, but I would love to learn to "keep my mind off everything else." Maybe exercise is the best way to do that after all. I feel my determination to "just do it" grow steely.

A few minutes later, I'm all dressed up and ready to make this happen—whatever "this" is. I do love these earrings, bardrop chandelier in sterling silver. They look... great!

I turn right out of the locker room and nearly collide into the pock-faced security guard, Larry Johnson.

"Excuse me," he says, his bad eye looking particularly bad today.

"No. Excuse me."

But instead of moving on, he looks me up and down with a sudden sneer on his lips, and puts his hands on his hips, giving me a stare that feels like he's considering putting a gun to my throat. What the hell? Does he know something? Does the guy ever *not* work here?

As I pass him by, my Big A turns on and I need to find a chair and sit down for a minute. Take some deep breaths... Whew! I'm trembling... I really do need to see Dr. Sharp tomorrow. I need to get out of this place. Get on with my life.

Finally, I stand. A few more deep breaths. Okay. I'm good. He's probably an asshole who sneers at everyone. I'm making mountains out of molehills. That's part of my Big A. Dr. Sharp has told me that many times.

"Kat, you tend to amplify things with a large dose of negativity, making them look far worse than they really are," she said once. "You need to learn not to do that."

Okay, then. Let's give it a shot. I turn on a smile and run a hand through my gorgeous new hair. Think on the bright side: There's no way they could know about me at this point. Besides, the important thing is that I'm all set for the evening and I plan to have fun. Screw Larry Johnson.

Hair—check, facial—check, nails—check, a bit of cleavage—check. Cool-looking dress. Check and check.

As I tromp along down a hallway, past a high-intensity interval training class, I run a hand through my newly dolled-up hair once again. I swear, that hairdresser is a miracle worker, I don't care what it cost, it was so worth—

"Ms. Noad?"

I know that voice. It's Jim Flanigan's, CEO of Great Fitness himself.

I'm walking past a spin class when Mr. Flanigan comes up to me. A high-energy song blares away. The well-built instructor, his voice booming through a microphone, is ordering everyone like a Marine sergeant: "Ready, set, let's crank this thing up! Let's go!"

"Hi," Jim says. "Kat Noad, right?"

"Guilty as charged," I reply, trying to laugh, then realizing that the joke isn't funny, given my circumstances.

"I want to tell you that your application for the childcare worker position is already being processed since we're so desperate for help. No DUIs or anything, I hope?" He grins and gives me a good look at his perfect teeth. I would love to give him a good cleaning. There's something so satisfying about it. When you're done removing all the plaque and shining them up, it's like you've played your small part in setting the world right, one set of teeth and gums at a time.

"No. None at all." I cringe, but it's true. Fortunately, my one DUI was expunged. I have my father's excellent lawyer to thank for that.

"So, we can probably call you in for an interview tomorrow. Donna Collier will be reaching out to you. She's my H.R. admin. I was wondering, would you be available to start work as soon as this Friday, if everything clears?" he asks. "We are really desperate. We have to have a certain staff-to-child ratio or we can't even offer the service."

"Sure," I say quickly. "My father's coming in from the airport on Friday at two, and I told him I'd pick him up. But other than that, I'm completely free all day."

"That would be great!" He studies my ensemble then, after a pause, he says, "Heading to the bar?"

Ah, a mind reader/detective as well as a CEO.

"Yes, I am, indeed. Get a little water at the old watering hole," I say, trying to make a joke as I feel my nervousness begin to rise.

"You're, uh, here quite a lot, aren't you, Ms. Noad?"

"Well... uh..."

"You're not thinking about moving in, are you?" When he

grins at me, his entire face crinkles up. Suddenly, my Big A shadow friend wakes up and takes notice.

I shake my head. "No. Not at all. I-I don't think I'm here all that much. I don't think..." My voice trails off.

"I'm only joking! But you know, my twin brother and I own this facility and three more in different cities, and see, about two months ago, the strangest thing happened."

"What was that?" I tilt my head, curious.

"Well, we found someone actually spending the night at our Great Fitness club in Chicago. Using our health club as his own apartment. He thought he could take advantage of us. Thought he could get away with it. We caught him though, of course."

I gulp. My good mood totally dive bombs. I feel my ears turn red and there's a buzzing inside my head all of a sudden, like bees circling a hive. "I-Imagine that," I mutter.

Mr. Flanigan nods. "I know. Can you believe some people? The audacity. When we finally caught him, we prosecuted. He spent a week in jail and was fined ten thousand dollars. That may seem harsh, but what he did breaks all kinds of insurance codes and it messes with our premiums. We simply cannot allow it."

"A w-week?" I stammer. "In jail?"

He folds his arms. "And he deserved every last minute of it as far as I'm concerned."

"I-I guess he learned his lesson, didn't he?" I'm barely able to get the words out.

"A great big expensively miserable lesson." For a long nearly unendurable moment, he doesn't say a word. Larry Johnson's glare flashes in my mind.

Mr. Flanigan rubs his chin again, as if he's going to say something, but then apparently decides not to. "It would take a real nutcase to do something like that. Someone really strange."

"The strangest." I wholeheartedly agree.

"Well, anyway..." He smiles again and that eerie doubt in

his eyes disappears. "Have fun at the bar, Ms. Noad. Tell Jack you can have your first drink on me."

"Thanks so much! That's so kind of you, Mr. Flanigan."

"Enjoy!"

When he departs, I can't seem to move, hands shaking, mind rattling, heart thumping. I don't know what to do. This is sick, awful... absurd. Someone did what I'm doing and got caught and prosecuted? I don't think Jim Flanigan was considering me as a trespasser... and yet... there *was* a certain look, as if he wasn't totally sure either. Why would he tell me that story if there wasn't a reason? Maybe he was warning me. But he still wants me to work at the daycare, so, in his eyes, I must be okay for now—I guess.

There is only one conclusion I can draw from this conversation: I have got to get the hell out of here—like tonight! I have no choice. No excuses. I *must* leave! The screws are tightening. No more farting around and telling myself this is some kind of therapy for my rattled life.

When I arrive at the bar, my anxiety is approaching Code Red. I need a drink so bad I can hardly stand it. My hands are trembling and my breaths are coming in quick in-and-out spasms.

"When we finally caught him, we prosecuted... He spent a week in jail and was fined ten thousand dollars."

Jail if Mr. Flanigan catches me, a psychiatric hospital if I call Dr. Baldwin and tell him what's what—a fine choice, indeed. Talk about being caught between a rock and a hard place.

Good news: Marcus is at the bar and, as distressed as I am, a wave of teenage giddiness flows through me just seeing him. Gorgeous Marcus, personal trainer par excellence. Someone who I can trust in my lonely world, I'm sure.

He's sitting with two women and a man. But these aren't regular people—I see that right off. These are creatures from a different species, a different planet. Humanus Maximus. Something like that. Gods and goddesses of superior health and fitness, people with sculpted bodies who look like they could conceivably double as Greek and Roman statues on the side.

Marcus spots me and waves exuberantly. "Kat!" he calls, motioning to me. "Come join us!"

I nod, shoot him a smile, and sidle up to the bar next to him.

"How's it going?" he asks with a jovial smile.

"Great!" I say quickly, lying my ass off. "Really great."

The women are long-haired and beautiful. One's a blonde with sky-blue eyes, wearing workout attire that looks like a new form of skin encapsulating her trim and muscular body. The other woman is red-haired, with full lips and deep-set eyes. The man, who's taller than Marcus by a few inches, has the thin, wiry look of a marathon runner and a rich mane of dark hair. They are laughing at something as I sit down on a barstool.

A variety of people are surrounding the bar: two men who look like a happy couple, dressed to perfection in jackets and open-collar shirts, sipping white wine; a fortyish man wearing a tennis outfit and sloshing back a beer by himself; a silver-haired man and woman—slim and trim. They could have easily stepped out of a travel magazine as models for AARP. They're both drinking cocktails.

Marcus stands and gives me a quick hug and for a split second, our bodies do a bit of talking on their own. I pick up a vibe. He smells good too, that same manly cologne. "You look great!" he says.

"Thanks," I say, beaming. I run a hand through my hair. I wonder what Sam would say if he could see my hair now.

"Amy, Dave, Marissa," Marcus says. "Meet Kat Noad. She took my free intro class today. She's a newbie."

"Hey everybody," I say, gazing around. Amy's the blonde,

Marissa, the redhead.

"They're all personal trainers here at the club," Marcus says. "Dave does personal training and admin too."

"Sounds great," I say, unable to think of anything else. I take a long breath, trying to get my bearings.

"Nice dress," Amy says. "Don't they sell that at the shop here?"

"They do," I say. I run a hand down the side and smooth it out.

"Looks good on you," Marissa says, smiling. "And I love your earrings."

"Thanks." And then I get right to the point. "So, what are we all drinking? I know *I'm* ready for a splash of the good stuff —maybe more like a bath." I laugh. After my little talk with Mr. Flanigan, I need something that'll knock me on my ass—fast.

"Fiji water for me," Marcus says, raising his glass. "With lemon. Cheers." He gives me a wink.

"O'Doul's for us," Dave, Amy, and Marissa say, clinking their glasses of non-alcoholic beer together.

"Oh." I'm sure the disappointment on my face is there for all to see. Should have known they'd all be sipping alcohol-free drinks. Is there a point when too much good health is *bad* for you?

Sadly, probably not.

I was all geared up to order another Moscow mule— couldn't wait, actually. The last ones were downright therapeutic, at least for a while.

"Hey, if you want a drink-drink, go right ahead," Dave says, reading my mind. "Don't let us stop you."

"We're not anti-alcohol," Amy says diplomatically, touching my hand. "It's just not for us."

"Yes. It's just not our thing," Marissa agrees, wrinkling her nose.

Jack is stationed behind the bar, cleaning a glass when I call to him. He's all dressed up in a dark-blue suit tonight, looking polished and suave, yet there's that same old ruggedness to him as well. Sexy through and through.

"Hey, Jack. How about a nice, stiff Riesling?"

"Comin' right up." Jack offers up a broad smile and our eyes meet for more than a second. Once again, it feels like Jack and I share the same wavelength. We're both party-goers from way back. We've got wireless transmission. He seems to be feeling me out, wondering why I'm with the stars of the club.

I decide to do a little snooping right off, just in case I do have to stay another night.

"Everything's so clean around here," I say. "Do they have some kind of, uh, midnight cleaning crew?"

"We used to," Dave says as he takes a sip of his drink. "The cleaning crew's been working days lately, at least most of the time. I think in about two weeks, they'll start coming in at night again. Something about a new contract."

"Really? I didn't know that about the cleaning crew." Amy is listening as she checks a text on her phone.

The cleaning crew situation is good news. But, really, I *am* leaving tonight. I have to. What Mr. Flanigan said about that guy in Chicago flashes through my brain and for a moment, I can barely focus.

"Love the bar here," I say, looking around.

"Yes. We think it's a great addition for the members. It's a big draw, especially on Friday nights. A lot of people come here and relax after work," Amy says.

"Plus, it keeps me employed," Jack offers, listening in.

We all laugh.

"Have you tried the float tank yet?" Dave asks.

"No, but I definitely plan to," I reply.

"You'll love it," Marcus says. "I was the first one who got in it when they set it up. I fell asleep in it. Woke feeling like a new person. Seriously."

I wish I could wake up feeling like a new person. That renewed feeling from my salon experience has worn off and I feel like plain old Kat again, anxieties and all.

Marcus's eyes meet mine. I catch a glimmer of interest in those deep blues of his. Or am I fantasizing?

Jack brings me my white wine. I sniff as I roll the wine glass around, getting oxygen into it, and then take a taste. Everyone watches me as if I'm some famous wine connoisseur. "Nice. Hits the spot. Thanks, Jack."

"It's a Louis Latour. Better than the Riesling." Jack gives me a supportive wink, as if he's cheering the one alkie on from the sidelines. "It's got more depth and body. You'll like it."

"Sweet." I shoot him a smile. Jack so gets me.

"You two know each other?" Dave asks, looking at Jack then back at me.

God, who is this guy? Mr. Perceptive?

"I was here last night. Jack fixed me a drink," I say, feeling embarrassed. And caught.

"I see." Dave gives me a look as he soaks up this info. God only knows what he's thinking.

"Mr. Flanigan said he was buying me my first one," I say to Jack.

"I know. He already texted me."

"How do you know our boss?" Dave quickly asks.

Lord! This guy sticks his nose in everything!

"Just met him, uh, today," I lie. "Cheers." I hold up my glass.

A warm glow seems to settle over us all as we clink glasses and bottles. A little thrill runs through me when I clink my feminine wineglass against Marcus's masculine bottle. It makes a nice ring.

"How do you know Jim Flanigan? For a newbie, you do get around," Dave says and laughs.

"Yes, I do," I say and shrug. I get around more than he knows. "Always been that way. When I was in first grade, I'd already preplanned a meeting with the principal—wanted to make sure I got immediate training on my ABCs on day one."

They all chuckle.

As I'm drinking my wine, the guy who I'd seen at the bar two nights before walks toward us. He struts like a pelican, head first followed by the rest of his body. He's wearing a dark-blue sports coat and a light-blue tie, and smells of cheap cologne—too sweet and sharp. I hold back a sneeze.

"Hey guys," he says. The rich quality of his voice makes me think he could have been a broadcaster in another life—or maybe he is a broadcaster, who knows?

"Harry!" Marcus says to the him. "How's it going? Meet Kat. Kat, this is Harry. Harry's a born-again drinker, aren't you, Harry?"

Harry laughs. It's a big laugh with lots of gusto. "Used to be a teetotaler, but not anymore. Drinking changed my life. I saw the light through whiskey glasses. Hallelujah!" Harry turns to Jack. "Jack! My man!" Jack smiles at Harry as he wipes the bar. "Give me a bourbon, would you? Neat. That single barrel Maker's Mark oughtta do." He extends a hand to me. His palm is dry and soft. "Harry A. McGraw. Nice to meet you."

"Hi," I say. "Nice to meet you."

"Guess you're wondering what a guy like me's doing in a place like this, huh?" Harry slaps his round belly as he looks at me.

"Well, uh..."

The others giggle.

Amy turns to me. "Actually, Harry's our chief of security. He uses that line on all the women."

Chief of security?

Hearing those words spins my anxiety into overdrive. My heart starts thudding like a bass drum and I swallow a dry lump.

"Well, it hasn't worked yet," Harry says. "But I keep trying."

"Maybe one day." Marissa gives me a friendly wink.

"Harry has a nose like a bloodhound," Dave says.

"And a body like a rubber tire," Marcus adds.

"I see." I stay diplomatically silent. I sip on my wine, though I am dying for some stiff liquor right now. Literally dying.

Jack gives me a long look and our eyes connect. I smile at him as I take another sip of my wine. I swear he knows what I'm thinking.

"By the way, get this," Harry says after Jack brings him his drink. He takes a quick swig. I stare at the gold liquid in the glass and lick my lips. He puts his glass back down on the bar.

"Get what?" Marcus asks, leaning forward.

"Breaking news. We found evidence that someone's staying overnight here," Harry says.

What?

"You're kidding," Marcus says. He whistles. "That *is* breaking news. Do they think this place is the Holiday Inn?" He laughs and finishes off his drink. "Stowaway at health club. I can see it now on the nightly news."

I suddenly wish I could disappear. Or make like a roly-poly, ball up and hide. My hands go slick and I'm doing everything I can to control the shakiness of my knees. How could they possibly know? I sip my wine carefully, trying to give nothing away. Inside, I'm a tornado of emotions.

Harry goes on, rubbing his hands together; he's obviously enjoying this story, really relishing it. "A security camera on the second floor picked up a dark shadow and a leg of some unknown person walking past it around one forty-five in the morning two nights ago."

Shit!

"Maybe it was a ghost," Amy says, laughing.

"No ghost," Harry says. "That was a human leg if I ever saw one."

So that's what Mr. Flanigan was getting at. I see now. And Larry Johnson too. That stare of his.

I feel my ears burning. I take another gulp of my drink, but this time nearly choke on it. I start coughing.

"Whoa there, wrong pipe?" Marcus asks, patting me on the back.

For a minute, I can't speak. I can't breathe. I wheeze. I feel my face turn red and my heart is now nothing more than a quivering tom-tom drum. "Yeah. I'm... uh... I'm good," I say finally. "I think." I put a hand to my chest.

"Do you think it's some homeless person?" Marissa says. "If *I* were homeless and needed a place to stay, this would be it. You've got showers, pools, hot tubs, and saunas. Happy hour snacks at the bar. They could probably snooze at night on one of the massage tables, who would even know, right? Why *not* stay here?"

"Interesting," Dave says. "It's true. If you can somehow slip into this place... It's wide open. You'd have access to anything you'd want. How would you even get caught?"

I set my wine glass down on the bar. I spill a few drops, hands shaking.

The others don't seem to notice, but Mind-Reader Jack sure does. He stares at my hands, and then catches my eye. He raises an eyebrow at me and I gulp. Oh, God! Wireless transmission without batting an eye. Is he thinking what I'm thinking he's thinking? Let's face it; I've been coming here three nights in a row. I can't stay away. I drink like a fish. I'm alone. Don't I kinda sorta stand out?

"The boss says there's no way we're going to start checking cards at random," Harry says. "We're not going to start saying, 'Pardon me, but can I see your membership card?' Nope. Not gonna happen. We are, however, working on this new facial recognition system. And installing more cameras. And I think he's getting software that will make a check-in procedure last for only eight hours and then you have to check in again."

"That sounds good," Dave says.

Harry continues. "These days, security's more important than ever. Did you hear about that active shooter in Milwaukee yesterday?" He shakes his head. "Terrible. Anyway, Jim's pissed as can be. He's ready to press criminal charges if we catch whoever it is. You know this happened in our Chicago club already?"

"No. Really?" Marcus asks.

"Seriously?" Dave says.

"Wow," I say, pretending it's the first time I've heard about it too.

"It sure did. It actually made the local news. Some businessman who was down on his luck. Thought he could make a go of it until he found a new place. He lasted a week before they caught him."

"Could be a woman too, you know," Amy offers all too helpfully. Thanks for nothing, Amy.

"Yeah." Harry says. "Sure. Crime's an equal opportunity employer. So, anyway, guys, if you see anything suspicious, let me know. Keep your eyes and ears open."

"Sure," Marcus says. "Will do."

"Likewise," Dave replies.

"Jack, hit me with another one," Harry says.

"Sure thing." Jack nods, gives me a long look, then pours Harry a strong one.

Harry turns to me, putting on a friendly face. "So how long you been coming here, Kat?" he asks. He takes a sip of bourbon and strokes his mustache.

I knock back my wine. I can barely get the words out. "Oh, just, just, uh, I just started."

"That's great! Glad to have you on board. Hope you enjoy it here. There's so much to do."

"So, when are you going to let me train *you?*" Marcus asks Harry, whose glass is now empty again. I still can barely breathe.

"Soon," Harry says, turning serious. "Still getting over my hernia operation. But it won't be long now."

"He's been saying that for a year," Dave says to me, rolling his eyes, and we all laugh.

"*I* could sure use some training," Amy says with a sexy tone in her voice, staring at Marcus.

Marcus slips his arm around Amy's waist and, as I watch, my romantic dreams evaporate like morning dew. Marcus kisses Amy on the lips. A quick kiss, but a more-than-friendly kiss for sure. They even rub noses. Amy is on Marcus's level, after all. I am not. He says, "Later, baby," and everyone laughs.

"Hey, I heard we're getting some new treadmills for the upstairs weight room, new Nordics EXPs, latest models," Dave says, and then the rest of the conversation goes off on a variety of tangents. I don't say much, which is not like me. Normally, I'd be telling all kinds of stories at this point, dominating the conversation as I kept on drinking, like for instance, I'd tell them about the time I was cleaning this woman's teeth and asked her to "open wide" so I could get to her back molars, and she said to me, point blank with a straight face, "I don't open wide for my husband, so why the hell should I open wide for you?" As a dental hygienist, you hear all kinds of crazy things! Now, however, I finish my wine, and when Jack tries to make eye contact with me, I avoid his stare.

As soon as I can, I excuse myself, saying that I need to get home.

"Got a dog to feed," I say, thinking of Lilly all of a sudden. I miss her so badly. "A... uh... G-German shepherd."

Oops. Jack is listening and I'd told him I had a Chihuahua at home. Another eyebrow of his goes up. This time, he's not smiling.

"*And* a Chihuahua," I add a second later. "I call him Mo. The German shepherd's name is Ron."

"You mean like Mo and Ron?" Dave says and laughs.

"Yep. You got it. I got a pair of Mo-Rons."

Everyone laughs.

"Anyway, see you around," Dave says.

Leaving my newfound friends at the bar, I disappear from their view then head for the outdoor pool and collapse on a lounge chair under the bright stars and the inky night sky, the full moon an eyewitness to my anxious foolishness. The air is cool and refreshing. You would think I'd be close to heaven. But the reality is: *I am so screwed!* It's nearly eight o'clock now and the night is starting to roll in. The newly appearing stars and moon are doing nothing but laughing at me.

You really think you can pull this off? If you keep spending the night here at Hotel Great Fitness, you're going to get nailed and they're going to press criminal charges and then... If you don't get out of here now, you'll wind up in jail for a week, just like that businessman in Chicago. And fined too. Not that I could pay ten thousand dollars. What do they do to you if you can't pay your fine?

I stand, intending to head toward the locker room where my stuff is, determined to leave this place for oh so many reasons... And yet, already, my head is spinning as I think about confronting that horrible front door once again.

Can't stay. Can't leave. I'm trapped like a mouse in some kind of maze and if I go left I get shocked, and if I go right I get shocked too. What does a mouse do in a situation like that?

Probably freeze.

Still, I try to leave and again, I fail miserably. Nervousness, heart racing, dizziness. It's all there. I simply cannot do it. I cannot make myself move through that door. I nearly pass out when I take a few steps in the door's direction, just like I've done before. Dejected, desperate, I make for the women's changing rooms, put my things back in a locker and instead of calling Dr. Baldwin and waiting for an ambulance to rescue me, at the last second, I change my mind. No way am I going to succumb to an ambulance and a psychiatric hospital. Not at this point.

If I *must* stay here tonight—again!—knowing all the risks and possible consequences that could result, I need to take action.

I need to find a safer place to stay for the night, number one, and I need to get my car out of the parking lot, like, ASAP. I cannot let it sit there overnight again. It would surely arouse suspicion and then they'd trace the license plate to me, and that would be it.

Sitting down on a chair near one of the smaller weight rooms in the back of the facility, I phone Carla who thankfully answers on the fourth ring.

"Carla! I need you to do me a big favor," I say.

"What kind of favor?" Carla's smooth-as-bourbon voice pours into my ear. "You mean you're too drunk to drive again, and you don't want to call a Lyft because you're afraid you might throw up in their car like you did last time? They've got you marked as a hurler, right?"

I blink. She *is* right. It's damn difficult for me to get a Lyft or an Uber. I've been reviewed as a, ahem, not-so-great passenger. I have a one-star rating. That's me. I can't even ride in the backseat of a car without causing trouble.

"No. Nothing like that." I blush, recalling that incident, the night when I lost it in an Uber. The driver, who told me he was from Pakistan and worked two jobs trying to feed his family while studying molecular biology at the college, said it's people like me who give the human race a bad name. I came back with such a creative quip and profound wit, I swear it was genius: "Oh, go f— yourself!"

I really *haven't* grown up, have I? I *am* a female Peter Pan. The realization slams into me like a ton of bricks. What kind of human being am I? Maybe I *do* give the human race a bad name. I wipe a tear away. Truth hurts like a cracked tooth, all inflamed and sore.

"Listen. I need you to come to Great Fitness. I'm kind of desperate."

Not kind of. Desperate doesn't even begin to describe my situation. Still, for lack of a better word...

Carla sounds confused. "Great what?"

"Great Fitness." I take a breath, trying to mute the trembling in my voice. "It's out in south Nashville, on ninety-six. It's this huge exclusive workout place. Google it and you'll find the address."

"But why?"

God, I hate this. I hate asking her. I grow dizzy and weak in the knees. Should I just tell her the true story and spill the beans? Would she understand and help me?

I like Carla as a person, but the problem is she's not the best when it comes to sticky situations. She told me about how when a pipe burst and water went all over the floor of her apartment once, she went into panic mode, slipped on the floor, twisted her ankle, then limped out of the house screaming for help. She was a complete mess. No, I'm not sure she could handle my situation with anything near aplomb, and I'm afraid to even begin to give it a try. If I told her the whole truth, I'd probably have to help her more than she'd help me. No telling how she'd react. Chances are, she'd probably get hysterical once she learned how panicky I become near the door, and I'd get hysterical watching her get hysterical, and then someone would have to rescue both of us. Besides, I still think I can handle this on my own if I just play my cards right. Walking through that horrid door can't be this hard!

"I need you to Uber out here and then drive my car back to my apartment. And park it somewhere on a side street, not where I live. And, above all, don't tell Sam what you're doing if you happen to run into him."

"Drive your car back?" The confusion in her voice resounds in my ear. "Why in the world do you want me to do that?"

"Carla. If I tell you, I'd have to kill you."

"Oh, shut the front door!"

"I'm serious. Now listen. Listen. I've gotten involved in something strange and weird and downright messy, and that's... that's all I can say for now. Just do it and keep this a secret between us? Please? Okay? It's in the back of the lot."

"What is?"

"My car, silly."

"Oh." Carla doesn't say anything for a minute. "I'll need the key, then."

"Okay. Okay. When you get here..." I gulp, swallow, my nerves, my nerves! "Just text me, walk into the front door of the club, meet me at the fountain in the front in reception—it's this huge fountain, you can't miss it—and I'll give you the key."

Carla's voice turns wary. "Are you sure you're okay, Kat? Have you gotten yourself into some kind of trouble?"

"It's not what I've gotten myself into. It's more like what I'm trying to break out of. Anyway, don't worry. It's no biggie. I just need you to do this for me as soon as you can. As soon as possible. I mean... can you come, like, now?"

"Fine. You'll owe me a free teeth cleaning, though."

"You got it. Promise. I'll whiten your teeth for you too. Once I land a new job."

"You mean you lost your job?"

"Uh, yeah. Dr. Pierce and I had a falling out, that's all."

"Okay. I'll be there as soon as I can."

"Thanks, Carla! You're the best!"

I wait near the fountain, playing games on my phone, trying as best I can to allay my anxiety. I try to close my thoughts down, to turn them into thought bubbles and let them pop. But

I *can't* let them pop. These aren't thought bubbles—they're thought bombs. Thought IEDs. I'm anxiety-locked inside this health club and I have Mr. Walrus Mustache on my tail along with one-eyed Larry Johnson. Sam is gone. My job is gone. My anxiety is nearing eleven. I can't stop shaking and the sadness that's filling up my heart is painful, aching, the kind of sadness that's on steroids, hitting the topmost point of my emotional barometer. My ears are ringing as well.

But the craziest thing of all is that when I turn to my right, a guy who looks like he could be Brad Pitt's younger brother walks by, all decked out in workout attire, a gym bag slung across his shoulder. Am I dreaming all of this? I really think I'm losing my mind.

Plan of action: stay here and not get caught until I figure a way out of this. And I need to do it on my own. I firmly believe this is the only way, the best way. I can't bring any friends or family into this. I don't want to become a burden to them, to worry them—especially my parents, who I've worried enough my entire life—and to become the person in their eyes who can't cope with their own mental illness. Unless there's no hope for me at all. *Then* I'll contact a friend or my mom or dad. But surely, there's still hope. There has to be.

Half an hour later, Carla enters Great Fitness and spots me right off. I walk up to her and hand her the key. I am so glad to see her! A friend. At last. This is good. *Should* I tell her what's going on? Just let it all out and see what happens?

"God, Kat. Are you sure you're all right?" Carla's lined brow matches the worry in her eyes. She has a round, full-moon face, and is all fixed up in a cute cutout dress, her tan skin exposed at the waist. Gold earrings too and high spiky heels. She smells sweet and her shoulder-length auburn hair shimmers as she looks me over. "Where'd you get your dress, Kat? It's gorgeous!"

"Just bought it. You like?" I spin around for her.

"I love it! And your hair! What have you done to your hair? It looks amazing!"

"Thanks!" I run a hand through my hair and break out in a smile. "I found this hairdresser—she's a magician."

Carla studies my face and I can tell by her frown and the hard stare she gives me that she doesn't like what she sees. "What's really going on here, Kat? I want to know. Come on. Let it out."

For a too-long, emotion-wracked moment, I don't say a word. I look away. I look up. My stomach transforms into an airplane runway again, planes crashing. My heart plays bongos in my chest. I choke back a tear.

No, I decide. I *can't* tell her. If I did, she'd get all freaked out and then I'd get all freaked out and the next thing I know, I'd be boo-hooing and she'd be boo-hooing and then she'd call my psychiatrist after wrenching the number from me, and he'd say call 911—what else is he going to say?—and I'd wind up in Insanesville, once again, swept away by ambulance for sure. Once they determine that you are mentally off-balance, they handcuff you while you're sitting in the back of the ambulance on the way to the psychiatric ward. Isn't that great?

I decide that I'd rather be caught by Mr. Flanigan and face jail. I've already had the mental ward experience—may as well broaden my horizons, right? After all, how bad could jail be for one measly week? Though I'd get handcuffed going to jail as well. Plus lose ten thousand dollars.

In the end, I realize that I can't confide in Carla. It's too risky. I have no idea how she'd respond. Instead, I shoot her the fakest, most plastic, most Saran wrap-around smile of my life. "I'm fine, Carla. Okay? I really am. I just need you to do this for me, that's all." I look her up and down, all dressed up herself. I raise an eyebrow and take a long breath to quell my nerves. "So where are you headed?"

Carla straightens her dress and her eyes suddenly sparkle.

"To the Gulch. Got a friend I'm going to meet up with." She fingers one of her earrings.

"A friend? Do tell." Even in my lousy situation, still, inquiring minds want to know.

Carla's smile is suddenly as bright as headlights. "We found each other on Match. He's a pharmaceutical salesman. Really cool guy. Just gonna have a drink or three. He works for J 'n' J. Johnson and Johnson."

"So how's his Johnson?"

"What? Oh, hush." She blushes as she waves a hand in the air.

We both laugh.

"By the way, my car makes this clanky noise sometimes when you accelerate, but don't worry about it. It's okay. It gets you from here to there."

Carla gives me a wide-eyed look, one I've never seen before. "Kat, this is so strange. Are you *sure* you're okay?" Her eyes bore into me as she touches my arm.

I swallow. I want to tell her... I really do. But I can't. I can't bring myself to give her the facts right now. Besides, it's so embarrassing. I don't want her to think I'm some kind of freak— even though I know now that I most certainly am.

"Yes! I'm fine. I'm okay! I couldn't be better." I stand firm.

She looks unsure. She narrows her eyes at me and it's obvious that she doesn't totally believe me. It doesn't take a rocket scientist to figure out that's something's up with me. "Well, I just hope you're not into something stupid, that's all. I don't see why you can't simply drive your own car off the parking—"

"Look, Carla. I need your help, okay?" Panic underscores my voice and I feel the blood rise on my face. "That's all I can say. Are you going to help me or not?"

I'm doing everything I can to hold back a tear. One tear is all it would take. I know I would not be able to stop crying after that. I'd just lie down on the floor and lose it, right here and now.

Carla's sympathetic look is reassuring. She sighs. "Fine, Kat. I'll help you. Don't worry."

I instantly regret the way I just spoke. We hug. My body tremors against her.

"Thanks, Carla," I say. "You're a real friend, you know that?"

"Look. If you're cheating on Sam—"

"I'm *not* cheating on Sam. Actually, Sam and I have parted ways."

"Oh, I'm so sorry, Kat. I had no idea!"

"Hey, it's not that big of a deal. We simply thought we'd be better off ending it, that's all."

"Wow, you really *are* going through some changes."

"I am." Changes isn't half of it. But that's all I'm going to say about how it feels like life is cramming me into a blender and mixing my ass up.

Carla gives me one final look, searches my face for some sort of clue to my bizarre behavior, and then it's done. The transaction's complete. She all too easily walks out the front door, taking my car key with her, and I am so jealous I could scream. She leaves the building with such unhindered ease, heading out into the real world, into her life, while I remain a prisoner. Stuck. Trapped.

I watch through a window in the front as she finds my car, unlocks it, starts it, then turns on the headlights, and drives off the lot. There she goes. Loneliness digs into me, deep and wide, turning my heart into a vast emotional hole. There's a thickness in my throat that hurts and an unimaginably powerful ache in my chest.

I head to the locker room. I've got to face it: Things are getting serious. I am now officially in this up to my eyeballs.

CHAPTER 13

THURSDAY

I wind up trying to sleep in an out-of-the-way shower stall for a while, but it's miserable. I can't sleep at all. My back starts killing me. And then Carla texts me at 1:37 a.m., telling me my car is safely stored back in my neighborhood on a side street, and that her date had been fun—until she choked on a piece of steak at El Greco's Steakhouse, and he rescued her with the Heimlich maneuver.

Wow! You okay?

It was scary, but he knew exactly what to do. He saved my f-in life!

Sweet.

How's that for a first date?

Exciting!

Yeah. We're going to meet again tomorrow. Maybe just eat soup

Ha! Sounds like a plan.

Yeah I'm fine now. But not so sure about you.

I'm not either.

A half hour later, still unable to sleep, I sneak down the hallway in the dark, avoiding all cameras—I'd checked the route out earlier—heading for a wood-floor dance room where I plan to lie on some exercise mats. No pillow. No blanket. Nothing. Still, it's better than a tiled shower stall and sharing the space with other people's germs. Not that I'm a germaphobe—BUT I AM!

As I'm creeping down the hallway and right before I turn on my cellphone for the flashlight mode, I suddenly bump into... something? No!

It's somebody! I cannot believe it! I gasp. My heart pounds, I choke up and my legs almost buckle. No... There cannot be...

"What the hell?" I whisper. I stare at none other than Lura! Even in the darkness, I can make out who it is. She's *still* in her workout attire—as I am—and my heart is pounding away now, nerves buzzing, adrenaline rushing, sweat dribbling down my sides. Her eyes are open wide as she switches on her cellphone flashlight and I switch on my cellphone flashlight and we go at it, streams of light blazing out at each other like light-swords in some sci-fi movie. Blinding each other. I swear, she looks like she's about to pass out. Ditto for me.

"What are you doing here?" I whisper.

"What are *you* doing here?" she whispers back directly in my ear.

"I asked you first."

"I asked you second."

"*I'm* the one who's been here the longest!" she mutters under the breath, baring her teeth at me. "I told you that. Don't even try to compete with me!"

"What do you mean compete?"

"Oh, you know what I mean."

I don't. "Look. Just get out of my way!" I say.

"Get out of *my* way!"

And then the next thing I know, Lura quickly goes around me and heads down a hallway to the left, giving me the finger in the process. I switch off my flashlight and remain rooted to the spot, shocked, amazed, dumfounded. Has the woman completely lost her mind?

I finally make it to the dance room, all atwitter, and lie down on a mat, heart still hammering away. I can't believe her. Then a thought makes me freeze. What if she turns me in? No. She wouldn't do that because she knows I would turn her ass in as well.

She's staying here overnight too? It's insane!

I finally fall asleep and then, next thing I know, it's 4:15 a.m. according to my cell, which quietly sounds its alarm. At exactly 4:31 a.m., I am out of that dance room like a bat out of hell, slinking past security cameras, trekking downstairs—legal again —and feeling surprisingly good.

I've made it through another night, safe and secure, Lura Nutjob notwithstanding. The image of the shocked look on her face flows through my mind. I surprised the heck out of her. As she did me. Serves her right; serves us both right, I guess.

I stretch and yawn. I sure hope I don't run into her anytime soon. Actually, I hope I never run into her again. I merge with the other people entering the facility, blending right in. I change into my bathing suit and find an empty hot tub where I soak soak soak my weary bod'. Relief at last.

Now it's nearly 9 a.m. and I'm back in the flow of the club, just another member doing her exercise-thing. But I *have* to leave today. This is getting ridiculous. Surely, Mr. Flanigan and Harry are going to step up their security operations. I won't be able to hide from them, and eventually, I'll be found out. I've got my appointment with Dr. Sharp at five-thirty too. I can't afford to miss another one. If I do, she may refuse to see me any longer and I'd hate to have to start over with another therapist. Not cool.

I formulate a deadline as my stomach roils. Today. 4 p.m. I need to get home and change and get ready for my appointment with Dr. Sharp and just get the hell out of here. See what's going on at the apartment, sans Sam. No excuses! I'm going to stand up to that horrid door and face it and then I'm going to walk through. I will not let it push me around any longer.

Until then, however, life at Great Fitness goes on, smoothly, inevitably, and healthily. I've already scheduled a yoga class for today on my app. That's where I'm headed as I pass by the daycare center. I spy the dark-haired girl who was crying the other day and I wave at her. She waves back and now gives me a wonderfully toothless grin. She's so cute and seems in a much better mood. I hope my background check comes through quickly so that I can start working there. Mr. Flanigan said I would know on Friday—that would be fine with me. I'd love to sail back in here and work with her and the other children—at least until I land another dental hygiene job. Or maybe I'll end up switching to childcare? It seems a lot less stressful.

What are my goals in life? Overcome anxiety is priority one. If I could learn to do that, I'd be so much happier. I've got to learn to be more mature with my choices too. Goodbye, Peter Pan. Approach this anxiety more systematically. Actually go see Dr. Sharp and get help. I know I need it now. That's one thing

I've learned by staying here. I can't rely on booze for the rest of my...

Wait, I have a text.

Ms. Noad, can you come in for an interview today at 4 p.m.? Thank you, Donna Collier, H.R.

I text back:

Yes. That would fine. Looking forward to it.

I guess I'll change that deadline to leave to five o'clock, then. No biggie. This will still give me time to get to Dr. Sharp for five-thirty, since her office isn't that far away. I'll probably wear the new dress to the interview—a bit on the fancy side, but it's better than anything else I have right now.

Anyway, once the interview's done, I'm out of here. It's a definite.

For now, though, I need to expand my horizons. Ten of us—four men, six women—sit on the floor in front of our instructor. The yoga studio, second floor, is not far from Pilates. It's a large room with mirrors on two walls and hardwood flooring on which we've all placed our yoga mats. A light-blue *Be Your Best!* sign hangs on the door, commanding as usual. Maybe I could sleep here too... *No, dummy, you're going to leave, remember?*

I wind up in the back of the class, next to this tall, lanky thirtyish guy with curly black hair. Lura's in the class too, coming in at the last minute. God! This is ridiculous. She's everywhere! She's all decked out in the brightest blue Lululemon I've ever seen. She gives everyone a great big hello. It's like the whole room's happy to see her, as if she's running for president of the club or something. She takes her place in the middle of the room, next to a woman with gray hair, who is wearing purple Lululemon. They hug. Then Lura hugs the red-haired woman behind her. Is there anyone she doesn't know here? When she turns around to see who else is here, our eyes meet. I freeze. She freezes. My heart booms and my stomach tightens up. She glares at me. I stare right back.

The instructor, a woman with deep-set black eyes, starts us out with a meditation. We all lie on our mats and close our eyes.

"Follow your breathing," she says in a soft, mellow voice. She's playing that spacey meditation music in the background, and there's a soothing lemongrass scent wafting throughout the room. She walks around as she speaks to us, her gentle tone almost hypnotic. "In... out. In... out. Slowly, take your time, elongate your breathing, slow your breathing down. Keep your mind attuned to your breathing. Remember, breath is life. Stay in the present moment... Feel your body... If your mind wanders, slowly bring it back to the present..."

Already, I'm at a loss. God. I can't follow my breath at all and my mind is nothing but a chatterbox. I can't stop thinking about my situation, all my mounting problems. My Big Problem. *Breathe.* I need to relax... I feel so safe in the club. So protected. At least until midnight's closing bell. I keep seeing that carrot-topped teen in my mind as he crosses the street staring at his phone. Life out there is so fraught with all kinds of dangers. Yes, fraught, as Sam would say. While in here...

Breathe...

Maybe I can find someone who'll slip me a Xanax. But who? At least two more weeks before I can fill my prescription. All I need is one measly pill—I'm sure it would do the trick and settle me down enough.

"Breathe... breathe... Stay in the present moment..."

Breathe...

Suddenly, an idea strikes. Maybe Marcus could help me exit this place. Yes. What about Marcus? He's such a nice guy and for some reason, I feel like I can trust him. Of course I could be completely wrong, but still... he seems like someone who would understand my problems. He wouldn't get all rattled like Carla and he wouldn't call 911 like Dr. Sharp or my dad or Dr. Baldwin. He could be my ticket out of here. I think he'd understand that I need something different than an ambulance and a psychiatric hospital. Maybe with him by my side, holding onto him tight, I *could* make it out without passing out. Maybe he could even pick me up and carry me...

"Breathe... breathe... Stay in the present moment and elongate your breaths..."

Present moment, my ass.

What if we sat down and talked? What if I told him what I'm going through, that my anxiety has me locked up in here, that I'm having bad panic attacks every time I approach the door? What would he do? How would he react? Would he help me work through this...?

"Okay, then," the instructor says. "Good. Now everyone. Let's try our first pose. Is everyone relaxed?"

No. I am *not* relaxed! And I'm also the world's worst meditator.

I follow the instructor's poses as best I can, but while the others seem to be speaking fluent yoga, my body is stammering gibberish. I am as stiff as the tin man in *The Wizard of Oz* after he woke up and needed oiling. Trying to do a leg stretch in the standing position, I fall over and collapse on the mat. I squeal, and for a small, embarrassing moment, heads turn my way.

"Sorry," I say to the class, blushing.

Lura turns and laughs at me in a mean way. That woman is the pits, I swear!

"You're fine," the instructor says.

I can't help but notice that the guy next to me is as limber as a string of wet spaghetti. Surely, he's some kind of yogi master. He's standing, sitting, twisting into all kinds of contortions and pretzel stances, pose after pose. Out of the corner of my eye, I watch him stretch his legs out in a sitting position, then slowly, ever so slowly, lower his head as he touches his nose to his knees. When he stands, he keeps his knees locked and touches the floor with the palms of his hands. Incredible.

I'm not too bad at the lion's pose. It's simple. All you do is sit on your legs and open up your mouth as wide as possible. You stick out your tongue and try to touch your chin with it. Then you give a little roar. Opening my mouth as wide as possible is one thing I *can* do. I've had lots of practice.

When the class is finally over, Spaghetti Guy turns to me and shoots me a sympathetic smile. "First time?" he says in a smooth voice.

"Could you tell?" I ask, feeling embarrassed.

He shrugs. "Well, kinda. Don't worry. We all have to start somewhere."

"You're like Stretch Armstrong's brother."

He laughs. "My parents are yoga instructors. Been doing yoga ever since I was a kid."

"I believe it."

For a moment, we don't know what else to say. He's cute. Smooth complexion, big brown eyes, black hair that's long and thick. Really well-built in a lean machine way; like an acrobat or a dancer or something.

"Want to grab some breakfast?" he says in a smooth voice. He peers at me through trendy dark-framed glasses as he rubs his squared-off jaw. "I'm starved."

Wow. Bold and upfront too, but I'm flattered.

"I've already had breakfast."

"You should always eat *after* yoga class. Keep your stomach empty for the poses."

I put a hand to my stomach. He's right. It does feel a little mushy there.

"Look," he says. "Sit with me while I eat. I'll buy you a latte. They make great lattes at Yummy's, did you know?"

"I do, actually."

"Well, I... uh..." Just then, Lura walks quickly past me and "accidentally" bumps against my shoulder.

"Know her?" he asks, laughing.

"Kinda. Sorta."

I try to roll up my mat but don't do a very good job of it.

"Here, let me help you." He takes the mat from me, then expertly rolls it up in two quick movements and hands it back. "So? A latte?"

What else do I have to do?

"Good session, Linda," he turns and calls out to the instructor.

"You should help me teach it next time," Linda calls back.

"So?" he asks, turning back to me.

I run a hand through my hair. *Stick a toe in the water, see how it feels.* The words pop into my mind. Crazy.

"All right. If you insist. A latte it is." I shoot him a smile, making sure he gets a good look at my teeth. These babies are like white gems.

"Great!" he says.

We exit the yoga room and head to Yummy's together. I would love it if Sam came in right about now and saw me with this cute guy whose name is...

"I'm Josh," he says, as if reading my thoughts. "And you are?"

"Kat."

"Well, it's a pleasure to meet you, Kat." He looks genuinely pleased. His big eyes shine as he grins.

We wait in line behind five people and finally order. Josh gets an egg-white burrito and a green juice. I order a soy latte and smile at my newfound discipline. Normally I'd have coffee loaded with extra cream, extra sugar and anything else I could get my hands on.

"I'm new in town," he says after we sit down at a table in the back. "Just moved here from the wild wild west—LA. Don't know a lot of people here in Johnny Cashville."

I laugh at his play on words. "You mean Noshville?"

"Huh?"

"Oh, there's this deli here and it's called 'Noshville.' They have the best Reuben sandwiches ever."

"Oh. Yeah. I see. Noshville. Okay."

Music flows out over the speakers, some country song I can't identify, something about Momma and a house. Yummy's is really hopping. I spy Lee with another staff member sipping coffees. It's Lee—definitely—not Jake. At least I think so. I hope he doesn't see me.

"Well, I've lived in Johnny Cashville all my life," I say. "It's a pretty friendly place. I was in LA once and the Los Angelinos, is that what you call them? They didn't say hi or even smile at you when they passed you on the street. Here, everyone at least *smiles* at you."

"I know. I don't know what to think of it. I guess it's just the way the south is, right? Extra polite?"

I nod. "It is. We always say please and thank you before and after we beat you over the head."

Josh laughs. Finally, his food arrives along with my latte. I take a long sip. Nice. It hits me with a fine caffeine jolt.

Josh takes a bite of his burrito and I watch as the sides of it spill over with red sauce.

"I love the food here," I say. "And it's all organic too."

"Yes. I know." He takes another bite. "I guess 'organic's the real buzz word these days, right?"

"Seriously," I agree. "Once I bought this completely organic Margarita mix with all these pure, natural ingredients to which I was planning to add a hefty amount of tequila, and then I thought: Oh, great. At least I'm killing my liver and gray matter organically."

Josh laughs. "That's funny. I know. I know."

"So what do you do, Josh?" I ask, taking another sip and raising an eyebrow at him.

"I'm a songwriter." He wipes his mouth with a napkin.

"Really? You mean you do it professionally? Like getting paid for it and everything?"

He pushes his glasses up the bridge of his nose. "Yep. Was working in LA, but my publishing company sent me to Nashville to make some background tracks for a few artists. I'll be staying here for six months, then it's back to LA."

"That's so cool!" I'm impressed. Practically everyone who moves to Nashville is a wannabe songwriter or singer. But so few ever make it. It takes amazing talent. And even then, it's kind of like winning the lottery.

"I'm very fortunate. Had my own band for a while, but then I was lucky enough to get signed with Sony Music as a songwriter and I couldn't resist. No more traveling. And a royalty check is one of the greatest wonders in the world. Right out of the blue, it just shows up in your bank account. You can't beat it." Josh takes another bite of his burrito, scratches an ear, and suddenly looks a little shy as he presses his lips together. "Hey, I was wondering..."

"Yes?"

He pauses a moment before speaking. "You think you'd like to see John Mayer tomorrow night? My publishing company has two great seats, right up front. They're giving them away. I'd love for you to come with if you want, I mean"—he lowers his head, then stares at me—"I just thought I'd ask."

This guy works fast. I'm actually on the verge of saying yes. But should I? I don't even know him. I'd love to see John Mayer, though. I've listened to "New Light" at least a hundred thousand times.

He's looking at me expectantly as he chews on his burrito. My eyes do an around-the-world over his face again. He seems nice enough.

But there's a problem. My father's coming in tomorrow and we're supposed to have dinner together, me, him, and Wanda. I have to pick him up at the airport at two o'clock. Still, maybe I could pull it off. I could explain to Dad that I desperately want to see a concert and I'd have an early dinner with him and then take off. I'm pretty sure it would be okay with him. He typically likes to do no more than eat, talk, and run. Besides, when will I next get the chance to see John Mayer with great seats? Probably never.

"Sure. I'll go," I say, taking the leap. What's life without taking a few chances? "I'll meet you at Bridgestone in the front."

Surely, I will have freed myself from my emotional incarceration by then. Besides, seeing John Mayer will *definitely* be a motivator for me to leave.

"Doors open at seven-thirty. What's your number? The concert doesn't start until eight-thirty," he says with a grateful smile.

"I can meet you there around eight, then."

I give him my number, tell him goodbye, and then as soon as I walk near the entrance and the fountain, on my way to the ladies' locker rooms, Lura appears out of nowhere, grabs me by the arm, and pulls me aside.

"You really think you're going to defeat me?" Her eyes have that other dimension look, somewhere between an alien on *Star Trek* and a person who's been stuck alone on an island for, like, a year.

"I'm... I'm not trying to—"

"Oh, I know your type. Look. I want you to see something. Follow me."

"Fine," I say, pressing my lips together.

She leads me into the room that houses the TWR screen. *BE YOUR BEST!* is written in large letters above the TV monitors.

"You see my name there?" Lura says and my eyes go to

where she's pointing. Turns out that Lura still happens to be number one in every single category except lap swimming. Even though she's number two in lap swimming, she still has the best Total Workout Rating (TWR). She's ahead of someone named James Dudley by three points, a slim lead, indeed. Monica Zales isn't far behind either.

"No one's taking me down from my number one spot, see? Not Jimmy, not Monica, and definitely not *you*." She pushes a finger into my chest. "Do you understand me?" She narrows her eyes at me. "I know what you're up to."

"I'm not trying to take you down," I say. "I'm really not."

"Right. I don't believe that one bit."

Lura stomps off without saying another word. Seriously? This chick is definitely out there. But why is she staying overnight? Did she only do it that one time? Or is she some kind of permanent resident?

I stare at the monitors. In a flash of inspiration, I quickly install the TWR app on my phone—it's different from the yoga app I already have—and scowl. "That bitch doesn't know who she's dealing with." My fingers are flying. "If it's a fight she wants, it's a fight she'll get."

Who's to say I can't give her a run for her money? I'm younger than she is by a good ten years—if not more. And after all, I did run track in high school. If I start trying really hard, who knows what I might achieve?

Then as soon as I walk out of the room and turn to my right, I spy Sam coming into the club and my heart takes a wild elevator ride, cables broken, all the way down to the deep dark basement of my soul.

CHAPTER 14

Sam... *So fondue of you...* I forget about Lura, John Mayer, and everything else—even the fact that my hair seems to be losing some of its body at this point, which totally sucks. Our eyes meet and for a momentous, barely endurable, unimaginably difficult second, it's just me and him. In the bubble. The moment stretches and elongates like a rubber band. Finally, I look away, trying my best to ignore him. I run my hand through my hair, hoping he'll notice my new look, even though it's slightly fading. I cannot talk to him right now. I would probably break down and let it all out—*everything*. How I feel so alone and how I can't escape from this health club and how much I still want him back and how so very good the Moscow mules are here... and how this nutcase Lura woman is stalking me competitively... and on and... I mean, if there is a black donut hole in the space that holds the human heart, I'm basically stuck down in it.

I practically run to the outdoor pool and plop down on a lounger, with my friend, the Big A, following me at breakneck speed, heart thrashing, my shoulders tight, my entire body feeling suddenly stiff. I need to relax and prepare for my interview and then my exit at five. Relax. Chill. Yes. Get ready. I can't think of Sam now.

Breathe.

But how can I relax when, poolside, Larry Johnson's counterpart is walking around, checking things out? A short, burly guy in slacks and a blue golf shirt—damn if there isn't a gun attached to his belt. Let's face it: Security's an important issue these days with all these assaults and, I hate to say it, active shooters; it can happen anywhere. I read an article on the internet about how fitness clubs—the upscale ones especially— are providing more security measures than ever. He must work the day shift. He looks out at the pool with his hands on his hips. He has a bored expression. Then his eyes wander to my area. I swear, in the next moment, he seems to be staring straight at me. And then he makes a call on his cell. He couldn't possibly be spying on me, could he? The inner spring in my nervous system tightens at the thought.

Relax, Kat. Just relax.

Children are jumping into the pool and teens and mothers are sunbathing. The song playing over the speakers at the moment is Bruce Springsteen's "Born to Run." I sigh as I listen to the words. It's all about being free. Breaking out of your environs. Finding your "better self." At least, that's what it means to me. Obviously, freedom is something I lack as I spend my days and nights anxiety-locked inside Great Fitness. But on the other hand, freedom comes with too many variables, too many choices and, for a person with anxiety, that can be dangerously debilitating.

Maybe this romancing of freedom business isn't all it's cracked up to be, Bruce Springsteen notwithstanding. Earl comes to mind, the orange-striped goldfish I had when I was a child. Dear Earl. He wasn't free at all. But he didn't seem to care, at least I don't think he did.

But I don't *want* to be Earl-like. I *can't* be Earl-like. I need to somehow learn that I can't let my anxiety get the best of me. *Be Your Best!*

BE your best.

Let go of the fears, face the fact that life *is* a roller-coaster ride, and there's nothing you can do but hold on and go with it. Welcome the unknown. Embrace it. Buckle your seatbelt and enjoy the ride. Maybe *this* is what they mean by "growing up." Okay. I get it. Just hold on and go with all the incoming variables. Don't freak out. *Be Your Best!*

Accept the possibility of carrot-topped teens wherever you go.

I stretch out on the lounger, basking in the sun, as these illuminations hit me where it hurts. Don't fear freedom. It's kind of like an epiphany... Wait! I've actually never had an epiphany before—which is... an epiphany in itself!

Suddenly my mind hits reverse. I can't help it. I travel back to a long weekend Sam and I spent in St. Petersburg, Florida, what, nine months ago now? Something like that. Surely, when Sam and I were together, really loving each other, I was being my best. *WE were BEING our best.*

We splurged and got a hotel room at the Don CeSar, a slam-dunk gorgeous hotel, noted for its unusual pink façade and waterfront views; gorgeous. We had this large, first-class room with a balcony overlooking the Gulf of Mexico and a well-stocked mini-bar. (Love those well-stocked mini-bars!) We kissed as the sun went down, standing on the balcony, the water stretching out into infinity, meeting the horizon, a warm breeze blowing through our hair. The sky was glowing red and orange, dissolving into the sparkling water. I was drinking a lemon drop martini: vodka, lemon juice, and triple sec. It tasted like candy on my tongue. God! I *do* tend to catalog my life around drinking events. Note to self: *Must stop that.*

As the sun slowly set, we promised each other we'd stay together no matter what, because what we had was too good to let go, relationships like ours were too hard to find, and that when you *do* find that special kind of love, you need to hold onto it and nurture it, through good times and bad.

"I love you, Kat," he'd said, summing things up, staring into my eyes. "I mean it. You and me. We're the best. I want it to always be us."

"I love you too, Sam." I meant it too. All of me wanted all of him.

He'd taken my hand and led me to the king-size bed where all heaven broke loose, skin to skin, heart to heart.

But what about the other moments? When I complained to him constantly, when I practically lived on our couch, eating, drinking, days and nights of laziness so wondrously and deliciously wrong that I'm sure he was fed up by it all. Instead of withdrawing from him, I should have reached out and talked to him, at least tried to. I basically took our relationship for granted and now I see: When you take a relationship for granted, you're playing with fire. Relationships are only as good as the effort you put into them. The thing is, Sam also failed to put his efforts into what we had, working all the time instead, so focused on things like locating exotic mushrooms to serve his customers and discovering a new supplier of harissa that he forgot to care about something far more important—us. Our future together. What we had. It wasn't *all* my fault, that's for sure.

My question now is: How do I move on? How do I push Sam into the background and step away from the past? And then a little bug in my ear answers: *If you can't move on, at least move forward.*

Move forward... Move forward... That sounds good to me.

Finally, I wind up snoozing off. This, I do like a champion.

.   .   .

One hour later, just as I'm starting to get on a rowing machine, Lura sits down on the rower next to mine. I've only tried rowing twice before, so I'm still kind of new at it.

"Let's race," she says.

I stare at her and frown. She is really starting to annoy me.

"Fine." I don't even hesitate. I'm not backing down from her.

She clicks a few buttons on her phone and our rowing machines link via the software app. She sets up a race pattern on our screens, a winding series of waterways, and then three... two... one... We're off!

She beats me right out of the gate, of course, her strong arms moving quickly. We glare at each other, but a minute later, I start gaining momentum as we finish the first cycle. Next thing I know, I'm not that far behind as we pull into a long stretch. I'm rowing with all my might as I draw closer to her and then, two minutes later, wonder of wonders—we're even! We stay that way for five minutes before I begin to tire and she shoots ahead. But as we come down to the last three minutes, I sense fatigue in her movements, and I summon up the will to work as hard as I can. Suddenly, we're neck and neck right down to the wire. Ten... nine... eight...

It's Lura, it's me, it's Lura... Here comes the finish line. Go! Go! Go!

She beats me by five seconds. Damn! I'm more exhausted than I've ever been in my life, even more tired than when I partied so much in Vegas once that I fell off the stage after doing a pole dance on amateur night. I look over at her and she's mopping her brow with a towel.

"You did better than I thought you would," she says. She stands and gives me a maniacal smile. "For an amateur. Honestly, I was hardly trying."

"I doubt that," I say. But all she does is walk away, grabbing a bottle of water from the fridge.

I'm exhausted. But I almost had her. If I keep training, I'll be able to beat her. I know it! It's simply a matter of putting my mind to it.

Feeling good about my performance, I hit the showers and get ready for my interview, putting on my new dress. My muscles are aching, but I have new resolve. My goal is to beat Lura—and soon.

The 4 p.m. interview for the daycare job goes off smoothly—at least for the most part—I think. Donna Collier, head of H.R. Admin and a tall, lanky woman who looks like she could have played basketball in college, seems convinced that I am daycare material by the end. Maybe I am, who knows? She goes over my resume and starts talking about how the daycare provides so much benefit for the clients and how it's so important for the club. She's totally serious. I try to match her seriousness. I don't have to lie—for once.

"I really do enjoy those children," I say. "It gives you this good feeling inside. I just love being around them."

"I must say, you've already gotten some compliments from the parents." She smiles at me, then looks down at my resume which is sitting on her desk. "But aren't you a dental hygienist professionally?"

"I am," I say, forcing a laugh. "But I'm taking a sabbatical. You know? Just trying new things for a while."

"I see." She presses her lips together.

"Actually, I think I may be going back to school to study early childhood education. So, working at the daycare would be a real opportunity for me."

"Hmm... Interesting. Change of careers?"

"I'm looking into it, for sure."

"Jim Flanigan says you're quite the exerciser too."

"Oh, I try." I feel myself blushing.

"That's marvelous." She taps her pen on her desk. "I need to get out there more myself. Lately, I've been kind of lazy."

"Be your best," I say with a Life-Is-Great smile. "You know?"

"I do. Yes. So very true." She speaks thoughtfully. After asking me a few more questions—what do you like least about working with children, what age groups do you most like to work with, how do you handle misbehavior? "Oh, I carry an electric prod with me—just kidding!"—she floors me. Before I even know what's happening, she reaches into her mouth and pulls out a partial denture. Just like that.

"What do you think?" she asks as if what she's done is as natural as air.

I can't believe it! I stare at her, at the partial, then back at her. Is she for real? But when I realize she's serious, I play along. I stand up and get closer to it and she turns it over for my inspection.

"Nice," I say, trying not to laugh. "Really good job."

She pops it back in her mouth. "I think so too. It's better than my first one, that's for sure."

I give her my best professional opinion as she opens wide and I stare into her mouth. "Hmm... It looks like it fits well. Truly."

"Lost my lowers in a car accident."

"Sorry to hear that."

I wonder if she lost a bit of her mind as well. What in the world was she thinking?

It's 4:55 p.m. when I emerge from the interview. I have to head to Dr. Sharp's for my five-thirty appointment ASAP and my nerves are now buzzing. Will I finally be able to exit through the door?

I collect my things from the locker and head for the door. This is it. I need to see Dr. Sharp, no doubt about it. I am determined. I have to get out of here! But there's that door again, the outside world and all its unpredictability, and I stand at the fountain and just stare at it. Outside, I can see through a window that it's starting to rain. Then thunder claps overhead. *Be your best... be your best...* I repeat the phrase like a mantra. But it doesn't help because suddenly, like a car whose driver can't take his foot off the accelerator, I hit an emotional wall head-on. I crash and launch into panic mode. My breaths get shallow and my heart gallops away.

Oh, God! No! A kind of thunder booms inside me, matching what I hear from the sky. As it starts to rain harder, I realize once again that I cannot go near that door! I simply can't do it!

I text Dr. Sharp after finding a seat next to the fountain. My hands are shaking so much I have to dictate it. *"I'm sorry, but I'm unable to make the appointment after all. I've been detained"*— by my own insanity, I want to say—*"I hope we can still meet in the future. Kat Noad."*

I feel miserable. Sweat dribbles down my face. I'm a mess all over again. The thunder's in the distance now, as slowly, gradually, my heart beats return to normal. I sit here, staring into space. My head starts to hurt, my temples are pulsating. Finally, I head back to the locker room and change into my bathing suit, feeling defeated, beaten, at a loss. I go get a sauna and try to relax—and finally I do.

But things aren't all bad. An hour and a half later, just as I'm heading to Yummy's for a vegetable bowl with rice and shiitake mushrooms, I receive good news: Donna texts me, telling me I got the job! Mondays, Wednesdays, Fridays, and Saturdays, the morning shift. The background check went through without a hitch.

We expedited everything. Can you start tomorrow?

Absolutely

I'm so thrilled I do a little dance right here in the hallway. I can use the job to pay some bills until a new dental hygienist job comes around—if dental hygiene is still what I decide to do.

Best of all, I get to be around the children.

I sleep in a back office that night, afraid that a security guard might nose around the massage area as a logical place for someone to stay. I lie awake almost all night, however, too afraid to nod off. My mind whirls around all my problems: losing Sam, my career path, my anxiety and panic, Lura, even starting at the daycare... If I can't leave tomorrow, I'll have to call my father and tell him to find his own way from the airport... and what about seeing John Mayer? Am I going to have to nix that too? And then there's Mr. Flanigan, Harry A. McGraw, and that security guard, Larry Johnson with his weird right eye, as well as the new burly guy. Jail. Yes. Jail! And the 10k! If they catch me, I am so screwed. And surely, they'll catch me.

Still, I got lucky for now—I guess. I stumbled on this small, unlocked, out-of-the-way office located behind one of the indoor pools. It belongs to an athletics director/swim coach, someone named Andrew Zurkin, and there's even a comfy couch in it. There's a picture of his family on his desk, a lovely family. Two boys and a baby girl, all smiling as if they're prepping for a toothpaste commercial.

It's a green, two-seater, this savior of a couch, but it works for me. Earlier in the day, I bought two large beach towels from the club's Pro Shop, and now I slide under them. The pillows on the couch are fluffy. It beats a massage table by miles. Still, I toss and turn for hours on end.

I so miss Lilly. I remember how she changed when she got cancer, how that great big lover of life turned weak and tired and full of pain. It was heartbreaking watching her decline like that. It changed me. When she hurt, I hurt. I've never been the same since. That was when I started drinking even more. When I started to let things slide at work. Nothing else seemed to matter. Watching Lilly suffer—I could hardly stand it. I finally fall asleep thinking of the good days with Lilly, when we took walks together in the park, when she looked up at me with those dark, trusting eyes, and when she laid her body next to me, nestling against me like a, well, like a child.

CHAPTER 15
FRIDAY

The daycare serves as a nursery for working parents as well as a drop-in center for parents who want to work out at Great Fitness. I show up as requested: 6:15 a.m. dressed in shorts and a blue blouse which I purchased yesterday at the Pro Shop. The commute is brief, of course. I order a latte along the way. The barista swirls the foam in the shape of a flower. Lovely. Surely, the world can't be all bad if people are taking the time to turn coffee foam into the shape of a flower.

I'm surprised that only four children are here when I arrive. Cute little munchkins. The frail-looking dark-haired girl who I'd noticed before is one of them. She's sitting at a yellow plastic table, studying flash cards, murmuring to herself. Once again, I'm immediately drawn to her. She's completely adorable, a doll of a child.

Helen Triol, according to her nametag, a fortyish woman with an ample, bosomy figure, and a thin nose set on a round face, is the supervisor of the program. When I ask about the dark-haired girl, Helen tells me that her name is Rosie and that her mother drops her off for the entire day, Mondays through Fridays while she goes to work.

"She's so cute," I say.

"She is. She's quiet, though. Hardly talks to anyone."

Wanting to see if I can break through, I walk up to the little girl and immediately try to engage her. "Hi. I'm Kat. What are you playing with?"

She doesn't smile and keeps playing with her flash cards. She doesn't even look up at me.

"Can I sit with you?"

Rosie still doesn't look at me. I try a different route. "Please? Pretty please with chocolate on top?"

Finally, she nods. "Okay."

Rosie has a red bow in her hair, which is tied up and pulled to one side. She's wearing an apple-red dress with black polka dots. She has an olive skin tone. Greek? Italian? Spanish? Her dark eyes, large and alert and round, are like a pair of moons. I could just eat her up in bits and pieces.

I sit down at the table with her. She suddenly turns my way and gives me an adorable smile.

"I'm playing a counting game. Can you count past one hundred?" she asks. Her childish voice rings with sweetness and innocence.

"Well, let's see now. I think I can. One hundred, one hundred and..."

I wait for her to fill in the blank.

"One?" she says.

"Yes! Then one hundred and..."

"Two?" She holds two fingers up.

"You got it!"

A boy who looks about two years old, with crumbs on his face and freckles across his nose, sits down with us at the table. He makes a motorboat sound. "Vrrrrrmmmm..." He has some soldier toys with him and he pours them into my lap. He doesn't say a word. He merely points at the soldiers and grunts. I stand the soldiers up on the floor, one by one, and start pretending they're fighting each other.

"Bang! Bang!" I say.

The boy suddenly breaks out in a "Ratatatatatat..." He makes machine gun fire sounds with his lips.

"Ratatatata..." I reply, mimicking him.

He aims a finger at me. "Bang!" he says. "Bang!"

"His name's Alex," Rosie says. She whispers in my ear. "He cries when his mommy leaves."

"That's too bad," I say. I frown and curl my lower lip in sympathy. "Hey, Alex. You don't need to be sad when your mommy leaves."

"Want Mommy." He lowers his head and curls his lower lip. I tickle his stomach and a second later, he's shooting at me again. Mommy forgotten. I love a child's sense of the past; they never dwell on it.

As I continue playing with the children, I realize that I feel comfortable with them. It's as if I've found a new place in this world to exist in. It's so much easier than dealing with grumpy dental patients. Maybe this *is* a good fit for me. If I'm not going to have a child of your own—a fact which seems fairly likely, given the way my life is going—I may as well play with them in daycare for a while. It's kind of fun.

I was so hungover in college when I went to that daycare, I really didn't know what I was doing. "You look sick, Miss Kat," this freckle-faced boy said to me back then. "Oh, I'm—" And then just as I stepped toward him, I tripped on some plastic stacking boxes and fell, landing right on top of Buzz Lightyear, who looked, in my condition, shockingly too much like this nerdy chem major I was dating. Talk about freaking out! "Damn!" I'd cried out loud, and that same freckle-faced kid said, "Miss Kat cussed! Miss Kat cussed!" All I knew was I wanted to get out of that daycare ASAP. Now a rush of happiness runs through me, lifting me up as I look around the room. It's a totally different story.

"Ratatata..." Alex fires back.

"Got me," I say, smiling, holding my hands up. I fall to the floor dramatically as if I'm dead, playing along.

"When my mommy leaves me, I don't cry. I used to cry, but I don't anymore," Rosie says brightly, coming up to me.

I stand and brush myself off. "Good for you," I say. I touch her shoulder and she moves closer to me. Next thing I know, she's leaning against me and smiling into my eyes. I smile back and stroke her hair. My heart goes out to her.

"What's your name?" she asks.

"I'm Miss Kat."

She smiles at me. "Like a kitty?"

"Yes. Meow."

We play a while longer, a variety of games. I try to teach the alphabet to a few kindergartners who arrive thanks to summer vacation. Rosie continues to stay by my side and I love that. She becomes my shadow. I think it's because there's something about her that seems to require more than just my attention. She's like a flower in need of real nurturing. I have the feeling that she's not getting what she needs at home, and that something is really bothering her. She seems anxious too, distracted at times, and aggravated by little things. Once, when a new child entered the room accompanied by her father, a tall well-built man with a beard, she grabbed hold of my hand and wouldn't let go, squeezing so tight it almost hurt as she leaned against me, her body trembling.

"Everything okay, Rosie?"

She didn't say anything. She just stuck her thumb in her mouth. Her little hand in mine, squeezing it like that, made my heart flutter. Her hand was wet too. An anxious little hand; just like mine.

She reminds me of, well, me. We attract each other. Similar

emotional structure, I guess. She is only a child, but we are both human beings and we both seem to be living in pain. I can see it in her eyes when she looks at me.

Toward the end of my shift, I find myself having a quiet conversation with Rosie. Just the two of us sitting on the floor in a corner of the room. Where do stars come from? she asks. Why does it rain? Is God crying when it rains? For some reason, she really opens up to me. She needs to speak, as if she's been holding in so much.

Finally, she says, drawing closer to me. "Miss Kat?"

"Yes, Rosie?"

"Are you married?"

"No."

"Why not?"

I find myself sighing. "Well, I guess the right one hasn't come along yet." I laugh. "It's a long story. Maybe one day."

"I don't want to get married," Rosie says, her eyes turning dark.

I look into her eyes. "Why do you say that, Rosie?"

An unchecked tear suddenly drips down her cheek. She wipes it away with the back of her hand, and then sniffles. I get a tissue and wipe her face for her, letting her blow her nose.

"Thank you, Miss Kat."

She lets me pull her close as she goes limp in my arms. "My mommy's scared of my daddy. My daddy's mean," she says softly. She leans up against me. I feel her body trembling.

"Mean?" I ask.

She nods slowly, but doesn't say anything else. Then she says, in barely more than a whisper, "My daddy hits my mommy. He's mean."

When I finish at the daycare at ten-thirty, I change into my newest workout attire as Rosie's last words still ring inside my head. I feel so sorry for her I can hardly stand it. I have no idea what to do for her. I talk to Helen Triol, the supervisor, and she says social services are aware of the situation already.

"And that's all I'm allowed to say about it," she says. She always seems muddled with so many children around her all the time, as if she's forgotten what to do next—I think she has Old Woman Who Lived in a Shoe Syndrome.

"I feel so bad for her. Is there anyone I can call and talk to? Anything I can do?"

She shakes her head. "Social services have been notified. I really don't think there's anything else we can do at this point. They're supposed to be looking into it."

"Okay, then. That's good."

"I saw her latching onto you, Kat, and I'm so glad." Helen pats my hand and gives me a smile. "Rosie needs to have someone at the daycare she can put her faith into and you seem to fit the bill."

At eleven, Veronica's already on her treadmill and I'm glad to see her. For some reason, she wasn't here yesterday. She's wearing another brand-new outfit. This time, it's a one-piece sports body suit. She looks fabulous in it. I was so excited to work out with her that I arranged this time off at the daycare.

When I arrive, she's talking with this immense, short-haired male figure who's about as large as a refrigerator, at least six five in bare feet with muscles all over and a huge thick neck supporting a large broad face. He's laughing at something Veronica is saying.

"There you are," she says when she sees me. "Morris Washington, meet Kat, Kat, Morris."

"Hi," I smile and shake his huge hand. Surprisingly, it's one of the softest male hands I've ever shaken. The name is familiar. He's wearing two gold rings on each finger and a gold necklace.

"Morris is the defensive tackle for the Tennessee Titans," Veronica says.

"It's so nice to meet you!" I immediately start gushing like a schoolgirl. "I know you! You led the NFL in quarterback sacks last year. Right? I'm a huge Titans fan."

"You got it." He laughs. His deep voice nearly knocks me back. "I hear you're Veronica's new workout pal."

"I am, indeed." I feel a glow inside when he says this; yep, that's me. Workout pal to the stars.

"I hope she doesn't talk your ear off."

"Oh, stop it," Veronica says, waving a hand in the air. She breaks into a huge grin. "I don't talk anyone's ear off."

"Not so sure about that," Morris says, winking at me. "Well, anyway, I need to get going. Gotta get back to the house."

"So, you'll visit Chamber Elementary next week, then?" Veronica asks, gazing up at Morris.

"For you? Anything. Sure. Just text me the details."

Morris gives Veronica a long squeeze-hug, and when he's gone, she says to me in one breath, "God, he's sexy."

"Are you going out with him?" I ask.

"No. But..." She smiles. "There's a possibility. I'm always trying to get the Titans to volunteer for these projects that the TV station keeps coming up with. Working at the food bank. Coaching kids in after-school programs, things like that. And Morris is great. He never turns me down. He does anything I ask."

Veronica is so inspiring. It's crazy!

"I think he has a crush on you, Veronica," I say.

She stares at me and considers this, running a hand through her hair. "You think?"

"Heck yeah. I can tell by the way he looked at you. All puppy-like, you know?" I open my mouth and hang my tongue out and pant. We both laugh.

We step on our treadmills, hit "Quick-start," and start talking right off as we match each other's strides.

"What kind of work do you do anyway, Kat?" Veronica asks.

"Oh, you know, the usual... CIA agent, astronaut, that is when I'm not doing acrobatics in the circus."

"Seriously."

"Actually, I gave all that up to do something *really* cool. I'm a dental hygienist."

She laughs. "Okay."

"But I'm kind of in-between jobs right now. Taking a sabbatical from it while I do a little daycare on the side. Got some money saved up, so... thought I'd take a break."

The possibility strikes me: Should I ask Veronica to help me? Would she? Could she? But she might turn me into a story for her news show. And how embarrassing would that be? No. I decide right there: I cannot trust her.

"Good for you! I once took a sabbatical. It lasted less than a week. The station couldn't do without me." Veronica adjusts her speed, picks it up a bit. "You married, Kat?"

I shake my head. "Nope. Just got out of a five-year relationship. All in all, it's been a real bummer." I wince inside at the thought of losing Sam once again. "I've been hanging out here a lot, trying to get over everything, you know? It's been rough."

"How so?"

God. She keeps asking questions. Is this some kind of interview? Do I really want to get into it with Veronica Ray of Channel Five News? Miss Perfection? How would she even begin to understand what anxiety is like? She's probably never had an anxious moment in her life.

"Well." I take a breath and then dive in. What the hell. "Honestly? I... I suffer from anxiety." Even now, my Big A is listening in. I say the words slowly, carefully and suddenly feel my face burn. I increase my speed on the treadmill. Veronica does the same. "And it holds me back. I get, like, panic attacks, you know? That's actually why I'm on this, uh, sabbatical. I'm trying to get myself together, you know? But it's hard. I'm taking it one day at a time."

Veronica looks straight at me. Her next words floor me. "I suffer from panic attacks too, girl. I know exactly what you mean. And you're right. One day at a time is about the best you can do."

"*You* have panic attacks?" I'm beyond stunned.

"Sure do."

"But you seem so calm on TV, and you... Are you sure?"

She chuckles. "Sure I'm sure. And I get them on TV too, believe it or not. I hyperventilate and for a second or two, I can't breathe. I don't get them a lot, but every now and then... it gets scary. When I'm doing the news, there are times when my eyes'll glass over and I'll start blinking really fast. I've learned to cope with them, though. But trust me, it isn't easy. When I first started broadcasting, once I had an attack on the air that I couldn't control, I was hyperventilating like crazy, and they had to go to commercial. I wobbled off to the bathroom and just sat in a stall and practiced my deep breathing. Ran cold water over my face. The works. It was not a good moment."

"You really cope well," I say. "I have to hand it to you. I would have never ever guessed."

Veronica turns serious. She wipes her brow with a towel and drinks from her water bottle. "It's something I've worked on through the years. And some days are better than others."

I nod. "I know what you mean."

"What do you do for your anxiety?" she asks.

"My best thing is taking long cold showers, Xanax as needed, of course, deep breaths, and wait until it's over. Sometimes I just curl up on a bed somewhere and try to sleep it off." *Oh, and, you know, locking myself in a gym 24/7,* I refrain from saying. "What do you do?"

"I'm on Prozac," she says. "And I meditate every morning,

which seems to help. I went the Xanax route, but I started getting addicted, so I had to nix that."

I consider my own relationship with Mr. Xanax. He's a tricky partner, indeed.

Veronica looks at her phone, which is lighting up.

"It's Morris. He's texting me, asking me out to dinner." She smiles, and then frowns, indecision written all over her face. "Should I go?" She wrinkles her brow in consternation, biting her lower lip.

"Of course!"

"I don't know... Not sure I want to get involved."

At that moment, Sam enters the workout room. Instantly my heart flutters and I emit a little anxious gasp. I rub my temples as I stare at him. He has his weight gloves on again. I point him out to Veronica. "There he is. My ex-boyfriend."

Veronica looks to where I'm pointing. "Cute," she says with a smile that consumes her entire face. "Really cute."

"I know."

I take a long drink of bottled water as my nervousness flutters inside me, my pulse racing. For a moment, I squeeze my eyes shut. "God. I so miss the sex." I whisper the words out loud, but they were really supposed to be an inner thought.

Veronica laughs. "Good, huh?"

"Once we did it in an elevator between floors, stopped the elevator and everything. Crazy, I know. But that's how hot we were for each other."

"My, my."

A minute later, she texts Morris back. When she's done, she says, "I told him we're on." She swallows. "And already, I'm feeling panicky."

"You'll do fine. Just meditate before the date."

When we are finally done working out on the treadmills, Veronica says, "Monday at eleven?"

"Same time, same station," I say, smiling.

After Veronica leaves, radiating a kind of inborn energy as she walks away and turning several members' heads, all I can do is gaze at Sam from afar. I stand in a corner and watch him. He's lifting weights now. First, over his head. Ten times. Then he bench presses. I wipe my face with a towel. Oh, please. *Must* he come here? I know I shouldn't, but I find myself sidling over to him as he's doing curls, really pushing it. He finally puts the weights down in the holder. Ten curls. Fifty pounds.

"I'm impressed," I say.

He studies my face. "So you're not staying at the apartment, then." It's not a question.

"I'm... I'm... Of course I am." *What is he talking about?*

"Not according to Gloria." He wipes his glove-hands together.

"Gloria? What do you mean?"

Gloria, my next-door neighbor. A real snoop as far as I'm concerned.

"Gloria said she hasn't seen you in, like, two days. I was over there packing up my stuff when she came and knocked. We talked. So, what's the story?"

"The story is that there is no story. I am staying at the apartment," I say. "I've just been out late, that's all."

"Out where?"

"None of your business."

"Okay." Sam raises his hands in the air as if I've pulled a gun on him. "If you don't want to tell me, that's fine."

God, I'm so tired of the lies. No, it's *not* fine. Nothing's ever fine with me. *NOTHING'S EVER FINE, OKAY?* I suddenly want to let it all out into the open. I want to tell him everything. Why I'm stuck here; my panic attacks. Spending the night in this place. How my Day of Change has turned into a Nightmare of Horrors...

Through a large window, I stare into the blue sky beyond, the clouds floating by, an airplane in the distance and, for the first time since I've been stuck inside Great Fitness, I suddenly feel trapped. Caged. Was that how Earl felt after all? Swimming around and around in his bowl, feeling like he was terribly, miserably confined? Poor Earl. Poor me. Suddenly, my phone rings. It's my dad again. He's called me three times, but I haven't had the courage to answer. *Sorry, Dad. Now's not the time to talk.*

I sigh and scratch my wrist. I decide that I can't tell Sam what's going on. If Sam knew what was happening to me—unlike Carla, who'd probably undergo her own meltdown—he would get all stiff and stern and call my psychiatrist and send for an ambulance without even a second thought. I know him through and through—that's just how his mind works. He wouldn't even begin to listen to my side of the story, that I need to figure this out on my own, that I simply need time, that traitor of a thing.

Now he goes on, unconvinced of anything. "But tell me this, then. Because I don't get *this* at all."

"What?" I put my hands on my hips, waiting for his question.

"Why are you here all the time, Kat? I don't get it." He scratches his head as he frowns at me, staring into my eyes. "You used to hate even the thought of exercise. But now, it's like that's all you do. It's crazy. Something's not right with you." He narrows his eyes. "You're acting *too* healthy and I don't like it one bit. It's weird. It doesn't make sense."

"First I'm not healthy enough and now I'm too healthy? Seriously? I can't win with you, Sam. I just can't win!"

"I mean—"

"Besides," I say, interrupting him, "it's none of your business anymore."

Then before I say something I regret, I simply walk away from him—until I hear him say behind me: "Your father called me, by the way. And I told him everything."

What?

I swing around. Stunned. I bite my lower lip. God! I walk back up to him and square off, hands on hips. "My father called *you?*"

Sam nods. "He says you weren't answering and he was calling to tell me he was coming to town and if I knew anything about where you were."

They have a good relationship, my father and Sam. They talk from time to time. My dad's a real foodie and Sam knows practically everything about food, and so they interact well. They've even gone out to eat together several times, Sam practically giving my father a dissertation on the best way to cook steaks (besides cooking sous vide, salting a steak thirty minutes before cooking is one of Sam's favorite techniques), my father drinking it in.

"So, that's how you marinate a filet. Now let's talk chateaubriand..."

"What did you tell him?" I ask.

"The truth, for starters. That you lost your job, that we broke up, and the reasons why, that you're coming to this fitness center every single day, which is so unlike you... that you're acting like a different person—"

I could kill him right about now. Fury sweeps through me like an Oklahoma tornado. "You *had* to bring my father into this? You have no right, Sam. Do you realize how much he's going to worry about me now? He's *already* worried about me and now..."

"Well, he needs to know."

I take a breath. I stab a finger into Sam's chest. "Look. I'm fine, all right? I'm simply trying to get healthy, that's all. My father doesn't need to know anything."

Lee and Lura walk by, laughing. Their words, "That many planks, huh?" flow past. Lura hard-stares at me and I hard-stare right back at her. Earlier, I'd checked my Total Workout Rating on my app and saw that, already, my score has jumped fifteen points. I'm gaining on Lura and she knows it.

"It's just so... confusing." Sam sighs. "Bewildering as a Leibniz esoteric."

A what?

"You look different too, your hair, your face, it's all different. I'm worried about you, Kat. The thing is, you're looking *too* good. What's wrong?"

I laugh. If this wasn't so sad, it would be hysterical. "Maybe breaking up with you's the best thing that could have happened to me, Sam."

But it's as if he doesn't even hear me. He rattles on. "Your father's coming to town and he says you and he are going to have a pow-wow. A 'meeting of the minds,' as he put it. We also talked about getting some tickets to see the Braves play."

We break up and Sam's going to see a Braves game with my dad?

"Did you talk to my mother too?" I ask, afraid to hear his answer.

Sam shakes his head. "No."

I'm sure my father will call my mother, who will in turn attempt a long-distance rescue. They're used to attempting long-distance rescues. To them, I'm still that little girl nearly drowning in the swimming pool—not ready for the deep end yet.

Maybe they're right. I honestly don't know anymore.

I feel like sobbing, but I hold it back. I swear, I cannot catch a break.

Thanks, Sam. You're ruining everything for me.

As I turn and start to walk away again, he grabs my shoulder and says, "I just want to know why you're never home, that's all. Are you out partying that much these days? Will you please tell me the truth?"

I don't answer. I merely fold my arms. Finally, I say, "Look.

If you want to know the truth, here it is. I'm staying with Val for a while, okay? I'm... I'm lonely without you..." Which *is* true... "And Val's place helps me feel better. She doesn't mind at all. I'm sleeping on her couch with Alf, her terribly handsome Shih Tzu. He likes me more than you. He wags his tail whenever he sees me and he doesn't snore."

You must immediately text Val and tell her what's what so that she can verify your story. But how are you going to explain your story to HER? Another conundrum, as Sam would say.

"Val, huh?" I can see him working the concept around in his formidable, Oxford-educated mind. He rubs his chin, scrutinizing me. "Hmm..." Sam, the detective, Sam the sleuth. He's definitely on the hunt for answers to the puzzle. "So, you're staying with Val?"

"Yep. Val. Did you put the key under the door?"

"I did."

I open my mouth but suddenly, the words won't come.

"What?" he asks. "What in God's name is going on with you, Kat?"

I don't reply, staying silent and taking him in. Finally, I say, "Look, Sam." I sigh. "A lot's happened, okay? A whole lot's happened. We broke up and I got fired. All in the span of a single day. So, now, I'm working on myself, all right? I'm trying to be a better person. And by coming here, I'm hoping I've found the right path. I'm using this Great Fitness place as my therapy zone. See?"

He seems to accept this. "Okay, Kat." He takes a breath and steps back. He nods and speaks softly. "I understand. Sure. That makes sense." He shoots me a smile. "Did you like that crab cake Benedict I left you?"

"The what?"

"The crab cake Benedict. It has the special hollandaise sauce on it, remember? I left it for you."

"Oh, that. No. I was so mad at you I didn't touch it."

Sam lowers his head. Was that a trick question? He would have seen that I hadn't touched it if he'd opened up the fridge.

Fooled him.

"Okay," he says. "I understand."

A few minutes after Sam and I go our separate ways, I head toward the juice bar when Lura comes up to me and taps me on the shoulder. She looks seriously ruffled today, and there's a dark intensity in her eyes that's almost frightening, as if there actually *is* a horror novel about treadmills and she's in it—the one who can never get off.

"Treadmills?" she says.

"Not now."

"Scared you'll lose? What's wrong? Are you a scaredy pants?"

"Not now!"

When I turn my back on her, I literally feel her breathing down my neck, she's standing that close to me. Finally, she walks off in a huff, thank God. I shiver inside. Wow! To use one of Sam's words, that woman is "intractable."

Members stream around me, bags slung over shoulders, studying their phones, or talking to other members. Just as I'm about to enter the juice bar, my phone rings. It's my dad. I take a deep breath as I answer. Oh, Lord... Here we go.

"Kat? You there? Kat?" My father's voice booms in my ear. He sounds serious and concerned, seriously concerned, and angry, parentally angry. "Kat!"

"Yes, Dad." I give him my life-as-usual voice, the one that's tinged with boredom and a bit of sadness thrown into the mix.

"What's this about you losing your job? What in God's name is going on?"

I'd texted him earlier and told him I couldn't pick him up at the airport as we'd planned because I was "busy." God. The lies keep mounting. Thankfully, he said that would be fine—he'd go straight from the airport to his business meeting on West End Avenue. But now, I guess, he's come out of the meeting to talk to me.

I roll my eyes. "I lost my job, okay? But it's no biggie. Trust me. I'm fine."

"No biggie? How's that? I thought you liked working for Dr. Pierce. This is disconcerting, Kat. It really is. You said she was understanding, that she didn't pressure you. I don't get it."

"She didn't pressure me—at first. But lately, she was cramming cleanings down my throat like I was some kind of octopus with eight arms. One right after the other. It was crazy." I release a weary sigh. A guy walks past me who, I swear, looks like Chris Pine. So handsome I could croak with those steely blue eyes and brown hair swished back. "It just didn't work out, okay? It wasn't what I was looking for."

"So what *are* you looking for?" His voice is gruff, stern.

"I-I don't know, Dad. I'm looking for what I'm looking for, okay?"

"And you don't know what it is? Thirty-two years old and you still don't know? And in the process, you lose Sam? You two broke up? And he says you haven't even been in your apartment for the last few days. Where the hell are you staying?" His voice thunders.

He cares for me so much. That's why he's angry—because he cares. I get it. And it touches me, it really does, but still, I have to remain firm. *Sorry, Dad. I'm sorry I'm your problem child. Isn't there one in every family?*

"Sam broke up with me. And now I'm staying with Val," I say quickly, hating that I'm lying to my father.

"Val, huh?"

"Yes. Val. Me and Val. Val pal. You know?"

He is not satisfied. "This is all such a surprise. You lose Sam, your job, you're staying with Val. You are really going through some changes here."

Tell me about it.

My father sighs into my ear, and I think back to how he used to pick me up and throw me in the air when I was a little girl. How we'd play Adventure Mountain, in which I'd buy an imaginary ticket and ride his big body and how he'd make me squeal and giggle as I climbed all over him, both of us lying on the living room floor. How does a person's life go from playing Adventure Mountain with their dad to becoming a prisoner inside a health club? What kind of journey *is* that?

"I'm exploring my options," I say finally.

"Exploring your options. You and Christopher Columbus. Right. Exploring. I remember when I was your age, me and a friend of mine, we were going to start a lobster business, yeah, that was exploring too."

I roll my eyes as he continues talking. It's one of his lectures. He won't stop until he's done.

"We had a plan to buy lobsters up north and bring them south and expand to California. We were sure we'd make millions."

"Lobsters, Dad? Really?"

"Yeah. Didn't work out one bit and we lost a pile of money. We were exploring all right."

"Well..."

"Look, Kat. Don't make the same mistakes I made. Do yourself a favor and get back to dental hygiene as soon as possible. You know it through and through. You're a damn good hygienist. Don't turn your back on that. It's your profession. You can do it for the rest of your working days."

"I know Dad, but—"

"Don't you see? You're being way too impulsive. Why throw away a perfectly good, solid career?"

"I'm not throwing away a solid career, I'm just—"

But he's not listening. "Now, look. I have to push back our dinner to Monday night, I'm afraid, though I hate to. I really want to see you, but if I don't get down to Chattanooga tomorrow, I'll miss out on a meeting with Ed Sutherland, and he's going to show me this property that has an auction deadline. Is Monday okay for you? I'll meet you around six."

"Sure. Monday. That's fine."

It's more than fine. For a moment, I go still as relief sinks into me. I've bought myself a bit more time to figure things out.

"So, where do you want to eat? I'm looking for something really special. Got any ideas?"

"Let me do some checking, Dad," I say.

"Okay. I want a good steak. And a great wine selection."

"You got it."

My father's voice turns serious and this time, deep and low. "Kat. Are you okay? I mean, honestly."

Honestly. His question digs deep. It reaches me like only a father can reach his daughter. I know he loves me so much too. It all makes me resonate with sadness.

I swallow. For a long moment, I don't say anything. I can't say anything. Finally, I get it out: "I'm fine, Dad. I'm great! No worries at all. Never been better."

"Okay. Fine. I'll make myself believe you. I'll see you soon, then. And Kat?"

"Yes, oh father of fathers?"

"There's something you should know."

"What's that?"

My father hesitates a beat before speaking. "Oh, never mind. I'll let it wait until our dinner."

What could it possibly be?

It's no surprise when my mother calls about an hour later, just as I'm getting ready to hop on a rowing machine. Ah, my mom. Elizabeth Noad. Maiden name: Shock.

My mother is the most self-absorbed woman I've ever known. More self-absorbed than I am—and that's pure talent. She raised me and my brother with one eye on us and one ear on the phone, constantly talking to her socialite friends about when the next women's luncheon would be or plans for the next golf tournament. We had nannies, daycare, babysitters, and an army of substitutes. I was always looking for my mom to give me her undivided attention and yet she hardly ever did. Not that that's what made me anxious, of course. But it certainly didn't help... Still, she *was* a fairly good tooth fairy. Whenever I left a tooth under my pillow, I always got cash for it, waking up to see two or three dollars the next day. Once, however, I didn't receive any money and my tooth was still under my pillow. I remember the next morning she said, "Sorry, Kat, but the tooth fairy was busy last night. She was at a fancy party with other tooth fairies, having fun. At least that's what I heard."

"Mommy, why are your eyes so red?" I remember asking.

Looking back, I'm sure she was hungover. Guess that's where I get it from...

Now, she sounds fairly lit, which is pretty much par for the course. I can imagine my father's call to her, saying, "Liz! Kat's been fired and she broke up with Sam and I'm sick about it. Just plain sick. You need to call her and talk to her. And do it now..."

"Hi, Mom," I say, using my best daughterly voice.

"Kat, darling. I heard you and Sam broke up." Her tone is sympathetic. A noisy atmosphere resounds in the background: laughter, bubbling conversation, a jazz band playing something tinkly.

"Did Dad call you?" I ask.

"Of course he did. What happened?"

I can so easily imagine their conversation. *"Do you know*

what our darling Kat's up to now?" "Don't tell me, I'm afraid to ask."

"It's not over. We're just... kind of sorta working on things. Dad was exaggerating." I can't tell her the truth. I don't want to upset her. I've upset her enough as it is. I took my mom through some nasty years when I was in my teens, kept her waiting up all hours of the night until I came home so many times when I was in high school, and dealing with my anxieties, not to mention the Oreo incident, my dear rabbit. I definitely put her through the mother–daughter ringer.

"Are you sure?" she asks.

"Don't worry. It's all good." I feel like the President's press secretary: *That's NOT a nuclear missile heading our way. Don't worry. The media's exaggerating, as usual.* "We've just had some issues. How's Hawaii?"

"Oh, Hawaii is wonderful, dear. Stunning." My mother's voice turns instantly happy—too happy. "We're staying on the big island and Sidney and I went horseback riding in the mountains yesterday, can you believe it? The sky here is so bright and blue and this beautiful parrot flew right past us, squawking away—it was so colorful, red and blue and yellow! Our guide told us it was a macaw. And the people are so friendly here too."

"How's Sidney?" I ask.

She laughs like a schoolgirl. "He's still my regular Jack-in-the-box. Vigorous as ever, the old dog."

God. I shudder at the image.

There was something irreplaceable in my life when my parents were still married. Something that Sidney and my mother could never match. Even with the benefit of time I'm still unable to get over it—the sad fact that my parents split up and let our familial bonds dissipate.

I must admit, though, Sidney J. Ensworth is one good-looking dude for his age: slicked-back silver hair, clear blue-gray eyes, that bold, adventurous chin of his. He owned a small chain of hotels, but made his big money from a shopping center investment. Plus, he bought Apple stock when it was, like, twenty-five dollars a share or something. I mean, the guy bleeds money.

Unlike my dad—who's always asking us to repeat what we say—Sidney's perfectly willing to wear *two* hearing aids, one in each ear. They're beige-colored tiny things that fit sleekly inside his ear canals. I think they're kind of fascinating. They even connect via Bluetooth to his iPhone.

"Are you anxious, dear?" my mother asks, her own voice growing more serious.

"Mom, you know me. I'm always anxious."

"How's your drinking, darling?"

"I've tamped it down. No more than two drinks per hour."

"Oh, stop it."

"Actually, lately, I've been drinking a lot less. I feel much better."

"Well, good for you, dear. Cheers! That's the spirit." She turns away from the phone and I hear her say in a commanding voice, "Sidney, order me another chocolate martini, will you?"

And then I hear Sidney's deep voice: "Tell Kat I said hello."

"Sidney says hi, Kat." My mother states this with a kind of impending-world-crisis conviction. She's obviously tipsy, a fact that gives me comfort. My mother completely sober is not a fun person. She gets very irritated very quickly. "Sidney's such a doll. Anyway, after Hawaii, we're thinking about an Alaskan cruise. I've always wanted to see Alaska. Don't you think that would be fun? We might even go dog sledding. Tourists can do that, you know." She lowers her voice and sighs. "Are you going to be all right, Kat? Do I need to worry? Tell me the truth."

"I'm fine, Mom."

"Good. That's good. You're not still thinking about Lilly, are you?"

I swallow and my eyes moisten. Of course I'm still thinking of Lilly. "No, Mom."

"Okay. Good. Listen, I have to run now. Sidney's lap looks so empty." She shouts, "Coming dear."

"Bye, Mom."

"Goodbye, Kat. And really, do try to take care of yourself, all right? I hate it when I have to worry about you. Just be happy. Can you do that for me just once?"

"Sure, Mom. I will. Be happy. Promise."

I end the call, staring into the vacuum of Great Fitness space as the lavender scent drifts around me and streams of members pass me by. My heart squeezes tight. Whenever I talk to my mother, I feel like I need a drink. I generally take a deep dive into the dark and dank pool of misery and dejection, actually. It takes me a while to get over our calls, which are usually chock full of emotional complexities, many of which are never spoken out loud, but are, still, as real as rain. I guess it's all the possibilities of what we *could* say to each other that really hits me so hard. This call was shorter than I expected and that's fine by me. But it's these lies that I keep on telling, one after the other. That's what really gets me.

Suddenly, Lura walks up to me—from out of nowhere *again*. Was she watching me? Is she stalking me? "Don't think you're going to beat me," she says. Her serious tone makes me edgy.

"Where are you staying at night anyway?" I ask, staring straight at her. This woman has caught me in a bad mood and I've just about had it with her.

"That's none of your business. You're here as much as I am. I've been watching you, you know." She points a finger at me. "I'm not going to miss out on the award for Most Time Spent At Great Fitness."

Is she serious? I really think she is. An award? "Look, Lura. We'll answer this over rowing machines. Tomorrow at noon."

"You got it," she says with a flash of a smile.

"And now," I say, "if you'll excuse me, I think I'll go take a sauna."

"The one upstairs nearest the shower is best," she says.

But I don't hold back. "I like the one downstairs, in the locker room in the back."

She shrugs and says, "Suit yourself, bitch," then stomps away.

Once again, I try to leave. I give it all I've got, stepping as close as I can to the door. But as before, the door casts a spell over me —maybe it's producing invisible waves, I don't know—that makes my heart pound so hard I can hear it in my ears, as my head whirls, I nearly lose my balance, and in the end, my Big A wins again.

It's so frustrating! I put my clothes back in a locker and realize that I may as well give Josh the bad news. It looks like I'll be missing John Mayer. Damn! This sucks entirely! Missing out on this is a new low. Can it get any worse than this? I guess I'll quick-text Josh and...

Wait! What about Val? She could go with him!

Val loves John Mayer too—even more than I do. We actually talked about going to see him once about a year ago. She's getting in from San Diego today, and since we won't be hanging out, why not? I smile to myself as I grab my phone and text her.

How'd you like to see John Mayer? Free. Great seats.

Are you kidding me?

I think I can arrange it. ☺

How?

I met this awesome guy. He's got tickets and I can't go, so I thought of you.

Why can't you go?

Busy.

Are you serious?

Yes! I can text him and see what he says and get back to you.

I'm getting into Nashville at three. Can you pick me up?

Sorry. No can do. ☹

Why?

Working. BTW... Sam thinks I'm staying with you.

What? WTF?

Just go with it, okay? Please do that for me?? Please!

You're crazy. Okay. Will do. But I need to know!

You will. In time. Just trust me on this.

Fine. Set me up with Mayer ya biatch.

☺

Lie after lie after lie. Cascades of lies. I'd planned on telling Val about my situation and putting the solution in her hands. But I couldn't make myself do it. I don't want her to know how messed up I am. And besides, she'd start crying and I'd start crying, and, knowing her—and just like Sam—she'd wind up taking the situation into her own hands and calling an ambulance and my psychiatrist no matter how much I'd try to stop her. And I'd hate her for doing it too. Our relationship would end. It would be horrible. No. Val is *too* close to me. I need help, but it has to be from someone who's more distant and objective: someone I can trust—but not a close friend or family member.

A kind of thickening sense of guilt washes over me that makes me shiver inside. My head starts to throb. It's as if I'm blowing up a balloon in my head filled with hot air and a crazy amount of lies, and that balloon's basically got to pop. When it does, it won't be pretty.

I text Josh, apologizing and telling him I can't go after all.

I have someone who can go with you though. Her name's Val. She's a veterinarian. She loves John Mayer! What do you think?

Well, sure.

Great! I'll get her to text you and you can take it from there.

Lord. How easy was that? I still feel regretful though, missing out on the concert. It's like I'm shooting myself in the foot. I had a chance to see John Mayer with great seats, and now... I gave it away!

I put my phone away and rub my hands together. It's kind of funny in a roundabout way. I've become a matchmaker. Val's been looking for the right guy. Who knows? Josh could be the one, her "It" man.

After playing matchmaker, I lie back on a lounger near the pool and stare up into a cloudless sky, an infinite blue masterpiece. It's another warm, humid day; breezeless; typical

Southern heat and once again, birds fly above me, free to go wherever they want. My own wings are clipped.

I know I shouldn't, but an anxious woman's gotta do what an anxious woman's gotta do. I buy a skirt, underwear, and blouse from the Pro Shop, take a long, luxurious shower, change, then hit the Great Fitness bar around five o'clock. It's Friday. TGIF. Happy Hour. Time to Be Happy. Right? An entire hour is dedicated to the entire process. What's not to like? But the big question is: Why don't more people take advantage of such a wonderful weekday rite? I'd like to be at my regular haunt, The Classroom, a bar in East Nashville where, instead of "Be Your Best, " *their* motto is "Get An Adult Education!" But hey, you can't have everything.

Jack pours me a red. He says it's from a special collection that Mr. Flanigan recently added. It's a Joseph Phelps Insignia, 2016, and it goes down smooth and delicious, with echoes of chocolate and plum in the background. That's what I call tasty. I munch on some wasabi nuts, and start feeling happy already. The bar is definitely crowded—at least twenty-five people packed in tight. I don't see any of the trainers, until I spy Lee at the other end of the bar. He's slapping some hunk of a man on the back and they're laughing loudly. Then I hear his boisterous voice: "That's great, Charlie. Just great!" I turn away. I really don't want to make eye contact with him. I must stay invisible. I must *become* invisible. No way do I want to be considered another Lura. I don't want anyone to know who I am.

"Just bought a new car today," Jack says, interrupting my trance. "Brand-new Camry." He's looking fine. Smooth shaven now. He's wearing jeans and a crisp white shirt open at the collar. He's got a hairy chest and I love that rugged, sexy look. It's really quite a turn on.

"That's what I have. But mine's about three years old."

"You like it?"

"I do. It needs a repair, though. Something's making a noise somewhere in the whatchamacallit."

"You mean, uh, the engine?"

"Yeah." I laugh. "The engine. Man, sure is getting crowded around here."

"It's Friday night. Time to party with Bacardi," he says with a grin.

Despite our easy banter, my wireless antennae aren't so sure about him. He studies my face a bit too long, rubbing his chin. The guy definitely seems like he can read my mind. God only knows what he's thinking.

Suddenly, from out of nowhere, as if blown in by an evil wind, Harry A. McGraw himself pulls up a stool beside me. If my life was a movie, I'd say: "Cue the dark music." I gulp and my entire body goes haywire. If there's a negative lottery out there, certainly, I would win it. I instantly want to get up and go, but how would that look? Suspicious as hell, of course. My heart knocks inside my chest, rattling my ribcage, as if there's a small person inside of me who wants out.

The chatter around the bar increases. Everyone seems to be in a good mood, but now, I'm terrified. My teeth chatter. Instead of another wine, I order my favorite bourbon, Maker's Mark, one of the best, born and bred in Loretto, Kentucky. I order it neat, and quickly knock it back. It's so warm and comforting going down.

"Hit me again, Jack," I say with urgency in my voice.

He raises another eyebrow at me and stares at me for too long. "Sure thing."

When he serves me again and I take another gulp, I burst through the clouds in my mind. I enter blue skies and sunshine. I'm flying.

Jack brings Harry a Maker's Mark, neat as well, and he too lifts the glass and slugs the gold liquid back. "Cheers. One more,

Jack. That's what I call fine stuff. Top drawer." He turns to me. "So, how you doing?"

"Me? Oh, I'm great!" I say quickly with the brightest, most confident, most energetic smile I can manage, while inside, I am now a four-alarm fire. It feels as if bees are buzzing in my head.

"You're really working out a lot, aren't you? I see you here, like, *all* the time." Harry laughs with an open mouth and I quickly see that his dentition needs serious work. Chipped teeth, recessed gums. A mess. It's amazing how people don't think their teeth are that important—until it's too late, of course. Then they come running.

Harry's comment about my constant presence at Great Fitness terrifies me. I use a napkin and wipe my brow. This *is* a nightmare. *Dear Mr. Stephen King: Can you please write me out of your horror story? I realize that my Big A is a monster, but really. I have had enough. Sincerely, Katherine Noad, otherwise known as Peter Pan.*

"Well, I'm trying." I give him another bright smile, white teeth dazzling, then rub the back of my neck. I can barely breathe. Is it hot in here, or is it me? "It's not easy, though. I'm taking it one day at a time." Another forced megawatt smile while my heart is nothing but a judge's gavel.

Harry doesn't seem to notice my anxiousness, however, which relieves me somewhat. He stares at me, but I don't think he even sees me. He looks into his drink as if it's some sort of wishing well. "I sure wish *I* could get going like you." He rubs his hands together, then adjusts the watch on his wrist. I can't look in his eyes and so I stare at his ears. He has a little skin tag on one of them and they're kind of hairy. "I just don't have the willpower. Been like that my whole life. I like to hunt—that's my thing. Deer season's my time of year. But the doctor says that if I don't start exercising, I'm headed for heart attack city." He shakes his head. "I can't seem to get started. Plus"—he pats his belly—"I don't eat the best."

"Hey. Don't think you're alone, Harry. I know exactly what you mean. *I* was the same way for so long too. I used to think that exercise was for everyone else but me. I had that mentality, you know, go take a nap when you get the urge. It's so much easier and you don't need expensive workout clothes. Right?"

He points a finger at me. "Exactly."

"But once I started coming here, I don't know..." I swallow. "It was like something kicked me in the butt and now I enjoy it. Treadmills, weights, you name it. I can't believe it either. But it's true. It's like I've been converted or something. It's like I've seen the light. Crazy, I know."

"Well, good for you."

"And I try to eat at Yummy's whenever I can as well," I continue, unable to shut myself up. "The menu's limited to healthy things so you can't go wrong. You can't, like, say... down a donut with your coffee and then go get a cinnamon bun and stuff your face."

"I know. I know." Then Harry turns to Jack. "Set me up, big guy," he says.

"Ditto," I say, holding up my empty glass.

Jack pours our drinks, sets them down on the bar, and after we say "Cheers," Harry and I kick them back in sync as if we are old drinking partners. It feels so natural that I relax a little. Harry has no idea that the person he's hunting, the person overnighting it here, is sitting right next to him. How wild is that?

Should I try to scope Harry out? Ask a few leading questions about the latest on the rascal who had the audacity to use Great Fitness as his or her own apartment?

I decide not to. He might sense something. I'd better play it safe.

"Well, that's it for me," Harry says a few minutes later, his face flushed from the alcohol. He gives me a smile. "Gotta get going. Son's playing in Little League, I don't want to miss it, and my ex can't make it. She's working late."

"You're divorced?" I ask.

Harry nods. "As divorced as they come, honey. Hey Jack. What about you? Divorced, married, or single?"

"I've undone I do," Jack says, turning to Harry with a smile. "I turned the page and I'm outta the cage. I untied the knot."

"You know what the judge told me at our settlement?" Harry says, touching my shoulder. "He said, 'I've decided to give your ex-wife eight hundred dollars a week.' And I said, 'Why, that's mighty kind of you, judge. I might chip in a few dollars myself.'"

Jack and I laugh. It's funny. Harry is quite the character. But still, he's chief of security, he's on the hunt, and *I'm* his prize game. Harry tells Jack and me goodbye and leaves—thank goodness—just as Marcus comes walking into the bar. He's wearing his Great Fitness uniform and slides into the place that Harry left.

Marcus.

In my state of alcoholic enlightenment, I shoot Marcus a ridiculously overzealous smile and gaze into the universe of his twinkling eyes. Me? Inebriated? Surely you jest.

"That Harry's something else," I say to Marcus.

He pulls up a stool next to mine. "Tell me about it."

Jack brings Marcus his usual sparkling water with lime. Members come strolling into the bar, finding seats. Some are wearing their workout clothing, others are dressed casually. Conversation bubbles around me.

"You learn to get used to Harry," Jack says, smiling. "It just takes time."

"Yeah," Marcus says. He takes a drink and sets the glass down. "He's still hunting for that overnight occupant too. That's the latest. And that's what we're calling him now. Or her. The Big OO. Who knows? We don't know if it was merely a one-night stand, or something more long-term and serious. But he's still on the lookout."

Hearing this, I see black spots before my eyes and my stomach turns rock hard.

"Have you been following my schedule?" Marcus asks me.

"Uh, what?" I blink, for a moment, not quite able to comprehend anything. The words "still on the lookout" keep echoing in my brain.

"I asked if you've been following my schedule?"

"Oh, yeah... that." I take a long breath, feeling the slickness of my hands. "Yes. Actually, I have." I shift in my seat. "To the letter."

"Great. By the way." He takes another sip of his sparkling water and squeezes the lime juice into the glass. The juice causes the water to fog up ever so slightly and we both stare at it.

"Yes?"

"Was wondering. Do you know someone named, uh, Sam Steele?"

My heart freezes.

"Uh, yeah. Well, kinda," I answer slowly as I frown. "Why?"

"He signed up with me for a six-month training package. We started talking and I mentioned that you were a new client of mine who was throwing everything at it—but I had no idea he was your ex." Marcus grins as my heart leaps from the high diving board and does a cannonball in my stomach. "He says he's surprised you're here so much. That you were the most non-exercising person he'd ever known. It's like you've done a one-eighty turnaround."

"Well—"

"So, good for you! And he was babbling on about not knowing where you were staying or something. Anyway, I told him I couldn't talk about other clients and shut it down, but I thought you should know. He seemed a little... upset about it all. I take it you've moved out of your apartment then?"

I wave a hand in the air as inside, my mind is like a major intersection and the traffic light has suddenly gone on the blink. I don't reply for a long moment. Finally, I say, "The truth is... that... I'm, well, I'm... staying with someone new, okay?" Lie, lie, lie! "I didn't want to tell Sam because I knew he'd get jealous."

Marcus blinks, taken aback. "Oh, I'm... I'm sorry, I didn't mean to..."

"No prob. Inquiring minds want to know, I guess."

A minute later, I finish up my drink, and leave the bar, totally caught off guard.

I *am* a rat lost in a maze, blindly turning this way and that, looking for a way out, seeking an answer that is nowhere in sight. My throat closes up and I wipe away a tear from my cheek. Standing alone near the Barre room on the second floor and staring out a window like the trapped animal I am, I come face to face with the guilt I feel. It hurts. Lying to Marcus like that, rushing away from the bar, all this emotional fakery. It's as if there's no end in sight.

Still, it's one more night in Hotel Great Fitness. Alone, hidden from view. All by myself. I take a breath and for a long moment, close my eyes.

So where should I stay? On a massage table? A yoga mat? Lesson learned: When one is anxiety-trapped inside a health club, one must be creative with one's accommodations.

The yoga mat in one of the yoga rooms, I decide. Yes. The room's nicely tucked away at the end of an infrequently used hallway on the second floor. I can lie here in a corner, totally out of the way of everything. With the lights out, I should be pretty invisible. I sure hope I can stay away from the prying one eye of Larry Johnson.

CHAPTER 16

SATURDAY

I make it through the night again, thank God—a yoga mat is certainly no bed, that's for sure—and now it's nearly eight o'clock, on my second day at daycare. (Sure love the commute, still!) Rosie seems withdrawn. Helen told me that her mother had dropped her off before I arrived. I was surprised because she's supposed to be in daycare from Monday through Friday only. We play a game called "Fried Egg," in which we sit on fluffy pillows and try to flatten them. Three or four other kids join in. The one with the flattest pillow gets to call out: "Fried Egg!" And then we pretend to eat the pillow—no match for the free-range, cage-free eggs they serve at Yummy's, of course. Still, no matter what I do, I can't seem to get Rosie out of her shell.

"Miss Kat?" a little boy says to me. He looks frail, with beady black eyes that are always darting around. "Do you like turtles?"

"I sure do, Mikey," I say. "Do you?"

He wears thick glasses. He won't look me in the eye, but aims his focus on the center of my forehead. "I love turtles. I know everything about them. Do you know the difference between turtles and tortoises?"

"What is it?"

"Tortoises live only on land, but turtles live mostly in water. Tortoises have more rounded shells and turtles have thinner shells." He sticks his neck out like a turtle's head poking out of its shell. "I'm a turtle!" he says.

"I'm sure you are," I say.

"He always thinks he's a turtle," a girl with pigtails says, one of the oldest. She stands next to Mikey and tries to give him a hug, but he backs away.

"No hug!" he cries. "No hug!"

"Miss Kat?" Rosie tugs at my hand and drags me to an isolated corner of the room. She's fidgeting and she rolls down her lower lip. She seems hesitant, almost afraid.

"What is it, Rosie?" I ask.

She looks down then away, afraid to meet my eyes. A hand goes to one eye and she rubs it. She goes silent.

"What do you want to talk about? You can tell me." I bend down to her level. "Are you doing okay?"

I touch her hand and when I do, she finally looks me directly in the eye. She stands on her tiptoes, whispers into my ear, and her words go straight to my heart: "My mommy cries all the time because my daddy hit her again."

When my shift is done, I walk out of the daycare center in a fog. It's awful what Rosie is going through. My heart aches for her. A tear leaks out of my eye and I wipe it away. Is there anything I can do? Are social services on the ball or what? Surely, there's someone who's handling this. But why aren't they taking control? I go back inside and talk to Helen about it yet again but all she says is that it's out of our hands.

I walk down to the fountain and find a chair to sit. I've heard about domestic abuse and read about it in the news, but I've never seen it up close and personal. It's the worst. No child should ever have to experience what Rosie is experiencing. I swear, something needs to be done. Standing in a hallway near a weight room, I look up social services and dial the 800 number, asking how to report domestic abuse. After all, Rosie certainly does not need to be living under those circumstances. When a woman finally comes on the line, I start telling her the story about Rosie and her parents, but she keeps putting me on hold, then finally asks, "Has the child been physically hurt?"

"No, as far as I can tell, not physically, but definitely emotionally, and I still think the family needs some kind of intervention."

At this point, all she does is tell me to go to a website and file a report with as much documentation as possible, then hangs up quickly before I can ask her any more questions. Man! What kind of system is that?

And then I have second thoughts. Maybe getting involved isn't something I should do after all. Helen told me they were handling it and maybe she's right; maybe I should simply let the system work. Besides, her mother might not appreciate me sticking my nose into it. People can be sensitive and then the next thing I know, she's complaining about me.

The relationship between my own parents was painful too, though I never saw them come to blows. They stayed together thirty-two years before finally going their separate ways. My father moved out, leaving my mother in tears and angry. Her drinking got worse and her time spent on the phone increased exponentially.

I was never privy to the real causes. There were arguments all the time. My mother turned to her country-club friends and practically lived at the club; my father wanted to be left alone. He grew inward and quiet, and then at times, would rage about something my mother did, and she would fire back. I'm sure there were affairs on both sides as the dissolution became an erosion that turned into a landslide. My brother and I were shepherded back and forth between our parents, treated like pets in cages. An outing here, a conversation there. It was miserable. I tried to think of all kinds of ways to make my parents stay together, but nothing worked. I wanted it desperately.

When I think of Rosie's plight, I feel miserable for her. Her situation is so much worse than mine was. Poor girl.

I find myself staring out the door while Lee is at the front desk, checking people in, bubbly as ever. I see a gorgeous blue sky, the parking lot crammed with cars, and in the distance, a group of nondescript office buildings surrounded by a cluster of maple trees. A feeling of intense sadness takes me by the hand and then embraces me. It's like Mr. Loneliness has turned into a friend, my one and only friend, and in a way, a guide, maybe even a teacher. God, I need my old life back.

No, you don't. Your old life? You want a new life, a different life. One that is moving forward and far less filled with anxiety.

I sniffle and rub my nose. My stomach forms into knots. And then as soon as I wipe the one tear away, another one returns.

Why can't I just do it?

Yes! Just do it! No preparation. Nothing. Get your ass out of here. Now! Quick—before you even have time to think about it. I clench my fists, summon up my will, and step toward the door, one foot, and then the other. For some reason, my heart's not beating hard and I'm not breaking out in a sweat. Closer. Closer. Could this be it?

Just do it! Just get out of here and walk outside!

I'm three feet away from the door when, suddenly, the words, *You're not ready for the deep end yet* flow through my mind and it happens all over again. A black tunnel appears before my eyes and the door seems to move away from me, going, going, fading into the blackness. I feel like I'm going to faint. I grow dizzy and my heart starts banging away, slamming against my chest. I'm sweating and feeling cold simultaneously. Panic City. I'm right in the heart of it. I'm frozen. I lose my balance and then—

"Oh, hey there." It's Marcus, a worried look on his handsome face, his forehead all wrinkled. "You need to sit down. You look pale, Kat, and you're sweating like crazy. Want some water?"

I nod slowly, as he leads me to a comfy chair near the fountain. I hold onto his shoulder as I walk.

"There," he says as I collapse into the chair. "Take a load off."

"Guess I worked out too hard," I say. I rub my temples. "I have low blood sugar. Sometimes I get a little light-headed." (Lie number six million forty-nine thousand.) Ugh!

He speaks sternly. "I told you about taking it easy, you know."

"I know. I'm a fool."

"No, you're not. You're overeager, that's all."

No. I'm a fool.

Marcus brings me chilled bottled water and I drink it down gratefully. *Breathe... Breathe...*

"Better?" he asks a minute later, standing over me.

It might be if you had a Xanax.

I nod. "Yes."

He puts a hand on my shoulder and for a long moment keeps it there. Our eyes connect again. I feel it, the chemistry between us. It's real. But this isn't a romantic thing—it's only a friend thing—at least I think it is. A good, open and honest friend is what I need so badly right now. Someone who I can talk to. Someone who won't go all ape shit when I tell them my secret. Someone who can look at my problem objectively and help me figure it out from a logical viewpoint. But I can't help the voice in my head questioning: *Could we be more than friends?*

"Is she your girlfriend?" I ask after another long swill of water.

Marcus blinks, surprised, as his mouth falls open. "Who?"

"Amy."

"Oh." He takes a breath, his expression turning serious. "We see each other, but honestly...? It's nothing major. We're really mostly friends. Why do you ask?"

"I'm nosey. And I'm a snoop. Why wouldn't I ask?"

He laughs and strokes his bold chin. I dive into his eyes. He dives into mine. "If you must know, I'm basically unattached," he concludes. "What about you? Aren't you with someone new?"

Would he actually be interested in me? I don't see how. I'm no Amy. And yeah. I'm with someone new, all right. My imaginary boyfriend who I'm living with ever since Sam dumped me. See where lying leads? Now Marcus thinks I have a boyfriend when I'm so unattached right now I could scream.

"Well," I say, "I'm kinda sorta breaking up with him after all." (Lie number six million forty-nine thousand and one.) I shrug as if I were tossing away nothing but an empty beer can. "It wasn't working out. Can't stand to live with a man who won't take care of his teeth and who's incredibly messy. You should see his side of the sink."

I smile while my heart is playing bongos and tom-toms. Why did I say that? *Can't stand to live with a man who won't take care of his teeth? Are you kidding?*

We are silent for a long moment. I'm feeling better now. I look into Marcus's eyes and study them, searching for an answer. Is he really someone I can trust?

"Hey, wanna meet at the, uh, the bar around six tomorrow night?" Marcus speaks shyly and I find it completely touching.

He obviously had to work his courage up to ask me. "I'd like to go over more of your training schedule."

Is he seriously asking me out? No. Impossible. It's my training schedule he's interested in. Not me. Or... maybe he is. Could he be? Wouldn't that be something? "Uh..." Still, I play it cool. *Don't act like you're jumping up and down inside—even though you one hundred percent are.* "Yeah. Sure. I can do that." I look down at my hands. "I've got some time."

That's a laugh.

"Okay, cool. See you then... then. Oh"—he blushes so sweetly—"you know what I mean."

Val texts me close to midnight:

You up?

Yep.

I had a great time!

I'm glad for her, sure I am but still, *I* wanted to see John Mayer! Damn!

What do you think of darling Josh?

He's so cool! We're planning to go out again. Seems like a great guy. Thanks for hooking us up! Where are you? I want to see you. We need to talk.

Been busy.

My neighbor said that Sam was parked outside of my apartment the other night until two in the morning.

I put a hand to my face and gasp.

God, Val. That's nuts! When I told him I was staying with you, I didn't think he would actually stalk your apartment!

Well, he obviously did. He's going a bit crazy. What's this all about? I want answers!

Wish I had some.

We need to get together and go out, plan a strategy. What about tomorrow night? Drinks at Louie's?

Can't, Val. But very soon. I promise.

Are you sure you're ok?

Yes!

Are you?

Yes!

Why won't you meet me? What the hell is going on? I still don't get why you're telling Sam you're staying with me. You're acting so strange. Is it another guy? I know you too well. WHAT IS GOING ON WITH YOU??

I'm doing GREAT! I really am! Gotta run. Glad you liked Josh.

And now, here I am once again lying in the dark on a yoga mat, feeling like a fool, trying to sleep, and hopefully avoiding prying eyes. There is some good news, however: I've learned that when you stack four yoga mats on top of each other, it actually makes a fairly comfortable mattress. It's really not that... Oh, crap. Who am I kidding?

CHAPTER 17

SUNDAY

How long can I keep this up? Fooling everyone in my life. Hiding out at Great Fitness, too afraid to face the world beyond its doors. I'm losing my mind. This is crazy. And it can't go on forever. Sooner or later, I know I'll be found out. It's only a matter of time.

Still, this "great" thing that everyone seems to throw out around here is sort of contagious. When you start saying the word, even if you don't believe it, it casts a kind of spell over you. *How are you doing? Great! How's work coming along? Great! You just got kicked out of your apartment and you're now living in your car? Great! You've been sentenced to die in the electric chair? Gr... well... maybe not so great on that one.* I don't know. Still, it seems to kind of lift you up—even if your life is heading downhill.

It was another frightful night, and now, all day, as I go through my exercises, I think of meeting Marcus. That's about all I can think of. Finally, as it approaches 6 p.m., I wander over to the bar. I wait for Marcus as butterflies flutter around inside me. Today's exercising made me feel good and now I have a nice fatigue settling into my bones. A fine soak in the hot tub and time in the steam room helped as well. I bought another new outfit for the occasion, a black wrap dress with a sleeveless bodice and an enticing surplice neckline. New earrings, too. Dangling gold hearts with tiny diamonds in them. I had to have them. I hope Marcus likes the dress. It was expensive, but I splurged anyway. Why not? Sometimes you just have to go out in style.

Just before I enter the bar, I run into Lura. She's in gray and pink athletic apparel, her eyes blazing with intensity.

"You don't give up, do you?" she asks. She actually pushes a finger into my shoulder.

"Why don't *you* give up?" I push her back.

We stand there, eyeing each other like gunslingers in the wild wild west. She licks her lips. I lick my lips.

"I never give up," she says.

"Nor do I."

"Bitch."

"Ditto."

She stomps off, joining three other women as they pass by— "Hey, Lura!" "Hey, girls!"—and talking energetically. They disappear into a spin class. Does that woman ever *not* exercise? Surely, there's a room in a mental hospital somewhere waiting for her.

A minute later, I sit down at the bar. There's a couple next to me and some cute guys at the end of the bar, joking about this newscaster who got confused and embarrassed last night on TV and instead of saying, "Here are the tick-picks," referring to tickets people won, she said, "Here are the dick-picks." I laugh with them.

"Hey, Jack Hammer," I say, when he comes up to me.

"Hey yourself. How's life treating you?"

"Couldn't be better." I snicker quietly to myself.

"What's so funny?" he asks.

"I know Jack."

"Huh?"

"You know that saying: 'You don't know Jack?' Well, now I do." I smile and shrug.

He chuckles. "What'll ya have?"

"How about a red?" I say quickly.

"I've got this Bordeaux that's literally begging to be tasted."

"Perfect."

Jack's eyes meander across my face. "You look great by the way."

I feel myself blush as I run a hand through my hair. "Thanks."

Jack pours me a glass, then gets busy, cleaning glasses, swooping past me, giving me a smile as he fixes other drinks.

Finally, Marcus arrives and Jack, seeing what's going on, frowns as he rubs the side of his face, his disappointment obvious. I feel sorry about that. But what can I do? Sometimes the things that happen in life are out of your control—like insanely hot personal trainers asking you out—and this is unfortunately one of them. Marcus has changed into jeans and a button-down white shirt, all freshly showered. He looks amazing. My stomach swirls and I feel an adrenaline rush. My senses feel heightened. He grabs the stool next to me. Cologne, with an orangey musk and a hint of lemon, drifts toward me. It's definitely not the cheap, Harry A. McGraw kind. Jack brings him a Perrier right off.

"How's your drink?" Marcus asks.

I take a soothing sip of the red. "Simply fantabulous." But it's not what I'm drinking that's important, I suddenly realize; more significant is *who* I'm drinking with. "How was your day?"

"Great! I got two new clients to train. Things are booming."

I eye his Perrier. "Do you ever drink alcohol at all?" I ask.

"Now and again I'll have a beer when I watch a football game."

"Oh, one beer. Oh, my. Call the Alcohol Police."

Even though I have a glass of red in front of me, I feel like ordering something stronger, like a neat Maker's Mark. But I don't dare. Not in front of Marcus. I need to learn to be more Marcus-like and less Harry-like, less Kat-like too—at least the old Kat, that is.

We clink glasses. "Cheers," I say, suddenly feeling buoyant. Lee is right. Great Fitness *is* great! "To good health."

Marcus's eyes sparkle. "And to the fountain of happiness," he says.

"To happiness," I reply. Of course. Happiness. Always and forever.

"No," he says. "The *fountain* of happiness. That's what we call our big fountain in front. The fountain of happiness. And that's where we were when I asked you out."

I laugh. "Okay, then. To the fountain of happiness. Cheers." I'm touched. Lord, maybe this *is* more than a friendship thing.

Marcus takes another sip, and then grabs some almonds. "By the way, the other trainers and I have seen your name climbing the TWR board rapidly, I'm impressed. We all are. Don't think you're going unnoticed."

Crap! That's the exact opposite of what I want.

He opens up a page on his phone and shows it to me. A new schedule for "Kat Noad."

"Interesting," I say.

"Yeah. I've tweaked some things. More push-ups, more cardio. And I've added jump rope. Jumping rope is really a fantastic way to build up your legs, your core, and your cardio simultaneously. I'd like you to try it."

"Sure. Why not?"

"I'll email you the schedule and you can see what you think."

"Thanks."

"Absolutely." He takes a swig of his drink. "You know, we are all wondering, all of us personal trainers, what your motivation is? I'm actually doing research on motivation and why some people have it and some don't. I want to write a book about it one day. You've gone from someone who doesn't do any exercise, according to your ex, to someone shooting up the scoreboard here. Honestly, you are one of the most motivated people I've run into."

I swallow more of the wine and grow thoughtful. What *is* my motivation? Good question. The fact that I'm stuck inside this exercise palace and can't get out seems to be all the motivation I need. Maybe I've stumbled upon a therapy program. You want change? Get locked up inside a health club for about a month. Simple!

"I don't know," I say. "I feel so much better after I exercise. I just like it, I guess." I shrug. "It's changing me, I think. Making me a better person. More disciplined, you know?"

"I want to show you something." Marcus pulls out his phone and thumbs through some photos. Finally, he lands on what he's searching for. The guy he shows me in the picture is definitely rotund with chubby cheeks. He's on a beach, lying on the sand and drinking some kind of cocktail which he raises at the camera.

"Who's that?" I ask.

Marcus clears his throat. "That, my friend, is someone I know very, very well."

"Your brother?"

He shakes his head. "Nope. It's me, about five years ago."

I put a hand to my chest. "Seriously? No way!"

Marcus nods. "Yes. Way. Before I had my big change, I used to be, basically, a human wreck. No job, no education. Nothing. Actually, I died for about twenty minutes."

I blink. "How's that?"

"I was in this bad car wreck on Nolensville Road. Traffic was terrible that day and someone slammed into my rear end as I was waiting at a stop light. My car lurched forward and hit the truck in front of me. My head hit the steering wheel because my airbag didn't go off. Concussion and spinal compression. While they were transporting me in the ambulance, I had an out-of-body experience."

I take a sip of wine. It's smooth and rich with a hint of plum and black currant. "You're kidding."

Marcus's expression turns ultra-serious. "Nope. Not at all. I saw the tunnel, the light, the whole thing. When I came to, all I know is that I was a totally changed person. I don't know what happened to me in that span of time, but something inside me got tuned up, lifted up, cleansed, I don't know. Six months later, I finally healed. But it was my vision that changed the most. I started seeing the world in a different way. I saw that everything I did, *every* moment of my life, actually had value, importance. I also learned that whatever you do or say comes back to you in one way or the other. See? That's why you have to be careful with your decisions. If you want good to flow to you, you have to be good to yourself and to others. What you do has a ripple effect and causes these invisible waves to flow out into the world."

"That's incredible!" I see that. I really do. Be good to yourself. And to others. It's that simple. *Be* your best. I get it, I think. Learn to *be* your best all the time, and life will work out for you. I think that's what Lee was getting at. As I move forward, this is what I need to keep in mind. I guess it's what you'd call a good old-fashioned dose of maturity. Hmm... Not a bad concept after all for a Peter Pan like me. Could I really learn to *be* my best at all times?

Marcus goes on after taking another sip. "Now I see the world from what I call a helicopter point of view. Everything I do has a far-ranging consequence. I mean literally everything. And so I tread very carefully. I think through all of my decisions and take responsibility for them. There's no one to blame but me for the way I am and the way my life is going. That's the truth and the light." Marcus smiles at me. "So there. Now you know."

"That's such a heartfelt realization. I mean, seriously." I am blown away. I've never heard it put like that before, but it seems to make so much sense. "That's quite a story," I say.

"I know." He looks down and then when he raises his head, his dark eyes burn into me. "It was a life-changing event. And you know what else?"

"What?"

Marcus gives me a crooked smile and his eyes light up. "I see people differently now too. I kind of sense what people are feeling and thinking, their states of mind. And guess what I sense about you?"

Oh, no. I hate to even hear it.

"What?"

"I sense that you feel, well... trapped. There's some kind of emotional box that you can't get out of. Am I right or wrong?"

I don't say a thing. He's so right I can't even believe it.

My Big A hammers me and inside I quiver. Twinges of sadness nick at my heart. Should I confide?

"It's a long story, Marcus, and..."

He puts his hand on top of mine briefly before moving it away again. A crackle of electricity flows through me. Does he feel it too? "Hey. I understand. And whenever you're ready to tell me about it, I'm all ears, okay? Friend to friend, you know what I mean?"

I nod.

For a moment, he stares at me and it's as if something passes between us, a hint of compassion, kindness, maybe even a sense of real love—not the romantic kind, but the kind that does, at times, exist between people, when we allow love to break through our own fears. He blinks and the moment is gone.

We finish our drinks, then Marcus touches my hand again.

"Hey. Let's get out of here and go have dinner. What do you think? Ever eaten at the Pharmacy? It's entirely organic."

My heart flutters and now I feel like I'm on the edge of a cliff, just about to make myself jump off. I'm both excited and anxious. It's like my body doesn't even know what to do with itself.

"I can't, Marcus," I reply, my voice like lead. I lower my eyes and feel myself blushing. I rub my hands together. My lower lip starts to tremble and for a moment, I think I might break down right here and now. Sam, my job, my captivity, poor Earl... and... Lilly... It's all coming to a head.

"Why not?" He studies my face and frowns. I sense that he senses that I sense that he senses something's not right about me.

I take a long breath, take another sip of my drink and grab a huge handful of almonds, which I stuff down my mouth. Stuff those emotions down. Don't let them surface. Marcus raises an eyebrow at me.

"I... I'm sorry. But... I just can't."

"What do you mean?"

I look away. I'm holding back a tear now. Oh, God. I rub my eye, pretending something's in it.

"I mean, I'd really like to, Marcus, but—"

Suddenly my phone rings. I check the caller ID and realize I can't miss this call. It's Dr. Fields, my old boss who I sent a resume to just the other day.

"Excuse me, I need to take this," I say as a wave of relief whooshes over me. I click the answer button. "Hello?"

"Is this Katherine Noad?" Dr. Field's voice is deep, steady, and all businesslike.

"Yes."

"Hey, Kat. It's Dr. Maurice Fields. I got your resume and I'd like to bring you in for an interview. Do you have any time on Tuesday?"

"Uh... yes. I do."

"I really need someone soon and I'd like to talk."

"Tuesday, then?"

"Tuesday's perfect. How's 10 a.m.?"

I confirm the time and click my phone to end the call. A feeling of blissful revenge flows through me. Screw Dr. Pierce! Screw Mr. Goldbaum. See? Getting a new job is easy. But besides the revenge, a warm glow of satisfaction courses through me. I'm wanted in the dental hygiene field. I'm no slouch.

"Job interview?" Marcus asks.

"You bet." I beam at him and find solace just staring at his face.

He smiles back, his eyes sparkling now. "Good for you!" Marcus finishes his drink. Then he says, "By the way, I have a favor to ask."

"Sure."

"My mother really needs to see a dentist but she's scared to death of them. Is there anything you can—"

"Are you kidding? Call her and I'll talk to her," I say quickly. I've had to do this before. I'm really good at soothing the fears of the patients who have dental phobia. I seem to know the exact things to say, despite what my former boss thought of me.

"You mean now?"

"Yes."

Gratitude shines in his eyes. "Thank you, Kat. I appreciate that a lot."

When Marcus gets his mother on the line, he says, "Mom, I want you to talk to someone."

He hands the phone to me and I introduce myself. "Mrs. Fletcher? Hi. I'm Kat Noad and I'm a dental hygienist."

"Hello. How do you know Marcus?" She speaks in a loud voice.

"He's training me at Great Fitness. He really knows his

stuff too. And he's very amiable." I smile at Marcus and give him a wink.

"I hope he minds his manners."

"He does, Mrs. Fletcher. He does. So, anyway, Marcus says you're afraid of dentists. Is that right?"

"I am."

"Well, I'm so sorry to hear that. Dentists are actually normal people, you know. They put on their pants one leg at a time, just like everyone else."

She laughs.

"But did you have a bad experience?"

She's silent for a moment. Finally, she says, "I don't even want to talk about it. It was a long time ago. And I haven't gotten over it to this day."

"Well, that's too bad, because the dentists these days are really well trained in helping people with their fears. They have nitrous oxide and specialized medicine that can put you at ease as well as soothing music and other techniques. The doctor I'm going to recommend for you is gentle as a lamb. He'll take good care of you. I promise. Would you consider meeting with him?" I ask gently.

By the time I'm done, she has agreed to set up an appointment ASAP with Dr. Ryan Brady, one of the best in the city at treating people who have dental phobia.

"Thank you, Kat," Marcus says when he's ended the call. "You are a saint."

I shrug. "A saint I'm not, but I hope that helps."

"I really owe you one."

Then before Marcus leaves, he kisses me on the cheek and gives me a tight embrace. The moment stretches out and I feel like I'm on a cloud. I don't want him to let go. His body against mine rings all kinds of bells.

"Well, got to get some food in me," he says finally. "I'm starved. Haven't eaten all day." He walks away and I watch him, wishing desperately that I could go with him. Yet I can't move a muscle.

The next thing I know, Jack is pouring me another glass of wine. "It's on the house," he says with a grin.

"Thanks, Jack! You're the best!"

I'm not going to turn down a free drink—no way. That's simply not in my DNA. I find that my sad mood suddenly dissipates, just like that. It's crazy, I know. Amazing what a free drink can do to your attitude—and your altitude.

Jack and I talk for an hour, yakking about anything and everything. It all revolves around alcohol too. We nail it: best drink for a first date—Vieux Carré; best drink for when you've been jilted—Long Island iced tea; best beach drink—margarita; best drink to loosen you up before sex—red wine, of course.

"Did you know a bottle of champagne has around forty-nine million bubbles?" Jack asks.

"Wow. I had no idea." I take a sip of the wine. "So, how about this? There are forty-two million protein molecules in a single cell. Talk about lack of elbow room!"

He laughs.

"So," I say, suddenly realizing something, "the number of bubbles in a bottle of champagne and the number of protein molecules in a cell are fairly close, then."

"And who says life doesn't work in mysterious ways? How'd you know that anyway?"

I shrug as I take another sip and taste the wine on my tongue. "Majored in biochemistry in college. I'm a science nerd."

"Cool," Jack says. Pours someone else a drink then returns to me. "You like magic?"

"I love magic."

The next thing I know, Jack fills up a shot glass halfway with water, pulls out a deck of cards from underneath the bar, and places the ace of spades inside it. He waves his hand over the glass, and then, when he pulls out the card—presto!—it's turned into the queen of diamonds.

"What? That's crazy! How'd you do that?"

"I'll never tell." Jack gives me wink, goes to serve another customer, then a few minutes later, he comes up to me and wipes the bar with a white towel. "Hey, let's meet at Randy's on Twelfth sometime. Now that's a real bar."

"Listen, Jack," I say, with a lazy grin. My mood suddenly lifts even higher. Getting asked out by a cute guy like Jack Hammer really ups my ego. "Right now, I've got a few things going on. But maybe next week. How's that sound?"

"Are you giving me the absolutely positively maybe routine?"

"No. Not at all." I shake my head. "Seriously. Next week. Let's do it." I flash him a toothy smile.

He points a finger at me. "I'm counting on it," he says.

God, I hope it's a promise I can keep.

That night, just as I'm coming out of a women's bathroom around ten minutes until midnight, getting ready to sleep on the couch in the office again, I hear footsteps behind me and turn around. It's Larry Johnson; his bad eye is still all messed up.

"We're about to close, ma'am," he says in a polite voice.

"I know. I know. I'm heading out. Thank you." I give him a Life-Is-Great smile.

He nods at me and keeps on walking. Then he stops and watches as I head to the elevator to descend to the first floor. When the elevator arrives, I give him another smile and push the down button. I exit the elevator and go toward the fountain. Now I'm at the door again, blending in with a group of young women who are loud and boisterous, boasting about how much they lifted today.

"I did fifty-pound curls!" one tall lady says.

Suddenly, instead of heading out the door, I quickly reverse track and slip into the stairway just as Larry Johnson walks past. There's a small door in between the first and second floors that I found this morning. It's a little hiding place that opens into an access unit and it eventually flows into the AC system and all the ducts that run throughout the building. Perfect for my needs.

I hear footsteps above me now and then Larry Johnson's voice, asking the front desk worker if he saw a blonde woman leave the building. Oh, crap! They're on to me.

"Yes," he says. "Went out with the weightlifting team, I believe."

"Okay, Ed," Larry says. "Thanks."

How about that for luck? I let out a huge breath of relief.

Minutes later, the lights are out and now I'm trapped. I don't dare move with Larry Johnson circulating the building. It's going to be one very long night. But once again, I succeeded. You've got to take this one night at a time, I'm realizing. And you have to be flexible. Ready to change sleeping spots at a moment's notice.

I finally fall asleep listening to the flow of air in the ducts, thinking about Lilly and how much I miss her warm body next to mine, the way she used to look me in the eyes and settle me down.

I dream of me and Lura racing against each other on rowing machines. We are down to the wire, neck and neck... and then I wake up in a sweaty panic.

CHAPTER 18

MONDAY

The next morning, anxiety overwhelms me. I also feel awful and depressed. How will I make that job interview with Dr. Fields? This is getting absurd; I haven't been home in days, and I lost the chance to see John Mayer. I'm making my father come here to eat with me at Yummy's—I told him that's where I wanted to meet. He can't believe I want to eat inside a health club (even I can't believe it.) I'm lying to all my friends. I've arranged my entire life around being captive at Great Fitness. I am a prisoner. And to think: All I did was come here on Monday to work out for an hour to start my Day of Change.

What the hell am I going to do?

The only things I can do: 1) change into my new workout attire I bought at the shop; 2) start exercising again; 3) try to maintain my sanity.

I work it all out on Mr. Treadmill, hoping he can counsel me. The faster I go, the better I feel. But an hour later, I am sitting on a chair next to a Nautilus bench press machine, a towel around my neck, wiping sweat from my eyes. Tears are welling and I'm feeling my face turn red. This is it. I've had it.

The balloon is about to burst. I do not see how I'm going to get out of this place on my own.

I am now on the verge of calling 911. Once I explain what's going on, the paramedics can come and give me a tranquilizer. Then they'll haul me away to that psych ward again—handcuffed, with everyone watching. Wonderful, right? A return engagement. I'd probably be a real headliner this time. I wouldn't be surprised if they'd have a sign out front: *WELCOME BACK, KAT NOAD!* I wonder if that woman's still there, the one who commented on my straggly hair.

The next thing I know, I'm staring up at Marcus, who is standing in front of me. Gorgeous as ever. "What's wrong?" he asks. "You look troubled."

"I am," I say as I sigh. And then suddenly I'm leaning against him. I start sobbing into his shirt. I can't take it anymore. I can't help myself.

He puts an arm around me. "What's going on?" he asks. "What's wrong?"

"Oh, Marcus. I have a problem. A big problem."

"Exercise addiction?" he says, trying to get me to smile. "It's a real issue, you know. There's a lady around here that—"

I shake my head. "No. It's not that."

"Then... what?"

"Do you have time to talk?" My heart is pounding so hard right now it feels like an animal trying to escape through my ribcage. I'm going to tell him everything, I decide. I don't want to worry Val or my parents, and Sam is totally out of the question. I'm going to put my faith in Marcus and see if he can help me. It's either Marcus or Dr. Baldwin. A personal trainer or a psychiatrist.

He looks at his fit-watch. "My next session isn't for another hour. Sure."

"Good. Let's go get a smoothie. I'm buying."

I'm flat-out in trouble. I have to face the truth. The truth isn't a coward; it's brave. I've got to be brave.

"Okay." He studies my face warily.

Now we both have green smoothies and are sitting at an out-of-the-way table at Yummy's. Two teenage girls are nearby. There goes Lura, walking alone. She glares at me as she passes. What is wrong with her? And then I remember; I'm gaining on her. I'm now number twenty-six in my overall rating. I'm sure she's pissed, maybe even a bit scared.

The teens are chowing down burritos. They're in their bathing suits, hair still wet, wearing flip-flops. They look so young and healthy and glowing.

My anxiety turns full on, Big A lighting up both the front and back burners.

Sure, Marcus could easily turn me in. Sure, I could be leaving this prison and heading straight to another. But I'm going to put it all on him. It's the best I can do. I have no other choice.

"Well?" he asks, raising an eyebrow. He takes a sip from his smoothie. "What's going on?"

"Oh, Marcus." A tear falls from my eye and I wipe it away. "I really have a problem." I take a long breath. "It's crazy, I know."

"What kind of problem?"

I dab at my eyes. "Let me start from the beginning. I want you to understand." I lay all my cards out on the table. The truth. At last. It spills out in a torrent and once I start, I can't stop: how I suffer from panic attacks and anxiety, how I came here with a hangover on Monday morning, intent on simply doing some exercising, and how I now can't even make it out the door, how I was dumped and fired within minutes, how I don't have any Xanax, which would help so much, and how I'm sleeping on the couch in the athletic director's office and other places, hardly sleeping at all. I tell him about Lilly and how it hurt so much losing her, and how I'm exercising, like, a lot now simply because I have nothing else to do—it's not some kind of fantastic motivation ability—and how I'm now effectively *imprisoned here*. Yes, I let him have it—all of it. I give it to him good. It takes about ten minutes for the entire story to unfold and, as the words tumble out of my mouth, the craziness of it all really shocks me.

When I'm done, I feel exhausted. He looks at me, eyes wide open, and, for a long moment, doesn't say a word. Eventually, he says, "So *you're* the one." He speaks in awe as if I'm the one who discovered gravity or Beyoncé or something.

I nod slowly. "Yes. I'm the one. And, look. I understand if you want to turn me in right now. Maybe that's what I need, anyway. But I'm also thinking, I don't know, I'm thinking that maybe you can help me somehow so that I *don't* have to turn myself in. Can you help me?" I lean forward in my seat. "I have to get out of here, Marcus. I've got a job interview coming up tomorrow, my life has been basically put on hold. I'm trapped. I really have to leave."

Marcus rubs his chin and doesn't say a thing.

"I mean, I can't stay here until I'm eighty!"

Finally, he speaks in a soft voice. "You know, I have a brother with panic issues. He's even been in the hospital for it. I feel so sorry for the guy. He doesn't do much more than work at a tennis club as an assistant—cleans the courts, sells racquets. If it hadn't been for his anxiety, he could have been a major tennis professional on the circuit, he could have played Wimbledon and everything. He had all the skills. It's really sad how his anxiety held him back."

Marcus looks me over, his eyes studying me. *Actions. Consequences.* "No," he says, finally. I draw a long breath. "No, Kat. I won't turn you in. As far as I'm concerned, this little talk of ours never happened. Okay? But you're going to have to leave sooner or later for your own good. You know that, right? I'm serious. You can't stay here forever."

"I know, Marcus. Of course. My father's coming tonight to eat dinner with me right here. I couldn't even meet him out somewhere. I'm arranging my entire life around living at Great Fitness. It's ludicrous. I *have* to get out of here."

Tears spill down my cheeks and I wipe them away with a dab of my finger. The teens look my way and stare at us. God only knows what they're wondering. They probably think that Marcus got me pregnant or I have cancer or I lost all my money investing in cryptocurrency.

"How can I help you?" Marcus asks. He furrows his brow as he stares me down.

"That's the problem, see? I don't really know. I don't know anything right now. I'm at a total loss." I lean forward toward him. "Can you think of something?"

"Should we call your psychiatrist?" he asks.

I shake my head. "That's the problem. All he'd do is send an ambulance for me and they'd shoot me up with Ativan and I'd be placed in a psychiatric hospital for probably a week this time, which will only make my anxiety worse, I'm sure. Plus, it'll scare my parents to death and I really don't want to worry them. They've had enough worrying over me already. I mean, I've practically put them in early graves."

"Do you have a friend you can call?"

"I do. But I don't want to. They'll get worried and start crying and I'll start crying. And then they'll think of me as some kind of mental weirdo."

"But you are a mental weirdo." He smiles.

"I know, Marcus. I know."

Marcus looks around and then stares into my eyes. It's as if he's searching for something, but I don't know what it is. I'm searching too, of course. Aren't we all?

"Okay, then. What if I walk you out? Or drag you out?"

"If you do that, and trust me, I've thought of it, I might have a breakdown and then you'd have to call an ambulance. It's risky. But if you think you want to try it, I'm game."

He sighs. The scene flashes in my mind. A crowd gathers around as I lie unconscious at the door and an ambulance comes and whisks me away, Larry Johnson glaring at me with his one good eye, Harry A. McGraw, open-mouthed.

"The woman's a nutcase, that's all there is to it," Harry would say.

"Let me think about it, all right?" Marcus says a minute later. I can practically see his mind whirring. "Maybe I can come up with something less drastic. I mean, I'm not going to risk my job over this, but if there's something I can do that's not too risky, I'll definitely do it. After all, you helped my mother too. Let me see what I can come up with."

CHAPTER 19

I feel better after confiding in Marcus. But I'm still on edge, nervous, panicky. Hell! I'm always on edge. I take some deep breaths and try to relax, but it's useless. Will Marcus come through for me? It's hard to say. All I know is that talking to him feels like a good move on my part—a possible way out. I hope.

After more of a workout on the weights and an aggressive engagement with a jump rope, plus some sit-ups, and push-ups —I'm up to fifteen push-ups in a row now—followed by another relaxing hot tub session, I have lunch at Yummy's: a veggie sandwich with sweet potato fries. Delish as always. Then, I head to the outdoor swimming pool and lie down on a lounge chair; probably take a dip in a few. It's another humid day with clear skies and not even the trace of a wind. Hot as a tamale. But still, it's great to be outside. A lone airplane cuts across the sky. Again, I wish I was on it.

Val texts me:

What are you up to?

Catching some sun.

Where?

By a pool.

Where? What is going on with you? I want to know right now!!!

Sorry. Can't. Soon, though, okay?

You're pissing me off, you know that?

What's up with you and Josh?

Classic deflection from me.

We're going out again! He's great! How'd you meet him anyway?

Met him in a yoga class.

Suddenly I realize: No doubt, Josh will tell Val that he met me at Great Fitness. But will it go any further than that? He only saw me here once—so no. I think I'm okay there. At least I hope so. Lord, this is getting so tangled up! Val, Josh, Sam, Jack, they're all nibbling around the edges of my deep secret.

You mean YOU did yoga? What is wrong with you? Are you not feeling well?

Thought it'd give it a try.

Unbelievable. Anyway, Josh slept over.

WHAT?? My, my. ☺

I owe you one, girlfriend.

You certainly do!

All that yoga he does sure comes in handy in bed, that's for sure.☺.

Ha! I bet it does!

He's like an f-in pretzel! Look. I need to see you!

Soon! I promise!

My entire body suddenly feels like an anchor, pulling me down. I hate it—lying to my best friend. But I have no other choice. I do not want to worry her and I do not want her rushing in here trying to save me. I have Marcus to help me now. He's the one I'm counting on.

As I stare at my phone a few minutes later—checking my progress on the ratings board—a woman wearing a two-piece yellow bathing suit sits down in the lounger next to mine. She looks Greek or Italian with her olive skin tone. She has long black hair, and Angelina Jolie lips that are glistening with gloss, and a curvy body—at least five feet ten inches if not taller. She's wearing these ginormous dark glasses that cover much of her face.

My jaw drops when I see that my favorite little girl, Rosie, is with her. The woman gives me a friendly nod and Rosie says, as if it's the most natural thing in the world, "Hey, Miss Kat." Then she immediately shoves a finger in her mouth. I recall that phone call I made to social services. Maybe I should have insisted on talking to a supervisor.

The woman looks at me, surprised.

"Hey, Rosie, how are you?" I say, smiling broadly. Then I

turn to her mother. "I just started working at the daycare here and Rosie's in my room. I'm Kat. Hi."

All that Rosie confided in me comes to mind again, the pain I saw in her eyes, the sadness, her little hand in mine. Should I say something?

"I'm Raline."

We shake hands.

Rosie says to her mother, looking up at her, "Miss Kat reads me fun books. She's nice."

"Oh, that's lovely!" Raline says. "What kind of books?"

I laugh. "Rosie likes books a lot," I say. "Let's see, there's *Mouse Man, Mermaid Tales, Harry and Marla and the Kangaroo Farm.* I could go on. I adore your little girl. She's my favorite, though that's a secret."

"Thank you," she says. "That's so nice to hear! She's my favorite too!" Raline's open-mouth smile reveals a beautiful set of pearly whites. She laughs and strokes her daughter's hair as she says it.

"Like Miss Kat," Rosie says, her eyes shining as she stares at me. She's wearing a pink bathing suit and she's holding pink sunglasses, which she suddenly decides to put on.

"She's such a cute thing," I say. "You should be proud of her."

"Oh, I am. She's such a doll. I love her to death."

"Love you, Mommy," Rosie says in an innocent voice. My heart melts.

Raline brings out a picture book from her bag and starts reading to the little girl, something about a family of rabbits in a field of bountiful carrots. For a while, the two of them do nothing but cuddle together and it looks to me like a lovely mother–daughter moment, one that I've always dreamed of having myself. I can't help but feel a pang of envy.

Suddenly, Raline gets a phone call, answers, and I can't help but overhear. She listens for a minute as I stare at my own phone. After a minute or two, she raises her voice—she sounds nearly hysterical—and it startles me: "No! That's *not* the way it's going to happen at all!"

I turn and look at her. Worry lines her brow. She lowers her voice, but I can still make out the words if I listen carefully. "I cannot do it that way. Look. I called my lawyer and told her exactly what's necessary. I really need protection. Don't you see? He's threatened me again!" She listens a minute longer, then ends the phone call and wipes away a tear from under her glasses.

"Come here, baby," she says to her daughter. "You want to lie down next to Mommy and nap?"

"Okay, Mommy," Rosie says. "Who was that, Mommy?"

Raline takes Rosie in her arms. "Oh, just something for adults. It's all going to be all right. Don't worry about anything, okay?"

"Okay, Mommy."

Raline strokes Rosie's hair and her daughter closes her eyes and a few minutes later, falls asleep. A warm breeze blows. Out of the corner of my eye, I watch as Raline tries to read her magazine, flapping the pages angrily.

I can't help myself. "Is everything okay?"

Raline looks down at her hands and sighs. She puts down her magazine. "God. Unfortunately, I'm afraid not. I've got this ex-husband. It's been a nightmare, that's all. A total nightmare." She raises an eyebrow. "Has Rosie mentioned anything? Does she ever seem upset?"

I don't hold back. "Actually, there are times when she does. I'm really sorry to hear what you're going through." I pause a moment before continuing. "I talked to my supervisor about it, and she said it was being handled through the proper channels. So, I didn't think there was anything else I could do. Is there?"

She shakes her head. "Unfortunately, I'm afraid not. The social service agencies are doing all they can. It's slow, though.

Terribly slow." Worry lines etch across her forehead. "But I deeply appreciate your concern. The thing is..." She takes a breath. "It's not me, it's Rosie that I worry about. I hate to have to expose her to this."

I nod slowly. "I totally understand." A lump forms in my throat.

Raline removes her sunglasses and I see now that one of her eyes is swollen, patched up with makeup, but with the effects of a blow still visible. She takes a deep breath and says, "I want to ask you something very important."

I sit up in my chair and stare straight at her. I grow tense inside. "I'm all ears."

"Please, don't ever let my ex take her from daycare. No matter what he says or does."

"Sure. Of course."

"I took him off the list so he wouldn't be able to. But I don't trust him. He may try to work around it somehow. He's wily as a fox."

"I'll definitely keep an eye out."

"He's threatened to steal her from me, see? He's angry that the judge awarded me full custody. He's an asshole, that's the only way to put it."

"I'm so sorry. That's awful!" Some people shouldn't be parents or spouses.

She stops speaking, trying to gain control of her emotions. She's shaken. I feel her pain, Rosie's too, a deep current of sadness that encircles them. I find myself choking back a sob.

Finally, she continues. "So, now..." She swallows as a tear slips down her cheek and she wipes it away, for a moment unable to speak. "Now, he's hired a better lawyer than the one he had before, and they're trying to undo the custody verdict."

"I'm so sorry."

"There's a chance, it's small, but it's still possible, that he might try to come for her at daycare, even though he's totally not allowed." She suddenly reaches out and grabs my arm. "If he ever does that, you call me, or the police ASAP. Okay? I'm serious." She blurts out the words as her lower lip trembles and her face goes pale. Her voice trembles with emotion. "He's... he's a real danger to me and to Rosie."

God. This is awful. The possibility of her ex-husband hurting Rosie, merely the thought of it, is more than I can stand. My fingers suddenly feel cold. "I understand."

I stare at Rosie as she sleeps peacefully, an innocent child caught up in a cruel adult world.

CHAPTER 20

My Big A is at it again. It's close to six o'clock now and my father should be here any minute. Even though we are eating inside a health club, I've dressed up for dinner, putting on my bandage dress once again with a new pair of shoes I've bought.

My father's bringing Wanda, which is another cause for my nervousness. I mean, I have nothing against her as a person, but I do find her wary of me, as I am wary of her. After all, she may become my stepmother one day if things keep going the way they're going, and it's an uncomfortable relationship to say the least.

As I'm waiting for my dad, standing next to the place where Marcus asked me out—the fountain of happiness—I suddenly see Josh walking in. Val's new man-friend—thanks to me. I smile. Mr. Pretzel. Stretch Armstrong. Having sex with a yoga master must be an interesting experience, indeed. I can't resist going up to him right after he flashes his card at the front desk.

"Hi, Josh. How's it going?" I ask. "How's Val?"

Josh puts his card back in his wallet and turns to me, looking surprised. "God. Kat," he says. He blinks at me. "I can't believe it. I mean, I really, really need to thank you for fixing me up with her."

"Hey, don't mention it." I wave a hand in the air. "I'm glad for you."

"I swear, she's the woman I've always been looking for. She's smart, funny. She's everything!"

I nod. "She's the best, Josh. There's no doubt about it. Are you around for a while?"

He nods. "I'm doing my legs today on the weight machines. And hey..."

"Yes?"

He takes on a serious expression. "If you ever need a favor from me—any favor at all—please, don't be afraid to ask. I'm all yours. Just saying."

I laugh. "You know? I may take you up on that. Glad to be of service. Anyway, have a *great* workout."

Just as Josh leaves me, my father and Wanda walk into the building, looking a bit confused. They're all dressed up too. I suspected they would be, even when they knew they'd be eating at a health club. My father is one of those jacket-and-tie people almost everywhere he goes.

The fountain of happiness roars in the background. Wanda looks superb. It shows you what newfound love can do to a person. She's all rosy-cheeked and relaxed looking, with a sparkle in her blue eyes that doesn't want to quit. She's wearing a tight blue dress and dangly earrings, and her long red hair is cascading around her shoulders. I would kill for hair like that. Her first husband was an insurance adjustor who ran away with another woman. Wanda, being the smart businesswoman that she is, remained unruffled, took him to court and won everything he had, and now I hear he lives in a small apartment, nearly broke, and the woman he took off with has vamoosed. I guess that's what karma does to a person.

Wanda's just like my father in many ways. They're both

real estate developers, extremely smart, business savvy, quick thinkers, and they read people very well—too well sometimes. This is definitely a cause for concern.

"Dad," I say, walking up to them both.

My father looks extra-healthy too. New love looks good on everyone. He's wearing a fashionable jacket and tie, with a blue silk pocket square in his front pocket. I give him a hug and inhale his old, familiar daddy smell, that manly scent that I've known since childhood.

"Good to see you, Dad," I say. I lean against him.

I give Wanda a quick hug, keeping a distance between us.

"Kat," my father says in his booming voice. "Let me look at you." My father's eyes go wide. He appears impressed. "You look great, Kat. Just great." Seems like he fits right in! He turns to Wanda. "Doesn't she look great, Wanda?"

Wanda nods vigorously. "You do, you do. What did you do to your hair?"

I run a hand through it. "They have this amazing salon here," I say. "They work all kinds of magic."

Yesterday, wanting to look good for my dad, I re-visited the salon and got another hair treatment, and another massage as well just for the fun of it.

"I should give them a try," Wanda says. "Maybe we can do it together, Kat. Me and you."

But I hardly hear what she said. All I can do is stare at the large ring encircling Wanda's left ring finger. Sadness slow-walks across my heart.

"So, what's new with you two?" I say slowly.

My father places his arm around Wanda and grins. She leans into him. They make a great-looking couple—if only my father were twenty years younger. "We've decided to tie the knot," he says.

I blink, taken aback. I mean I expected as much, but hearing the words still kind of bowls me over. "You are? Seriously?"

"We certainly are," Wanda parrots.

They stare at each other and quick-kiss in front of me.

"It'll be a simple civil wedding, nothing big," my father says. "We'll sign the papers at the courthouse and then head off to Vegas for a honeymoon. I have a suite reserved for us at the Wynn."

"Okay, then." Inside, I am a whirl of emotions.

"Aren't you going to congratulate us?" my father says. The two of them are practically glowing.

I blink again. "Sure. Of... Of course. Congratulations you two. I'm glad for you," I say without much enthusiasm.

"You don't sound like it," my father says, disappointment in his eyes.

"No. I am!" I fake it. "I am! I am totally happy for you two! Truly."

"Well then." My father clears his throat and looks slightly offended. "Anyway, shall we?"

"Shall we what?" I ask.

"Eat. I'm starved!"

Earlier, I'd arranged guest passes for them, and now I lead them through the club as we head to Yummy's. My father and Wanda look around, taking it all in.

"Big place," he says.

"It's huge," I say. "They have everything here. It's great!" I sound like Lee.

"Sam says you're here all the time, exercising like a fiend these days," my father says.

"I am."

"I'm so sorry that you two broke up," Wanda says. She touches my shoulder. "I'm sure what you're going through is rough."

"You have no idea," I say, sighing. *No idea at all.* "But let's not talk about the negative stuff. Let's eat."

"I still don't understand why you wanted to eat inside this health club," my father says.

"New trend, Dad. Everybody's doing it these days."

He looks at me, unconvinced.

"It's big in California."

He shakes his head. "Whatever you say, Kat."

The three of us get to Yummy's and order at the counter, standing in line. We form an interesting trio. The photos of the organic apples and pears, dotted with moisture droplets, seem to stare back at me, laughing their seeds off. I stare at the sign above me for support: *Be Your Best!*

I'm trying. I really am.

Already, I'm thinking: This will not be fun. My father will not hold back just because Wanda's with us. She's practically part of the family now. He's going to dig deep, delving into my issues: losing my job and losing Sam. Not to mention losing my sanity.

My father can't hide the disappointment on his face as he studies the menu. He looks glum, as if he's being asked to eat prison food. I know what's running through his head. *Can't we at least go to an Outback Steakhouse for some real food?*

"Hey, Dad," I say as we wait. "Did you hear? The Tennessee Titans eat vegetarian now."

"I feel sorry for them," he replies with a sigh and a frown. "That's a shame."

After ordering, the three of us find a table in the back, sit down, and wait for the server to bring us the food. I was given card number twenty-three and place it on the metal holder at our table.

The lights are so bright in here it's glaring. The ambience is not what my father is used to—not in the least. I knit my hands together. Look at me, making my father come to Yummy's to eat with me. Shame on me.

My father rolls his eyes as he looks around. He adjusts his

tie and tries to force a smile, a man out of his orbit. An uncomfortable moment grips us.

"So," he says, folding his arms and staring at me. "We need to talk."

Must he start in so quick?

I stare at Wanda for support.

"It's so big here," Wanda says, taking the hint. "It's really very cool."

My father takes the conversational bait. "They probably do a lot of business. I did a health club real estate deal two years ago in Charlotte. Atlas Clubs. They make millions."

"So, how'd your deal go here in town, Dad?" I ask. Anything to keep him off the elephant in the room.

At one time, my father had wanted me to get into the real estate development business with him, but it didn't suit me—just one more disappointment for him in the Great Big Wall of Disappointments I was building. I couldn't handle it: all that extra huffing and puffing and schmoozing and wheeling and dealing. It wasn't for me. He really never understood why. My brother wasn't interested in it either, but he does do legal work for some of my father's contracts, forever the golden child.

My father answers with: "My meal? What? I haven't eaten yet." He looks suddenly cross.

"Your deal!" Wanda raises her voice at him, then rolls her eyes. "Your deal. She was asking about your deal. We are definitely getting you some hearing aids. You promised you'd do it."

"I will, I will, as soon as we get back." My father looks sheepish. He adjusts his tie.

"Please, Dad. You really do need them," I say, speaking louder. We've been struggling with my father's hearing loss for years. "They have these small ones now and no one will even know you're wearing them."

"Frank Greer's wearing them now, dear," Wanda says. "He says he can't imagine living without them."

"I know, I know," my father says, looking irritated. "Anyway, the deal went well. I'm signing the contracts tomorrow. I bought some land near I-65 and I'm putting a hundred-unit apartment complex there. It's all set. I've got the financing in place and everything. Nashville's one of the hottest markets in the country. It's a no-brainer. Got it cheap too. Worked them down."

Wanda looks at my father with a sudden admiration all over her face, blooming love too. She turns to me. "Your dad's the best," she says. "Do you realize that? He's a whiz at development." She kisses him on the cheek.

"And you're a whiz yourself," he says, smiling at Wanda. Then he looks over at the counter for the food and licks his lips. He may love Wanda, but food's on his brain. I know my dad top to bottom. I can practically see what he's thinking.

The meals finally arrive and the waitress, Brandy, an MTSU college student, gives me a wink and a nod, having seen me here more times than I can count.

"How's it going, Kat?" she asks.

"Great," I say. "This is my dad and my soon-to-be stepmom. Wanda, Dad, this is Brandy."

"Hey, everybody!" She giggles. "Enjoy!"

I ordered a veggie burger and Wanda and my father ordered the succulent veggie casserole. It's no steak, of course.

"Okay, then," my father says. He looks at Wanda who returns his dissatisfied stare and once again, guilt crosses my heart.

"Oh, come on, Dad. It's tasty. Try it."

He clears his throat. "It'll have to do, won't it?"

"It's an adventure, Dad. Open up your palate."

"Some opening," my father grumbles. He takes his first bite and chews grimly. "Wanda, can you hand me the ketchup and the salt?"

"Sure, dear." Wanda passes them to my father, then bites

into a forkful of casserole. "Not bad," she says politely. "Not bad at all."

"So, look, Kat," my father says as he proceeds to smother the casserole with ketchup and salt and then takes another hesitant bite. He points his fork at me. "Let's get serious here. What's up with you? Sam says you're hanging out at this fitness center all the time now. I'm worried. You need a job."

"I have a job," I announce.

"What?"

"I'm working here at the daycare. A kind of stopgap job until something better comes along."

"Well, then," my father says. "Daycare?"

"Yes. It's just a temporary thing, Dad. I also have a job interview with a dentist tomorrow, so..."

"That's good. Okay, then." Still, there's that disappointment in his eyes, that look that I can't ignore. My throat tightens up as I stare at his face.

I push on. "But why are you so worried about me hanging out at a fitness center?"

"Come on, you know what I'm talking about. You lost your job and you've become this exercise fiend. It's not you at all."

"She's just trying new things, darling," Wanda chimes in. She takes a half-bite of the casserole and then drinks some water. "It's like I was telling you. When I was Kat's age, I hadn't even started real estate yet. I was still working as an administrative assistant at an insurance company and hating every minute of it. She's just spreading her wings, aren't you, Kat?"

"I am," I say. Maybe Wanda isn't half bad. I only wish I could fly out of here, that's the problem.

"Well, look," my father says. "I don't mind you trying new things, but dental hygiene's a profession, a solid career. Are you giving up on it?"

"No. Not at all. Like I said, I've got an interview with a dentist I worked with before. Dr. Fields, a nice guy. But for now, I'm taking a sabbatical. I'm living life. I don't see what's so bad about that. I'll probably be back at dental hygiene before you can say periodontal disease. Soon, I promise."

Wanda laughs.

My father frowns. He bites into the casserole and chews angrily. "Something else is bothering me, too, and I want to get it out into the open."

"What?" I take a bite of my veggie burger, and I try to enjoy it, but my anxiety is starting to fire off inside me now.

"You told Sam you were staying at Val's. But Sam said he watched Val's house for you to turn up and you never showed up. So you're *not* staying there, right? What the hell is going on? Where *are* you staying?" Ah! The million-dollar question. My father leans forward, his eyes, knowing and wise, drill into my own. I twist in my seat.

My throat tightens up. Deny, deny, deny, lie, lie, lie. Battle stations.

"Dad, I didn't want Sam to know, but I... I... well, I have a new boyfriend."

"A *new* boyfriend?" He raises an eyebrow at me, doubt written all over his face. He bombards his casserole with more salt. He then stares gloomily at his food, takes another bite, and then pushes the plate away as he throws his fork down. "I'm done," he says, throwing the napkin into his plate. "That was... different."

"Oh, come on, it's not that bad," Wanda cajoles.

I take a breath. "I didn't want Sam to know, Dad. Surely, you can understand that."

My father looks at Wanda. Then he studies my face. He says simply, "All right, then. Who?"

"Yes, who is this new boyfriend?" Wanda asks, leaning forward. "What does he do?"

Oh, God. I knew it. Details! They always want details!

"Well?" my father stares full on at me. "Let's have some answers."

Silence suddenly overwhelms me. There's a long uncomfortable moment. "He's... he's..." I swallow, and then spout it out: "He's... he's a s-songwriter who just moved here. From LA. Really nice guy. Rich too."

"See?" Wanda says, leaning back in her seat with a grin as she turns to my father. "There's nothing to worry about. I told you Kat knows how to take care of herself. She's smart, that's what I said. Kat's no fool." Wanda gives me a woman-to-woman wink.

"Well, I'd like to meet this songwriter person." My father grumbles. "I want to see what he's like. Songwriter? That's hardly a profession in my mind."

Before I can even stop myself, the words tumble out of my mouth. I'm going to show them both. Oh, yeah! "Actually, he's..." *What? Are you crazy! You can't pull a fake boyfriend out of thin air. Sure I can! Do it! Just do it!* I run Josh's offer through my brain. *And hey, if you ever need a favor from me... please, don't be afraid to...* "Actually, he's... here now," I say and simultaneously realize I'm making a big mistake—but it's too late now. Lie number six million four hundred thousand. I can't seem to stop. "He's, uh, he's, well, he's working out as we speak. Would you like to... meet him?"

"Yes. Of course. Introduce me to this fine young gentleman," my father commands, waving an arm in the air. "Go find him." He gives Wanda a wink. "Let's see what this young fellow is made of."

I take a sip of water. "Actually," I start backtracking. *You had to open your big mouth, didn't you?* "I'm not sure now is a good time. And we've only been dating for about a week. And... h-he's working out pretty seriously and he's pretty busy this evening..."

"Too busy to meet your father for even a minute? What kind of a boyfriend is that? I knew a songwriter was bad news!"

I'm stumped. If I stick to my story, it'll look like I'm dating a selfish ass. If I say yes... Will Josh even cooperate?

Wanda gives me another woman-to-woman smile. Dad is picking over his casserole again, tasting around the edges. The man looks starved.

I sigh and push back my chair. I feel sorry for him. "Okay, Dad. Be right back."

I stand, take a long drink of water, and walk around the fitness center until I find Josh in the weight room. He's on a leg machine, pushing hard against a one-hundred-and-fifty-pound weight. He's really going at it, his face an abstract work of grimaces.

I walk up to him and, when Josh's finished lifting the weight, I grab his arm, trying to stay calm, while inside, I am a fiber-optic bundle of nerves.

"Hey, Kat," he says, looking surprised. "What's up?"

His face is all red from the heavy lifting, sweat dripping down. He uses a white towel to rub his face, sipping on a bottled water.

"Josh." I try to contain the desperation in my voice, but it slips through. Still, I am *determined* to make this work. If my father wants to meet my brand-new boyfriend, I am going to produce a brand-new boyfriend—no ifs, ands, or buts. "Got a question."

"Shoot."

"Was wondering." I look around and there's Lee jogging past us, flailing an arm in the air as he says hello. "You said you'd help me out if I ever needed a favor, right?"

"Right. Absolutely."

"Well, I'm calling that favor in, right here and right now, if you don't mind."

"What? Sure." He looks perplexed. "Does your car need a jump?"

I shake my head. "No. Nothing like that. It's more family-oriented."

I tell him what I need and he listens intently at first, then with doubt in his eyes, then with a frown. "You mean you want *me* to be your stand-in boyfriend so you can impress your dad and his girlfriend? Like, *act* the part?"

It sounds even crazier coming from his mouth, but I nod eagerly. "Basically, yes. Would you? Please?" Standing in front of him, I clasp my hands together as if in prayer. "I'm kind of desperate."

"But you want me to lie," he points out.

I'm taken aback and flutter my eyes. "Uh... Yeah. I need to have a boyfriend so my Dad'll leave me alone and stop worrying about me. And if we can be, you know, like, kind of close with each other, so much the better. It'll take ten minutes tops."

He looks confused. "But still, I'd be lying."

Jesus H. Christ. The guy has integrity. With all the assholes in the world these days, guys who lie as easily as breathing, I cannot believe my bad luck—and Val's good luck, come to think of it.

I hold my first finger and thumb a half-inch apart. "It's just a little lie, Josh. A teensy-weeny lie. Nothing major. It's not like you're lying to a district attorney or something. It's not like you're being indicted for murder!"

"I don't know, Kat, I really don't..."

I raise my voice. "Please? I helped you find Val, remember? Amazing Val, woman of your dreams?"

Josh rubs the back of his neck. Finally, he gives in. "I guess. I mean, I do owe you one."

"Great! Just follow my lead. I'll buy you and Val a meal at Prime House. Promise. I'll pay for it and you two can go by yourselves. On me. Oh, and don't tell Val, okay? There's no need to bring her into this."

As we approach Yummy's, I take his hand, my fake boyfriend's. Voila! Though I'm wishing I had a *real* boyfriend to present to my father and Wanda, not this stand-in. My mind flicks to Marcus and those washboard abs of his.

I'm hoping Josh is a fair actor, but I have my doubts.

I stride up to the table and say, "Dad and Wanda, meet Josh. Josh Hannah. Songwriter extraordinaire."

My father stands and shakes Josh's hand. "Nice to meet you," he says.

Wanda remains seated, leaning across to shake Josh's hand too. She gives me a strange look, and then studies Josh. Her eyes flick back to rove over my face. I can practically feel her womanly intuition kicking in.

I kiss Josh on the cheek and then rub off the mark my lipstick has left. Josh gives us all this crazy, big, fake grin, as if he'd been ordered to smile for the camera whilst being prosecuted for espionage. Then, as if he's come down with a massive case of stage fright, he freezes. Practically turns into a corpse. A guy with integrity who's a terrible actor. Wonderful. Just my luck.

"So, Josh, how did you meet Kat?" my father asks in his loud, oh-so nearly offensive manner.

"Well, we—"

"Right here," I interject quickly before Josh can even finish. "Right, Josh? I was working out, no, it was yoga, right, honey? Yes, yoga. Josh is an expert at yoga. So, yeah, yoga, right babe?"

"Yes, uh, yoga. Right."

Suddenly, Josh's right eye starts to twitch. But what's worse is his ears are burning red now.

I catch Wanda's roving eye. She looks skeptical.

"Anyway, Josh has to get back to his workout," I say. "B-But I'm glad you had a chance to meet—"

"Songwriting, huh?" my father asks. "I hear that's one shaky profession."

"It can be." Sweat is starting to drip down his forehead. His eye keeps twitching. "But so far, it's been good to me."

"And what do you think of my Kat?" My father studies Josh —man to man—his daddy-antennae on high alert.

Josh looks at me and scratches his head. He shrugs. "Great," he says. "Really great."

The unimpressed expression on my father's face is all too obvious to ignore. There's a long silence that seems to cast a net over us. He crosses his arms and waits for more.

"She's really nice," Josh says finally, as if he's been handed the words on a cue card and he can barely read them.

Both my father and Wanda cock their heads and raise their eyebrows at the same time.

"Nice? In my book, she's the best," my father says. "And don't you forget it." He puts an arm around me and kisses me on top of my head. "She's my precious angel, Josh. She's my world."

"Well, Josh is, uh, itching to get back to his training routine, aren't you, babe?" I prod.

"Yes? Oh. Yeah. Yes."

He stands there. Frozen as a popsicle.

"See you, honey," I say.

"Huh?" He blinks rapidly.

"Bye."

"Oh, yeah. Nice meeting you."

Before he departs, I kiss him on the cheek and throw my arms around his neck. His arms hang limply by his sides.

When Josh has disappeared, I sit down. My father stares at my shaking hands, a not-out-of-the-ordinary sight for him, and then says to Wanda, "What do you think?"

"Is he really a songwriter, Kat?" she asks. "You know how practically everybody in Nashville is a would-be songwriter.

Or singer, or something. But so few ever make any money at it."

"I know. But he really is," I say. "He's the real thing. Google him. You'll see. Josh Hannah. He's amazing. He just got a cut on Brad Paisley."

"Brad Paisley, huh?" my father says skeptically. He sighs. "Well, I guess..." He sits back down and stares at the now cold casserole, which is probably turning into a fantasy filet mignon in his mind. "If that's your choice, Kat. So be it." He looks at me long and hard. "I've decided that I will no longer try to direct your life. Number one, I can't. And number two, you need to make your own decisions. Your mother and I can only do so much. Ultimately, it has to be up to you. You're too old now for me to do anything but watch you make your own mistakes, fall down, make some more, and hopefully learn from them."

These words hit home. *Oh, Dad. I'm still your little girl. And right now, I'm making the biggest mistake of my life and I don't know how to help myself at all. Can you rescue me again like you saved me in the pool? Can you simply say "pickle"—that magical word—and make us laugh together and make it all go away?*

Knowing that I really am on my own shakes me up. All of a sudden, I'm so close to breaking down and telling him everything. Letting my father take control. Just plain giving up and giving in. But I can't. I won't. I have to figure this out for myself. I am *determined* to figure this out for myself. It's time for me to finally grow up and take charge—for once in my life. Farewell Peter Pan.

Dad rubs his chin. "I just wish you hadn't lost your job, that's all." My father's eyes burn into me. "But at least I know where you're, ahem, staying. Moving in with a guy you hardly know? I don't like that one bit."

Again, his disappointment in me breaks my heart. "Sometimes you have to move on, Dad," I say.

Wanda gives me a smile. This much she understands, and understands well.

After we've all finished eating, my father cheers up a bit. "Why don't we go and get some ice cream? There's a good place just down the street. What's it called, Wanda?"

"Custer's?" Wanda says.

"I can't," I reply regretfully.

Dad frowns. "You've never turned down ice cream in your life. I'm not in town long, you can't take a half hour to join us? It's our tradition!"

I run a hand through my hair, searching for comfort in the new look, the new "me." When I was little, my dad would always take me out for ice cream, just me and him. It was such a treat. Now we always make time to do it whenever he is in town. "I can't, okay?" I swallow. "I have to go out with Josh. He's waiting for me. We're going dancing."

Could I make it outside if my father accompanied me? What if I broke down?

My dad sighs. He wants this. A half-hour with his daughter getting ice cream is important to him. "Oh, come on, Kat."

I look at Wanda who has this strange expression on her face. I can practically see her mind whirring. If only I could just tell them the truth and be done with it. Let them haul me out of here in an ambulance.

"I'm sorry, Dad." I start fighting back tears. "I-I just can't do it." I speak through clenched teeth. "I don't need ice cream!"

"Well. Okay, Kat," my father says. He holds his hands up in surrender. "Miss Health Nut. Whatever you say. Look. You take care of yourself all right? I just want you to be happy, that's all. Can you please be happy?"

"I am happy, Dad," I say, but I speak the words too strongly, too forcefully, and my father looks unconvinced.

"That's good," he says weakly. "When you're happy, I'm happy."

I hug Wanda briefly, and then I give my father another tight embrace. Maybe too tight.

As I watch them walk out through the front door, so effortlessly, so normally, a thick sadness overwhelms me. There they go. I would love to go with my dad to get some ice cream, the way we've done as far back as I can remember.

I stare out a window and watch them get into my father's rented car, a blue Buick, having driven in from the airport. My dad holds the door open for Wanda and they kiss briefly before she climbs in. They finally drive away.

I turn and head to the locker room. My skin prickles and my throat is tight as my lips slightly tremble. I change into my bathing suit and sink into a hot tub, feeling the bubbles all around me, the pressure of the jets against my back. Melting. Feeling sad and all alone, as if loneliness were a liquid, surrounding me. I'm swimming in it—Earl-like—this sad, liquid loneliness.

Oh, Kat. What are you going to do?

It's eight o'clock that night when Lura comes at me with switchblade eyes. I'm on an elliptical, really going at it. Trying to exercise my problems out of my mind. Lura looks at me as if I've murdered her child or something.

"Why don't you just go home?" she says. She pokes me in the shoulder again.

"Why don't *you* go home?" I give it right back, hardly able to breathe.

"Don't you have anything better to do?"

"Don't *you* have anything better to do?"

"But *I'm* the one, don't you get it? I'm the one!"

I put a hand to my chest. "No. *I'm* the one."

"Ugh! You're impossible!"

She waves a hand in the air, then stomps off, hops on an

elliptical herself, and goes at it full steam, glaring at me. We both work out like fiends. I refuse to stop. She refuses to stop.

Finally, we wear each other out and we both get off at the same time. I'm exhausted and so is she. I mouth the word, "Bitch!" She mouths it right back.

She's the one who needs to be in the psychiatric hospital—not me. She is definitely playing with half a deck. But I'm sure she's worried too: I've moved up eight more spots on the TWR workout charts.

That night, I sleep in the back office. The couch is like a Sealy Posturepedic compared to the yoga mat or the massage table. I have the Dr. Fields interview tomorrow at ten, but already I grow uncertain about whether I'm going to make it. The truth is that I am coming to doubt more and more my ability to leave, which makes me grow panicky just thinking about it.

Fortunately, once again, I go unnoticed by the security guard. The office is so neatly tucked away, it really does seem to keep me hidden from snooping eyes. Still, lying on the couch, mostly I toss and turn as all my troubles keep popping up in my mind. My trials and tribulations. It's the lying to my friends and my dad and mom that really gets me, though. This is what I hate most of all. It's miserable. I just can't keep it up.

CHAPTER 21

TUESDAY

As soon as I get off a treadmill around 9 a.m., Marcus steps up to me and whispers in my ear. His breath on my ear makes me shiver. "Come with me. Now."

"Why?"

"Just come."

He leads me down a secluded hallway beyond the fountain, then through a series of doors and down another hallway. The sounds of weight machines clinking and clanking reverberate around us. We finally arrive at this out-of-the-way door, which opens up to a basement. We walk down the stairs and enter a small room. He switches on a light. The room contains old signs, old chairs, and some dilapidated workout benches. We're all alone.

"What's this all about?" I ask.

Marcus keeps on walking, leading me by the hand, finally stopping in front of a door, an exit sign glowing above it.

"Go, Kat," he says. "Just go. Do it. Leave now. You can do this!"

I stare at the door, and then back at Marcus. What the hell?

It's all so sudden. And yet, maybe now is the time. *Is it now or never?*

He takes my hand again and leads me closer to the door. His touch is gentle but firm. I look into his eyes.

"Close your eyes and take some deep breaths."

I do as he suggests, trying to find my calm, but Panic is already holding court inside me.

"Breathe," he says.

I take more deep breaths, eyes closed. His hands are on my shoulders now, massaging me.

"Breathe deeply." He lowers his voice and whispers in my ear. "Relax. Relax."

A minute later, he says, "Now. Do it. Go. Relax and just do it!"

But before I can even take another step forward, here it comes. The quaking inside, hands trembling, heart pounding like a tom-tom.

Help me, Daddy. Help me! I'm scared!

That little girl inside me is screaming once again.

Help me!

And then it surfaces, that one suppressed memory that I've tried to keep in the dark closet of my mind for most of my life. It used to come up all the time when I was younger, but I learned to keep it down fairly well—until I'm totally stressed, like now! Sara Jane. That horrible day my father rescued me from drowning. *Not ready for the deep end yet.* Sara Jane, my best friend, actually drowned.

No! No!

"Come on, Sara Jane. Swim with me!"

I'd wanted to know what the deep end was like and as soon as we swam out to it, we were both immediately way over our heads. Seconds later, I could barely breathe. Sara Jane started gasping. I was somehow able to come up for air since I was older and stronger. I remember splashing and being scared and screaming. When the adults heard me screaming, my father leapt into the water and hauled us both out. I was able to survive, but Sara Jane... I can still see her body lying on the side of the pool, the adults gathered around her, someone using mouth-to-mouth on her. But she didn't come back.

And it was all my fault.

No! No! No!

I'M SO SORRY, SARA JANE! SO SORRY! CAN YOU EVER FORGIVE ME?

Tears fall from my eyes and I can barely breathe now. The memory does what it always does—it captures me, freezes me up inside, makes it so that I can barely even think. I go numb.

Marcus opens up the door and sunlight shines through, the Nashville heat radiating toward me, calling out to me. Outside, a woman is holding a child's hand as she walks across the parking lot. In the distance, a flock of birds fly in a V-shaped unit.

I'm trembling. "Marcus, I... I..."

"Go," he whispers in my ear. "Just do it."

"I-I c-can't. No! Please, Marcus. Don't make me. I can't. I'm drowning, Marcus."

Drowning. Daddeeeee! Dadddeeeee! Not ready for the deep end. Sara Jane! Sara Jane!

I backpedal. It's the only thing I can do. I slip my hand away from Marcus's and stumble back from the door. That carrot-topped teen rears his head at me. Manslaughter. Jail. Sam-lessness. Job-lessness. Rent. Out There. Hard concrete. An ugly world. I sit down in a corner of the room and start sobbing. Sara Jane's body rises in my mind, so close, I can nearly touch it.

"Marcus, I... I can't. I'm going to throw up. I'm going to pass out, I'm..."

As I stare outside into the sunlit day again, the next thing I know, my head swims with dizziness, a tilt-a-whirl, and then I pass out.

. . .

When I come to, Marcus is kneeling over me. He has a wet towel and he's placing it over my brow. I sit up.

"Here. Drink this," he urges.

He hands me a bottled water and I drink greedily. My breathing rolls through me like ocean waves. That's how it is when I have a panic attack.

"I think I need to go for a swim," I say a minute later. I feel so dejected. Rejected. Torn.

"Sure," Marcus says. "Understood." He gives me a long searching look. "I need to get back. I have a client to train."

"I'm... I'm sorry, Marcus. I guess I couldn't do it. And thanks for not forcing me through the door. That would have probably broken me."

"Sure. At least I tried. I was thinking of moving you outside when you passed out, but I wasn't sure you'd be able to handle it. It was too risky."

"I know. Thanks for not doing that."

"Let me see if I can think of something else."

"Like?"

"Let me think about it."

He gives me a goodbye hug and once again, for a brief moment, I'm floating on a cloud. But then the moment turns awkward and he lets go of me. His eyes scan my face.

"Kat, I..."

"What, Marcus?"

He shakes his head. "Never mind."

The silence between us is cavernous. Finally, we go our separate ways.

The whole entire thing leaves me in a kind of zombie state. Brain fog. I feel like I'm a delusion, my reality is so unreal. All I can do is text Dr. Fields and tell him that a personal issue has come up and I won't be able to make the interview. I stare at the words he texts back:

That's fine. When you're ready, just call. I'm still interested.

He's so understanding; that buys me some time. If I can ever get out of here...

Two hours later, Lura comes into the sauna I'm in. It's just the two of us. It's a redwood cedar sauna and the wood creaks and pops in the heat. I don't know whether to leave or stay. I wipe my face with a towel as I watch her sit down across from me. She gives me a tight smile. I return it the best I can.

"You're slipping," she says, taking a sip from a bottled water.

"What do you mean?"

"Your ratings are going down." She crosses her arms over her chest in a triumphant gesture.

"That's because I give up. You win. Okay? Now would you please leave me alone?"

"Now that's what I want to hear—I win." She smiles. And then a moment later. "Why are you staying here if it's not for the competition?"

"Why are *you* staying here?"

She looks down, then away. Finally, she says in a soft voice. "If you must know..." She takes a deep breath. "I hate going back home. I'm too lonely there. The place is huge. One of those homes built in the late 1800s, sitting on five acres in Franklin. I inherited it from an uncle of mine. It's gorgeous, but it's way too much space for me. Once I got my divorce and my awful ex moved out, it was too depressing being there. I never made many friends and the few friends I do have, well, one's moved back to Idaho and the other's always busy with her job. So, I'd rather stay at Great Fitness. I know people here. Lots of

people. I'm never alone, you know? I love it here. I just don't
want to face my empty house and walk those empty rooms."

"So you don't have a job?"

"No. I don't need to work. My divorce left me with more
money than I know what to do with. My ex was a banker, really
successful. Real dick though, too."

"Why don't you get a roommate?"

She shakes her head. "Couldn't live with anyone, and I
don't think anyone could live with me. I'm too manic. You can't
imagine how manic I am. But hey, it's not so bad here. I know
this place in and out. Besides, I have to keep my ranking up too,
you know. Most calories burned on the elliptical three months
in a row. That's me. And that's no small feat!" She lowers her
voice. "That Larry Johnson and Harry McGraw? I have them
totally fooled. They're dopes." She shrugs.

"You are really something else, Lura. I've never met anyone
like you."

"I know. But enough of me. What's your story?"

I sigh. I am unhappy. Trapped. I'm riddled with anxiety,
full of fear, and all I can do is roam around this place like I'm on
some sort of extended vacation that's not really a vacation at all.
How will I turn this around?

"I'm not here to beat you, Lura." Our eyes meet. "Trust me.
I'm really not. I promise. Your rating on the board doesn't
interest me at all. I have too many problems of my own."

"Like?"

I close my eyes for a second and swallow. "I'm here for my
health." My voice trembles. "I'm trying to improve myself by
being here," I halfway lie. "I'm using this place as a kind of treatment center. Where all the usual temptations are not in front of
me. There's not even a donut in sight. I'm surrounded by exercise equipment and positive, good-looking people and..."

"You're really not here to try beat my stats?"

I laugh sadly. I hold up a hand like I'm taking an oath. "No. I promise. I'm not."

She gives me a warm smile and finally I think I've gotten through. "You know what? I think I actually believe you. Truce?" she offers a hand.

"Truce." I shake her hand.

We sit there in silence as the sauna hisses steam and my dreams of leaving this place shatter like glass.

CHAPTER 22

I don't do much the rest of the day. I sit out by the pool, walk around, and basically feel miserable. I am the human version of Earl. I try to eat at Yummy's, but I'm not even hungry, just pick at a portobello mushroom sandwich. I do float therapy. An hour in a tank filled with Epsom salt. It's supposed to be good for your skin. I just lie in there and float on my back, trying to let my troubles ease out of my mind. By the end of the session, I'm completely relaxed, loose and calm. It's kind of wonderful. Definitely, I will do this again.

I take a beginner's yoga class around seven o'clock. Strange: I'm getting better at it. I can hold my postures longer now. I'm no Josh, but I think he'd be proud. When it's over, I consider heading to the bar. But no. I pass. Instead, I do laps in the outdoor pool, shower, change, then mess around on my phone, sitting in a lounger outside. I actually Google: "How to exit a health club when you're too anxious."

As expected, nothing of interest comes up. I stare up at the stars in the sky and beg for an answer. The moon is equally silent. I wait. Nine... ten... eleven o'clock... Finally, at five minutes to midnight, I slink into the same back office I've used before, settle in on the couch.

I'm exhausted and I fall asleep quickly... until...

I'm in a deep sleep when the overhead light snaps on. I have no idea what time it is, but I'm sure it's way past midnight. I rub my eyes, thinking momentarily: This must be a dream—but it's not. Standing before me are none other than Harry A. McGraw and Larry Johnson. They are looking at me as if I've committed serial murder. Larry's bad eye is flickering.

"Thought you could trick us, didn't you?" Harry's angry voice hits me like a blow to the head.

"I... I... was working out and fell asleep and..."

"Oh, no you weren't. We know what you're up to. I called Mr. Flanigan and he's on his way. You're not going anywhere until the police arrive."

The word "police" makes me sit up quickly. Panic ensues. Heart-pounding, pure, one hundred percent panic. Tears start flowing before I can stop them. I tremble all over.

"I-I'm sorry. I'll leave in the morning." My anxiety hits me full on, slamming my nervous system. "I promise."

Harry shakes his head. "Uh-uh. Not that simple. This is unauthorized use of our property. This is a crime and you're going to pay."

"Look. I'll leave right now if you want. I was just..."

Harry sneers at me. He's a completely different person. Gone is that friendly side. In its place is the hunter who has caught his prey.

"Are you homeless?" he asks.

"I'm..."

"You're gonna pay for this," Larry says in a thick Southern accent. "You think this is some kinda hotel? You think we're gonna put a goddamn mint on your pillow?"

Suddenly, I hear footsteps coming down the hall, and then

Mr. Flanigan enters the room. Even now, at this hour, he is immaculately dressed in jeans and a crisp blue golf shirt, hair combed to perfection. Staring at him makes my heart leap in my throat. His commanding authority makes my anxiety kick into higher gear. Anger surrounds him like a whirlwind, his eyes two beads of fury.

I feel so bad that I've let Mr. Flanigan down. He gave me a job and everything. I'm suddenly seeing black spots in front of my eyes and I can't catch my breath. "I'm sorry, Mr. Flanigan." Tears spring out of my eyes and leak down my cheeks. I wipe them away. I pull my knees up against my chest. I shake my head pitifully. "I'm so sorry. I'll leave. I promise. I just needed a place to stay for a while, that's all. My boyfriend left me and—"

He turns to Harry. "Did you call the police?"

"They're on their way."

I need to tell the truth. That's my only hope. Although anger is radiating from Harry, I *know* there's a kind side to Mr. Flanigan. Surely, he'll understand and have some compassion.

"I... I have anxiety and panic attacks, Mr. Flanigan," I say, turning to him and looking him directly in the eyes as I sniffle and wipe away tears.

"Panic attacks?" He furrows his brow, caught off guard.

"I've tried to leave, several times. I really have, but every time I try to walk out the door, I panic, I get dizzy, my heart races, I break out in a sweat and the next thing I know, I have to throw up. I nearly pass out. It's bad, Mr. Flanigan. It really is." I stop speaking and gasp for air. Finally, I continue, "My b-boyfriend left me and I got fired all on the same day, within the span of an hour, actually. Fired *and* dumped all on the first day I came here, can you believe it?" I pause again, put a hand to my head. "And now I'm afraid of going out into the real world." I wring my hands together. "I've... I've always had this panic issue. I'm basically trapped here. And I can't get my Xanax refilled... and I'm too afraid to do anything other than stay here at Great Fitness. I'm so sorry. I know it's wrong. If I could leave,

I would." I hang my head in shame. I've never felt so bad and humiliated all at once.

"Bullshit," Harry says. "That's total nonsense. You're doing nothing but looking for a free place to crash. Don't hand us that crap. You're a freeloader."

"You aren't doing anything but lying your ass off," Larry adds.

"No, no! I have my own apartment and I'm a paid-in-full member," I say. "And an employee. I love working at the daycare here."

"No one's entitled to stay the night," Mr. Flanigan says. "I have liability issues. If you were to hurt yourself while you were here over night, my insurance wouldn't cover me. It's not permitted under the terms of our insurance. And you've broken the member contract by staying overnight. I'm afraid this is rather serious."

"Can I at least go to the bathroom?" I ask quietly, lowering my head.

"Larry will walk you down the hall," Mr. Flanigan says.

As we walk down toward the bathroom, Larry says, "So, it *was* you flushin' that toilet, wasn't it?"

I nod. "Guilty as charged." I take a breath. "You sing really well, Larry."

Larry blushes. "Woulda had a record deal if it wasn't for my eye."

I somehow believe him.

When I return from the bathroom, I wait in the office again, sitting on the couch. I stare at the wholesome family pictures on the desk. Such a faraway world from mine. There's a painting on the wall—seagulls on a beach with the sun going down. *My* sun's going down. Harry and Mr. Flanigan have drawn up chairs.

"Some people think they can get away with just about anything," Harry says, glaring at me. I wonder if he marvels at my slyness, drinking bourbon at the bar with him; I was his precious prey, right under his nose.

"Now, now, Harry," Mr. Flanigan says. "Don't be rude. We caught her. That's enough of a shock as it is." Hearing this makes a tingling warmth in my chest. *Thanks Mr. Flanigan for standing up for me.*

When the police finally arrive—a bullet-shaped man and a pencil-thin woman both wearing blue and with guns in their black holsters—Harry simply points at me. "She's the one."

I turn, pleadingly, to Mr. Flanigan. "Please, Mr. Flanigan."

"You'll have to come along with us, ma'am," the police-woman intones, bringing out her handcuffs, which jangle as she holds them.

So, this is how it ends. Escorted out of the building by the police.

"Wait," Mr. Flanigan says. He rubs his chin and furrows his brow, his arms crossed over his chest.

The policewoman turns to Mr. Flanigan. "It's up to you, sir. If you want to press charges, we'll take her in and book her."

"Please, Mr. Flanigan. Please!" I'm begging now. It's the only thing left for me to do. Praying and begging, which come to think of it, are practically the same thing. "If you call an ambu-lance to come get me, the paramedics can give me a shot of Ativan and that will relax me enough so I can leave. And then I'll have to go to a psychiatric hospital." A tear leaks out of my eye. "I guess it's where I belong."

Mr. Flanigan looks me over, studying me. Finally, he says, "I tell you what. I'll call the ambulance for you, okay? And tomor-row, I'll have them here at 9 a.m. No point in doing it at this hour. You call your therapist or somebody and tell them what's going on. The paramedics will help you get out the door. It's that or the cops."

Harry throws his hands up in the air. "You mean you're gonna let her off the hook?"

"Say, what?" Larry says.

"I'm not letting her off the hook, Harry," Mr. Flanigan says. "I'm simply solving a problem. For her and for us."

"Thank you," I say. "Thank you, Mr. Flanigan. You won't be sorry. Thank you so much!"

He turns to the cops. "I'll take it from here, but thank you for coming."

"Okay, sir," the woman says.

Right before Larry, Harry, and Mr. Flanigan leave me alone in the office, Mr. Flanigan says, "I'll tell Lee to check on you when he comes in in the morning first thing." Filled with shame, my face tingles with heat. He studies me again, his eyes a mixture of anger and curiosity and... compassion. I can't help but wonder if he has any daughters and if he has problems with them. "For now, just try to get some sleep."

And then he locks me in.

Once again, I'm swaddled in silence and loneliness and fear and dread. Trapped again, this time in much smaller confines. Earl all over again. Surely, this is how he must have felt swimming around and around in that small glass bowl. Suffocating.

So, this is how it ends. Sam-less, job-less, Great Fitness-less. And completely controlled by my Big A. *You win, okay? You've pinned me down for the count.*

CHAPTER 23

WEDNESDAY

The door to the office opens at 4:45 a.m. I had fallen into a fitful sleep. Now Lee is standing there and I blink. Surely, it's Jake. I blink again. No, it's Lee.

"Eat this if you need it," he says, handing me a chocolate sea salt power bar. I stare at it blankly, like an archaeologist examining an artifact and wondering what its purpose was, turning it over in my hands.

Lee is as speechless as I am. It's such a strange situation for us both. I feel as shy as when I first met him, timid me asking if he could show me around. Lee swallows, shoving his hands in his pockets. He's not Mr. Red Bull now. He's calm and careful with me. The strange look in his eyes saddens me. Suddenly, everything's not so great at all.

"What a night for you, huh?" he says. "Mr. Flanigan filled me in."

"Yeah. I guess the jig is up. And now they're kicking me out. Sorry, Lee."

"You know, you really had us fooled. We thought you were some kind of exercise maniac or guru. I was getting ready to sit at your feet and let you teach me all you knew."

"That's a laugh," I reply.

Again, a long silence fills up the moment between us. Finally, Lee says, "Well, I'll come back and escort you down to the front about a quarter to nine. The ambulance should be here at nine."

I nod.

"Need to use the bathroom?"

"Yes, please."

Lee escorts me to the bathroom and waits outside as I do my business. Then he returns me to the office and I sit back down on the couch, knotting my hands together.

"Well," he says, "I guess you can sleep some more if you want. If you get hungry, you've got that bar."

"Thanks, Lee," I say. "You're a good guy."

"Good luck, Kat," he says sincerely as my eyes moisten. "I really hope you can turn things around."

He leaves and I'm so embarrassed and afraid and sad and everything else. I couldn't have dreamed this all up if I'd tried to. Life is way more far-out than fiction; this much is true, for sure.

I turn out the lights to the office and sit in the dark, stewing. Time is not my friend. I have three and a half hours left. Either I figure out a way to escape or I leave in an ambulance.

I fall asleep for about an hour, then wake up with a start. I'm panicking. My breaths are quick and shallow. It's like my body is riding a wild horse, galloping away and I can't control it. I pace the floor. I sit. My hands are slick and sweaty.

I call my therapist at 8:30 a.m. I know that's when she arrives at her office on most days. I tell the answering service it's an emergency and Dr. Sharp calls me back five minutes later. She's good that way—she's always on top of emergencies.

"Kat, what's going on?" she asks, in that serious but objective tone of voice she always uses with me.

"I'm afraid I'm in a bit of a rough situation, Dr. Sharp. I'm... well." I can't continue. My throat closes up.

"Yes, Kat?"

"Oh, Dr. Sharp! I'm such a fool!" Tears slide down my cheeks as finally, finally, it all comes out in one long stream of words. "See, I anxiety-locked myself inside this health club and they'll be sending an ambulance for me around nine this morning and I'm going to need a shot of Ativan to get me through the door and... it's awful, Dr. Sharp. Can you call Dr. Baldwin and tell him that they'll be taking me to Rolling Hills so he can admit me?"

Dr. Sharp doesn't say anything for at least a minute. When she finally speaks, it's with so much sympathy for me that I start crying all over again. "Oh, Kat. I am so sorry. Sure. I'll call Dr. Baldwin for you. No problem at all."

CHAPTER 24

Larry and Harry knock on the door and then unlock it with a key like a jailer. I'm a bundle of nerves as I watch them enter, still sitting on the couch. It's 8:48 a.m.

"Can I get my things from the locker?" I ask.

"Sure," Larry says.

I unfold myself and stand, then slowly head to the door. I am a prisoner. That psychiatric hospital had bars on its windows. I remember that much. And there was a sour stink in the air the whole time I was there. And that doctor, so full of himself. This is what I have to look forward to—again.

Larry walks with me as I exit the room. Suddenly, Lee comes up to us.

"You okay, Kat?" he asks.

"Never better," I say, forcing myself to smile.

I walk a few feet down the hallway and my breath quickens. I struggle for air. My hands grow slick and my head pounds. This is it. Another panic attack is on its way, heading straight through my entire nervous system. I take some deep breaths. It hardly helps at all.

After I get my things, the four of us head to the first floor on the elevator, step on floor one, then approach the fountain. The walk of shame. Me, flanked by the two security guards and Lee walking next to Larry. My hands are shaking. My joints hurt. My entire body feels like it's cascading in pain that's both emotional and physical. Members stare at us. They know something's up. It's so embarrassing I could puke. I'm being escorted out of the building. How *great* is that?

What if Sam comes into the gym and sees me? I'd have to explain everything. There's no way I want my ex-boyfriend to know how deeply I've sunk. This is the lowest of the low.

Suddenly I hear the cry of a little girl and something inside me resonates. I swing to the sound and spy Rosie. A man I don't recognize is holding her hand and pulling her past the fountain, rushing her along. He's a tall, mean-looking guy with a ring in his earlobe and a scruffy beard, bald. He's escorting her toward the door. No, not escorting, more like dragging her. How in hell did he get her out of daycare? This is exactly the scenario that her mother feared. This must be her father! I remember that there's a new worker today. Suzanne. I think that's her name. She probably doesn't realize that she's done the worst thing possible.

Rosie's obviously not happy and is refusing to cooperate. She's crying and trying to shove her father away. But the little girl is no match for him.

No one else even notices. I guess they assume it's nothing more than a case of a spoiled child being disciplined.

I stand in shock as the man stops and tries to give Rosie a piece of candy, but she knocks it out of his hands. They're so close to the door now, moving past the front desk. My heart goes out to her. I can hardly breathe for a moment.

"Lee," I say, grabbing his arm. "That girl. Come on."

"What?" he says.

I yell, "She needs our help!"

The next thing I know, I'm racing toward Rosie and her

father before the guards can even stop me, intent on only one thing: rescuing her. "Stop him!" I yell. And everyone turns my way.

"Kat! What are you doing?" Lee calls out to me. "What's going on?"

As soon as I approach them, Morris Washington, the Tennessee Titans player, walks in, carrying a gym bag, big as a locomotive. He practically blocks the door.

"Stop him!" I scream. "That man is kidnapping that little girl! Stop him now!" I point a shaking finger at him.

Rosie's father turns around and stares at me, his lip curling. Rosie turns around as well.

"Miss Kat!" she cries, jumping up and down, tears sliding down her cheeks.

"This man does not have legal custody!" I yell.

"Kat?" Lee says, coming up behind me flanked by the guards, their eyes wide. "Settle down now. What's going on?"

I'm breathing so hard I can barely speak. How can I even explain it to them before he gets away?

My heart is booming, but there's a newborn resolve inside me that I'm not going to squelch. Pushing past Morris, the father has dragged Rosie out the door now. If he gets her in his car, God only knows where he'll take her.

"No!" I cry.

Larry puts an arm around my shoulder to stop me, then Harry too, but I wriggle out of their grasp, totally determined, and run toward the door. In another minute they'll be gone. I reach the door and stop dead in my tracks.

"Kat? Are you all right?" It's Morris, standing there beside me.

"That man, that man..." I gasp for breath. Standing at the door, I can't get the words out of my mouth.

I watch as the dad hustles Rosie into a black Benz, trying to shuffle her into the back seat. But she's kicking him now, biting him, yelling out.

No!

The door that's been a cruel barrier between me and the outside world for at least a week is now all that stands between me and Rosie. I cannot let this happen. Suddenly, I feel like I'm outside my body and looking down from above. Everything starts to unfold in slow motion.

When I think of Rosie, the fear lifts away and the next thing I know, I'm out the door. Just like that. Saving Rosie is all I can think of. Nothing else matters.

Rosie!

Sunlight washes over me as I race toward the car.

"Stop him!" I yell. Several people are walking toward the fitness center and a few are leaving. But no one understands what I'm talking about.

I keep running and shout to anyone who is willing: "Please! Call 911!"

When no one seems to take any action, I whip out my own phone and call.

"Your emergency?" a voice quickly answers.

"I'm in the parking lot of Great Fitness, 1609 Greenview Drive, and there's a kidnapping taking place right before my eyes. Hurry! Please, hurry!"

I race toward the car. The father glares at me. A bead of sweat lines his brow. He twists his mouth into a grimace.

"Leave her alone!" I yell, standing in front of the car. My heart is a fist in my chest.

"Back off you lunatic," he shouts. "This is my daughter."

"You're not allowed to take her away from here!"

"I said back off!"

The man pushes Rosie into the back seat and tries to strap her in. She fights him. She squeals. "No! Help! No! Miss Kat! Help me!"

I *can't* wait for the police. The police are going to be too late.

He finally has Rosie buckled in. He's about to get into the driver's seat. I lunge, grabbing him by his shoulders and yanking him backward.

He pushes me off and I jump at him again, but he smacks me in the mouth. For a second, I see stars.

The pain in my jaw shoots throughout my body, stinging.

"Fuck off!" the father says, moving back to the car door. That's when we both realize we're surrounded by onlookers.

"Hey, pal, you're not going anywhere." The voice is deep and full of authority. It's Morris Washington, pushing through the crowd and now towering over Rosie's father. Her father stands back against his car, not looking so sure of himself now.

"This is my daughter!" he yells. "I have every right to—"

"No, he doesn't," I say. "He's not allowed to take her. He doesn't have custody. He's dangerous."

"We're going to wait for the police to come and sort this out," Morris states.

In the distance, sirens finally wail. Even more club members gather around. There's Lura—she doesn't miss a thing!—staring at me with a crazed intensity in her eyes as if she's daring me to try to break her attendance record.

"What the hell is going on?" Jim Flanigan asks, rushing up to us. "What's happening here?"

"Mr. Flanigan. Thank God." I wince as I point at Rosie's father. "This man does not have custody over his daughter and he's not allowed to take her from daycare. The new worker must have failed to check him against the approved parent list."

"Are you sure?"

"Dead sure, Mr. Flanigan. He's not on the approved list."

Helen, the daycare supervisor comes running out to us. She looks pale.

"Oh, God! Thank you, Kat. She's right, Mr. Flanigan! That

man does not have permission. I'm so sorry, I made a mistake. There was a new person at the desk and..."

Rosie's father looks all shriveled up. Morris's hand is around his shoulder, clutching him tightly. Mr. Flanigan stares at the father, at little Rosie, at Helen and suddenly looks relieved.

"Good work, Kat," he says. Surprisingly, he puts an arm around me and I lean into him. I'm visibly shaking as I wipe away a tear.

I gaze around at all the onlookers. They look shocked, pale-faced, some are talking on their phones, telling friends and family what's happened, a few are filming.

Two policemen arrive a few minutes later and Mr. Flanigan calmly explains everything. With the crowd still standing around, they handcuff Rosie's father, all limp and scared now, and then shove him into the backseat of the squad car. I take Rosie in my arms and she cries against me. I hug her with all my might. She clenches me, sobbing.

I look up and there's Marcus taking it all in, everything, and I catch his eye. A breeze of understanding passes between us. He stares at me and I give him a quivering, timid smile back. Brow furrowed, mouth gaping open, he looks as surprised as I feel.

"I want my mommy! Mommy! Miss Kat! I want my mommy!" A thumb goes into her mouth. Then, a minute later, when she settles down: "I was scared. I didn't want to go with him."

"You were so brave, honey," I say. "You really were!"

"Let's take you back inside where you can wait for your Mommy, okay?" Rosie embraces Helen and sobs. I see tears in Helen's eyes as well. "Your mommy will be here very soon. I'm so sorry this happened."

Helen gives me a sad, grateful look, then takes Rosie's hand and leads her away. As they head into the building, a wave of gigantic relief washes over me.

A minute later, Mr. Flanigan gives me a wink. "How does it feel to be outside?" he says in a low voice.

I take a big, deep breath. I *am* outside, aren't I? I look up at the sky, the clouds passing above, the sun shining down. I stare into the wide-open space of freedom itself. A warm, welcoming wind caresses my face and I burst into a smile. I feel like hugging myself. "It feels... great!"

The onlookers disperse at last. There's an ambulance, pulling up to the front of the building. That must be for me. My stomach turns over.

Mr. Flanigan goes up to the driver and explains the situation as I watch from a distance. A minute later and the ambulance leaves as even more relief, like a fresh spring shower, bathes me, drenches me all over my body.

"Thank you, Mr. Flanigan," I say when he walks up to me again. I watch as the ambulance turns down a street and disappears.

"Thank *you,* Kat. Honestly, you saved my ass. If that guy had taken that little girl away from here without permission... All hell would've broken loose from so many angles."

He shakes his head and then walks quickly away to talk to a dark-haired employee.

Morris comes up to me and asks, "Are you okay?"

The pain in my jaw comes back in a rush, but the truth is I've never been more okay in my life.

"I'm... fine, I think." I rub my jaw.

"You really put some moves on that asshole," he says. "You know that?"

"You did too, Morris," I say. "I guess we both stopped that perp from getting into the end zone."

We both laugh as we high-five each other. "You did good, girl," he says. Then Morris heads into the club, leaving me alone.

I am giddy. I look around again, stare up at the vast and

limitless blue sky, feel the wind against my face, and it feels as if I can taste freedom itself at last—yum; it's as delicious as a blueberry smoothie. I finally found an exit, a way out, and it came in the strangest way possible.

I've never been so glad to be outside.

Again, I take another deep and refreshing breath.

And then it's Marcus who comes up to me and the next thing I know, his arms are around me and we hug long and tight. *Marcus.* A smile blooms across my face as a brand-new warmth radiates through my chest and there's a sudden lightness in my limbs that makes me feel as if I could almost lift off the ground.

"I finally did it, Marcus!" I say. "Look at me. I'm outside! Can you believe it? It's real."

"I knew you had it in you." He stands before me and applauds. "See? You beat that door and tore it to shreds."

"I guess I did." I take a bow.

I feel so happy right now. It's as if I'm standing on my own Mt. Everest, looking out at the world and lo and behold, it's one gorgeous, breathtaking view.

The truth is that saving Rosie saved myself. It was that simple.

EPILOGUE

It's now one month later and I'm all shook up. (Isn't that a song?) Everybody's here; it's like a party, except it's not. My parents are in my apartment with their spouses, Wanda and Sidney, and Val and Josh are in attendance as well. Plus, Joey, who came all the way from LA. How could I leave out Joey? Tall with dark curly hair, and three days' growth of beard. I hadn't seen him in at least two years. He Ubered from the airport and we hugged as soon as he came through my door. My brother, the Golden Child. As far as I can tell, his life is still a smooth highway with his successful law practice, his wondrous wife, and his two sweet kids.

I'd found the courage to call my father and my mother and Val and Joey and ask, no demand, that they all come see me. When they asked why, I was firm: I needed to get things off my chest, I said. I wanted to tell them all exactly what happened at Great Fitness, the truth—and I wanted to tell them in person. (Everyone's here except Sam, but that's as it should be. We are done. I realize that I'm far better off without him in so many ways.)

It's Sunday in September and it's a beautiful day in Nashville, temperature in the non-humid low seventies. It's perfect outside, really, but inside my heart, with my family and close friends gathered around me, I'm cloudy and stormy and possibly on the verge of raining down a few tears.

Finally, everyone is seated and we're munching on crackers, and cheese, and drinking red wine, a smooth Sonoma County Cabernet, which has "fine structure with dark fruits," as Sam would say. And then, as they stare at me, wondering what's going on, I stand in the center of the room and explain everything, the entire messy story, and I apologize for all my lies, and manipulations. And then yes, here they come—a few tears leaking out of my eyes. Just as I'd predicted, this is hard: one hundred percent chance of pain.

"But why didn't you call me?" my father asks when I'm done, finishing off with Rosie and my final escape.

"I didn't want to worry you, Dad," I say. "I've always been a worry to you. I know I have. Don't deny it. And I thought I could figure it out for myself."

"Next time worry me, do you understand? Worry me!" He turns to Wanda, who has a sympathetic look on her face. I feel so sad and embarrassed right now. "Can you believe this kid of mine?"

"Do you forgive me?" I ask them all.

"Absolutely," they say quickly, each of them. "Of course."

It's the quickness of their answer that gives me the most relief.

"And"—I clear my throat—"there *is* good news. I have a new job. It's in *pediatric* dentistry! I can even wear a dinosaur costume at work if I want. I'll be around children every day and still be able to clean teeth."

"Oh, Kat," my father says. "I'm so proud of you! That's terrific!" His eyes sparkle.

"Excellent, Kat," my mother says as she finishes her glass of wine and pours herself another one. I'm sure she'll be hitting my

Maker's Mark before this is over. "Maybe you can be the tooth fairy there too."

That's a thought.

"Look, Kat." Wanda turns my father's head to the side so that I can see his right ear. "Your dad's wearing hearing aids now! Isn't that wonderful?"

"Best thing I ever did," he says. "I was a fool for putting it off so long. I'm hearing so much better!"

"What did you say?" I put a hand to my ear and we all laugh.

"And Josh," I say, turning to him and growing serious. "I just want to say that I am so sorry I made you my fake boyfriend. That was wrong. I don't even know what I was thinking. I put you in such an awkward position and I feel terrible about that. Can you forgive me?"

"Hey, not a problem. I totally understand," he says. "If it hadn't been for you, I wouldn't have found Val." He puts an arm around her.

"You are such a nut case," Val says, tears in her eyes now. "But I finally think you're growing up. No more Peter Pan for you."

"You think?"

"I do. I really do. But please, don't ever tried to hide something from me again, okay? You're my best friend forever, girl, and I want to know what you're going through—everything. Just like you would want to know what I'm going through too. Don't you see that?"

"I do, Val. And I'm sorry." I lower my head. "Friends don't let friends do stupid things. I hope you can forgive me."

"Give me a few days, okay?"

"Sure."

"Oh, Kat," my mother says, with Sidney sitting next to her. He looks supportive, sympathetic, and when our eyes meet, he gives me an encouraging look that says he knows how hard this is for me. "You have always been a conundrum to me. I cannot for the life of me understand you. You were always so anxious, even when you were a child. Is it my fault, darling?"

I don't hesitate. "No, Mom. Don't blame yourself. It's just the way I am, I guess. This anxiety of mine is something that's inside me and I don't think it'll ever completely leave. But you know what? Now that I've gone through this trial by fire, I definitely intend to get help, okay? And this time, I mean it. I've already started seeing Dr. Sharp again."

"That's good, dear. I'm glad." She takes a long breath. "I know I wasn't the best mother and I'm sorry, Kat." My mother's eyes start to moisten now. Her chin trembles. "I wasn't that involved. I left you alone too much. Both you and your brother. And then the divorce, I'm sure that shook you up terribly. I'm so sorry." And then it was my mother's turn to start crying.

"Don't blame yourself, Mom. You did the best you could. I don't blame you at all, truly, I don't. You're a party animal and I'm a party animal. It's in our bones."

The complex relationship between me and my mother is somehow satisfying when all is said and done, I realize. The heat and the warmth, so to speak, sometimes shed a little light.

"I hated letting you all down," I say. "And I want to apologize to all of you. I'm so sorry."

Another tear slides down my cheek.

"You're not letting me down," my father says quickly as my mother takes a tissue and dabs at her eyes. "You're my daughter. I love you. You can't possibly let me down. You should know that."

"Oh, Dad. But aren't I a disappointment? I know you're not proud of me like you are of Joey."

I turn to Joey who has a sorrowful look on his face. My father waves a hand in the air. "Nonsense. I'm proud of you both. Equally and always. Ever since I laid eyes on you resting against your mother in the hospital, Kat, ever since I saw your first smile, that precious look you have when you're excited about something, your quick mind. You're special, Kat. I want you to know that. I love you with all my heart."

"Oh, Dad."

And then the next thing I know, he's standing up and reaching out to me and we hug, a long embrace and I feel his love like never before, strong, deep Daddy Love. You can't beat it. He *is* my safe place to run to. "Oh, Kat. I love you so much."

"And I love you, too, Dad," I say. Then: "Oh! I almost forgot!"

I rush out to my garage and bring in my new puppy. A golden Lab I'd found on the same farm that I'd gotten Lilly. Cute as could be. I put his paw in the air and make him wave at everybody.

"Say, hi, everyone," I say. Oohs and ahhhs follow. "Meet Lloyd." He barks as if he's introducing himself. "My new friend."

"He's so cute!" Val says. I hand him to her and she cuddles him. "Bring him in and I'll check him out—if I don't keep him for myself."

"No way. He's mine!" We all laugh.

"A toast," I say, raising my glass a minute later. I look around at everyone, grateful to have these people in my life, grateful to have them here with me now. "Some say that we should drink to life, you know? But I say let's drink to love. For what good is life without love?"

"To love," everyone says, and we all raise our glasses and drink to that most mysterious thing of all, that which brings us together and keeps us together and gives us reason to live.

Love.

———

To be honest? In a way I'm glad I went through this whole thing, as crazy as it sounds. My big little adventure at Great Fitness was a (great!) growth process and I learned so much about myself, my limitations, but most of all, about my courage. I learned that real power, authentic power, actually and positively dwelled inside the breast of Kat Noad. It is something I didn't know I even possessed. It is something that I plan to call on for the rest of my days. How can you learn how much courage you have until you're put to the test?

I'm eating better too—vegetables and fruit and smoothies, although I do splurge from time to time. I don't go clubbing nearly as much. I see Lura around at Great Fitness, but she's not nearly as combative. In fact, we've been treadmilling together lately, just talking about anything and everything.

I've joined Veronica in an Anxiety Awareness campaign. After my interview on TV with her—yes, my story made the local news!—we got hundreds of emails in support of what I'd gone through, and now we have a website and meetings once a month. So many people suffer from anxiety. The more support we can give each other, the better.

I meet Rosie and her mother every so often at a restaurant just to talk and Rosie always has a new picture she's drawn for me and something to tell me with such excitement in her voice. "Miss Kat! I'm going to the zoo this weekend! Can you come with us?"

And that so-called dad of hers? The asshole's forming brand-new relationships in prison. Good for him.

Go where you're needed. I guess that about sums it up. That's what I've learned most of all. It doesn't matter what you want, or what you think you want. How much money you make or how famous you try to become. Just plain go where you're *needed*. And you know what? *That's* being the best you can be. If you do, you won't go wrong.

———

Now, it's two weeks later, and Marcus and I...

We're taking an after-dinner stroll in the night air, heading to the walking bridge that overlooks the Cumberland River in downtown Nashville. It's a coolish, windy evening and the promise of our future together hangs in the air. With the moon as our witness and stars in our eyes, we kiss, deeply, soulfully. Marcus puts his arm around me and I lean into him as we stare out onto the moonlit water. I know we have a connection, know it deep in my heart. It's only a matter of bringing it out.

"You're famous at Great Fitness, did you know that?" he says after our kiss ends.

"Famous for being a fool." I push some hair off my face.

"No. Not at all. Mr. Flanigan says that because you stopped Rosie from being abducted, you saved him from a major lawsuit. He wants to give you a free lifetime membership. And your interview with Veronica Ray about how you saved Rosie? That was amazing. It brought us all to tears. And then there's Jake Gyllenhaal."

"Yes...?" I wait expectantly.

"Well, he's not in the picture at all." He laughs. "But Lee is and he's totally impressed by you as are the rest of us. They all think you're great! The word is out, Kat. You're a star."

A star? Me? Unbelievable.

After taking in the night and the lights shining from the nearby buildings, we hold hands as we head back to his car. Love-butterflies are all over my stomach, fluttering around. I feel like one of those forty-nine million bubbles in a champagne bottle that Jack had talked about, rising to the surface, so happy I could pop at the top.

"Want to work on the elliptical tomorrow?" he asks.

"Sure."

"And by the way, I think you're ready to begin doing some pull-ups too. We'll start out slow and work you up."

"Sure, coach. Whatever you say. I'm ready and willing."

"And I'm ready and willing too," he says, his sparkling eyes diving into mine.

"Hmm..." I give him a beam of a smile. "I guess we both are."

Once we get in his car, we kiss again. And then, side by side, off we drive into a hopeful future and the meandering highways of the night.

A LETTER FROM ELLIE

To me, there's no greater joy than reading a novel that completely absorbs and immerses you. My hope is that you found yourself drawn deeply into the world of Katherine Noad, her trials and tribulations, her fears, tears, and joys. I also hope she lives on in your mind and heart long after you've finished reading. I want to say a huge thank you for choosing to read *Come Here Often?* If you enjoyed it, and want to keep up to date with all my latest releases, just sign up at the following link. Your email address will never be shared and you can unsubscribe at any time.

www.bookouture.com/ellie-center

Also, I would be very grateful if you could find some time to write a review for *Come Here Often?* I'd love to hear what you think, and it makes such a difference helping new readers to discover one of my books for the first time. And by the way, I love hearing from my readers – you can get in touch through Twitter or Goodreads.

Yours truly,

Ellie Center

 twitter.com/EllieCenter

ACKNOWLEDGMENTS

Thank you to everyone at Bookouture and especially Christina Demosthenous, editor extraordinaire. And thanks to Laurie Chittenden, Valerie Grey, Eve Hall, and Elizabeth Zack, who read this novel in its early form and made suggestions.